Th

PENGUIN BOOKS

The Templar's Code

The Templar's Code

C. M. PALOV

PENGUIN BOOKS

PENGUIN BOOKS

Published by the Penguin Group
Penguin Books Ltd, 80 Strand, London WC2R ORL, England
Penguin Group (USA) Inc., 375 Hudson Street, New York, New York 10014, USA
Penguin Group (Canada), 90 Eglinton Avenue East, Suite 700, Toronto, Ontario, Canada M4P 2Y3
(a division of Pearson Penguin Canada Inc.)
Penguin Ireland, 25 St Stephen's Green, Dublin 2, Ireland (a division of Penguin Books Ltd)
Penguin Group (Australia), 250 Camberwell Road, Camberwell, Victoria 3124, Australia
(a division of Pearson Australia Group Pty Ltd)
Penguin Books India Pvt Ltd, 11 Community Centre, Panchsheel Park, New Delhi – 110 017, India
Penguin Group (NZ), 67 Apollo Drive, Rosedale, North Shore 0632, New Zealand
(a division of Pearson New Zealand Ltd)
Penguin Books (South Africa) (Pty) Ltd, 24 Sturdee Avenue, Rosebank, Johannesburg 2196, South Africa

Penguin Books Ltd, Registered Offices: 80 Strand, London WC2R ORL, England

www.penguin.com

First published 2010
001

Set in 12.5/14.75 pt Garamond MT Std
Typeset by TexTech International
Printed in England by Clays Ltd, St Ives plc

ISBN: 978-1-405-93177-9

www.greenpenguin.co.uk

MIX
Paper from responsible sources
FSC www.fsc.org FSC™ C018179

Penguin Books is committed to a sustainable future for our business, our readers and our planet. This book is made from Forest Stewardship Council™ certified paper.

To Chester and his merry band

'I lived in this world of darkness for myriads of years
and no one ever knew that I was there.'

– Gnostic Hymn

Prologue

1524

The New World, Arcadia Colony

Isabelle d'Anjou threw herself at the foot of the black-robed priest. 'Mercy! I beg you!'

'*Haereticus!*' the Jesuit screamed, his thin, ascetic frame shaking with fury's passion. 'By this cross you will know Him!'

An armed soldier, red surcoat emblazoned with a white cross, roughly grabbed Isabelle by the waist and hauled her away from the priest. Shrieking, a wild animal caught in a snare, the terrified girl grabbed at the beads dangling from the Jesuit's hand. A desperate plea that went unanswered, the soldier plunging a falchion into Isabelle's left breast. Blood arced through the air, splattering the priest's cassock.

Raising his gaze heavenward, the Black Robe made a ritualized motion. Above to below. Left to right. '*In nominee Patris, et Filii, et Spiritus Sancti.*' With upturned hands, the Black Robe continued his Latin chant . . .

. . . As the mounted knights slashed and swung their broadswords . . . As the soldiers ravished the village women . . . As the orange flames consumed the thatched huts in a fiery blaze . . . . As the pitiless and unrelenting devastation raged all around.

Horrified, Yann peered from beneath the upturned cart. He watched as a bearded man, the Stone Keeper, fell to his knees, hands clasped to his chest. Blood dripped from a hideous gash on the side of his face. For one brief instant, their eyes met.

'Yann! You must—' The cry went unfinished. An armoured horseman, brandishing a broadsword in his gloved hand, took aim at the bearded supplicant, severing both hands with one pendulous swing as the blade sliced through the Stone Keeper's torso. The morning sun glinted off a silver ring still attached to a detached hand.

Suddenly, a village farmer, sharp scythe gripped in his hands, charged through the mêlée. '*Beauséant!*' he yelled. The hoarse cry was the last word the intrepid farmer uttered, a soldier embedding a double-edged axe into the top of Didier's skull.

And on it went. As though the gates of Hell had opened up and swallowed the village of Arcadia whole. A killing field. Sickles and scythes no match for broadsword and war hammer.

Fear rooting him in place, twelve-year-old Yann remained crouched beneath the wooden cart. Blackness threatened to overtake him. Dark spots swirled before his eyes. The entire village was drenched in blood. Everywhere he looked. Headless torsos. Sprawled legs. A trampled hump, all that was left of César the blacksmith.

And standing near the front gate, presiding over the bloody mass, the duplicitous Black Robe.

Yann shuddered, blinked, commanded his body to move.

I must escape!

Crawling from under the cart, he dashed towards the blacksmith's shop, orange flames shooting from the roof. From there he charged across the Bertrand croft with its newly planted Lenten crops. Barley and beans. Glancing up, he saw the mended battle standard that undulated in the breeze above the village longhouse. *Splayed red cross on a black-and-white background.* A different cross to the one sewn on to the surcoats of the marauding soldiers.

Yann charged towards the stone wall that bordered the back of the village, hoisting himself up and over. He gracelessly landed in a bramble bush. Sharp thorns pierced his hose. Dizzy, he leaned over and retched.

On the other side of the stone wall, he heard a knight angrily bellow, 'Kill them! Kill them all!'

Flagging energy renewed, Yann lurched out of the bush and kept on running. Towards the forest, with its dense greenery and long shadows. The perfect place for a boy to vanish from sight. *To escape the carnage.*

Since the time of the great sea journey, two hundred years ago, the people of Arcadia had lived in harmony with their neighbours. Each year, the Arcadians paid tribute to the local *sachem*, bushels of dried fish ensuring peaceful coexistence. A small price to pay.

But the Black Robe could not be bribed. He did not want their gold. Nor their silver. Nor a basket of dried pike. He wanted their sacred stone. And he was willing to kill every man, woman and child in Arcadia to get it.

But the Black Robe would come away empty-handed. The ancient relic was not kept in Arcadia. It was safeguarded in a specially built sanctuary, a league away. A fact known only to the Stone Keeper and the seven members of his inner circle. *All dead.* Put to the sword. Which meant that Yann was the only Arcadian still alive who knew the secret. The reason why he now ran through the forest. Heart pounding. Shins aching. Breathless.

Gasping for air, Yann came to a shuddering halt and leaned against a sturdy oak tree. Shafts of sunlight streamed through the interlaced branches, dappling moss and rock.

Hearing something other than his own laboured breath, Yann jerked his head away from the trunk. Craning his neck, he fearfully peered behind him . . . just in time to see two Narragansett warriors, faces painted, black hair roached, emerge from the shadows. One man held a war club, the other a tomahawk.

Uncertain whether they were friend or foe, Yann placed his right hand over his racing heart and bowed his head. 'I am Yann Gugues . . . the Stone Keeper's son.'

I

Present Day

Washington, DC

Afraid that he'd been followed, Jason Lovett scanned the crowded subway platform as he pushed his way through the slow-moving throng.

Not seeing the pretty-boy bastard who'd been tailing him, he noisily exhaled.

So far, so good.

The exit turnstile was at the other end of the Dupont Metro Station and he was in a big-ass hurry. The lecture was scheduled to end at one o'clock. It was his only chance to speak with Cædmon Aisquith. And, hopefully, to make a proposition the English historian-turned-author couldn't refuse. He had fifteen minutes to get to the lecture hall.

Shit. Could these people move any slower?

'It's like bovines being loaded off a cattle car,' he muttered, now sandwiched between a pudgy soccer mom and her equally plump teenage daughter. Afraid he would get stuck on the escalator behind a couple of lard asses, he squeezed past.

No sooner did he clear the obstacle than a dude in an even bigger hurry bumped into him, prying loose the book Lovett had tucked under his arm. He made an awkward save, catching the hardcover volume before it hit the deck. The subway had seemed a good idea at the time; now he wasn't so sure. Earlier, he'd gone to Union Station where he'd bought a train ticket for Richmond. He'd even boarded the train, bailing out just before it left the station. Moments after that, he caught the eastbound subway. An elaborate hoax to make the pretty-boy bastard think he was leaving town.

God, he hoped the ruse had worked.

Feeling a trickle of sweat roll down the side of his face, he wiped his shirt sleeve across his brow; the humid air inside the cavernous station jungle-like.

Finally reaching the turnstile, he snatched his subway ticket out of the metal slot and rushed towards the escalator. Head bent, he sprinted up the left side. Glancing upward, he groaned, the escalator at least a city block long. Ten years had come and gone since he rowed crew at Brown University, his lung capacity not what it used to be.

A few moments later, wheezing like an old fart with emphysema, he stepped off the escalator. He glanced around the urban neighbourhood, disorientated. Dupont Circle was a hip hodgepodge of cafés, book stores and high-end art galleries. The nearby traffic circle didn't help, at least six streets radiating out in all directions.

He stopped a middle-aged suit rushing past. 'Excuse me,' he huffed, still working on catching his breath. 'I'm looking for the House of the Temple.'

The suit pointed to one of the radiating streets. 'Two blocks up New Hampshire. Turn right on S Street,' he brusquely replied, clearly annoyed that the last five seconds of his life had been stolen from him.

Lovett nodded his thanks. Ignoring the traffic signal, he darted in front of a yellow cab. His jaywalking incited several motorists to lay on the horn.

Up yours! I'm in a hurry.

Figuring he'd catch his breath at the other end of the line, he jogged down New Hampshire Avenue, the tree-lined street relatively free of pedestrian traffic. The embassies of Zimbabwe, Namibia and Nicaragua passed in a blur.

He peered over his shoulder.

Fuck. There was a dark-haired man about a block back. He didn't think it was the pretty-boy bastard. *But then again, it might be.*

Catching sight of the basement of a nearby townhouse, he veered off-course, ducking into the brick stairwell. He scrunched out of sight, wedging himself between a metal garbage can and a blue recycling bin. Worried he might puke, or even pass out, he ripped open the Velcro flap on his cargo pants and removed a prescription bottle. The doctor at the walk-in clinic had prescribed the Xanax to help manage his anxiety. He'd taken one an hour ago and so far it hadn't done jack.

Fumbling with the child-proof lid, he popped another tablet into his mouth.

A second later, his courage in freefall, he peered over the brick retaining wall. The dark-haired man was now half a block away. Still too far to make out his features.

Lovett shoved his hand back into his pocket, this time removing a small digital voice recorder. He'd been keeping a verbal diary. *Just in case.*

Fearing the worst, he switched it on. Then, in a lowered

voice: 'If someone is listening to this – Shit. It means the fucker finally caught up to me. Just so we're clear, I'm not paranoid. I *am* being stalked. But there's too much at stake to tuck tail and run. No way in hell I'm going to let that pretty-boy bastard take what's mine. If he wants the treasure, he's going to have to—'

The dark-haired man strolled past.

Lovett sagged against the brick wall, relieved.

Hoping the Xanax kicked in sooner rather than later, he shoved the recorder back in his pocket and climbed out of the stairwell.

At S Street, he turned right. About a hundred yards down, he caught sight of the House of the Temple, a colossus of stone that took up an entire city block.

Christ.

What kind of drugs were the Freemasons taking when they constructed this ungodly structure?

The House of the Temple looked like an ancient Greek sanctuary with a truncated pyramid plunked on the top of it. The truncated pyramid bore an uncanny resemblance to the one on the back of the dollar bill. Which no doubt gave conspiracy theorists a hard-on. Add to that the giant pair of sphinxes that flanked the imposing granite steps and the whole thing put him in mind of the Temple of Mausolus at Halicarnassus. Which was kind of ironic since he'd spent a summer at Bodrum working on an archaeology dig. Slaving away, actually, grad students forced to do all the grunt-work. But then he dug up a gold earring. Talk about an adrenalin rush. It sure beat the hell out of sifting through potsherds.

Deciding there and then that the real glory was in treasure hunting, he spent the next summer at Key West, volunteering with the Fisher expedition. *Man alive.* It was an adrenalin rush on steroids, gold and silver bars strewn across the ocean floor, there for the picking. But not for the taking, the Fisher folks were a real proprietary lot. Possessed of a first-class education and a burning desire to make his mark on the world, he figured he could find his own treasure trove.

And he was damned closed to doing just that.

But he needed help.

That's why he was standing in front of the butt-ugly building.

Knowing he only had a few minutes before the clock struck one, Lovett took the steps two at a time, counting thirty-three of them. At the top, he opened a massive pair of bronze doors. About to step inside, he glanced over his shoulder.

The pretty-boy bastard was nowhere in sight.

Mission accomplished.

2

'. . . leaving no question in my mind that the Ark of the Covenant was a form of ancient technology inherited from the Egyptians,' Cædmon Aisquith told his audience, more than a few of whom had a copy of his book, *Isis Revealed*, in plain sight.

'Next question?' He pointed to a woman sitting in the front row of the library reading room. At least four dozen jurists' chairs had been placed in the middle of the room, turning the book-lined chamber into a makeshift lecture hall.

The bespectacled attendee glanced from side to side, verifying that she was, indeed, the chosen questioner. 'Yes, I'm, um, curious about your recent trip to Ethiopia, which you briefly mentioned in the lecture. How do you know the Ark of the Covenant isn't hidden there?'

Discreetly glancing at his wristwatch, Cædmon saw that there were nearly five minutes left in the Q&A session. Ample time to flesh out the answer. Stepping over to the nearby table, he scanned the thumbnail picture gallery on his laptop. Image selected, he accessed the PowerPoint display, projecting a map of Ethiopia on to the screen behind him.

'For those of you unfamiliar with the tale, Menelik, the illegitimate son of King Solomon and the Queen of Sheba, supposedly stole the Ark of the Covenant from his father's fabled temple in Jerusalem and took it to Ethiopia in the mid tenth century BC. Where it's reputedly still hidden, safeguarded by the priests at St Mary of Zion located in Axum.' Using a laser pointer, Cædmon indicated an area in the north-eastern quadrant of Ethiopia; Axum was located one hundred kilometres from the Red Sea.

'Keen to explore the theory, my research assistant and I travelled to Ethiopia this past January.' He gestured to a woman with long curly brown hair standing on the sidelines, leaning against a bookcase. Attired in an ankle-length denim dress with a crimson red shawl tied not around her shoulders, but around her hips, she was the lone peacock in the drab-feathered flock. 'At this juncture, allow me to introduce my travelling companion, photographer Edie Miller.'

As if on cue, every head in the group swivelled to the left.

Edie Miller acknowledged the collective stare with an amused half-smile.

Introduction made, he next pulled up a stunning photograph of St Mary's taken at sunset, the stone building bathed in a tangerine glow.

'After visiting numerous monasteries and chapels, examining scores of illuminated manuscripts, and interviewing the chief priest at St Mary's, I can now punch a very big hole in the Menelik theory.' He took no pleasure in the announcement, certain at one time that he'd find the Ark in Axum. 'While a *tabot*, that being the Ethiopian word for ark, is safeguarded within the church sanctuary, it is, alas, a twelfth-century replica of the Old Testament original.'

He put the last image on to the screen, a line drawing

of the Ark of the Covenant based on the description in the Book of Exodus.

'Our field research in Africa was conclusive: Menelik did not take the Ark of the Covenant to Ethiopia.' Scanning the group, he squinted, barely able to see in the dimly lit library, the window shutters closed tight. 'All right, who'd like to take the next stab at me? Yes, the gentleman in the blue pullover.'

A stout middle-aged man rose to his feet. 'Well, if Menelik didn't steal the Ark, who did?'

'There are a number of suspects in the rogues' gallery. What we do know is that the Ark of the Covenant disappeared from the pages of the Bible soon after the construction of Solomon's Temple. Whether captured or hidden, its current whereabouts is unknown. But rest assured, the Ark *is* out there . . . waiting to be discovered.'

Out of the corner of his eye, he saw Edie pointedly tap an index finger against her watch crystal.

Warning bell sounded, Cædmon cleared his throat. 'Yes, well, that concludes our discussion of the Egyptian origins of the Ark of the Covenant. I would like to thank the chief librarian at the House of the Temple, Mr Franklin Davis, for hosting today's lecture.' He motioned to a grey-bearded man in the front row. He'd met the librarian at a Washington book-signing some months back. When an invitation had been extended to speak at the national headquarters for the Scottish Rite of Freemasonry, he'd gladly accepted. 'And, of course, I would like to extend a warm note of thanks to a most inquisitive audience.'

As the overhead lights came on, Cædmon acknowledged the polite applause with a self-conscious smile.

Uncomfortable in the role of public author, he knew such venues not only sold books, but attracted individuals with a keen interest in Egyptian history. And mystery. The latter near and dear to him. While he'd been trained as a historian, he preferred to think of himself as a 'rehistorian', legend, lore and mysticism at the heart of his research endeavours. An unholy trinity that compelled several book reviewers to wrongly accuse him of being a conspiracy theorist.

Glancing around the room, he could see a few nattering clusters milling about, most of the attendees en route to the refreshment table set up in the adjacent banquet hall. In dire need of a thirst-quencher, the obligatory lecturer's glass having already been drained, he bent over the wooden table and proceeded to shut down the laptop computer.

As he pecked away, Cædmon noticed a rail-thin man approach, a copy of *Isis Revealed* clutched to his chest. Shaggy-haired and dishevelled, the man looked out of place in the clean-cut crowd.

'I've got some information about the Knights Templar that might interest you,' the tow-headed man announced without preamble.

Removing his fingers from the keyboard, Cædmon straightened, giving the man his full attention.

Long years ago, when he'd been a doctoral student at Oxford University, he'd written his dissertation on the Knights Templar, his research leading him to conclude that during their tenure in the Holy Land, the Templars had been secretly initiated into the Egyptian Mysteries. To his chagrin, the dissertation he'd meticulously researched was publicly ridiculed by the head of the History department at Queen's College. Realizing his advanced degree would not be conferred, he left Oxford, tail tucked between his legs.

Whereupon he'd promptly been recruited by MI5, the UK's security service.

MI5 actively sought men like him, defrocked academics keen to prove their worth. Such men made good spies. He'd spent eleven years in Her Majesty's Service before returning to his first love, history. No longer concerned with how his controversial theories might be received, he'd written *Isis Revealed*.

Although he suspected the opening gambit would lead nowhere, Cædmon inclined his head towards the shabbily dressed younger man. 'Pray continue.'

Visibly anxious, the blond man used the ball of his shoulder to wipe several translucent beads from his upper lip. Then, a determined look in his hazel-blue eyes, he thrust the copy of *Isis Revealed* in Cædmon's direction.

'Open it.'

Thinking the impolite command odd, Cædmon took the proffered volume.

A half-second later his jaw slackened as he read the handwritten message scrawled on the inscription page.

The Templars brought the Ark to the New
World in the 14th century.
I have the proof!

3

Saviour Panos opened an oversized bronze door and stepped inside the House of the Temple. In no hurry, well aware that the blond-haired archaeologist was now trapped within the confines of the stone colossus, he stopped at the guard station located just inside the vestibule.

A green-eyed man of mixed race, his drab uniform hugging a trim figure, looked up from the book he'd been reading. 'Welcome to the House of the Temple.'

'I am pleased to be here,' Saviour replied in a cultivated accent that had taken years to perfect. He glanced at the battered-copy of *The Iliad* splayed on top of the podium, greatly amused. Beware of Greeks bearing gifts . . .

'English Literature major at Howard,' the other man offered, noticing the direction of his gaze. Warmly smiling, he gestured to the nearby cloakroom. 'Would you like to check your jacket?'

'No, thank you.' Saviour returned the other man's smile. He frequently used his physical beauty to advantage, well aware that one could conquer the world with a smouldering glance.

Pleased that he'd so easily found his quarry, he stepped into the atrium. No sooner did he enter the dimly lit space than he came to a sudden halt, taken aback by the lavishly designed chamber.

'It's magnificent,' he murmured, dazzled.

Well acquainted with ancient architecture – Thessaloniki, the city of his birth, inundated with churches, towers and Roman arches – the atrium was wholly different from those grandiose monstrosities. While the expansive chamber with its massive granite columns had the heft and gravitas of a basilica, this was no Christian sanctuary. There were no Byzantine saints casting down their stern disapproval. No lavishly painted enthroned Madonnas. In lieu of the Stations of the Cross, there were bronze medallions with bas-relief symbols. The square and the compass. The sun and the moon. The All-Seeing Eye.

The temple proudly flaunted its pagan origins.

Beautiful. Erotic. Like a muscle-bound youth.

Enthralled, he walked towards the centre of the room, drawn to the gargantuan marble table supported by carved double-headed eagles. Marvelling at the superb craftsmanship, he ran his palm across the top of it. As he did, he envisioned a certain blond archaeologist, naked, sprawled on top of the marble slab.

A dagger through his heart.

Out of the corner of his eye, he saw the security guard approach.

'That table is a replica of one they found in the ruins at Pompeii.' The other man held his gaze a second too long.

'I have always wanted to visit Pompeii,' Saviour replied. Then, exploiting the overture, he lowered his voice to a husky whisper. 'I was supposed to meet a friend here. Perhaps you saw him, a blond-haired man.'

There was no mistaking the flash of disappointment. 'Yeah, I saw him. He came through a few minutes ago.

Asked where the lecture was being held.' He motioned to a placard set on an easel near the entryway.

Saviour examined the publicity photo of a red-haired man. 'The Egyptian Origins of the Ark. A Lecture by Author Cædmon Aisquith.'

'This lecture, where is it being held?'

The guard pointed to a hall on the other side of the atrium. 'Take the stairs to the basement level. Then walk through the portrait gallery. The reading room's on the right. Can't miss it.'

'It is a beautiful sanctuary,' Saviour murmured, glancing about one last time. 'You, my friend, have an enviable job.'

The other man shrugged. 'There are better jobs.'

'Trust me, brother, there are far worse ways to earn a living.' Degrading, humiliating ways. For a few coins, the price of two oranges at the fruit vendor's stall, he'd learned that man's depravity knew no bounds.

Saviour shoved the unpleasant memories aside. Those days had passed. He had reinvented himself. A feat no other wharf rat could lay claim to.

He stepped towards the staircase, his stride purposeful. Perhaps it was the energy exuded by the exotic chamber, but suddenly he was excited. Invigorated. A Greek warrior about to launch an attack against the unsuspecting Trojans.

He'd been following the blond-haired man for the last week. Ever since the archaeologist dug up the mass grave site. There could be no witnesses to the massacre. Not even nearly five hundred years after the fact.

Not now.

Not ever.

4

'Shit, where are my manners? Like, I forgot to introduce myself. I'm Jason Lovett. *Doctor* Jason Lovett,' the blond-haired man quickly amended. 'Which makes me a bona fide archaeologist rather than some Templar nut job.'

A statement no doubt meant to assuage any misgivings or preconceived notions.

Misgivings aplenty, Cædmon politely nodded as he shook Dr Lovett's right hand. 'I am pleased to make your acquaintance.'

He detected a tremor in Lovett's arm. *The man's a tangled package of nerves*. Like a downed electric wire flapping in a gale-force wind.

'Okay, I know that what I wrote on the inscription page is *way* out there –' the shabbily dressed archaeologist jutted his head at the copy of *Isis Revealed* still clutched in Cædmon's hand – 'but I found it. Or rather, I'm *really* close to finding it. I just have to decipher some Templar symbols. Which is why I need someone who's not only well-versed in Templar symbolism but who can think outside the box. Dude, you're an academic renegade. I couldn't put that damned book down. And I'm not even a big fan of Egyptian mysticism.'

'Such high praise puts the blush to my cheek. But returning to your assertion regarding the Ark of the Covenant . . .' He let the opening dangle, hoping to steer the anxious archaeologist back on course.

'The Ark. Right. I checked out your web page and saw that you're a Templar expert. So, I won't bore you with any details about the Templars and their sordid tale. You know the facts better than most.'

Indeed, Cædmon was well acquainted with the 'sordid tale'. An order of warrior monks, the Knights Templar were founded during the Crusades, the Church-sanctioned series of bloodbaths that attempted to free the Holy Land from the Muslim infidel.

When Acre, the last European stronghold in the Holy Land, fell in 1289, the Templars lost their *raison d'être.* With no more wars to fight, the Templars returned to France, a move that gave the French king, Philip le Bel, fitful sleep. *What monarch of sane mind wanted the powerful Templars encamped on his doorstep?*

Strapped for cash, the French king concocted a stratagem to have the entire Order arrested en masse on heresy charges, enabling him to confiscate the Templar treasury. With Pope Clement's blessing, the plan was enacted on 13 October, 1307. A Friday. On that fateful morning, the Templars were arrested by the king's seneschals and turned over to the Inquisition. Accused of everything from worshiping Satan to ritualized sodomy.

So went the conventional history.

From his doctoral research, Cædmon knew that was a slanderous myth. During their tenure in the Holy Land, the Templars were exposed to the Egyptian Mysteries. That exposure had a profound effect on their religious beliefs. When the Templars returned to France, they were Catholics in name only. The religious *volte-face* was the *real* reason for their downfall.

‘I am well acquainted with the Templars,’ Cædmon replied, keeping his thoughts to himself.

‘Then you know that the Templars were obsessed with finding the Ark of the Covenant.’

‘Their search proved futile, the Ark’s whereabouts is still a mystery.’ As he said it, Cædmon wondered if the youthful archaeologist had even been present for his earlier lecture.

Extending his arm, Lovett jabbed an index finger against the book cover. ‘Like I wrote, I’ve got proof to the contrary.’

‘Indeed.’ Out of the corner of his eye, Cædmon saw Edie Miller approach, bearing a capped water bottle. Seeing him, she broke into a grin.

‘What do you know? Conspiracy theorist makes good.’

‘A conspiracy theorist? You’ve obviously been reading my reviews. Regardless of what the critics write, I am but a simple man trying to earn an honest quid,’ he retorted, feigning indignation. Having met four months ago, he and Edie were taking a stab at a transatlantic relationship. Currently they were in that hazy stage between the hay and the grass.

‘Great lecture by the way.’ She offered him the plastic bottle. ‘Here. I thought you might need to wet your English whistle.’

‘Dr Jason Lovett, allow me to introduce you to Edie Miller. Edie shot all of the photographs during the recent Ethiopian trip.’ Tucking the unopened bottle under his arm, he opened the book cover, allowing Edie to view the scrawled inscription. ‘Interestingly enough, Dr Lovett is an archaeologist.’

Edie's brow furrowed. Just as he knew it would.

'Correct me if I'm wrong, but there's a glaring historical fact that you seem to have overlooked . . . Columbus didn't discover America until 1492,' she stated baldly. 'My medieval history is a little rusty, but weren't the Knights Templar rendered null and void in the early fourteenth century?'

'Columbus never set foot in America. Besides, Irish monks and Norse Vikings reached these shores long before ol' Chris ever set sail,' Lovett countered, his feathers clearly ruffled.

Cædmon joined the fray. 'The Templars had Arabic sea charts acquired in the Holy Land during the Crusades. Moreover, they were able to navigate with a primitive but effective lodestone compass. Making a transatlantic journey entirely possible.'

Edie rolled her eyes. 'You are *such* a history wonk.'

'Who happens to be right on the money,' Lovett remarked. 'The standing story is that the mighty Knights Templar were laid low by the French king. While it's true that a general arrest warrant was issued for every friggin' Templar in France, only a handful of them were actually arrested. Meaning that a whole slew of them managed to escape.'

'Rumours have swirled ever since as to how the missing knights managed to elude the royal seneschals,' Cædmon added, the centuries-old rumours still hotly debated amongst Templar *cognoscenti*.

'Someone tipped them off, maybe even the Pope himself.' Jason Lovett shrugged, the how of it clearly unimportant to him. 'It doesn't matter. When the royal seneschals stormed the Templar stronghold in Paris, the fabled Templar treasure trove had vanished into thin air.' The archaeologist peered over his shoulder. Verifying that no one outside their small circle would be privy to his remarks, he said, 'I'm pretty certain that the Templars transported their treasure trove by wagons to their naval base at La Rochelle. From there, eighteen galleys, all flying the skull and crossbones, set sail. *Never to be heard from again.*' The last utterance had about it the clichéd foreboding usually reserved for a low-budget horror film.

'You just referred to the Templar "treasure trove".' Edie punctuated the two words with a pair of air quotes. 'I thought we were talking about the Ark of the Covenant. What are you saying, that the Ark is part of a much larger hoard?'

'That's the working theory.' Jason Lovett stepped closer. Again, he glanced over his shoulder. When he did finally speak, his voice was little more than whisper. 'With the price of gold being what it is, we're talking about a treasure worth somewhere in the neighbourhood of a hundred billion dollars.'

5

Concealed by a floor-to-ceiling bookcase, Saviour Panos stood at the back of the reading room, frowning. At the front of the room, he espied the archaeologist conversing with a tall red-headed man and a curly-haired woman. The red-haired man he recognized from the publicity photo; the woman he'd never seen before.

Admittedly, he was surprised that Lovett had taken anyone into his confidence. It didn't fit the pattern. In the week since he'd been following Lovett, the archaeologist had not spoken to a single person.

Uncertain how to iron out the unforeseen wrinkle, he surreptitiously observed the trio.

Feeling the muscles in his legs tighten, he slowed his breath. A trick he'd learned long years ago. Placing his hand under his jacket, he slid his fingers over the scabbard attached to his belt. His very first weapon had been a fillet knife that he'd stolen from a fisherman's tackle box. Only thirteen years of age, he'd slept with it gripped in his hand as he'd huddled in an abandoned shack near the piers, afraid of being sodomized in his sleep. In time he'd become skilled in its use, spending hours tossing the knife at a crudely painted target. Once, during a particularly nasty street brawl, he'd plunged the knife into another boy's belly. Not deep enough to kill. That came later.

In the years since, he'd owned any number of knives. But none as exquisite as the antique dagger he'd selected for this special occasion.

Slowly, not wanting to attract attention, Saviour removed the dagger from the leather case, careful to keep the blade hidden from view. In his mind's eye, he could see the centuries-old weapon, forged of steel, the hilt gold-plated, inlaid with twenty-four small rubies set in an eight-pointed star pattern. The Creator's Star. With his thumb pad, he fingered the tiny stones. A blood-red cluster. 'In the beginning God created the heavens and the earth.'

The ornately fashioned blade had been a present from his benefactor, a man known to him simply as Mercurius. The Latin name for the Greek god Hermes. The divine messenger. In truth, his divine salvation.

When Mercurius became his patron, he'd not only seen to his education, he had also provided Saviour with a penthouse apartment in Thessaloniki's upscale Kalamaria neighbourhood. In return, Mercurius asked only that Saviour be his eyes and his ears. A secretive man, Mercurius kept to the shadows. Saviour was the polar opposite, naturally drawn to the light. Together, he and Mercurius formed a perfect whole. Like the bronze medallion he'd seen in the atrium depicting the sun and the moon. Or the two squares that comprised the Creator's Star. Pairs of opposites.

He stared at the trio still huddled at the front of the room, well aware that he had but one knife.

He'd not planned for three enemies. Only the one. A mistake.

Which of the three posed the biggest threat?

The curly-haired woman he quickly dismissed. Which left the archaeologist and the tall red-haired man.

Saviour sized up the two men, deciding who to take out.

6

As he had several times already, Jason Lovett nervously glanced over his shoulder. 'Actually, a hundred billion is a conservative estimate. But we need to, um, keep the dollar amount on the download. If you know what I mean.'

'Loose lips sink Templar ships,' Edie deadpanned. Or something equally asinine.

A hundred billion dollars. Was this guy for real? Talk about selling something off the back of a truck. She glanced at Cædmon, wondering if he was buying Lovett's egregiously tall tale.

Outwardly calm, her companion opened his water and took a measured sip before placing the plastic bottle on the nearby table.

Edie's gaze shifted between the two men, struck by the startling difference between them. With his plaid shirt tails, baggy cargo pants and wispy soul patch, Jason Lovett looked like he'd arrived on a skateboard. Add to that a barely contained frenetic energy and it made her wonder if the youthful doctor had got trapped in a caffeine-laced grunge time warp. Cædmon, on the other hand, attired in a tailored wool blazer paired with a zippered turtleneck and black denim jeans, exuded an air both casual and sophisticated, a feat only a European could pull off. Six feet three inches in height with a thatch of red hair, he stood out in a crowd. She always thought that if you fused some of history's famous red-heads – Erik the Red, William Shakespeare, Thomas Jefferson – you'd end up with Cædmon Aisquith.

'How did the Templars amass such a large fortune?' It seemed the obvious question to ask.

'How indeed?' Cædmon seconded. 'Granted, all new recruits were forced to sign over their property to the Order and the European aristocracy was generous with their donations. But even that would not account for so massive a sum.' Cocking his head to one side, he shot Lovett a penetrating stare. 'Pray don't tell me that you're one of those misguided chaps who erroneously believes that, while in the Holy Land, the Templars discovered a treasure hoard buried beneath the ruins of Solomon's Temple?'

Lovett raised his hands. A show of surrender. 'Hey, you got me mixed up with some other dude. By the time the Templars came along in the twelfth century, the Jerusalem treasury had already been pilfered. Being a history wonk, you know that in 70 AD the Romans razed the Jerusalem temple to the ground. But not before they looted the joint. It stands to reason that the Ark of the Covenant was included in the booty since the sacred relic was housed inside the temple. Along with a *very* vast fortune in gold, silver and glittery gemstones.'

'So, in other words, all roads lead to Rome,' Edie said, unconvinced. Then, deciding to play hard ball, 'Okay, suppose, for argument's sake, the Romans did ransack the Jerusalem treasure – how did the Templars get a hold of it eleven centuries later?'

Clearly up to the challenge, Lovett smirked. 'This is

where the story gets interesting. In the early fifth century, the Visigoth hordes sacked Rome. Their chieftain Alaric made off like a barbarian bandit, stealing the treasury that the Romans had stockpiled in the previous centuries. Now, we're not just talking about the Jerusalem treasury, we're talking about loot plundered from all over the then known world. A big honking treasure by anyone's definition. Bigger than anything Mel Fisher and his crew found in the wreckage of the *Atocha*. That's for damned sure.'

'You still haven't answered my question,' Edie said, refusing to be sidetracked.

'I believe that he has,' Cædmon said, coming to the younger man's defence. 'After sacking Rome, Alaric returned to the Visigoth stronghold in the south of France and promptly buried his pilfered treasure trove. In the year 1150, the Knights Templar took up residence in the same hills and dales once inhabited by the Visigoths.'

'*Where* –' mimicking a gunslinger, Lovett pointed both index fingers at Cædmon's chest in a quick draw – 'you guessed it. The Templars found the friggin' Visigoth treasure. That's about the time the Knights Templar started to live large, building their navy and buying up thousands of manors all over Europe. Suddenly, over night, they had more venture capital than anyone else on the continent. No one could touch these guys. They were a financial force to be reckoned with.' Lovett's hazel-blue eyes gleamed, Edie was certain she could see dollar signs superimposed over his pupils.

'You are, if anything, well-versed in Templar history,' Cædmon remarked.

'Hey, I've been boning up.' Lovett cackled softly. 'Get it . . . archaeologist.' He patted his chest in a 'Me, Tarzan' kind of way. 'Boning up.'

'It's an intriguing theory,' Cædmon continued, ignoring the *shtick*. 'But without more proof, it's thin gruel.'

'Personally, I think the whole story is ludicrous,' Edie said, adding her two cents. Figuring that was the real dollar value of the Templar treasure.

'Hey, this isn't some pie-in-the-sky crackpot theory. I've got the proof. Maps, artefacts, archival records. I've devoted the last year of my life to following the Templars' trail.'

'Mmmm.' Pursing his lips, Cædmon cocked his head to one side. Edie could see that he was mulling it all over, giving serious consideration to the story just told.

And that had her worried.

Couldn't Cædmon see that Jason Lovett was a Templar wannabe? He probably liked to dress up in chain mail and pretend he was a medieval knight.

'Where exactly in the New World did the Templars hide their treasure trove?' Edie made no attempt to hide her scepticism.

'I'm pretty certain the Templars made landfall at Newport, Rhode Island. From there, they moved inland, setting up a colony about twenty miles west of Newport. I partially excavated the site. Looks like some sort of massacre took place. That said, I'm not exactly certain where they hid the treasure.' Not nearly as cocky as he had been, Lovett turned towards Cædmon, a beseeching look on his face. 'This is where your expertise would come in handy. I found some Templar symbols carved on to a boulder.

I think it's a signpost or maybe a secret code. Since you're a Templar expert—' The archaeologist stopped in mid-sentence. Bug-eyed, he teetered unsteadily on his feet.

'Are you all right?' Cædmon solicitously enquired.

Still swaying, the archaeologist frantically reached behind him. Like a man trying to scratch his back, but not quite able to reach the right spot. 'The pret-ty-boy b-bastard . . .'

Without warning, he lurched, toppling the projection screen as he fell, face forward, on to the parquet floor.

An instant later, Edie screamed, horrified to see a jewelled knife hilt protruding from Jason Lovett's back.

7

'Good God!' Cædmon bellowed, shocked beyond belief.

Jason Lovett had just been felled by an assassin's dagger.

Craning his neck, he glimpsed a dark-haired man sprinting towards the exit at the back of the reading room. A lone assassin.

Cædmon turned to Edie. 'Call the police! And whatever you do, don't leave this room until they arrive.' Orders issued, he dashed towards the rear exit.

'Where are you going?' Edie yelled at his backside.

He made no reply, the portcullis about to come crashing down. The assassin had at least a five-second lead, the man having already vanished from the reading room.

Charging through the back doorway, Cædmon burst into an interior hallway, then was immediately brought up short. Panelled in dark wood punctuated with elaborately framed portraits of thirty-third degree Freemasons, the picture gallery had about it a claustrophobic eeriness. Particularly since, other than the immortalized Masons, there wasn't a soul in sight.

'The bastard only had two choices, right or left,' he muttered, silently cursing the fact that the killer was so fleet of foot.

Instinct told him the assassin would steer clear of the banquet hall to the right and the nattering lecture-goers still availing themselves of free refreshments. *Why risk being tackled to the ground by an over-zealous onlooker?*

Hoping his instincts proved correct, he tucked into a runner's pose, taking the road less travelled to the left.

At the end of the hall, he veered in the direction of the polished marble stairs that led to the atrium. Unless he hurried, the bastard would soon be clear of the building.

Taking the steps two at a time, he grabbed hold of the brass banister to keep from falling on his face, leather soles slipping on the smooth surface, his shoes not designed for a foot race.

At the top of the staircase, he swung to the right. Peering through the granite-columned corridor that framed either side of the spacious atrium, he sighted the front exit. And the lone security guard manning his station at the door, unaware of the tragedy that had just occurred below deck.

About to summon the guard, the shout snagged in this throat . . . stifled as he sighted a bit of movement out of the corner of his eye.

He pivoted just in time to see one side of a double door silently swing shut.

Is the wind in that door?

Cædmon stared at the closed door panel, wondering if a trap had just been set. Wondering if Lovett's assassin was the wind that blew shut the swinging door.

'Only one way to find out,' he murmured, stepping forward.

8

'Somebody! Quick! I need a doctor!' Edie Miller hollered, dropping to her knees and scrambling across the downed projection screen to reach Jason Lovett's side.

Oh, God. Was Cædmon really chasing a cold-blooded murderer? What if the killer had a gun? Or another knife? Or was a martial arts—

Cædmon is okay, she silently affirmed. He'd been trained as a spy. Which meant he knew how to handle himself in a dangerous situation.

A paunchy middle-aged man rushed into the reading room.

Edie didn't know if it was the blood, the sprawled body or the jewelled knife hilt, but the first responder skidded to an abrupt halt, his cell phone limply plastered against his cheek. 'What the . . . !'

'Stop gawking and start dialling! Tell the emergency operator that a man's been stabbed at the House of the Temple on 16th Street,' she instructed, having made the assumption that, like most people caught up in an emergency, his brain had just turned to mush. Then, hoping to avert yet another catastrophe, 'After you make the call, I need you to corral everyone into the banquet hall until the police arrive. The killer is still on the loose.'

The man's shock instantly morphed into visible fear.

'But I . . . I've got a w-wife and two k-kids. Why do I have to be hall monitor?'

'Just do it!' Edie screeched, on the verge of lurching to her feet and delivering a heavy-handed slap to his face. 'If this man dies, it'll be on your head!'

The guilt trip worked, the man jabbing away at his cell phone as he spun on his heel and ran out of the door.

Just then, Jason Lovett, amazingly still conscious, rolled from his stomach to his side. The movement cost him, the archaeologist gasping for breath.

'Can I get you anything?' Belatedly realizing it was a stupid question, Edie brushed a hank of blond hair away from his face.

His hair was so soft. Baby fine. Maybe because he was just that, a baby. *Somebody's baby. A mother's beloved son.*

Her eyes welling with tears, Edie placed her hand against Lovett's flushed cheek, willing him to stay alive.

Staring at her with a pain-wracked expression, he found the strength to whisper weakly, '*Aqua sanctus . . . aqua sanctus.*'

'I . . . I don't speak Latin,' she sputtered, not even sure that was the right language. 'You need to – Of course! *Aqua* means water. You want a drink of water.'

Relieved that she'd correctly interpreted the request, she leaned forward, snatching Cædmon's water bottle from the table. Hands trembling, she uncapped the bottle. Then, gently lifting Jason Lovett's head, she placed the bottle to his lips.

Tersely shaking his head, he slapped the bottle out of her hand, splashing water down the front of his chest. '*Aqua sanctus!*' he hissed, this time more urgently.

'Which means *nothing* to me. Cædmon's the one who speaks Latin.'

'You have to . . .' Grimacing, Lovett fumbled with a Velcro flap on his cargo pants.

'Don't move,' she ordered, afraid he might cause greater harm. If such a thing was possible.

Lovett ignored the order, grunting as he ripped open the flap and shoved his hand into his trouser pocket. A prescription bottle plunked loose, rolling a few inches on the parquet floor. Edie glanced at the label. *Xanax*. An anti-depressant. Jason Lovett liked to pop pharm candy.

'The ambulance is on the way,' she told him, wondering how much longer Lovett could hold out. 'We'll have you at GW Hospital in a jiffy. It's a straight shot down New Hampshire Avenue. Won't take but a few minutes to get there.'

Again, Lovett fumbled with the flap on his cargo pants. Wincing, he raised himself up slightly, struggling to remove something from his pocket.

Edie reached over to help him . . .

. . . only to jerk backward when she saw the glint of a gun.

9

Cædmon pushed open the swinging door.

Aware that he might be walking into a trap, he cautiously advanced into a small reading room. Glass display cases lined one wall; a wooden table laden with stacked volumes dominated the centre of the space.

He scanned the cosy jumble. *Marble busts of famed Greek philosophers. A stuffed bald eagle. A glass case displaying Abraham Lincoln's death mask.* As near as he could tell, the room contained nothing but old books and morbid curiosities, Lovett's assassin nowhere in sight.

About to take his leave, his nostrils suddenly twitched, his olfactory senses detecting a scent other than old leather and aged paper.

Cologne.

Yes, he was certain of it, a faint scent of sandalwood clinging ever so gently to the molecules in the air.

He followed the scent.

Entering a two-storey library, he approached an oversized desk nestled between two freestanding cabinets. A narrow staircase on his right led to a cantilevered catwalk suspended overhead.

The scent of sandalwood grew stronger.

The assassin was near.

No sooner did that thought take root than Cædmon heard a quick intake of breath – the only warning he had before the assassin lunged at him. Grabbing hold of the metal post that secured one side of the staircase to the floor, the other man catapulted his body into the air.

Before Cædmon could register what was happening, two leather shoe soles forcefully slammed against his chest. Hurled backward, his head violently swung to the right, his skull smashing into one of the cabinets, causing the imposing piece to totter precariously.

Christ!

A nauseating bolt of pain instantly surged from his right temple all the way down his arm. He spat out a mouthful of blood, red spittle flying through the air, spattering the inlaid glass on the cabinet door. He staggered several feet. Proverbial stars erratically flickered. Disorientated, he heard a low cackle.

The bastard was laughing at him.

He shook off the pain.

Jaw clenched, Cædmon charged his attacker.

Quick on his feet, the other man grabbed a heavy bookend from the desk, hurling the gold-leafed monstrosity at Cædmon's chest. He dodged to one side. Unarmed, he snatched the nearest item at hand – a brass lamp on a nearby end table. He roughly yanked the cord from the wall as he ripped off the lampshade. Makeshift club in hand, he went on the offensive.

'*Bugger!*' he silently cursed when the other man seized a pair of scissors from the desktop arsenal.

Mirthlessly smiling, the assassin came at him, the scissors aimed at his soft underbelly.

Tempted to go for a head shot, Cædmon instead swung the brass lamp at the killer's right hand. Metal slammed against flesh, making a hideous sound. *Thwack!* Like a carrot snapped in two. The scissors clattered onto the floor.

'*Argh!*' the assassin bellowed.

Galvanized into action, Cædmon made a quick, left-handed grab, wrapping his fingers around a suede-clad arm. Snarling, his adversary parried with a vigorous knee jab. A direct hit to the kidneys.

Cædmon grunted. Swallowed back a mouthful of stomach bile. The assassin pulled free from his grasp, dashing up the staircase that led to the second-storey catwalk. Gasping for breath, he gave chase, clambering up the narrow flight of steps. At the top he saw a flash of brown suede, the assassin some twenty feet ahead of him on the catwalk. Ten feet beyond that, the catwalk dead-ended.

Tightening his grip on the brass lamp, Cædmon slowed his step, the game finally drawing to a finish. Cornered, the assassin stood with his back to him.

'Why did you stab Jason Lovett?'

The question met with a soft chuckle.

'Do you find that amusing?'

'I find this entire situation amusing,' the assassin replied . . . just before he vaulted over the railing.

In stunned amazement, Cædmon watched the other man sail through the air, landing nimbly on his feet.

'Bloody hell!'

Flinging the brass lamp aside, Cædmon ran down the staircase. Heart pounding in his ears, he headed for the atrium, bursting through the swinging double doors just in time to see Lovett's killer run past the abandoned security station.

Still determined to catch the bastard, Cædmon raced across the atrium and out of the front door. *Too late!* The assassin had already descended the flight of steps and was sprinting towards an idling bus.

I don't bloody believe it . . . he's going to make his escape on a city coach.

His energy flagging, Cædmon gracelessly charged down the granite stairs.

By the time he reached the thirty-third step, the assassin was already onboard, the coach doors pneumatically closing behind him. An instant later, the vehicle pulled away from the kerb. Rushing forward, he swung his arms above his head, flagging the vehicle. The stone-faced driver didn't give him so much as a sideways glance.

'Shag it!'

Furious, Cædmon banged his palm against the side of the departing coach. In the far-off distance he heard the blare of multiple sirens.

Having seated himself at the rear of the bus, the assassin calmly turned and looked at him.

Cædmon returned the impudent stare, imprinting the man's face on his memory – dark shoulder-length hair, wide-set brown eyes, a proud nose, slightly pouting full lips. Expecting coarse, even loutish features, he was taken aback by the assassin's physical beauty.

I've seen his face before, he realized with no small measure of surprise. At London's National Gallery there was a painting by Botticelli, *Portrait of a Young Man.* Jason Lovett's assassin could have stepped right out of the fifteenth-century canvas, the resemblance uncanny.

Smiling slightly, the assassin raised his right hand to his lips, blowing Cædmon a kiss.

'Cheeky bastard,' he muttered in disgust, the killer's smugness the last insult. The 'Young Man' well aware that he had just got away with murder.

10

'The American soul is hard, isolate, stoic and a killer.'

The thought popped into Cædmon's head as he re-entered the Masonic reading room, D. H. Lawrence's assessment strangely apropos.

Although he wasn't altogether certain that Jason Lovett's assassin *was* an American. The audacious young man had the air of a fashionable boulevardier combined with the physical beauty of a Mediterranean gigolo. Not exactly the image that came to mind when envisioning a cold-blooded American hit man.

Edie, her face streaked with tears, rushed towards him. The crimson-red shawl that was tied at her waist flared behind her like an unfurled sail.

'Thank God, you're all right!' she exclaimed, flinging herself at his chest.

Cædmon wrapped his arms around her quivering backside, belatedly realizing that he was shaking as well. For several moments they held each other, both of them murmuring words of comfort.

Hearing the shrill blare of sirens outside the building, he pulled away and awkwardly patted her shoulder. Four months ago, fate had, literally, thrown them together when they were both marked for execution by a religious zealot intent on finding the Ark of the Covenant. Had it not been for that dangerous episode, their paths would never have crossed. Given that he maintained a flat in Paris and Edie lived in Washington, their paths didn't cross on a regular basis. In fact, he'd just flown into Dulles Airport only the evening before; the first time in nearly four weeks that they'd seen one another. He supposed that a bit of bumbling was to be expected.

'Yes, right.' He cleared his throat, directing his attention to Jason Lovett's sprawled body. 'Where is everyone? A brutal murder usually brings out the morbidly curious.'

'The security guard has the lecture-goers cordoned in the banquet hall.' Edie scowled at him. 'I know that you got your book smarts from Oxford and your street smarts from MI5, but seeing you chase after the killer scared the bejesus out of me. Who do you think you are, Superman?'

'My apologies for scaring the lady. Unfortunately, my superpowers left something to be desired,' he confessed. Like any male of middling years, it pricked his ego that he'd been bested by a younger man. Stronger of both wind and limb. 'The bastard made a clean go of it. Like chasing the Artful Dodger.'

Gnawing on her lower lip, Edie glanced over her shoulder at the dead archaeologist. 'Before he died, I thought Lovett was about to pull a gun on me.' Slipping a hand into her dress pocket, she removed a small chrome-coloured device which she wielded like a handgun. 'Bang-bang! *This* is what I mistook for a loaded weapon,' she said, handing him a digital voice recorder.

'How curious. Given the tragedy that's just transpired, I suspect Jason Lovett wasn't the only person actively searching for the Templar treasure. Although his unfortunate death makes me think that—' Suddenly noticing the jewelled knife hilt protruding from Lovett's back, he stopped in mid-sentence.

Good God. Surely he was seeing things.

Well aware that the authorities would arrive at any moment, Cædmon walked over to the corpse. Going down on bent knee, he examined what appeared to be a finely crafted centuries-old dagger.

'I don't believe it.'

Clearly perplexed by his reaction, Edie stared at the jewelled hilt. 'What is it?'

Taking care not to touch the murder weapon, he indicated the small inset rubies that formed a distinctive eight-pointed star.

'It's an octogram star, the age-old symbol of creation.' Perplexed at seeing the symbol on a murder weapon, he stood upright. 'In ancient Egypt, the octogram star was known as the *ogdoad* and was used by the creation cult that sprang up at Hermopolis. The number eight is highly significant in many esoteric traditions, the Gnostics, the Kabbalists, and, of course, there are eight points—'

'On the famous Templar cross,' Edie said, beating him to the punch. A split-second later, her brow furrowed.

'Do you think this star has something to do with the Knights Templar?'

'I think that Dr Lovett's murder has something to do with the Templars. As for the star . . . I don't know.' Cædmon shrugged, wishing he had a better answer. The eight-pointed star was one of the most complicated symbols in history. *Two interlaced squares. The seven days of Creation followed by the eighth day of regeneration.* Paradise regained.

Lost in thought, he glanced upward, his gaze alighting on the Egyptian hieroglyphics that adorned the ceiling. The unusual motif reiterated the premise of his Oxford dissertation – that the Knights Templar's exposure to the Egyptian Mysteries was at the heart of their brutal demise. And though he'd been derided for a lack of corroborating evidence, he still held firm to the belief.

The Templar treasure. The octogram star. The Egyptian ogdoad. *A dead archaeologist.*

Was there a connection between the seemingly separate sine qua non?

'The Knights Templar are at the heart of this mystery. I can feel it in my blood.'

Edie waved a hand in front of his face. '*Hel-lo.* Jason Lovett was murdered before our very eyes. I suppose you're going to tell me *that's* an occupational hazard of being an archaeologist.' She shook her head, putting Cædmon in mind of a harried mother chiding her ill-behaved child. 'Until now, I thought your obsession with the Knights Templar was relatively harmless.'

'I am not obsessed,' he replied, taking issue with her word choice.

'Well, if you aren't obsessed, why did you chase Lovett's killer?'

'Strangely enough, I had a great many questions to put to the brute. First and foremost, I wanted to know why he executed Jason Lovett.'

Edie's brown eyes opened wide, as though he'd just made the most outlandish of statements. 'Man's greed knows no bounds. Money is the root of all evil. Yo-ho, yo-ho, a pirate's life for me. Take your pick.'

Before he could reply, a bevy of uniformed police officers and a medical emergency team, stretcher in tow, rushed into the reading room.

'What about the digital voice recorder? Should we turn it over to the police?' Edie enquired anxiously.

Cædmon glanced at the uniformed policemen shoving their way through the crowd. Then he glanced at the small digital voice recorder that he still held in his right hand. Finally his gaze landed on the open book that was on the floor beside the dead archaeologist.

The Templars brought the Ark to the New World in the 14th century. I have the proof!

'Mention the digital recorder to no one. Our slain acquaintance bequeathed it to us for a reason.' With the tip of his shoe, he closed the book.

Hopefully, no one would think to open it.

11

Saviour exited the city bus.

At a glance he could see that he was in a Latino neighbourhood, the shop signs all in Spanish, the pedestrians darkly hued.

Still in a heightened state of exultation, he strode towards a cantina half a block away. Admittedly, he enjoyed being pursued, finding it highly erotic. Although in the early years he'd done his share of chasing. Begging. Pleading.

'Pick me. I can pleasure you better than those other boys.'

In need of an espresso, he entered the rundown cantina. Almost immediately, he was assaulted with the combined scents of cinnamon, jalapeño peppers and heated lard. Confidently striding to the back of the establishment, he seated himself at a table covered with a stained white cloth. In the centre of the table, there was a vase of plastic flowers; a pitiful attempt to beautify what was essentially a very ugly café.

A squat woman with dark eyes and even darker hair approached the table.

Assuming she spoke no English, he initiated the exchange. '*Un café exprés, por favor*,' he told her. Having spent a summer on the Costa del Sol, he knew enough Spanish to satisfy most of his physical needs.

Stony-faced, the waitress returned a few moments later,

placing a demitasse and chipped saucer in front of him. Raising the cup to his lips, Saviour immediately felt a stab of pain in his right hand. *Katadikazo!* His pursuer had scored a direct hit with the brass lamp, the surge of adrenalin having masked the injury.

Grimacing, he took a sip of the bitter brew, the pain causing his thoughts to turn to the red-haired man who'd given chase. Did Lovett tell him about the excavation? If he did, it meant that Cædmon Aisquith knew about the massacre and the treasure that initiated the bloodbath. As God was his witness, he wouldn't have shared that information with his own mother. The bitch.

An unmarried woman, Iphigenia Argyros earned the condemnation of her family and neighbours when she was raped by a Libyan refugee. Like hundreds of his countrymen seeking asylum, Saviour's father arrived on the island of Chios in a rickety fishing boat, having braved the treacherous seas to get there. Apprehended by the Greek coast guard, he was transferred to a detention centre in Thessaloniki, managing to escape in short order. First he satisfied his hunger. Then he slaked his lust.

Saddled with an unwelcome bastard, whom she named Saviour out of spite, Iphigenia blamed her miserable lot in life on the child born of that violent union. The fact that his father was a 'filthy, dirty Muslim' made Saviour sub-human in his mother's eyes.

On his thirteenth birthday, enraged that his mother had refused to mark the occasion, Saviour stormed out of the two-bedroom flat in Vardalis Square. It had been the only home he'd ever known.

The first night of his newfound freedom had been

terrifying. Curled in a foetal position, he'd slept in a doorway. The second night, he sneaked into the Agía Sophía, the Church of Holy Wisdom. Lulled to sleep by the soft glow of devotional candles and the strangely erotic scent of incense, he'd been rudely awakened the next morning by a bearded priest who dragged him across the tiled floor, bodily tossing him through the ornately carved church doors. Holy wisdom obviously did not include Christian charity.

His belly aching from hunger, he'd had no choice but to steal food from the Modiano market. A fiasco, as it turned out, a furious fruit vendor beating him with a rose switch. Sobbing, his backside a mass of raised welts, he feared what would happen to him come nightfall. As fate would have it, that's when he met Ari, a street-smart fourteen-year-old who'd been homeless for nearly five years.

Putting a brotherly arm around his shoulders, Ari shared a loaf of bread and a bottle of Coca-Cola with him. Then he invited him to the abandoned cannery that was home to half a dozen runaway boys. Ranging in age from ten to fourteen, they were a close-knit family, Ari the acknowledged leader.

To earn money, the older 'brothers' hit the wharf each morning just after dawn, giving blowjobs to the dock workers arriving for their day's labour, jockeying for business with other homeless runaways. Using a banana, the two of them laughing uproariously, Ari had shown him how to arouse a man in record time so that he was on his knees only a minute or two.

Soon his days fell into a pattern. Morning 'wages' in hand, he and Ari would buy a pack of cigarettes and a box of *kadaifi*, a nut pastry drizzled in lemon syrup. They would then spend the next few hours lounging on the beach, mocking the dockworkers who, like donkeys, had earlier grunted and brayed as their hips spasmodically jerked. He and Ari had names for them. Hairy Ass. Scrunch Balls. Blow Torch. Little Stump. Late afternoon ushered in another round of blowjobs when the fishermen came in with their daily catch, the boys often paid with fresh mackerel. Pooling their meagre funds, the 'brothers' would buy several bottles of retsina to wash down the fish which they grilled on an open fire pit.

While it was far from a perfect life, it was a vast improvement over the one he'd had. With Ari at his side, no one dared to call him a bastard.

About to lift the demitasse to his lips, Saviour felt a soft vibration against his waist. Lowering the cup, he gingerly reached for his mobile phone, the pain in his right hand having intensified in the last few minutes. He didn't have to look at the Caller ID to know that it was his beloved Mercurius.

'Did you use the dagger?'

'As instructed,' Saviour answered, annoyed that the question had even been asked.

'I assume that it went well?'

For a brief moment, Saviour contemplated lying. Thinking better of it at the last moment, he truthfully replied, 'I dealt with the archaeologist. However, there was an unforeseen complication. The archaeologist may have revealed his findings to a man and woman whom he met here in Washington.'

'Their names,' Mercurius demanded, uncharacteristically brusque.

'The woman's identity is unknown. The man is named Cædmon Aisquith.' He spelled the unusual name.

On the other end of the line, Saviour could hear the soft peck of fingertips striking a computer keyboard. He assumed Mercurius had just keyed the name 'Cædmon Aisquith' into an Internet search engine.

'Who is he?' Saviour enquired, curious about the red-haired man.

On the other end of the line, he heard a ponderous sigh.

'A dangerous threat.'

12

A dangerous threat, indeed, the man known as Mercurius thought as he hung up the kitchen phone and walked over to the stove. He peered into the *cezve*, the Turkish coffee-pot; the brew had started to froth. Using a small spoon, he skimmed the light brown *crema* into a small cup.

As he knew all too well, the world was full of dangerous threats. Always lurking. Ready to spring forth when one least expected a knife to the throat, a gun to the temple. Such was the nature of our earthly existence. And though he felt deep remorse over the archaeologist's demise, Mercurius knew that Jason Lovett would have sold the sacred relic to the highest bidder. An action that would have prolonged the misery, the relic mankind's only hope for escaping this wretched world.

Turning off the gas burner, Mercurius carefully poured the hot coffee as close to the side of the cup as possible, the froth slowly rising to the top. That done, he opened a tin, removed a sugared candy and placed it on the saucer beside the diminutive cup. A piece of rosewater-flavoured Turkish Delight to cleanse his palate. Mercurius carried the cup and saucer to the study, his olfactory senses assailed by the rich aroma that wafted through the air.

As always, the pungent scent reminded him of that long-ago night in 1943.

How could it not?

Cybele, their aged housekeeper, had just set a large tray of Turkish coffee and powdered sweets on the table in the elegantly appointed drawing room. All of the furnishings – the elaborately carved cabinets, the gilt mirrors, the upholstered settees – had been imported from France. At no small expense, Thessaloniki a lengthy sea journey from Marseille. His mother, lounging on a velvet-covered divan, was in the process of smoking a lemon-scented cigarette. His grandmother plied her hand to a piece of petit-point embroidery. His two sisters played cards at a table specifically designed for that purpose. And his father sat in a tufted leather armchair, deep in conversation with his best friend of more than forty years.

Suddenly, a knock sounded at the front door.

Every head in the drawing room had swivelled towards the entry hall. Osman de Léon, a Muslim *Ma'min*, glanced at the man sitting next to him, Moshe Benaroya, a Jewish Kabbalist. In years past, their friendship would have attracted no notice. That was when they'd both been subjects of Sultan Abdul Hamid, Thessaloniki part of the fabled Ottoman empire. Before their respective religions had been hermetically sealed off, one from the other, in the aftermath of the first of the world wars.

Of course, as anyone familiar with history knows, those same fierce winds had blown across central Europe five hundred years earlier when Thessaloniki – named for Alexander the Great's sister – had been conquered by the Turkish sultan, Murad II. In the aftermath of *that* war, the name of the city was changed to Salonika. When the winds died down, a new era of prosperity and religious tolerance was ushered in. As evidenced shortly thereafter when the sultan welcomed to Salonika thousands of Jews who'd been banished from Spain by the radical Catholic monarchs, Isabelle and Ferdinand. Learned, skilled and entrepreneurial, the transplanted Sephardi, as they were known, adjusted quickly to life in the Ottoman city.

While the Sephardi businessmen helped Salonika to prosper, it was the Sephardi holy men who made an indelible mark on the 'new Jerusalem'. Mystical rabbis, known as Kabbalists, studied the esoteric secrets embedded within the Hebrew alphabet, convinced that those twenty-two letters, bequeathed to Moses by God, were at the very heart of creation. The Kabbalists of Salonika were renowned the world over and regarded with high esteem by the mystics of the Christian and Muslim faiths.

Until the year 1666, when a Jewish Kabbalist named Sabbatai Zevi proclaimed himself the Messiah.

In the religious frenzy that ensued, thousands of Jews sold their belongings and hitched themselves to the Zevi wagon, certain that the end of the world, as prophesied in the Book of Ezekiel, was near at hand. The sultan did not take kindly to any of this and had Zevi arrested and sentenced to death. However, being a fair and just ruler, the sultan exercised leniency at the last and gave Zevi the opportunity to recant his sins and convert to Islam, thereby saving himself from a sharp scimitar. Not only did Zevi recant, but he urged his thousands of followers to follow his lead and convert to Islam. Which they did willingly. As only Kabbalists could, these new adherents to the Muslim faith saw their conversion as a redemptive act of gathering up the Divine sparks of the universe so they could live a more holy life in the material world. They called themselves *Ma'min*, the Faithful.

At the turn of the twentieth century there were ten thousand *Ma'min* in Salonika. A strong, vibrant community that had fused together Sephardic culture and Kabbalistic beliefs, and had wedded those to the Muslim religion. They read the Koran, attended mosque, but still contemplated the secret teachings of Moses. The *Ma'min* were the perfect bridge between the two People of the Book, being the Muslim followers of a Jewish messiah. This fluidity of faith extended into their personal lives, the *Ma'min* intermingling and intermarrying with both Muslims and Jews.

Which is how, in those tumultuous last years of the *fin de siècle*, a wealthy *Ma'min* family named de Léon hired a Jewish wet nurse who hailed from the humble Benaroya family. Their respective sons, only three days apart in age, grew up side by side. *Milk brothers.* So inseparable that one would have been forgiven for thinking they were blood brothers.

No sooner did they reach manhood than the fierce winds blew yet again.

In 1922, in the aftermath of the *first* Balkan war, Salonika became a Greek domain. Overnight, five hundred years of Ottoman rule ended, the mosques shut down, the distinctive minarets that pierced the skyline were destroyed. The physical destruction was paltry compared to the human toll – the Greek government heartlessly decreeing that all Muslims be deported to Turkey. Only those with extraordinary circumstances would be exempt. Osman de Léon was one of a handful of *Ma'min* granted permission to remain in the newly renamed Thessaloniki, having wisely wed a Christian woman from an influential Greek family.

And so the two 'milk brothers', Osman and Moshe, were able to continue the friendship that began in infancy.

The bond strengthened over the next two decades. Although on that spring night in 1943, it was threatened yet again. This time by a fateful knock at the door.

'May it be good news,' Moshe Benaroya murmured, as Cybele scurried to answer the door.

It wasn't. Not unless one considered it 'good' to have an armed SS officer pay his respects.

Rudely refusing the offered cup of coffee, the SS officer at the front door ordered Moshe to leave the house. Since Osman and his family were non-Jews, the SS officer had no interest in them. If he wondered why a wealthy tobacco merchant was hosting an impoverished Jew, he made no mention of it.

'You cannot take him!' Osman had protested, clearly upset. 'Moshe Benaroya is my brother!'

The SS officer smiled mirthlessly. 'Then you will want to accompany him to the train station.'

A stunned silence ensued. The adults in the room were well aware that it wasn't a suggestion; it was an order.

Although he was only five years of age, Mercurius intuited that something momentous had just occurred. Running across the drawing room, he threw himself at his father.

Bending at the waist, Osman scooped him up in his arms and held him close. 'You must always remember, little one, that you were named for the Bringer of the Light.'

Moshe Benaroya, standing beside them, placed a comforting hand upon his tousled head. 'Do not fear the Light, Merkür. For it will lead you to your life's purpose.'

Osman de Léon never returned from the station. And neither man ever returned from Auschwitz.

As the throng of 'passengers' bound for Poland were marched through Plateia Eleftherias – Freedom Square – the citizens of Thessaloniki had stood silent. Yes, some cried. And a few helplessly shook their heads as the bedraggled stream of humanity passed before them. But no one raised a gun, a finger or even a voice in protest.

Mercurius and his mother had stood silently with the other bystanders. Terrified, the entire time he'd clutched her leg. Overhead, cotton clouds turned blood red, saturated with the rays of the setting sun. Day was dying and he feared a new day would never dawn.

It did. But not before three thousand Jews and one *Ma'min* Muslim had been tightly packed on to the waiting train. Leaving behind their property, their history and their cherished memories of the 'new Jerusalem'.

Over the course of that heartbreaking spring, nearly forty-five thousand Jews from Thessaloniki were transported to Auschwitz. Most, when they first arrived, were handed a bar of soap and sent directly to the 'showers'.

Lost in the horrific memory from that long-ago spring night, Mercurius raised the small cup of Turkish coffee to his lips and took a measured sip.

On that fateful day in 1943 when the unexpected knock sounded at the front door, he'd been taught an invaluable lesson . . . that evil is birthed in silence.

13

'I don't care what the homicide detective told us,' Edie said as she walked into the living room of her Adams Morgan row house. 'I'm not buying that it was a crime of passion. It was . . . I don't know, too much like an execution. An aggrieved lover wouldn't kill from a distance. A person consumed with jealous rage would have stabbed Jason Lovett thirty or forty times. At least that's how it always plays out on those true-life crime shows.'

Carrying a brown paper bag, Cædmon followed in her wake. 'I, too, am lukewarm to the scenario concocted by the police. However, there's a possibility that it was an act of violence aimed at the Freemasons. The group has incurred many enemies over the centuries.'

'Again. Doesn't ring true,' Edie countered, taking the paper bag from him. 'The lecture was open to the general public. And if someone was PO'd at the Freemasons, wouldn't they have gone on a rampage?'

As she spoke, Edie removed several food containers from the bag and placed them on an oversized bronze platter. Supported underneath by a matched pair of Indian stone elephants, the gigantic platter did double duty as a coffee table. Her next-door neighbour Garrett never failed to mention that her living room looked like the inside of *I Dream of Jeannie*'s bottle. Cædmon was too much the gentleman to comment. Having spent several weeks at his

Paris flat, she knew that he preferred the dark woods and fabrics one expected to find in an English library.

With her free hand, Edie gestured to the plastic containers of sushi and the small sake bottle. 'I'll serve up the fish while you pour the libations.' Garrett had just returned from a business trip to Tokyo and had smuggled a couple of bottles of sake in his luggage. Anxious to give the stuff a test drive, she placed two demitasse cups on the platter next to the cerulean-blue bottle.

Cædmon seated himself on the velvet sofa. About to plop down on the sisal carpet, Edie instead cocked an ear towards the doorway. Hearing the *whhrr* and *hum* of the fax machine, she said, 'Sounds like we've got an incoming. What do you wanna bet that's the fax you were expecting?'

'Trent is, if anything, dependable.'

'Stay put. I'll go check.' Motioning him to remain seated, Edie walked across the hall to her home office. Sure enough, there were several sheets of white paper in front of the fax machine. Earlier in the day, Cædmon had contacted his old group leader at MI5 to request a background dossier on Jason Lovett. *Must be nice to have friends in high places.*

In addition to the faxed sheets of paper, she snatched up her laptop computer before heading back to the living room.

She set the laptop on the sofa then, holding the fax aloft, said, 'Do you want to read it or should I?'

Cædmon's brow slightly furrowed. 'Er, by all means,' he deferred, indicating that she should do the honours.

Seeing that creased forehead, Edie belatedly realized she'd overstepped her bounds. She handed him the faxed sheets of paper. 'On second thoughts, it *is* addressed to you.'

A tad self-conscious, Edie seated herself on the floor and made a big to-do out of opening the food containers. Stilted interludes like that made her wonder how they were ever going to make a transatlantic relationship work. Because of the lengthy amounts of time spent apart, when they did hook up it often seemed as if they reverted to Square One – the awkward 'Getting to Know You' stage. Off-kilter conversations. Mumbled apologies. *Sharing the bathroom!* The only time they were in sync was in bed. However, man cannot live by bed alone.

Amused, Edie giggled.

Cædmon glanced up. 'Care to share the joke?'

'Nope. So, what's the scoop on the dearly departed archaeologist? Any deep, dark secrets?'

Setting the fax aside, Cædmon shook his head. 'No red flags, if that's what you're asking. According to the dossier, Jason Lovett had a Bachelor's degree in Cartography and two advanced degrees in Archaeology. After graduation, he spent some time in Key West working with the Fisher team, trying to locate shipwrecked Spanish galleys.'

'Politely put, he was a professional treasure hunter.' Ravenous, she used a chopstick to smear a healthy amount of wasabi on top of several sushi rolls. That done, she opened a packet of soy sauce with her teeth, slathering it over the green-coated rolls. 'Which begs the question . . . Do you think the fabled Templar treasure is really as big as Lovett claimed?'

'I don't know if it would be worth so staggering a sum as a hundred billion dollars. However, if it does exist, the

Templar treasure would be sizeable,' Cædmon replied, partially validating the dead archaeologist's outrageous claim. 'And if the Templars had the Ark of the Covenant in their possession, the sacred relic would have been smuggled out of France along with the monetary treasure. As you know, I'd give anything to get my hands on the Ark.'

'We *are* talking about events that occurred seven hundred years ago.'

Edie reached for a California roll, sushi one of her favourite take-out meals. Probably because she got to eat it with her fingers. Cædmon, on the other hand, veered away from the wasabi, used chopsticks and always kept a napkin at the ready. Just another reminder that they were polar opposites. The fact that he'd gone to Oxford and she'd spent time in the foster-care system after her junkie mother overdosed meant they had grown up in two different worlds.

No doubt, his highbrow education was the reason why Cædmon sometimes acted with a cerebral detachment, whereas she tended to act on her intuition. Head and heart. She was still trying to figure out if, together, they made a complete whole. Although as far as jobs went, she thoroughly enjoyed being Cædmon's research assistant. Never a dull moment.

'I don't mean to burst your Templar bubble, but the treasure may already have been discovered,' she said, pointing out the obvious.

'The evidence suggests that the treasure has not been found.'

'Really? And what evidence is that?'

Cædmon dabbed at his lip with his paper napkin before

answering. 'When the Spanish returned from the New World, their ships loaded with Indian gold, silver and gemstones, the country suffered from massive inflation because of the sudden influx of capital on the Spanish markets. Had the Templar treasure been found, a similar thing would have happened. Since there's no record of an unexplained capital influx in the European markets, we can safely assume the treasure has not been discovered.'

Edie stared at the digital voice recorder in plain view on top of the bronze platter. 'Earlier today, Lovett presented a *very* fanciful theory. Unless he's got a map with a big "X" marks the spot, listening to that thing is going to be a colossal waste of time.'

'Perhaps Dr Lovett will flesh out his fanciful theory on the voice recorder,' Cædmon countered in a measured tone. 'Besides, I have a morbid curiosity. Dead man talking from the grave, and all that.'

'Speaking of which, Lovett was out-of-his-mind delirious right before he, um –' she searched for a tactful phrase – 'passed over. I didn't mention it earlier, but he kept repeating the words "*aqua sanctus*".'

'*Aqua sanctus* . . . how curious. It's Latin for "holy water".' Cædmon reached for the digital voice recorder. 'An overly anxious archaeologist babbling in a dead language. This should prove interesting.'

14

The man behind the wheel of the leased Audi A6 braked to a full stop and cut the ignition. The burnt-out street lamp, suspended from an iron base adorned with paper flyers that gently flapped in the evening breeze, provided a dark pocket in the otherwise well-lit residential neighbourhood.

Leaning across to the passenger seat, Saviour Panos opened a hard-sided case. From its depths, he removed a parabolic dish with microphone, headset and tape recorder. The same surveillance equipment he'd used to good effect with the archaeologist.

This night he had a different target; his beloved Mercurius was anxious to ascertain how much Cædmon Aisquith knew about the massacre site and the Templar treasure.

Acting on a hunch – that he'd find the Brit at the police precinct – Saviour had earlier followed the red-haired man from the police station to the row house situated on the other side of the street. To his surprise, the historian was still in the company of the curly-haired woman from the Masonic temple. Curious as to the nature of their relationship, he'd made enquiries of a plump middle-aged man walking a ridiculously shaved miniature poodle. The gossipy dog owner had been a fount, Saviour learning that Edie Miller, a photographer by trade, was romantically involved with the British writer, the two having just returned from a trip to Ethiopia.

The information had been freely given. But, of course. Beautiful people rarely came under suspicion – a defect in human nature that Saviour often exploited to his advantage.

Able to see two blurry shadows through the sheer fabric that hung at the window, Saviour aimed the parabolic dish in that direction.

'*. . . he spent some time in Key West working with the Fisher team, trying to locate shipwrecked Spanish galleys.*'

Smiling, he turned on the recording device, his two love birds coming in loud and clear.

Able to relax finally after a hectic day, he retrieved a box of Dunhill cigarettes and a silver lighter from his jacket pocket. The lighter, engraved with the Creator's Star, had been a birthday gift from Mercurius. A man of deep religious convictions, Mercurius had an almost fanatical attachment to the eight-pointed star. In much the same way that his mother Iphigenia had been slavishly devoted to the Virgin Mary, their squalid flat inundated with her unsmiling image. Personally, Saviour preferred the image of Jesus on the cross, a writhing half-naked man in his death throes.

As he flipped open the lighter, Saviour cursed under his breath, his right hand, now swollen, throbbing from the earlier run-in with the Brit. Somewhat clumsily, he lit the cigarette dangling from the corner of his mouth with his left hand. Inhaling deeply, his lungs filling with smoke, he savoured the calming effects of the tobacco. A gift from the gods.

However, the gods had not always smiled so favourably upon him. There was a time when he could barely afford to buy one or two cigarettes, let alone an entire pack. That was when he knew what living on the knife's edge meant. The hunger. The fear. The utter exhaustion. The simple desire for a soft bed and a full belly had become an obsession. But not for himself. He could do without. Instead, he coveted the small luxuries for his beloved Ari.

When Ari first took ill with a bad case of the chills, they naively assumed the hacking cough and elevated fever would soon dissipate. A few weeks later, he began to spit up blood, the respiratory ailment worsening, Ari so weak he could barely make the ten-block walk to the hospital. When the doctors diagnosed his friend with having a virulent strain of antibiotic-resistant pulmonary tuberculosis, Saviour had refused to believe.

My God! It was a death sentence. He'd been sorely tempted to grab one of the shiny instruments off the bedside tray and jab it into the doctor's soft underbelly. He was that enraged. And when the hospital staff quarantined Ari, refusing to release him until the danger of contagion had passed, Saviour had to be dragged from the hospital by two burly security guards.

Painfully aware that his friend needed more comfort than his meagre income could provide – sucking dock workers' cocks kept him fed and shod but paid for little else – Saviour quickly devised a plan to earn more money. Even a seventeen-year-old wharf rat knew that the male prostitutes who paraded along the Leoforos Nikis were in great demand, wealthy tourists and businessmen paying a hefty price for the pleasure of their company. Saviour also knew that those same tourists and businessmen had discriminating tastes. Meaning he had to somehow transform himself from a dirty wharf rat to a stylish escort.

Determined to provide for his ailing friend, he spent hours studying the haughty young men who strolled the Leoforos Nikis, the café-lined promenade that hugged the Thermaic Gulf. He spent even longer hours staring into a cracked mirror, affecting an aloof expression that conveyed a purposefully ambivalent message: that he might deign to spend some time with a client – provided the price was right. Even then, it wasn't absolutely assured. Because in those hours spent on Leoforos Nikis, he'd noticed a curious phenomenon – for the wealthy men with the well-padded wallets, it was all about the ritual of the hunt.

Needing to outfit himself properly for the ritual, he must have sucked a hundred cocks before he had enough money to buy a pair of white trousers, a striped boat-neck jersey and a small bottle of Paco Rabanne cologne. In a cost-saving measure, he'd stolen a pair of hand-made leather loafers from a five-star hotel, sneaking in while the maid was changing the bedclothes.

His thick wavy hair professionally styled, his body bathed and scented, Saviour was now ready to join the other beautiful young men on the Leoforos Nikis.

His first night, a Saturday, a tall Dane with a memorable lack of body hair hired him for the entire evening. Saviour proceeded to spend what seemed like an eternity on his hands and knees. The next few nights passed in a blur. An entire group of Japanese businessmen. An American professor at Aristotle University. A French diplomat. At week's end, he had enough money to rent a small one-bedroom flat just south of Egnatia Street. Close enough to smell the wafting incense at Agía Sophía. On Sunday, his well-deserved day of rest, he splurged on lamb and green beans. The next day, Monday, the doctors agreed to release Ari to his care. As he ushered his pale, pathetically thin friend into their new residence, he bit his lip, worried that Ari might not like the sparsely furnished flat. Side-by-side, they stepped across the threshold, the sun streaming through the newly washed windows. Ari reached for his hand. Too moved to speak.

In time, Ari's illness forced Saviour to reinvent himself yet again.

Saviour lit another cigarette. Suddenly hearing a static crackle in his headset, he readjusted the hearing device. Detecting a third voice, he turned up the volume.

'It's been said that every great treasure hunt starts with a centuries-old rumour.'

At hearing the dead archaeologist's voice eerily transmitted through his earpiece, Saviour nearly choked on a mouthful of smoke.

Skata!

It was like a ghost whispering into his ear.

15

'It's been said that every great treasure hunt starts with a centuries-old rumour. My hunt is no different. Flashback five years ago to when I was a PhD candidate at Brown University. That was the year I had an internship with the department chair, Dr Cyrus Proctor, an expert on American-Indian archaeology. A ground-breaking ceremony doesn't take place in Rhode Island until Dr Proctor has examined the site to determine if it has any cultural significance. God help the commercial developer if Dr Proctor finds Native American artefacts buried in the soil. But I digress.

As fate would have it, I was sitting in Dr Proctor's office grading mid-term exams the day that a middle-aged Indian dude walks in unannounced. The dude tells Dr Proctor that his name is Tonto Sinclair – yeah, Tonto, I kid you not – and that he needs help tracking down Yawgoog's treasure, Yawgoog being a mythic Narragansett folk hero. A scary-looking dude, Tonto had the words "red blooded" tattooed across his knuckles. It didn't take much to imagine him all done up in war paint with a tomahawk in one hand and a bloody scalp in the other. Anyway, Tonto produces a gold coin supposedly minted in the Middle Ages and a photograph of a large boulder carved with a medieval battle standard. He said the gold coin and the boulder were gifts from Yawgoog to the Narragansett tribe. Needless to say, Tonto had my undivided attention.

Not nearly as impressed, Dr Proctor dismissed both items, claiming the gold ingot could be purchased on eBay and the carved rock, which he'd seen before, was part of an eighteenth-century colonial hoax. Pronouncement made, Dr Proctor sent Tonto packing.

For the next five years, the incident haunted me. I kept thinking, "What if there really is a treasure hidden in Rhode Island?" Determined to answer that question, my first task was to research this Yawgoog character. To that end, I tracked down the Indian dude, Tonto Sinclair. Mistakenly thinking I was there to help the Narragansett find their lost treasure, Sinclair regaled me with the Yawgoog legends. While I'm no folklore expert, it was obvious the Narragansett Indians look upon Yawgoog as some sort of man-god. A couple of the tales, in particular, snared my attention. Like the one about Yawgoog, decked out in an apron, constructing a stone bridge across a river. Or Yawgoog hanging out in a cave large enough to house a small tribe. And last, but not least, Yawgoog liked to ride around on big whales.

Pleased to be taken seriously, Tonto took me out to the middle of the Arcadia Management Area, a wilderness preserve in the southwestern part of the state. First he takes me to see Yawgoog's stone bridge. And, yeah, it's a bridge made of stone ledges that spans a raging river. Then he shows me this big-ass freestanding boulder which he claims had been carved by Yawgoog.

Man, imagine my surprise when I saw a cross pattée, the famed Templar cross, prominently carved on the boulder. And that's when it hit me – Yawgoog had been a Knights Templar.'

Wearing an incredulous expression, Edie abruptly shut off the digital voice recorder.

'Can that possibly be true?'

'I believe the tale has merit,' Cædmon replied. 'But where it's headed is unclear. If the Knights Templar did make landfall in Rhode Island in 1307, they would have been technically more advanced than the native peoples. Which explains why Yawgoog had been deemed a man-god.'

'Okay, I'll buy that. But how in the world did a Knights Templar get the strange moniker "Yawgoog"?' Holding the sake bottle aloft, Edie silently enquired if he wanted a refill.

Cædmon wistfully stared at the proffered bottle. A fondness for alcohol was a burden borne by many ex-intelligence officers. An expedient way to soften the violent memories. And his memories were more violent than most. Five years ago, the Real Irish Republican Army had detonated a bomb in a crowded London tube station. He'd lost the woman he loved in that blast. Out for revenge, he used his MI5 resources to track down the RIRA leader who masterminded the attack, gunning him down on a Belfast street corner.

That act of cold-blooded vengeance did nothing to assuage his pain. Plunged into a state of inconsolable grief, he spent months in an inebriated state. Until his taskmasters at Thames House forced him to dry out.

Although tempted, Cædmon shook his head, declining the refill. Edie knew nothing of his battles with alcohol. Easier to remain silent than make the shameful confession.

'The name Yawgoog might possibly be a butchered pronunciation of a medieval French name,' he said in answer to Edie's question. 'Curious name aside, I'm intrigued by the notion of Yawgoog donning an apron to build a stone bridge.'

'That caught my attention too. Didn't medieval stone masons wear aprons?'

He nodded. 'A leather apron was used to carry the tools of the trade: the mallet and chisel. And a sturdy apron protected the mason from flying chips and stone dust. But there's also an ancient tradition of mystical adherents donning an apron. In its esoteric guise, the apron symbolizes purity.'

'Probably because it covers the lower portion of the body,' Edie correctly deduced.

'In the Old Testament, the Levite high priest wore an apron as part of his ceremonial attire. The *ephod*, as it was called, had to be donned before the high priest could stand before the Ark of the Covenant.'

In the process of raising a piece of sushi to her lips, Edie's eyes opened wide as she dropped the tasty titbit on to the plastic container. 'Well, *that's* an interesting factoid. Certainly throws Yawgoog's apron into a whole new light, huh?'

'While it doesn't bring us any closer to finding that most sacred of relics, it is a curious coincidence.'

'Change of subject,' Edie said abruptly, picking up the abandoned piece of sushi. 'Lovett said that Yawgoog liked to ride around on a whale. I'm thinking that might be a quaint Indian description for a Templar ship which, sizewise, would be comparable to a humpback whale.'

'How very astute.' An unusual mix of Victorian grace and quirky modernity, Edie Miller was also possessed of a nimble mind. All of which engaged his heart, his brain and various other organs. And not infrequently at the same time.

Always intrigued by an intellectual conundrum, Cædmon got up from the sofa and walked over to the CD-player on the other side of the living room. Opening a clear plastic case, he removed Erik Satie's *Gymnopédies*. Music helped to hone his thoughts. His belly full, his mental pencil was in need of sharpening.

His dinner companion theatrically rolled her eyes. 'Any excuse to play drippy piano music. That particular CD makes me feel like a character in a French film. You know the character I'm talking about, the one who only wears black, smokes *way* too many cigarettes and speaks in existentialese.'

'You forgot to mention the beret.'

He assumed the jibe had to do with the fact he lived nearly four thousand miles away in Paris. While he was content with the arrangement, he suspected that Edie had reservations. As for their professional relationship, she ably assisted in his research from a distance via email, fax and text messaging.

'It's kind of morbid, listening to a dead man's voice. Lovett's so conversational, it's like he's right here with us.'

'Indeed.' He glanced at the digital voice recorder, a twenty-first-century memento mori.

'So what do you think of Lovett's theory so far?'

Cædmon took a moment to consider his reply. Then, of two minds, he said, 'The man was either brilliant or out'n'out bonkers.'

16

Standing in the shadow of Edie Miller's front porch, the intruder stared at the unlatched window lock.

Stupid bitch.

Face pressed to the glass, Saviour peered into the darkened room. *Desk. Filing cabinet. Shelving units crammed with boxes and books.* It didn't appear that the Miller woman kept anything of value in her home office. Not that he was looking for something to steal. He had a different purpose altogether for wanting to break into the house.

Having already verified that no one lurked in the street, Saviour braced his hands on the top of the sash. Slowly, he slid the window open. Just enough so he could bend at the waist, swing one leg over the sill and –

– duck inside the darkened room with no one the wiser. *Yes, a* very *stupid bitch.*

Still bent at the waist, Saviour slipped off his shoes, shoving them into the waistband of his trousers. The house had wood-plank flooring; he could noiselessly glide across the polished floorboards. Straightening to his full height, he recalled an old Greek saying: '*I locked the house, but the thief was inside.*' Amused, he bit back a chuckle.

Ready to go exploring, he first slipped a hand into his jacket pocket and removed a switchblade. He pressed the smooth nubbin on the handle, releasing the three-and-a-quarter-inch stiletto. Fingering the blade with his thumb, he felt a slight impression, the word 'Milano' incised on the honed steel. The Italians were only good for two things – making shoes and stilettos.

Silently sliding to the open office door, Saviour stood in the shadows and listened, able to hear every word that emanated from the room on the other side of the hallway. Little birds cooing silly nothings. *How sweet.* Soon enough, he'd rip the wings from their squawking bodies.

The archaeologist actually recorded a digital diary!

If he could, Saviour would gladly kill the blond bastard all over again. *And after he killed him again, he'd piss on the grave!* Because of the recording, the Brit and his woman knew everything. So, the chickadees had to be smothered. Silenced, once and for all.

Glancing into the darkened corridor, he saw a light emanating from a room at the end of the hallway. *The kitchen, more than likely.* He headed in that direction, careful to keep his movements as smooth and even as possible. An angel of death flitting past.

A few moments later, Saviour surveyed the tidy kitchen with its row of glass containers all neatly lined on the counter. *Flour. Beans. Pasta. Sugar.* And at the end of the row, a cell phone nesting in its charger.

Perfect.

In order to call the police, the little birdies would have to come to the kitchen. All he had to do was lie in wait.

About to slip his shoes back on, Saviour saw something out of the corner of his eye – a small metal door in the middle of the kitchen wall. The panel box for the electric circuit breakers. *Even more perfect.*

He softly padded across the kitchen and opened the grey metal door.

The last piece of the plan just fell into place.

17

'I'm casting my vote for bonkers,' Edie stated for the record, suspecting that Jason Lovett was spinning an imaginary web. 'The hunt for the fabled Templar treasure makes for a great Hollywood movie, but it's just an urban legend.'

'Many legends have a basis in fact,' Cædmon was quick to inform her, just before he pressed the START button on the digital voice recorder.

'Now this is where serendipity and Sarah Sanderson come in. Within days of meeting Tonto Sinclair, I got a text message from a woman I used to date at Brown. Sarah suggested that I check out a centuries-old circular stone tower that's located on a knoll overlooking the bay in Newport, Rhode Island. A local oddity – nobody's ever been able to figure out who built the damned thing. Although – and this is where the story gets interesting – the Italian explorer Giovanni Verrazano made mention of the circular tower when he explored Rhode Island in 1524. Verrazano is credited with being the first European dude to come ashore in New England. Curious as hell, I drove to Newport to check out the stone tower for myself. A careful examination of the site convinced me the tower had been built in the fourteenth century by the Knights Templar.

Certain there was a connection between Yawgoog, the Newport Tower and the Templars, I asked Tonto Sinclair if he knew where exactly Yawgoog and his extended family had lived. While he didn't know the location of Yawgoog's cave, he was able to show me where the family maintained an above-ground settlement. As with the carved boulder, the settlement was located in the Arcadia Management Area. Anxious to conduct a field search, I rented a cottage that was conveniently situated at the crossroads just outside the park entrance. Since it's off-season, I pretty much have the place all to myself. That enabled me to set up a large site perimeter without having to worry about nosey rangers and curious hikers.

On my preliminary field walk of the site, I discovered slightly raised patterns on the ground surface. A little digging revealed that a substantial rubblework structure, probably a fortification wall, had been erected at the north-west corner of the site. I'm guessing that, in its heyday, a settlement complex covering a ten-acre swathe had been built at Arcadia. Although, for some unknown reason, all visible traces of the settlement have been obliterated.

Needing to prove that this was a Templar settlement and not an Indian village, I used a metal detector to scan the area. It didn't take long before I hit gold – literally – nearly shitting on the spot when I excavated half-a-dozen gold coins minted in the late thirteenth century. I also uncovered bits and pieces of early-sixteenth-century weaponry, a sword hilt engraved with a Maltese cross, part of a rosary with a Sacred Heart of Jesus medallion and a silver ring. The year 1523 was engraved on the rosary medallion. I then checked the historic record and learned that there were Maltese knights aboard Verrazano's ship, the Dauphine.

Since six gold coins and one tarnished ring does not a treasure make, I decided to bring in the heavy artillery and use ground-penetrating radar to scan below the surface. Imagine my surprise when I discovered a mass grave containing at least two hundred bodies on the outskirts of the settlement.'

*

Edie switched off the device. 'Whoa! I didn't see that coming,' she exclaimed, the tale having taken a dark turn.

Cædmon's brow furrowed. 'A mass grave can mean only one thing . . . after more than two hundred years, the Inquisition finally found the Templars in their New World hideaway.'

'Since we can't verify that this mass grave even exists, maybe we shouldn't jump to premature conclusions. Or make sweeping generalizations.'

'When the Age of Exploration began in the fifteenth century, I suspect that the Church fathers in Rome belatedly realized the Templars had escaped to America in 1307,' Cædmon conjectured, ignoring her suggestion to put on the brakes.

'Maybe the Narragansett Indians attacked the settlement.'

'The Indian custom was to leave the bodies to rot where they fell. They wouldn't have dug a burial pit nor razed the settlement to the ground. And the Maltese and Jesuit relics uncovered by Dr Lovett point to an entirely different villain. In the early sixteenth century, the Jesuits took over the Inquisition. However, as ordained priests, they could spill no blood.'

'Let me guess . . . they contracted the Knights of Malta to do their wet work.'

'The Maltese knights giving new meaning to the phrase "Submit or die".'

She shook her head, still trying to make sense of the centuries-old massacre. 'This is what I don't get – why kill the Templars' descendants? They committed no wrongdoing.'

'One of the more onerous edicts of the Inquisition was to sear the offspring with the heretic's brand.'

Shuddering, Edie switched on the digital voice recorder again.

'According to Tonto Sinclair, Yawgoog faded from the scene when the white colonists arrived. Although, and this is key, right before his stage exit, Yawgoog made the Narragansett the custodians of his vast treasure. Soon thereafter, colonial land grabs and King Philip's war pretty much wiped out the tribe, who have only recently made a comeback. Which means Tonto Sinclair may be the only Narragansett Indian who's ever heard of Yawgoog's treasure.

My gut feeling is that the treasure is stashed in Yawgoog's subterranean hideaway. But the Arcadia Management Area comprises some seventeen thousand acres. The cave could be anywhere. The only clue I have is the carved Templar boulder, which I'm convinced is an encrypted signpost. I also found some weird primitive writing on one of the foundation stones that I excavated, although I doubt the inscription has anything to do with the treasure. Kinda hard to read a signpost that's buried underground.

Even though I've only found six gold coins, there's no doubt in my mind that we're talking about the largest treasure in the world. I am so close. I even defaulted on my student loans so I'd have the cash to fund the search. But I've hit a roadblock. I need someone who can decipher the damned Templar carving. I'm going to DC to see if I can interest Cædmon Aisquith in the job. The guy's a real academic renegade. I read his book Isis Revealed *and, according to his bio, not only is he currently working on a book about the Templars, but he's interested in the Ark of the Covenant. While the Templars didn't leave an inventory list, it's possible the relic was part of the cache. Since I need a man with Cædmon Aisquith's skills set, I'll use the Ark as my calling card. God, I hope he'll agree to help. If he does, I'll give him a decent cut of the action. Of course, any number of folks would love to elbow me out of the way. We are, after all, talking about a shitload of money. I can't be too safe. No one knows about my wilderness crash pad. Or so I thought until I caught someone prowling around. Said he was a hiker who lost his way, but . . . this guy did not look like a trailblazer. Unless we're talking the strip in Vegas. A real Rico Suave, decked out in tight cargo pants. That's why I've got the artefacts and all of my research notes well hidden at the cottage.*

If someone is listening to this – Shit. It means the fucker finally caught up to me. Just so we're clear, I'm not paranoid. I am *being stalked. But there's too much at stake to tuck tail and run. No way in hell I'm going to let that pretty-boy bastard take what's mine. If he wants the treasure, he's going to have to—'*

The recording abruptly ended.

Cædmon stared at the digital recorder as he thoughtfully tapped his index finger against his chin. 'Lovett knew the *enfant terrible* was watching his every move.'

'This Rico Suave guy was probably hoping that Lovett would lead him right to the fortune. Although why kill the gilded archaeologist *before* he finds the fabled treasure?'

'I don't know. But I would be interested to examine this boulder with the Templar cross pattée carved on to it.' Pulling the computer on to his lap, Cædmon quickly accessed an online travel agency.

'You're going to Rhode Island, aren't you?'

'Ah! The Hope Valley Inn is located just a few miles from Arcadia.' He glanced up from the computer. 'And, yes, I am going to Rhode Island. Lovett presents a compelling case for the outlawed Templars taking their treasure to Rhode Island. The Ark of the Covenant may well have been part of the treasure trove.'

'Hel-lo! Did you even listen to the recording?' Exasperated, Edie answered her own question. 'No, you did not. Because if you *had* listened, you'd know that Lovett used the Ark to lure you into the showroom. He didn't provide one scrap of evidence to prove the Ark is part of this fabled—'

'Even if the Ark isn't included in the treasure hoard,' Cædmon interjected, 'I can't ignore the fact that the Knights Templar may have established a secret colony in the New World. That, alone, warrants further investigation.'

Folding her arms across her chest, Edie carefully considered her next move. Not only did Cædmon have an obsessive interest in the Knights Templar, he also had a chip on his shoulder, courtesy of the History department at Queen's College. Although he rarely spoke of the long-ago incident, he resented the dons at Oxford who'd trashed his unorthodox dissertation, bitter waters running *very* deep. So, no surprise that he wanted to uncover a new twist on the Templar tale. If he succeeded, it'd be the ultimate '*Up yours!*'. And, as his paid research assistant, she did have a vested interest. Particularly since her other career prospects weren't exactly paying the bills.

Edie glanced at the matted and framed photographs of Ethiopian women that she'd placed around the room. Some were candid shots, others were posed. All were photographs of women. No doubt, her degree in Women's Studies had something to do with the content. The collection was her first foray into the realm of social documentary photography. She'd shown the photos to a couple of local dealers, managing to snag a week-long show at a Dupont gallery that specialized in African art. Several of her photos had also been purchased by the Ethiopian Embassy and would be displayed in their main reception hall. It was a small start. A baby step, really.

'I agree that "The Lost Templar Colony" will make an exciting chapter in your next book.' Cædmon would get no disagreement from her on that score. 'But Jason Lovett was killed today because of something he found in Rhode Island. We have no idea what we're going up against. And, according to the now *dead* Jason Lovett, the Catholic Church mounted a sneak attack on the Templars' New World colony, slaughtering the inhabitants outright. We are treading on *very* dangerous ground.'

'First of all, the slaughter occurred nearly five hundred years ago. The Church has long since abandoned its search for hidden Templar treasures. As for Jason Lovett's tragic murder, we have nothing to fear; the killer doesn't know that we're privy to the digital recording.' Cædmon's clipped tone made him sound like the calm voice of British reason.

Edie took a moment to digest the rebuttal; he'd punched big holes in her case. Persuasive as always.

'The phrase "*aqua sanctus*" might possibly lead to Dr Lovett's hidden research notes,' Cædmon continued. 'I won't know until I get there.'

'You're gonna need a research assistant. I'll go upstairs and pack a bag,' she announced, her mind made up.

'After what happened today at the House of the Temple, I'm concerned that—'

'Don't say it.' She threw up a hand, forestalling his

objection. 'I know that you're concerned for my safety, but as you just pointed out, Jason Lovett's killer doesn't know that we have the recording. Besides, you pay me to do a job. Although I prefer to think of myself as your partner in crime and not just a business deduction on your taxes.'

Cædmon smiled at the jest. 'In that case, be sure to include a pair of sturdy boots.'

'And I'll toss in a bottle of sunscreen and a— Whoa!' she exclaimed in mid-stream, startled when all of the lights in the house suddenly went off. 'I think we just blew a circuit.'

'On the floor! Now!'

'*What!?*'

18

Edie heard rather than saw Cædmon dive off the couch in her direction. An instant later, his chest ploughed into her shoulder, shoving her to the floor. Stunned, she opened her mouth, sucking in a gasp of air.

'Wh-what's going on?' Then, a split-second later, the realization dawning: 'Oh, God . . . it's him, isn't it?' *Him* being Jason's Lovett's killer.

Cædmon pressed his mouth to her ear. 'Where's your mobile phone?'

'Um . . . kitchen . . . charger . . . on the counter,' she rasped, unable to speak in full sentences.

'Right.'

Crouching over the top of her, Cædmon grabbed her by the hand and pulled her off the floor, dragging her to the staircase in the hall.

'Now what?'

'I want you to go upstairs and lock yourself in the bathroom. *Do not* under any circumstances come back downstairs.'

Shock having mushroomed into full-blown terror, Edie obeyed, taking the steps two at a time. Stumbling near the top, she made a wild grab for the banister. But not before painfully banging a knee against one of the stair treads. Her kneecap throbbing with pain, she hobbled down the landing.

Moments later, door securely locked behind her, she scanned the porcelain and tile confines of the bathroom.

She needed a weapon!

Lurching towards the cabinet above the sink, she yanked it open and took a quick inventory – medicine bottles, cosmetic bag, hair brush, Band-aids. Nothing even remotely dangerous. Panic swelling, she wiped a clammy hand against her skirt. Somewhere, in the shadows of her house, a killer lurked, intent on . . .

Plunger! The thick rubber cap was attached to a sturdy wooden handle. If need be, she could use the shaft like a billy club.

With that thought in mind, she rushed over to the toilet bowl and snatched the plunger from its hidey hole behind the porcelain tank. Tucking the plunger under her armpit, she went to the window. Palms pressed against the lower sash, she shoved upward.

The window refused to budge.

'Come on!' She balled her fist and pounded on the sash.

Teeth clenched, she tried again. *Success!* Opening the window to half mast, she scanned the alley. The fluorescent street lamp on the corner buzzed and flickered, casting a surreal tangerine glow onto the row of parked cars and trash receptacles that lined the rutted lane. Several streets over, a dog repeatedly barked. Directly opposite, on the other side of the deserted alley, a light shone in the window.

Edie cupped a hand to her mouth. 'Hey, you! Over there! Open the window!'

No one answered the summons.

The jackhammer inside her chest thumped faster. *What*

if Cædmon couldn't get to her cell phone to call the police? Rico Suave could kill them just like he killed Jason Lovett.

To hell with that! Grasping the plunger between her hands, Edie took aim and –

– hurled it across the alley at her neighbour's window.

The rubber end hit the screen window before bouncing off and landing in the alley below. Edie held her breath, hoping someone inside the house would investigate the commotion.

Nearly twenty seconds passed before a small Latino boy tentatively pulled aside the curtain and peered out of the window.

'I need you to call the cops!' Edie hollered.

The child shook his head, uncomprehending.

She put her right thumb to her ear and her pinky to her mouth. The international sign for 'phone call'. '*Policía! Urgente!*'

The little boy's eyes opened wide. A few seconds later, he ran from the window. Edie had the sickening feeling that her plan just backfired. That rather than eliciting his help, she'd scared the bejesus out of the kid.

Her stomach painfully cramped, she stumbled over to the locked door and put her ear to the small crack between the jamb and the door. Cædmon was downstairs, in the dark, defenceless.

'Please, please, please,' she whimpered to the powers that be.

Because, in that terrified instant, it suddenly dawned on her . . . she no longer had a weapon.

19

Hearing a floorboard groan under a heavy weight, Cædmon froze.

The killer was inside the house.

His field of vision reduced to shadowy shapes and dark objects, he stood motionless. Holding his breath, he listened for a footfall. A swish of fabric. Anything to pinpoint the intruder's location.

The entire house was silent as the grave.

Clever bastard, cutting off the electricity, he thought grudgingly as he tiptoed into the kitchen. Made him think the assassin had preternatural senses. Or the advantage of night-vision goggles.

He came to another standstill, taking a moment to review the kitchen's layout in his mind's eye – refrigerator on the right, stove on the left, Edie's mobile on the counter next to the back door. And, most importantly of all, carving knife in the third drawer. He pivoted in that direction. In the near distance, a police siren shrilly blared.

Suddenly, nostrils twitching, he detected a familiar scent. *Sandalwood.* The same cologne worn by Jason Lovett's killer. The bastard was here, somewhere in Edie's kitchen. Hearing a sharp, breathy inhalation, he intuited the deadly spring was about to uncoil.

Damn!

Like a mortar fired from a cannon, Cædmon launched

himself at the cabinetry. Grabbing a knob, he yanked open the third drawer. Sundry kitchen tools loudly rattled. No time to choose, he grabbed the first utensil he laid his hand upon – a steel sharpening rod. Armed, he spun on his heel, weapon raised.

Just then, a beam of golden light hit his ocular nerve. Blinded by the unexpected burst of illumination, he shielded his eyes with his left hand while his right arm furiously slashed through the air, warding off an attack.

'Cædmon! It's me!'

His pupils contracted, enabling him to see that Edie stood in the doorway, a flashlight grasped in her hand.

'Get the bloody hell out of—'

'He's gone.' She pointed to the opposite end of the kitchen.

Craning his neck, Cædmon saw that the back door was wide open.

'The neighbours called the cops. I'm guessing that when Rico Suave heard the police siren, he got spooked and ran off.'

Indeed, the strident blare had become louder in the intervening seconds.

'Thank God.' Exhaling a ragged breath, he walked over and closed the door, securing it with the chain latch.

'Lucky for us, Rico Suave's survival instincts are stronger than his killer instincts.' Although the remark was uttered with a fair amount of bravado, the worry lines between Edie's brows belied the bluster.

'Trust me, the latter are finely honed.'

Worry lines deepened. 'Maybe we should cancel the trip to Rhode Island.'

Opening the metal door that housed the electric panel, he flipped the main circuit, flooding the kitchen with fluorescent light. 'The sooner we leave Washington, the better.'

With Jason Lovett's killer on the prowl, it would be foolhardy to remain.

20

'You must follow them to Arcadia.'

Heavy-hearted, Mercurius hung up the phone. While not dire, the situation *was* troubling. Earlier today, one problem had been resolved only to have another emerge in its place. Jason Lovett had taken the historian Cædmon Aisquith into his confidence. Not only did the Brit know about the Templar colony, he was determined to find the sacred relic.

Mercifully, the Brit had no idea what he sought.

Worried what danger the new day would bring, Mercurius trudged down the hall towards his study to keep vigil. As was his custom, he stopped in front of the framed photographs that hung on the wall. His gaze slowly went from one heart-wrenching image to the next. *The massacre of Armenian Christians. The extermination of European Jews. The slaughter of Bosnian Muslims.*

Bodies . . . Blood . . . Bones.

'And they utterly destroyed all that was in the city, both man and woman, young and old, and ox, and sheep, and ass, with the edge of a sword,' Mercurius softly whispered, the verse from Joshua ironically apropos. Ironic because three millennia ago, a terrible evil was spawned; an abomination that fostered hatred, promoted bigotry and incited intolerance. Darkness followed in its wake. The evil manifested into the cult of monotheism. Judaism, Christianity,

Islam – within the bosom of each cult beat the heart of darkness.

Crusades . . . Holy wars . . . Jihads.

Could anything be more reprehensible?

So much hatred and violence. Century after bloody century. One could sweetly dream of a peaceful planet, but with the dawning of each new day, the nightmare returned. Indeed, mankind could be forgiven for viewing the world with suspicion. A suspicion germinated from the niggling fear that perhaps our gods have played us false. That we've been duped into believing this world was created by a benevolent and merciful God.

What if it was all a hoax?

For *there*, in each haunting picture, was the incontestable proof. A thousand words not nearly enough to convey the unrelenting anguish.

'*. . . and darkness was over the face of the deep.*'

Confronted with this pervasive darkness, what man didn't yearn to be free of the torment? Drugs, sex, food, shopping, gambling, just a few of the sedatives that mankind used to anaesthetize the pain.

As always, his gaze returned to the framed black and white image of emaciated corpses haphazardly tossed into an earthen pit. He reverently touched the glass that covered the 66-year-old photograph. *Auschwitz.*

'*Lest we forget . . .*'

While that atrocity still haunted, who would mourn the slain Templars tossed into a mass grave at Arcadia? Mercurius didn't need a photograph to envision that brutal episode. The Templars' descendants had been hunted for their heretical beliefs, but massacred on account of the sacred relic that they'd safeguarded. For all their vaunted courage, in the end, the Knights Templar could not bring themselves to use the relic to eradicate the evil in their midst. Perhaps they'd harboured an ill-fated hope that the world could be redeemed.

A hope shared by so many.

Save the world. Save the earth. Save the planet.

The desperate cry of the anguished souls who refused to acknowledge that the Creation was flawed. Had *always* been flawed. Defective. One had only to turn on the cable news channels to ascertain that the hate mongers, the dictators and the vicious thugs dominated global politics. Always threatening to pull the trigger. Start a war. Drop the bomb. It was now as it was in the beginning.

Mercurius tore his gaze away from the framed photographs. He refused to countenance such a world. A pragmatic man, he could reach but one conclusion – this world was not worth saving.

21

'The Templars referred to the Holy Land as "Outremer", meaning "the land beyond the sea". A fitting name, as well, for this far-flung Rhode Island promontory.' As he spoke, Cædmon stared at the two-storey stone tower on the other side of the wrought-iron enclosure, stunned anew, the medieval circular structure out of time and out of place.

'After getting a look at this, it's no wonder Jason Lovett was so convinced the Knights Templar set up shop in the New World.' Standing beside him, her dark curly hair blowing in the chill bay breeze, Edie shot several digital photos. 'Too bad the roof and flooring have rotted away. I bet it was something to see in its heyday.'

'Indeed.' Situated in the middle of a small Newport park, flanked by nineteenth-century mansions, the rubble-work masonry struck a surreal note. Approximately eight metres in diameter and an equal measure in height, the structure was supported by eight Romanesque arches resting upon eight stone pillars. Were it not for the fact that the Italian explorer Giovanni Verrazano mentioned the circular tower in his 1524 ship's log, he would have dismissed the unusual structure as a Victorian folly. A wealthy man's attempt at recreating an idealized medieval edifice.

'While there's no conclusive evidence that the tower

was built by the Templars, the design is highly suggestive. As you no doubt know, the circle beautifully illustrates the concept of infinity.'

'It's most definitely a medieval-style structure, although –' Edie's brow furrowed – 'Lovett maintained that the Templars established their colony not on the coast, but inland at Arcadia.'

'This was, more than likely, a watch tower to signal to ships in the bay.'

'Which raises an interesting point . . . did the Templars travel back and forth between the New World and the Old?'

'It's quite possible that there was sea travel between Rhode Island and, say, Scotland. In the aftermath of the *auto-da-fé*, a contingent of Templars escaped to the Highlands, the Scots sympathetic to their cause. As Oscar Wilde once famously quipped, "Many people discovered America before Columbus, but most of them had the good sense to keep quiet about it."'

'I'll say it again, way cool. It certainly warrants a chapter in your next book.' Edie scanned the photos on the camera's display screen. 'Love to take some snaps at sunset.'

'Time doesn't permit a lengthy excursion.' Cædmon glanced at his wristwatch. A few minutes shy of three, they had just enough time to drive to Jason Lovett's cottage in Arcadia.

'Okay, scoutmaster, I'm ready to hit the road.' Playfully winking, she stuffed the digital camera into its case.

As they strolled back to the rental car parked at the kerb, Cædmon slung a companionable arm around Edie's shoulders. Unable to resist, he turned his head and took one last look at the stone tower that so convincingly mocked the history books.

'I suppose the great unknown at its most dangerous was a safer bet than the Inquisition on its best day,' Edie remarked, correctly deducing his thoughts. 'And what better place for the Templars to hide themselves and their treasure trove than on an undiscovered continent that nobody in the early fourteenth century even knew existed.'

Key in hand, Cædmon unlocked the front passenger door on the rental car. 'Until they were discovered by Verrazano and the Knights of Malta. By the sixteenth century, the Age of Exploration was in full swing, the kingdoms of the Old World all vying for territory in the New. Only a matter of time before someone discovered the Templars' secret hideaway.'

'Doomed from the get-go.' Pulling aside her long woollen skirt, Edie eased into the sedan's front seat.

A few moments later, dark clouds scudding across a lacklustre grey sky, they drove away from what had to be the most unusual man-made structure in America. While not proof positive that the Knights Templar took refuge in the New World, it lent a certain credibility to Jason's Lovett's outrageous claim.

'Off to the land of Yawgoog,' Edie said cheerily. 'Where, hopefully, we will find riches beyond compare.'

Uncertain what they would find at the dead archaeologist's cottage, Cædmon made no reply. Only yesterday, Jason Lovett's dream had ended in a bloody nightmare. However, they trod a much safer path, the killer unaware that they had left Washington. After the unexpected break-in, they'd packed their bags and spent the night in a downtown hotel.

Approaching the toll bridge that went between Newport and Conanicut Island, Cædmon gestured to the bay in the near distance. 'This is the same sight that greeted the Templars when they first sailed into these waters.'

'*Sans* the oil tanker.' Edie twisted in her seat, softly grunting. The compact Toyota sedan afforded a modicum of comfort. 'There's something that's been bothering me . . . according to the legends, Yawgoog had "innumerable" children, but I thought the Templars were celibate.'

Cædmon manoeuvred the Yaris behind a dented pick-up truck hauling a plastic-covered mattress, the unwieldy object lightly bouncing in the cargo hold. 'Once they were excommunicated, the Templars were no longer bound by their vow of chastity.'

'Free to fornicate at will,' she retorted with a grin, the woman no prude. 'Although the only available females on Rhode Island were Narragansett.'

'The Templars may well have taken Indian wives. Or perhaps they warmed their beds with Scottish lasses.'

'The old "Seven Brides for Seven Brothers".'

'Without female mates, their secret colony would have been short-lived to say the—' He glanced into the rear-view mirror. An old habit ingrained from the years at MI 5, an enemy's most common avenue of approach from the rear. 'Strap yourself into the seat belt.'

'Why? What's wrong?'

'Unless I'm greatly mistaken, we're being shadowed.' For the last several minutes he'd been keeping an eye on the black Audi following in their wake, the vehicle keeping perfect pace. Not too close to be noticeable. Not so far as to lose sight of them.

Craning her neck, Edie peered out of the back window.

'The black Audi with the tinted windows,' he said. 'Turn back round. We don't want the driver to know that we're on to him.'

'Are you thinking what I'm thinking, that it's Rico Suave behind the wheel?' Although she appeared outwardly calm, he detected a note of panic in her voice.

'We're of like mind.' Pulling into the left lane, he accelerated past the pick-up truck. He then passed four more vehicles, tucking in behind a mustard yellow SUV. As expected, the Audi stayed put, the driver careful not to show his hand. On a heavily congested expansion bridge, he could follow at a distance, secure in the knowledge that they had nowhere to run.

'Once we get off this bridge, you do plan on losing him, don't you?'

Suspecting that would be a tricky feat to manage on an unfamiliar roadway, he made no reply. Instead, keeping one hand on the wheel, he rummaged in his anorak pocket for two crumpled bills to pay the toll. Up ahead, a neat line of booths materialized on the horizon, two lanes of traffic suddenly branching into six. He veered away from the garish SUV, heading for the toll booth on the far left.

Beside him, Edie groaned, having spotted the Audi in her side-view mirror.

'Guess who just broke away from the pack.'

'Remain calm.'

Slowing the Yaris to a crawl, he made his way to the toll

booth, coming to a complete stop once they were abreast of the uniformed attendant. He shoved his arm through the open window, handing two dollars to the overly plump female. About to put his foot back on the accelerator, he instead leaned his head out of the window.

'May I please have a receipt?'

'Are you crazy?' Edie hissed. 'He's right behind us!'

'As I am well aware.' Turning away from his agitated passenger, he directed his attention to the moonfaced attendant. 'Thank you so much.'

Slowly, in no apparent hurry to leave the toll plaza, he drove away from the booth, remaining in the extreme left lane. Up ahead, the six lanes funnelled back into two. Whereupon he had a choice: continue straight on to the high-speed expressway or take the far-right exit.

'Oh, I get it . . . you don't want Rico to know that we know that he's right behind us.'

He glanced into the rear-view mirror; the driver of the Audi was in the process of handing a bill to the attendant. 'Let's hope the bastard falls for the charade because –' he slammed his foot on to the accelerator, cutting in front of a boxy minivan, then a sporty red coupé and, finally, the mattress-laden pick-up – 'we're taking the next exit.'

The sudden burst of fuel catapulted the Yaris to sixty-five kilometres per hour, tyres squealing as he jerked the steering wheel to the right, barely managing to stay on the roadway as they veered on to the sharply curved exit ramp. According to the green sign that they'd just passed under, they were headed towards Jamestown, a seaside village on the southern end of the island. He sped through the stop sign at the end of the exit ramp.

Edie twisted in her seat to peer out of the back window. 'Punch it! Pedal to the metal! He's right behind us!'

'Damn! The bastard has quick reflexes,' he muttered, remembering how the beautiful young man had bested him at the House of the Temple. Their pursuer, driving a far more powerful vehicle, had no difficulty keeping pace.

He glanced at the speedometer: 120 kph. A safe enough speed on an expressway. A more precarious speed on a narrow two-lane coastal byway.

'Any idea how fast this old girl will go?'

Staring at the wobbling speedometer – as though by such action she could telepathically dictate a speedier progression – Edie groaned, 'Not fast enough.'

He spared another glance into the rear-view mirror, wondering how long they could maintain this high-speed chivvy. 'Can you – shag it!' he exclaimed a half-second later when, just ahead of them, a lorry suddenly veered on to the roadway from a side street. Still cursing, he slammed on the brakes, the Yaris fishtailing from side to side. A short ton broom sweeping the roadway clear of debris.

Beside him, Edie did a fair imitation of a crash dummy, her upper body propelled forward before the constraints of the nylon shoulder harness jerked her back into place.

No time to enquire how she fared, he stomped down on the accelerator as he swerved into the opposite lane, entreating the powers that be to grant them safe passage. At 120 kilometres per hour, they'd never survive a head-on smash-up.

'Godspeed is suddenly taking on a whole new meaning,' Edie rasped, her right hand cinched around the door handle, the left clutching the armrest.

Safely passing the lorry, he peered into the rear-view mirror, verifying what he already suspected: that the Audi had also successfully navigated the slow-moving obstacle.

'It appears that we're about to have an unexpected visitor,' he informed Edie, the Audi zooming towards them, still in the left lane. He wound down the driver-side window. 'Quick! Hand me your mobile phone!'

'By the time the state troopers get here, we'll be roadside fatalities. In case you haven't noticed, his is bigger. Meaning he can easily ram us off the road.'

'Just hand me the blasted mobile!' he impolitely ordered, thinking Edie's truculence strangely misplaced.

She passed her iPhone just as the Audi came parallel to them. Snatching the device in his right hand, he held it like he would a pistol. Then, his left arm rigidly positioned at a ninety-degree angle from his body – hopefully obscuring the fact that he wielded a mobile phone rather than a loaded weapon – he took aim at the parallel vehicle.

The illusion worked, the driver of the Audi hitting the brakes as he repositioned his vehicle directly behind them.

Admittedly relieved, he returned the iPhone.

Beside him, Edie insistently jabbed her finger in the air. 'Look! Up ahead on the right! It's a golf course!'

'Perfect.' He swerved abruptly to the right, the back end of the Yaris fanning, first to the left, then to the right, as they made the turn. Glancing in the rear-view mirror, he watched as the sleek Audi followed on their heels.

Passing the clubhouse, he headed straight for the green turf.

Mercifully, the course was closed for the season, the links deserted. Overhead, an osprey and an eagle glided through the air, casting their shadows on to the greenway, the two birds of prey vying for the same quarry.

'Oh, God! He's gaining on us!' Edie exclaimed anxiously as they sped along the fairway.

Cædmon looked into his side mirror. Repeating the move he'd made on the two-lane highway, the Audi pulled up beside them. This time, however, the driver used the much sturdier vehicle like a battering ram.

The Yaris shook on its flimsy metal frame, knocked in the direction of the towering pines that rimmed the fairway.

Cædmon slammed on the brakes. Rubber tyres dug into the thick grass, leaving pulpy furrows in its wake.

Just as he hoped, the Audi sped ahead of them, the driver *finally* thrown off his stride by the unexpected manoeuvre. Cædmon jammed his foot on the accelerator. The fourteen-inch tyres spun on the turf before they were spasmodically propelled forward.

They crested a green rise.

Only to be met by a glassy pond on the opposite bank.

'Bugger!' Beginning to think the golf course a less than inspired idea, he barely managed to escape the watery snare.

'The Audi is right behind us!' Edie informed him.

'These nine holes may prove our undoing. Brace for impact,' he ordered, sighting an ominous granite outcropping on the edge of the green.

To Cædmon's surprise, his co-pilot did the exact opposite, releasing the clasp on her seatbelt. Twisting in her seat, Edie snatched an overnight bag from the footwell.

He heard the metallic *rrrhh* of a zipper.

'Come on! Come on!' she muttered, frantically rummaging through the duffel. 'There's got to be something in here that I can – Yes!' She unfurled a folded bath towel. Then she unwound the passenger-side window and heaved her upper body through the opening.

'What in God's name are you doing?'

His shouted question went unanswered. A half second later, Edie released the oversized terry-cloth towel.

Like the eagle and osprey that soared overhead, the snowy white towel glided through the air. Only to crash land directly on to the Audi's windscreen. Completely obscuring the driver's vision.

The Audi zigged. Then zagged. A moment later, the luxury sedan cruised over a grassy incline. Airborne, the vehicle landed with what had to be a bone-jarring thud. Right into a sand trap.

Cædmon brought the Yaris to a full stop, he and Edie watching as the driver of the Audi, his upper body hampered by a white air bag, tried to extricate his vehicle from the pit. The powerful engine roared, but the Audi wouldn't budge, rubber tyres impotently spinning in the sand.

'Yeah, boy!' Edie whooped.

More relieved than exuberant, Cædmon wasted no time in driving back towards the clubhouse. 'That should buy us some time.'

Although not a large supply.

22

Cædmon opened the passenger car door. 'We mustn't tarry.'

'I know. Just a quick sneak and peek to find Lovett's research notes. Assuming we can figure out what "*aqua sanctus*" means.' As she exited the Yaris, Edie pulled the two sides of her jean jacket closer together. Though it was early spring, there was a distinct chill in the air. 'We left the golf course about an hour ago and I'm guessing it'll take at least that long for Rico Suave to get towed out of the sandpit.'

'Meaning we have a very narrow window.'

'And don't worry about the big dent on the driver's-side door. That's what auto insurance is all about. We'll tell the folks at Avis that it was a hit and run accident.' As she spoke, Edie assessed the one-storey 1950s cottage set some fifty yards from the main road. Situated in the midst of a towering pine grove, it looked ridiculously small. One menacing pine, heavy with sap, was bowed in a gravity-defying arch, it limbs brazenly brushing against the asphalt shingle roof. In addition to the cottage, there were half a dozen derelict trailer homes scattered across the grove.

'According to the chap at the local petrol station, this is Lovett's rental cottage,' Cædmon remarked.

As they walked along the dirt lane that served as a driveway, Edie cast a sideways glance at the nearest trailer. A rickety wood deck had been added to the turquoise blue frontage. Over the top of that hung a faded black-and-white-striped canvas awning. She knew without being told that the interior boasted threadbare wall-to-wall carpet, chipped Formica countertops and jalousie windows that had long since rusted shut. She knew this because, when she was six years old, she and her mother had lived in a trailer park outside Orlando, Florida. Her mother, Melissa, manned a ticket booth at Disney World and would frequently leave Edie unattended, unable to afford a babysitter. Since her only companion was a 13-inch TV, Edie knew all the plotlines and all the characters on the daytime dramas. Given the pendulum extremes of her own life, *Sesame Street* bored her to tears.

Unbidden, old memories suddenly flashed across her mind's eye. Her mother, sprawled on the trailer floor, dead from a heroin overdose, the needle still stuck in her arm. The song 'Sweet Melissa' playing on the tape recorder.

Don't leave me, Mommy. Please don't leave me.

On autopilot, Edie's brain hopscotched to the next chapter. The two and a half years spent on the foster care merry-go-round. The fear. The loneliness. *The unthinkable abuse.*

Unnerved by the flashback, Edie shook her head, flinging aside the painful memories like a wet dog shaking itself dry.

'There is a distinct *noir pastorale* to the environs.' Cædmon's observation made Edie think that she wasn't the only one creeped out by the setting.

'Is it my imagination or are we being watched?' She glanced at the turquoise trailer.

'An innate distrust of strangers is typical in a close-knit community.'

She sidled closer to Cædmon, well aware that distrustful people tended to keep a loaded hunting rifle at the ready. 'What if the police show up? After all, Lovett *was* murdered yesterday.'

Cædmon took hold of her elbow, assisting her up the brick steps that led to a covered stoop. 'According to Dr Lovett's recording, he told none of his acquaintances about the rental cottage. No doubt it will be a while before the police learn of its existence.' When they reached the stoop, he slid his hand into his jacket pocket and removed a slim leather case. 'I thought a lock-picking kit might come in handy.'

'Who carries a lock-picking kit with them?' She held up her hand. 'Don't answer. I think the correct response is "an ex-spy".' Several months ago, Cædmon had confessed to having once worked for MI5. Other than the one brief mention, he never spoke of his prior employment.

'You will thank me for my foresight when—' He stopped in mid-sentence.

'What's the matter? You've got a "something stinks in Denmark" look on your face.'

'The front door is ajar.'

Edie examined the outer edge of the door. Sure enough, it was open a fraction of an inch. Her stomach muscles instantly cramped. 'Maybe Lovett left in a hurry, forgot to lock the door and the wind blew it open.' Even as she said it, she knew that was an unlikely scenario.

Cædmon pushed the door all the way open. Frowning, he ran his hand over the door frame. 'The wood on the jamb is splintered. Someone used brute force to enter the cottage.'

'What do you want to bet that someone drives an expensive Audi sedan?' Edie glanced over her shoulder, suddenly worried that she'd miscalculated how much time it would take to extricate a vehicle from a sandpit. 'We have no idea if Lovett's killer is one step behind us or one step ahead of us.'

Cædmon put a staying arm across her chest, preventing her from entering. 'Remain here while I investigate.'

Not about to contest the order, she nodded wordlessly.

A braver soul than most, Cædmon stepped inside. As he disappeared into the darkened depths, Edie, arms protectively crossed over her torso, repeatedly told herself that it would have been flat-out impossible for Lovett's killer to have beaten them to Arcadia.

When Cædmon reappeared several moments later, Edie let out a pent-up breath, unaware that she'd even been holding it. 'I take it the boogeyman has vacated the premises?'

'So it would seem. I turned on all the lights and checked all the closets. But be warned, the place has been ransacked, the intruder leaving a ghastly mess in his wake.'

Bracing for the worst, Edie stepped across the threshold. Whoever ransacked Jason Lovett's cottage had done so with a wild abandon, chairs, lamps and side tables upended, books and magazines strewn helter-skelter. Seeing a red eight-pointed star painted on the living-room wall, she gasped.

A person didn't have to be a criminal psychologist to recognize the splotch of colour for what it was – an act of unrestrained violence.

'The late Jason Lovett was a man blessed with misfortune,' Cædmon said quietly. 'As you'll recall, the same symbol adorned the knife used to kill him. Blood and treasure. Throughout history, the two have walked hand-in-hand.'

Edie stared at the macabre graffiti, her gaze drawn to the red rivulets of colour that had dripped from the points of the star. 'Please don't tell me that's . . .?'

'Blood? Er, no. My apologies. I didn't mean to imply that it was. There's an open can of red paint in the kitchen.' Stepping over to the wall, he ran his hand over the mural. 'It's completely dry. From that we can safely deduce the artwork was created *prior* to Dr Lovett's demise.'

'Whenever it was done, it means we're not the only ones searching for the dead archaeologist's research notes.' Edie turned her head, nauseated by the chilling image. *So eerily similar to Jason Lovett's bloodstained shirt.*

Hearing a loud rasping sound, she abruptly turned on her heel. 'Oh, God! He's found—'

'It's just the pine tree scraping against the roof,' Cædmon interjected.

'Right. I knew that.' She laughed shakily. 'Steady as she goes.'

Not nearly as steady as she'd liked to be, Edie followed Cædmon into the kitchen. She wrinkled her nose, the paint fumes particularly strong. At a glance she could see the paint can had been unceremoniously dumped in the sink, the brush tossed on the counter.

She gestured to the blobs of dried red paint staining the countertop. 'Assuming this is Rico Suave's handiwork, there's a very real possibility that he found Lovett's research notes.'

'I think not.' Cædmon opened several kitchen drawers,

peering inside before closing them. 'The fact that he followed us to Rhode Island belies the notion. Although clearly the man is anxious to lay his hands on Dr Lovett's hidden papers.'

'Overly anxious,' Edie muttered, still rattled by the earlier chase. And grateful that it hadn't been the Yaris spinning sand. 'No wonder Lovett was popping anti-anxiety pills.'

Cædmon righted an overturned bin. 'The bastard even sifted through the rubbish.'

'Leaving no Coke can unturned.' She examined the odd assortment of empty food containers scattered on the linoleum floor. *Crushed aluminium soda cans. Tuna fish packed in water. Fruit cocktail packed in heavy syrup. Malt-flavoured Ovaltine.* 'Strange diet.'

'Strange man.' Opening the refrigerator, he examined the contents. A few moments later, shaking his head, he closed the door. '*Aqua sanctus . . . aqua sanctus.* What in God's name does it mean?'

'You said it meant holy water.'

'That's the literal translation. But, figuratively, what does it mean?'

She shrugged, as clueless as her partner. 'A dying man's words are often nonsensical.'

'To all but the dying man.'

'Who probably took the secret to his grave,' Edie muttered, the conversation having turned morbid. 'Come on. The clock is ticking. Let's hurry up and check out the rest of this hell hole.'

Walking down the hall, they stopped at the open bathroom door. As with the kitchen, it was a mess, bottles, tubes and containers littering the tile floor.

She plucked a pornographic magazine off the floor. 'Quite the trio of contortionists,' she said, tilting her head to one side as she examined a photograph, trying to figure out which oiled body part went with which naked person. 'Talk about a human pretzel. Obviously, Jason Lovett is, I mean, *was* no different than most men his age, totally obsessed with sex.' She tossed the magazine into the waste-basket, the contents of which had been dumped into the sink. 'Making the crucifix on the wall above the toilet a tad hypocritical.'

Hearing that, Cædmon's red head immediately swung towards the toilet. She watched as his gaze moved from the white porcelain bowl to the slightly crooked wooden cross.

'Ohmygosh,' Edie whispered, belatedly making the connection.

Cædmon turned to her, grinning.

At the exact same moment, they both exclaimed, '*Aqua sanctus!*'

23

'. . . lips sink ships. So, if you want me to batten the hatches, it's gonna cost you.'

Saviour Panos glared at the overweight idiot in the baseball cap and blue jacket. '*Nagamoti mana su stomai su*,' he muttered, enraged. *And your mother's mother while you're at it*. He didn't have to understand the other man's idioms to know that he was being bilked. To the tune of five hundred dollars. The price the tow-truck driver demanded for hauling the Audi out of the sand trap *and* not reporting the incident to the local police.

Able to detect the smell of pickled cabbage, Saviour wrinkled his nose. He hated the smell of sauerkraut. For that offence alone he should gut the man like a netted tuna.

The other man shrugged. Oblivious to the fact that he'd just been accused of committing a reprehensible act involving his mother's mouth. 'You're the one who drove into a sand trap. Now you have to pay the piper if you want to be on your merry way. And don't blame me . . . shit happens.'

Although furious, Saviour couldn't dispute the driver's prophetic assertion. Shit *did* happen. And always when you least expected it. The Brit had outwitted him. Yet again. And though he, Saviour, drove the more powerful vehicle, the English bastard bested him. But he knew where to find the pair. Having eavesdropped on their conversation last evening, he knew their entire itinerary. Even the name of the hotel they'd booked for the night. He already had the Hope Valley Inn plotted on his portable GPS device.

Arms crossed over his chest, Saviour impatiently paced the golf green, anxious for the tow-truck driver to haul the Audi out of the pit. Although temporarily delayed, he was still two steps ahead of the pair. Two steps because he knew where to find them and he possessed the power of life and death. A power bestowed upon him by his beloved Ari that long-ago dawn when he'd returned to the flat . . .

. . . having spent the night cruising the Enola Gay discotheque. It had been a good haul, his pockets flush with Euros. He could now buy the blue cashmere sweater for Ari that he'd seen in a boutique window. Easily chilled, Ari was prone to violent fits of shivering. Some days Saviour would cradle him like a baby, using his own body heat to warm his friend. A heart fire. Immune from the contagion, he was the perfect care giver. As it turned out, his mother had had him inoculated for TB when he was a child. According to the physician at the hospital, the BCG vaccine had protected him from contracting the deadly infection. How ironic. Iphigenia had given him life. She resented his life. And then she saved his life.

In high spirits despite the early hour, he'd regaled Ari with the silly chitchat he'd overheard at the disco. Inane babble spouted by preening pretty boys. Clearly uninterested, Ari motioned him to the bed. He obliged, sitting on the edge of the mattress. Wrapping a bony hand around his upper arm, Ari pulled him close so he could whisper something in his ear. Horrified, Saviour pulled away. *Okhee!* '*No! Impossible! Don't ask again!*' He lurched from the bed and stomped to the other side of the bed chamber. In desperate need of a cigarette, he flung open the window, reached into his pocket and removed the pack of Dunhill cigarettes that he'd stolen from one of the preening pretty boys. Ari continued to stare at him beseechingly. Saviour forced himself to return the stare. Determined to win the battle of wills.

This was not the first time that his beloved friend had pleaded with him to use his greater strength. To commit that final irreversible act. Each time, Saviour had adamantly refused. *The medicine still might work, yes?*

But that particular morning, something happened in the intervening seconds of stalemated silence. For the first time, he forced himself to look at the bloody rags that littered the floor. The disgusting sputum cup. The sloppy array of pill bottles. And then he smelled it – the fetid, foul stench of decaying flesh. In that instant, he *knew* . . . Ari was dying from the inside out. Dormant bacteria in the body had begun to necrotize the tubercles in his lungs.

No longer able to turn a blind eye, he relented. Walking towards the bed, he sat beside his beloved. *The angel of death in a striped boat-neck sweater.* He wrapped an arm around Ari's pathetically thin shoulders. With his free hand, he reached for the blood-splattered pillow. Ari smiled. The first smile in many days. Saviour placed the pillow over his friend's face.

Had he known that he would also be plunged into a dark void, he would not have done it; the ensuing guilt was unbearable. He'd always had a quick temper, never one to back down from a fight. But, after Ari's death, it took little provocation to incite a murderous rage.

The first time it happened, he'd been with an overly plump German who refused to pay the agreed-upon price. For nearly twenty minutes he'd been on all fours while the stout bastard huffed and puffed, enveloping him in the nauseating scents of sauerkraut and sausage. After the blitzkrieg, the Düsseldorf banker had the gall to say, 'I had hoped for something better.' Infuriated, Saviour refused to let the insult go unanswered. Acting on a whim, he smashed the empty Riesling bottle against the hotel dresser and slashed the fat man's throat. For the next week, he'd lived extravagantly on the wad of Euros that he'd stolen from the dead man's wallet. A new leather jacket. A pair of boots. A cashmere turtleneck sweater.

The German was followed to the grave by an Israeli tourist. Because of Ari's death, they *had* to pay.

Just as the Brit would soon pay for having bested him.

24

'Keep your fingers crossed,' Cædmon said as he raised the ceramic lid that covered the toilet tank.

Holding her breath, Edie looked inside.

Damn.

'Nothing but dank water and the standard plumbing apparatus.' Baffled, she glanced at the crucifix hanging above the toilet. 'Jason Lovett *did not* hang that cross so he could pray while on the pot.'

'We must assume it's a red herring.' Cædmon repositioned the lid back on the tank.

Unconvinced, Edie shook her head. 'I don't think so. We just haven't followed the *aqua sanctus* clue to its logical conclusion. For starters: where does the water in this tank go?'

Cædmon's brow furrowed. 'I imagine that it flows into the public-sewer system.'

'Nope. You imagine wrong. Since this is a rural area, there isn't a public-water system. With every flush, all of the *aqua sanctus* in the toilet bowl goes to a septic tank, which –' she stepped into the bathtub so she could peer out of the bathroom's only window – 'is almost always buried *behind* the house because, let's face it, who wants a cesspit in their front yard?' She scanned the unkempt backyard visible on the other side of the smudged glass.

'And you think Lovett may have hidden his research notes near the septic tank?'

She glanced over her shoulder. 'Got a better idea?'

'Lovett was using the spare bedroom to store his excavating tools. I'll grab a shovel and meet you in the back garden.'

Several minutes later, spade and pickaxe at the ready, they set out in search of the buried septic tank.

'I'm no expert, but most septic tanks have a hatch that's visible above ground,' Edie said, putting a hand to her eyes as she surveyed the surprisingly expansive lawn. 'The goose grass is thick and the foxtail knee-high. Lovett obviously didn't own a mower.'

'I suspect his preoccupation with the Templar treasure is the real reason for the overgrowth.' Cædmon jutted his chin towards the right side of the yard. 'You search that half of the lawn and I'll take—'

'Found it!' She pointed to an area approximately one hundred feet from where they stood. 'See that lush patch of weeds? What do you want to bet Lovett's bumper weed crop is being fertilized by the discharge from the septic tank?'

Cædmon slung both of the long-handled tools over his shoulder. 'Your powers of observation are commendable. If this is, indeed, where Dr Lovett concealed his research notes, we should be on the lookout for signs of disturbed vegetation.'

'How can you be so sure that Lovett *buried* his notes?'

'It's what *I* would have done.' Cædmon came to a halt at the edge of the thicket. 'Ah! I see a clump of snapped thistles. Evidence that someone very recently traipsed through here.'

'Could have been a deer or other wild animal.'

'Only if their hooves were shod in lug-heeled boots,' he retorted with a smirk, pointing to a cluster of visible footprints. 'This is newly turned soil. I suspect that Dr Lovett stomped on the loose earth after he refilled the hole.'

A blue jay perched in a nearby tree cawed, the harsh sound eerily similar to a rusty gate swinging on a hinge. Spooked, Edie glanced at her watch. Fourteen minutes had elapsed since they'd first arrived at the cottage.

'Yes, I know; the clock is ticking,' Cædmon remarked, accurately reading her thoughts. Unlimbering the digging tools from his shoulder, he handed her the pickaxe. Then, firmly planting his leather shoe on top of the shovel blade, he forcefully pushed down. 'Hopefully, our would-be fossor dug a shallow grave.'

He did. Steel struck metal in under two minutes.

'Eureka!' Edie exclaimed, going down on her haunches to better examine the upturned object. 'Looks like a metal tool box. Ooh! And it's *very* heavy.'

Cædmon grasped the container's handle. 'I suggest that we take our booty back to the cottage.'

'Good idea.' Standing upright, Edie furtively glanced at the turquoise trailer. 'I'm probably being paranoid, but I've got a hinky feeling that someone's snooping on us.'

25

Hansel and Gretel. Still mucking around Lovett's cottage.

Tonto Sinclair lowered the binocs and set them on the dashboard. He'd parked the Ford F100 behind an abandoned trailer. Out of sight. He figured that, like the candypants foreigner who had earlier trashed the joint, they were looking for buried treasure. White birds of an avarice feather. According to his buddy Bear Mathieson who ran the Gas 'N' Go station, Hansel was an Englishman.

How fucking ironic was that?

Cos anyone familiar with tribal history knew that it was the English motherfuckers who triggered the Narragansett demise. History 101. *They came. They saw. They conquered.*

In need of a smoke, Tonto reached for the pack of Marlboros in his shirt pocket. With an impatient shake of the wrist, he loosened one from the pack and clamped his lips around the filter, sliding it from the pack. *Another one of life's little ironies*, he mused as he clicked the lighter. Had it not been for a pack of smokes, he'd never have found out about Yawgoog. Or the treasure. Or what really happened when Verrazano and his knights made landfall.

It'd been hot as hell that July morning in 2003 when he'd pulled into the Charlestown smoke shop to buy a pack of Marlboros. He'd spent the previous night in the county lock-up on a drunk and disorderly charge stemming from a verbal altercation that he'd had with a redneck who made the mistake of calling him a drunken, shiftless Injun. The drunken part he owned up to; he *had* downed a twelve-pack of beer. But shiftless, he wasn't, having clocked fifty hours that week at the sawmill. His fuse short, he sought redress with the classic one-two sucker punch – straight jab, right to the body.

The fuse wasn't any longer the next morning when he staggered into the reservation smoke shop, foul mood courtesy of a thin, lumpy mattress, a bad hangover and a flatulent cellmate. He'd just handed a fiver to the gal behind the counter when a trio of Rhode Island state troopers suddenly stormed through the shop door. Two of the uniformed bastards had their weapons drawn. The third had a snarling German Shepherd on a lead. Lips curved in a malicious grin, the head trooper yelled, 'Everybody! Hands where we can see them!'

Endowed with an innate distrust of authority figures, Tonto made damned sure that the trooper who tried to arrest him – *for buying a fucking pack of smokes!* – got a good look at both his hands. Right before he balled them into fists and let the bastard have it with a hard right hook. Like it was the punch heard round the world, all hell broke loose inside the smoke shop.

In the end, everyone got hauled away in cuffs. Including a fifteen-year-old stock boy.

Although Tonto knew why he'd been arrested – aggravated assault against a state trooper – he had no friggin' idea *why* the troopers had led an armed raid against the reservation smoke shop. It wasn't until his arraignment hearing that the public defender informed him that the state of Rhode Island did not take kindly to reservation

Indians selling tax-free cigarettes. Screwing the state of Rhode Island out of one hundred million dollars in yearly tax revenue.

Jesusfuckingeronimo! He got sentenced to two years at the John J. Moran correctional facility because of an unpaid tax bill! Like his life wasn't shit already, no sooner did the judge bang the gavel than his old lady up and left him for a trucker she met at a travel plaza on I-95.

Real quick, Tonto found out that prison does one of two things to a man: either he becomes a better criminal or he becomes a better man. In his case, he became a better Narragansett. And wouldn't you know, the road to redemption started with a pack of smokes.

He'd been at Moran about three weeks when a tree trunk of a Native named Annawon Tucker hit him up for a cigarette. Down to half a pack, he grudgingly obliged the request.

'Ever think about getting a new name?' the impertinent bastard had asked.

Stuck with the moniker since he was a kid, Tonto shrugged 'Beats the hell out of Felix.' A name he'd always despised, Tonto was the lesser of the two evils. *And what was he supposed to call himself, Running Turtle?* Or some other dumb-ass Indian name?

'When you're ready to man up and hit the Red Road, you let me know.' With that cryptic remark, Annawon took his leave.

The Red Road.

A lot like the Yellow Brick Road except this one led to a traditional *peespunk*. A sweat lodge where men went to cleanse their spirits and purge their bodies. And didn't *that* scare the shit out of him. Although he lived on the rez, Tonto had never been a road warrior. Never been interested in tribal history or learning the traditional ways. *What was the point?* The white man had long ago decided that the Native peoples were a minority, not a nation. Wearing a *wampum* necklace wasn't going to change that.

But, for some reason, Tonto couldn't get the 'invite' out of his head.

Maybe it was the thinly disguised insult about manning up. Maybe it was the boredom of being in prison. Whatever the reason, for the first time in his life he was suddenly *curious.*

It started out simply enough, Annawon regaling him with tribal history while they shared a few smokes. Those first lessons were all about the glory days, the Narragansett once a powerful tribe, ruled by 'kings' who collected tribute from the lesser bands like the Wampanoag and the Niantics.

But all of that changed in the seventeenth century when the first white colonists arrived. From then on out, *nothing* went right for the Narragansett people.

First there was the smallpox epidemic of 1633. In 1643, the Narragansett invaded the Mohegan's turf and got their asses kicked. Then, in 1676, they suffered monumental losses when they went to war against the English motherfuckers. To punish their defiance, the motherfuckers rounded 'em up in droves and shipped 'em off to sugar plantations in the Caribbean. By the time the nineteenth century rolled around, the few remaining Narragansett in Rhode Island became unwitting victims of the government's 'detribalization' policy, the reservation sold right out from under them. In 1978, after years of legal wrangling with the federal and state governments, the Narragansett were awarded 1,800 acres. Small recompense given the centuries of broken treaties and empty promises.

After one of these depressing history lessons, Tonto conversationally remarked to Annawon, 'It's like we're a cursed people.'

'More truth in that than you realize. The day the white man stole Yawgoog's Stone, that was the day the Light left the Narragansett people. We've been wandering around in the darkness ever since.'

'Who the fuck is Yawgoog?'

It was a few moments before Annawon replied.

'Yawgoog was a white man like no other. For generations, he and his extended family lived in a village in the middle of the Narragansett territory. And then Verrazano and his knights showed up and slaughtered everyone in the village. Except for Yawgoog's son. The Narragansett gave refuge to the boy who, like the eldest son in each generation, took the name of the father, Yawgoog. The Narragansett shared the ceremonial pipe with Yawgoog. And, in return, he shared with us the secret of the sacred stone. When he died, Yawgoog entrusted the stone to the Narragansett. Not long thereafter, the English motherfuckers stole Yawgoog's Stone. And that's the *real* reason why our people were nearly decimated into oblivion. We broke our sacred trust with Yawgoog. We can't reclaim what's rightfully ours until we reclaim Yawgoog's Stone.'

Tonto didn't know it at the time, but his irreverent question, and Annawon's surprising answer, would change the course of his life. Because it occurred to him, and

Annawon was in complete agreement, that if Yawgoog's Stone could be found, the curse that had been hanging over the Narragansett for the last five hundred years would be lifted.

But, like most things in life, there was a catch. The infamous Catch-22. He needed the white man's expertise to find the damned stone. He wasn't an archaeologist. Or a historian. But, thanks to Annawon, he knew his tribal lore and the Yawgoog tales inside and out.

Sadly, Annawon no longer walked the earth, having succumbed to lung cancer in 2008. Which made Tonto even more determined to find Yawgoog's Stone.

Flicking his cigarette butt out of the pick-up window, he shifted on the bench seat, adjusting the bolt-action Winchester that rested on top of his thighs.

When cruising the Red Road, a warrior best have his tomahawk at the ready.

26

'Like every other room in the house, Lovett's office looks like a cyclone hit,' Edie commented. Stepping across the threshold, she turned full circle as she assessed the damage. The tools of the dead archaeologist's trade – spades, brushes, trowels and a large mesh sifter – were haphazardly scattered about the room. In a surreal nod to sanity, the fax machine, computer monitor and photocopier had survived the tirade unscathed. 'Okay, so now what?'

'Now we open Pandora's box.' Cædmon placed the exhumed metal container on top of a scarred table. Thrilled by the discovery, he hoped its contents would put them one step closer to the elusive Templar treasure. He gallantly swept his arm in Edie's direction. 'Since you so cleverly solved the mystery, I think you should do the honours.'

'Wish me . . . *What is that!?*' she screeched the moment the metal box was opened. She pointed an accusing finger at a skeletal hand nesting in a bed of Styrofoam.

'A casualty of war, I daresay, the skeletal appendage severed at the wrist.' And a clean cut, at that, indicating a *very* sharp blade had been used. He assumed that the rest of the skeleton was in the mass grave that Lovett had uncovered.

He carefully removed the Styrofoam tray from the box and placed it on the table. Beneath it was a neatly packed assortment of zip-lock plastic bags. He removed a large see-through bag and held it aloft. 'Good God! Unless I'm mistaken, this hilt came from a sixteenth-century hand-and-a-half wheel pommel sword.'

'Do you think we can get anything for it on eBay? *Just* kidding,' she added when he cast a chastising glance in her direction. Edie lifted a smaller zip-lock bag from the metal box, dangling it in front of his face. 'This silver ring looks pretty old. What do you want to bet it goes with the severed hand?'

Cædmon did a double-take. Stunned, he snatched hold of Edie's wrist, stilling the plastic bag's back-and-forth motion.

Could it really be?

'May I?' When she nodded, he took custody of the polythene bag.

Taking a deep, stabilizing breath, he unzipped the bag and, with reverential care, removed the tarnished silver ring. Utterly bowled over, he stared at the pair of armed and helmeted knights engraved on a circular disk.

Un-bloody-believable.

Weak at the knees, he walked over to the one chair in the room that hadn't been knocked asunder. Holding the chair back with his free hand, he eased himself on to the wooden seat.

Edie approached, clearly bemused by his reaction. 'Given your dumbstruck state, I have deduced that that is not your garden variety cocktail ring. Pretty valuable, huh?'

'It's a signet ring. When pressed into molten wax, it created a seal,' he informed her, finally regaining his senses. 'And, yes, I suspect it would fetch a pretty penny. Although its historic value is immeasurable.' And the reason for his dumbstruck state? 'Each Grand Master had his own unique signet ring with which he stamped letters and documents, enabling him to validate—'

'Back up!' Edie interjected. 'Are you saying that's a *Templar* signet ring that belonged to a Knights Templar Grand Master?'

He gazed at the ring still cradled in his palm. 'Yes, that's precisely what I'm saying. Proof positive that the Knights Templar landed on these shores and established a secret colony at Arcadia. The smoking gun, as it were.'

'Well, *this* I've got to see.'

Pronouncement made, Edie strode over to the far side of the room. Yanking open the middle drawer on Lovett's desk, she rummaged through its contents. When she didn't find what she was looking for, she opened another drawer.

''Bout time,' she muttered, removing a magnifying glass. 'Can't imagine an archaeologist without one of these at the ready. Now let me have a look at that ring.' She pinched the ring between her thumb and index finger, examining it under the magnifying lens. 'Hey, I recognize these guys. This is the famous image of two Templar knights riding one horse.'

'Symbolic of the Templars' vow of poverty.'

'Well, let's hope they didn't take the vow *too* seriously because I will be highly disappointed if we don't find a chest full of gold florins.' Brown eyes mischievously twinkling, she resumed her examination. 'There's a bunch of Latin inscribed on the outer rim of the ring . . . *testis sum agnitio*.'

'*Agni*,' he corrected. 'Typically seen on Templar seals, the phrase means "I am a witness to the lamb." As in the Lamb of God.'

'That's well and good, but this inscription reads "*testis sum* agnitio".'

His jaw slackened. 'My God . . . are you certain?'

'Here. See for yourself.' She handed him both the seal and the magnifying glass. 'Significant or just a medieval typo?'

Confirming that the inscription did, in fact, read *agnitio*, he slumped against the wooden chair. 'A most dangerous play on words,' he murmured. 'It means "I am a witness to knowledge". Knowledge, or *gnosis* in the Greek, refers to a transcendental understanding of creation. Mystics describe it as a momentary flash of insight. A glimpse into the mind of God. *Testis sum agnitio* . . . the heretic's creed.'

'Because the little people were supposed to kneel and genuflect and not ask any questions, right?'

He nodded. 'The medieval Church took great pains to ensure it was the sole proprietor of knowledge and was quick to condemn anyone who laid claim to spiritual knowledge that differed from their carefully crafted orthodoxy. All of which begs the question . . . what knowledge did the Templars possess?'

'Whatever it was, it brought the wrath of the Inquisition down upon them. And that, in turn, spelled the Templars' doom. Which is why they "loaded up the truck and moved to Beverly".' The last part of her remark was sung rather than spoken. Giggling, Edie apologized. 'Sorry. Couldn't resist. And from your blank expression, I have ascertained that you've never watched a single episode of *The Beverly Hillbillies*.'

'To get back on point, it's clear from both the Newport Tower and this signet ring that the Knights Templar *did* have a Doomsday plan that involved the New World.' They would have been fools not to have a contingency plan, their enemies not only numerous but virulent. 'I need to see what else is in that blasted metal box.'

As he lurched to his feet, Cædmon handed Edie the ring and magnifying glass. She, in turn, pointedly glanced at her wristwatch.

'Only fifteen minutes have lapsed since we entered the cottage. We have time,' he assured her, unwilling to wait until they'd checked into their hotel to examine the contents of the grey metal box. Having spent years studying the Knights Templar, Cædmon knew that trying to understand the elusive order of warrior monks was akin to finding a wisp of smoke in a thick fog. But the mist had just cleared, however briefly, Jason Lovett having unknowingly bequeathed to him an extraordinary artefact.

Testis sum agnitio.

His belly tight with anticipation, he lifted another bag out of the box. 'We next enter into evidence, several black rosary beads along with a very tarnished Sacred Heart of Jesus medallion. Inscribed with the year 1523, it is convincing evidence that the Jesuits were directly involved in the Templar massacre at Arcadia. An unpleasant smell, the stench of orthodoxy.'

'Being awfully melodramatic, aren't you?'

'Tell that to the poor souls who met their death at the end of a Maltese sword. Since the good Jesuits were forbidden to draw blood, the Knights of Malta were often used as their armed proxies.' He placed the plastic packet on the table next to the Styrofoam tray. 'Ah! This should pique your interest.' He removed a bag containing six gold coins.

Smiling broadly, Edie snatched it from him. 'According to Lovett, these were minted *prior* to 1307. Several thousand more of these babies and I'll be set for life.'

'Given the mass grave that Dr Lovett uncovered, it would seem that Chiron has been paid in full.'

Edie, her smile drooping at the corners, glanced at the skeletal hand. 'He charges a mean penny.'

'Indeed.' Having reached the bottom of the metal box, he removed a small field notebook. Inside the front cover was a folded map of the Arcadia Management Area. He wasted no time unfolding the map. 'I give you Yawgoog's domain. Marks to Lovett for thinking outside the academic box.'

'He's indicated four separate areas on the map: Yawgoog's settlement, the mass grave, Yawgoog's bridge and the Templar stone.' Edie tapped each of the landmarks with her index finger. 'Where do we start?'

Staring at the map, Cædmon gave the question due consideration, trying to determine the best course of action. 'It doesn't make strategic sense for the Templars to have hidden their most valuable assets within the settlement compound. Moreover, Lovett had already scanned the settlement area and didn't find anything of note other than the mass grave.'

'Leaving us with the stone and the bridge.'

'Which, according to the map, are within close proximity to each other.' Cædmon held up a hand-held GPS device that he'd found in the bottom of the box. 'This should make our scavenger hunt that much easier.' Decision made, he folded the map. 'We'll begin our hunt at the Templar stone first thing tomorrow morning. To that end, we should gather any of Lovett's archaeology supplies that we might need.'

'I saw an empty knapsack in the living room. We can use it for the small stuff, trowels, magnifying glass, bullwhips. You know, the Indiana Jones grab bag.'

Cædmon chuckled, Edie's quirky personality one of the things that attracted him to his American lover. That and her indomitable spirit.

As Edie trotted off in search of a rucksack, he gathered the larger items that they might need. Bending to retrieve a pickaxe from the floor, he noticed several sheets of paper protruding from the fax machine. Curious, he reached for the paper instead of the pickaxe.

Edie re-entered the office. 'What did you find?'

'Mmmm . . . I'm not altogether certain.' Puzzled, he showed her the two sheets of paper.

Holding one sheet in each hand, she examined them in turn. 'Well, this one is easy –' she gently shook the piece of paper in her left hand – 'it's a fax cover sheet to a Dr Lyon at Catholic University. This other one is just plain weird. It looks like a carved message written in a mystery alphabet. Mystery because I've never seen letters that even remotely resemble these.'

'Lovett did mention finding a primitive script carved on an excavated foundation stone. It's possible that he faxed the script to this Dr Lyon in the hopes that the other man might decipher its meaning.'

He stared at the curious script.

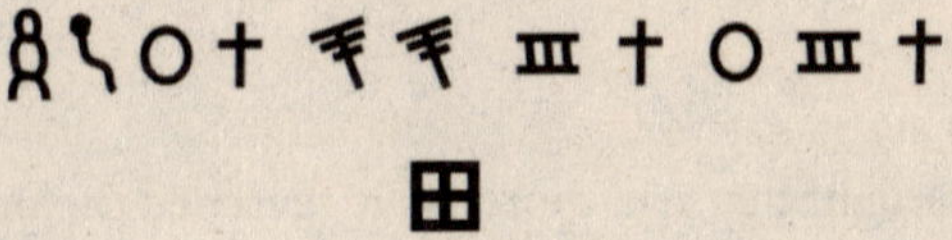

'It could be some sort of Indian writing.' Edie handed the two sheets of paper back to him.

'I didn't think the Narragansett possessed a written language.' He folded the fax sheets and placed them inside Lovett's field notebook. 'If, in fact, this was carved on to a foundation stone, its significance is negligible. As part of the building's footings, the foundation stones aren't visible. Chthonic in nature, such stones are symbolic of the grave and often carved with a message not meant to be seen by the living.'

'And on that cheery note, we need to hit the road.' She handed him the Templar signet ring.

About to replace the ring in its zip-lock bag, Cædmon had a sudden change of heart. Instead, he slipped it on his right ring finger. A perfect fit.

Noticing Edie's quizzical expression, he shrugged.

'For safekeeping.'

27

'But I thought that you thoroughly searched the premises,' Mercurius replied, surprised to learn that the meddlesome Brit had discovered something inside Jason Lovett's cottage.

'I did search it!' Saviour exclaimed, clearly agitated. 'But I tell you, I just saw Aisquith and his bitch haul a metal box into their hotel room. I'm so *vlaskas*! No! Stupid doesn't begin to describe me. How could I have missed—'

'Shhh. Calm down, *amoretto*. The pair have obviously found Dr Lovett's research material.' In the process of watering an indoor lemon tree, Mercurius set the galvanized can on the nearby potting table and shifted the cordless phone to his other ear. 'As with all problems, this one has a solution.' Although, at the moment, he didn't know what that might be.

'I can deal with those two the same way that I dealt with Jason Lovett.'

Mercurius hesitated. 'I'm in a quandary and must ponder this new development before I make a decision,' he said, stowing his ego lest he reach a poorly contrived solution.

'The Englishman is fucking his woman as we speak.' A child of the streets, Saviour chortled nastily. 'They're not going anywhere any time soon. Although if all goes according to plan, soon they'll both be coming.'

Mercurius let the crass remark pass in silence. 'I will speak with you shortly, *amoretto*.'

Sighing, uncertain how to proceed, he switched off the phone and set it beside the watering can. He then pinched a yellow leaf from a slender branch. As he rubbed it between his thumb and forefinger, the plucked leaf released a delicate lemony scent. Lamb meatballs wrapped in lemon leaves was one of Saviour's favourite dishes and always elicited an exuberant round of compliments. Given to strong emotions, his *eromenos* tended to overreact. An endearing quality, one that Mercurius had learned to temper with a firm hand.

Had Hadrian been forced to temper the high-spirited Antinous? he wondered.

An interesting question, the play of opposites the beating heart of pederasty.

In ancient Greece, the relationship between a mature man, the *erastes*, and an adolescent boy, the *eromenos*, had been idealized. And ritualized, with courtship an integral part of the relationship. The ancients recognized that mentoring was a key component in a boy's education. *How else did a youth learn to be a wise and prudent man?* Saviour Panos had been a swaggering, beautiful eighteen-year-old man-child when they first met. Seven years later, he was still beautiful but not quite as brash.

Picking up the cordless phone, Mercurius left the conservatory. Through the window, he noticed that his next-door neighbour had just pulled into the driveway. The neighbours would undoubtedly be shocked if they knew the true nature of the relationship with his 'nephew'. For nearly two decades, he'd resided in the same upmarket neighbourhood of lawyers and doctors and much-maligned financial planners. Good people who conducted their lives by the light of day, but lived in a state of darkness. No different than the 'good' people of Thessaloniki.

Once the Jews had been expelled from the city in the spring of 1943, the 'good' people went wild. Like devouring locusts, they looted vacant Jewish homes and warehouses, the Greeks convinced that Uncle Ezra had been hiding a fortune in gold and silver beneath the floorboards. Under the house. Even in the coffin, with the thievery extending to the Jewish necropolis on the outskirts of Thessaloniki. The Nazis contributed to the hysteria by dynamiting the city's synagogues.

To everyone's keen disappointment, there was no hidden gold. Although there were other valuables – furniture, pianos, clothing – all carefully packed and shipped to Germany.

Greek culture was saturated with the notion of divine justice, so the citizens of Thessaloniki paid heavily for their shameful behaviour, having to endure two years of privation, with food, fuel and other basic necessities in short supply. Hundreds perished from hunger. His own mother took in laundry and learned to cook, forced to let go of the servants. Mercurius and his two sisters collected tinder in a small red wagon to ignite their mother's pitiful cooking fire. One day, towards the end of the occupation, he saw a Nazi officer leaving his mother's bedroom. That night, a chicken miraculously appeared in their stewpot.

Soon after the war ended, the de Léon family emigrated to Chicago, a hirsute uncle with two spare bedrooms opening his door. In an episode similar to the one with the German officer, Mercurius caught his Uncle Nikos buttoning his trousers as he left his mother's bedroom. At the time, he'd considered it an act of disloyalty to his dead father. It wasn't until many years later that he realized Melina de Léon had been forced to trade the only commodity she had – her extraordinary beauty – to provide for her children. Not only did Uncle Nikos, a butcher, daily provide fresh meat, he provided something else which turned out to be priceless to Mercurius – a college education.

In his teen years, knowledge had been an escape – from the drudgery of mopping up entrails in his uncle's butcher's shop, from the shameful guilt of finding Rock Hudson more attractive than Elizabeth Taylor. In his twenties, while a doctoral candidate at the University of Chicago, knowledge became a gateway. A mind-blowing, consciousness-altering entry to the other side.

And then, like a mugging in a dark alley, knowledge became a dangerous thing.

It was 1966. Twenty years earlier, the first of the Dead Sea Scrolls had been discovered by Bedouin in the caves of Qumran. The scrolls, consisting of some nine hundred separate documents, had been hidden by a cloistered sect of Jews known as the Essenes. Contemporaries of the Christian Messiah, they'd maintained an impressive library in their secret grotto.

The amazing discovery proved to be the largest cache of biblical texts ever found. Moreover, the scrolls were of immense value to all three religions of the Book, containing writings from the Old Testament, non-canonical

Apocryphal texts and various sectarian manuscripts. All uncensored and unedited. And *that* worried religious leaders who feared the scrolls might ultimately prove 'sacrilegious'. A direct challenge to accepted orthodoxy.

Early on, Mercurius became fascinated with one scroll in particular – the famous Copper Scroll. He'd just completed his doctoral work in ancient and extinct Semitic languages and had finagled a prestigious appointment at the Archaeological Museum in Amman, Jordan, to study the unique metal scroll. Unique, because it was the only one, of all the hundreds of scrolls, *not* written on parchment or papyrus.

Unearthed in 1952, a preliminary translation was made, the Copper Scroll, once again, proving unique in that it didn't contain *any* biblical scripture or commentary. Instead, it contained a detailed list of sixty-four different locations where an immense treasure trove of gold and silver had *supposedly* been hidden.

Was it any wonder that he'd been thrilled at the prospect of travelling to Jordan to study those twenty-three pieces of copper?

From the onset, Mercurius thought it odd that the scroll had been inscribed on copper – *of all materials!* – and composed in an early square-form Hebrew script with intermittent Greek letters. An avid fan of Sir Arthur Conan Doyle, he approached the Copper Scroll like a detective rather than an academic.

'When you have eliminated the impossible, whatever remains, however improbable, must be the truth.'

And the truth was astounding.

Soon after his arrival in Amman, he uncovered a secret code embedded in the Greek letters that punctuated the

Hebrew script. But more surprising than that, the cleverly devised code spelled the name 'Akhenaton'. He knew from his studies of ancient Egypt that the Pharaoh Akhenaton had instituted a monotheistic religion that worshiped a sun god called Aten. The plot thickened when he discovered that Akhenaton and the Hebrew patriarch Moses had been contemporaries.

Suddenly, the biblical assertion that '*Moses was learned in all the wisdom of the Egyptians*' took on new meaning for Mercurius. *Could there have been a connection between the ancient Israelites and the monotheistic pharaoh?* If he could prove that a link existed, it would certainly shed new light on the origins of Judaism.

Excited by the discovery, he shared his findings with several of his colleagues. Who among those esteemed academics was responsible for the catastrophe that followed, he couldn't say. At the time, he didn't much care who was to blame. He was too devastated by the fact that *all* of his research – twelve months' worth – was stolen from his small, windowless office at the Archaeology Museum. And that a single word, punctuated with a bold exclamation point, had been scrawled on the wall next to his overturned desk – ***Heretic!*** Uncannily similar to the scare tactic used by the Nazis who would scrawl the world *Juden!* on a house or storefront before shipping someone off to Auschwitz.

Afraid that he might be dealing with the same kind of blind hatred, Mercurius heeded the warning and never again mentioned the secret code embedded in the Copper Scroll. The ransacked office bespoke an incontrovertible truth – that human institutions are fundamentally corrupt;

education, religion and government a sham foisted upon mankind to deceive us into believing that we have some measure of control over our lives. We earn a degree, we bend a knee, we cast a vote. It was mere stagecraft to camouflage the evil that lurked in our midst. The perpetuation of a 3,000-year-old deception. One that led all the way back to Akhenaton and Moses.

That long-ago day, as he stood in the small office, it simply sufficed that he'd discovered the heretofore unknown connection between those two disparate figures. Later, *many years later, in fact*, he would comprehend the significance of that connection. For it was the root of all evil.

As providence would have it, the incident in Amman was significant for another reason – it was the Second Sign that he had been consecrated at birth for a great and glorious purpose. The First Sign had been revealed twenty-three years earlier – on that fateful night when his father Osman de Léon and the Kabbalist Moshe Benaroya had been forcibly marched to the train station.

'You must always remember, little one, that you were named for the Bringer of the Light.'

'Do not fear the Light, Merkür. For it will lead you to your life's purpose.'

Another thirty-seven years would pass before the next sign was revealed to him. Thirty-seven years before he learned that his ordained purpose was to extinguish the dark fire that had brightly burned for countless centuries. By summoning a firestorm to douse the flames.

But to do so, he had to find the sacred relic.

Stepping into his study, Mercurius walked over to the

window to draw the drapes, the glass reflecting the setting orb in the western sky. He pulled the heavy fabric panels, catching a glimpse of the dormant rose garden just beyond the window, beautifully splashed with bloody streaks.

Again, he considered the metal box that Saviour had seen Cædmon Aisquith carry into the hotel room. *The more hidden a thing, the more holy.* He smiled, well aware of what the Knights Templar had hidden in their New World colony. He knew because Moshe Benaroya, his father's milk brother, had exposed the relic's provenance in explicit detail.

And Mercurius would let the Englishman find it for him.

Still holding the cordless phone, he accessed the speed-dial function. Saviour picked up on the first ring.

'I've reached a decision, *amoretto*.'

28

'I give you Arcadia. Heaven on earth.' As they entered a sun-dappled glade, Cædmon gestured expansively to the hard wood and evergreen backdrop. 'Indeed, if it didn't exist, we'd have to invent it.'

For the last hour, guided by Jason Lovett's GPS receiver, Edie and Cædmon had been traipsing through the Arcadia Management Area, a surprisingly remote and rugged woodland dotted with limpid kettle ponds, vivacious brooks and lush foliage. Beautiful to behold, it was an unspoiled landscape far different from the windswept coastline they'd explored the day before. Although the eastern coast and the western woodland did share something in common: a whole lot of rocks. Big ones. Small ones. They came in every shape and size, and Edie worried they might have trouble finding the so-called 'Templar Stone', the first of two landmarks on Lovett's map that they hoped to locate. The second landmark was a stone bridge supposedly constructed by a mythic Narragansett man-god known as Yawgoog, Jason Lovett convinced that Yawgoog had been a Knights Templar.

'Arcadia was an oasis for those brave knights mercilessly hunted by the Inquisition,' Cædmon continued. 'And one which abundantly provided the fugitive Templars with food, water and the raw materials to build their New Jerusalem.'

As he spoke, Edie envisioned Cædmon as a medieval knight decked out in chainmail. Last night she'd watched him as he slept, curled fists stacked on his chest. As though curled around an imaginary broadsword.

'Sounds great,' she replied, adjusting the strap on her knapsack. 'But I'm still trying to wrap my mind around a hidden treasure trove, the monetary value of which has as many digits as a long-distance telephone number.' Counting on her fingers, she began to recite her own telephone number, only to stop in mid-recitation. 'Unbelievable. Not enough digits.'

Cædmon glanced at the GPS device. 'We're within six hundred metres of the Templar Stone.'

Edie peered over her shoulder, verifying that they were still alone in the forest. Although Cædmon had repeatedly assured her that Rico Suave had lost their scent, she wasn't entirely convinced. A psychiatrist would probably diagnose her as having a deep-seated trust issue. But then that same shrink hadn't witnessed a man being murdered with a very sharp stiletto.

'What I want to know is how in God's name the explorer Verrazano even knew to look for the Templars here in Arcadia? Clearly, the knights went to great lengths to keep their secret refuge just that, a secret.'

Cædmon held back a fir bough, motioning her to pass in front of him. 'I seem to recall that the Indians sold Manhattan Island to Dutch explorers for about sixty guilders' worth of beads and trinkets. Roughly the equivalent of twenty-five dollars.'

'So, in other words, the Templars may have been sold out on the cheap.'

'Not necessarily by the Narragansett, but perhaps by a rival tribe who knew of their existence. We shall probably never know the specifics of how their demise came about.'

As they navigated their way through dense, overgrown brush, Edie irritably thought they should have brought a machete instead of the small hand-held pickaxe that Cædmon had tied on to his knapsack. A city girl at heart, clunking through the woods had never been her idea of a fun time.

'According to the GPS map, the Templar Stone is close at hand,' Cædmon informed her, blue eyes gleaming with excitement.

'Close at hand, but well hidden,' Edie said under her breath as they exited the piney wood and entered a clearing inundated with scores of hefty boulders. In the midst of the boulders were the remains of a demolished rock pile. A steep granite slope some fifty feet in height ominously hovered at the periphery of the clearing.

'We know from Dr Lovett's recording that a Templar symbol was carved into a large freestanding stone.' Poised in the classic buccaneer stance – feet wide apart, hands on hips – Cædmon surveyed the tumble of large boulders.

'But there's at least thirty boulders and a couple of hundred rocks out here.'

'Right. Time to divide and conquer. We can rule out the rock pile, the individual stones of which are too small to be carved upon. That said, I'll take these boulders on the western side of the clearing.'

'Okay, rock on.' She gave Cædmon the heavy metal hand salute. Seeing his bewildered expression, she chuckled. 'Or not.'

It took only a few minutes for hope to mutate into disappointment, Edie finding nothing that even remotely resembled a man-made carving. She shuffled back to the rock pile in the centre of the clearing. 'No carvings on my side of the street. You're certain that we're at the right map coordinate?'

Cædmon glanced at the GPS receiver. 'Quite. Unfortunately, Lovett made no written notation in his field journal regarding the Templar Stone, fearful, no doubt, that his notes might be confiscated.'

'In his digital voice recording he said that he was brought here by an Indian named Tonto Sinclair. Maybe we should give him a call.'

Her suggestion went unanswered.

Lost in thought, Cædmon circled the rock pile. 'This cairn was deliberately constructed. And, more than likely, these loose stones littering the base were part of the original stack.' He pointed to the hundreds of rocks haphazardly scattered on the ground.

'Perhaps this was a holy place for the Indians. You know, like a ceremonial burial ground.'

'Admittedly, my knowledge of the local native tribes is paltry; however, that doesn't ring right. If you'll recall, many of the Yawgoog tales involved our mythic man-god industriously working with stones. A labour that the Narragansett deemed peculiar.'

'So, what are you saying, that Yawgoog stacked these rocks? And, if so, to what end?'

'To answer that, we must envision this pile of rocks as it *once* appeared long centuries ago.'

Edie tilted her head as she stared at the nearly destroyed

cairn. She then blurted the first thing that popped into her head. 'It was shaped like a pyramid.'

Arms crossed over his chest, Cædmon again circled the pile. Smiling, he said, 'Yes, a pyramid. Brilliant.'

'And that's brilliant because . . . ?'

'Because a pyramid symbolizes the ascent of the sun into the heavenly sphere.' Raising his arm, he pointed to the top of the four-storey granite slope. The parent that gave birth to all of the strewn rocks. He next gestured to the pile of stones in front of them. 'This cairn would have served as a signpost to the initiated, instructing them to look skyward. Specifically, to the top of the granite tower in whose shadow we now stand.'

Edie looked upward, not liking what she saw. 'But we don't have any climbing gear,' she argued, pointing out the obvious.

Undeterred, Cædmon strode towards the tower. 'And neither did the fourteenth-century Templars,' he said over his shoulder. 'Leading me to conclude that there's a way to ascend this granite tower without breaking our bloody arses.'

Rooted in place, she watched as he disappeared behind the massive granite outcropping. She'd seen enough documentaries on the Discovery channel to know that it probably came into being a gazillion years ago when colliding land masses caused a giant geological burp.

'Just as I thought, there's a back staircase,' Cædmon announced upon his return. 'If we take care, we should be able to make the ascent.'

'Great,' she deadpanned, not completely sold. And not completely certain that if one of them slipped, they'd survive the fall.

'As you can plainly see, there are enough fissures, cracks and protruding ledges to enable us to safely scale to the top,' Cædmon pointed out, the man a real sword in the stone when it came to the Templars.

'Don't worry. I've got this climb covered,' she assured him with a big, fake, chipper smile. 'Last year I did the rock wall at a sporting goods store.'

What she failed to mention was that she'd had an instructor to guide her through every step, she'd worn a safety harness and there had been an inflatable mattress in case of a harness malfunction. *Bouldering in a vacuum.*

'To lighten the load, I suggest we leave behind the knapsacks and digging equipment.'

Refusing to go anywhere without her digital camera, Edie removed it from the knapsack. She then slid the strap over her head, carrying the camera bandolier-style across her chest.

Despite the fact that they had only their hands and feet to use for purchase on the granite slope, the climb proved easier than she had imagined. Reaching the top, she was relieved to find herself on a relatively flat ledge some thirty feet in length and twenty feet in width. A gusty blast of air lifted the hair off her shoulders. Standing above the tree line, she could see across a vast expanse of wilderness. 'Wow, what a view!'

'Indeed, it's quite inspiring,' Cædmon murmured, his gaze fixed on a lone boulder positioned at the far edge of the granite shelf. 'Unless I'm greatly mistaken, we have discovered our divining rod. Shall we?'

Edie eagerly fell into step beside him. 'Hopefully, there's a map and a big Jolly Roger carved on it.'

'Curious you should mention the Jolly Roger, given that the famous pirate logo originated with the Knights Templar and was frequently used to mark their grave sites.'

Walking around the boulder, they came to a standstill in front of a crudely incised carving.

'Well, it isn't a Jolly Roger.' She squinted to better make out the weathered image. 'Do you recognize it?'

'Most assuredly.' Going down on bent knee, Cædmon fingered the carving, the image incised in hollow relief. 'It's the Templar battle standard. Better known as the Beauséant.'

'Beauséant . . .' She accessed her memory banks, going all the way back to Madame Girard's high-school French class. 'That comes from the word "beau", which means beautiful, right?'

Cædmon nodded. 'However, in medieval French it translated more closely to "glorious". The Templars were known to shout "Beauséant!" as they charged into battle.'

'The medieval version of the rebel yell, huh? I think we should get a photo. For the family album,' she added with a playful wink. A few moments later, photo taken, she showed him the images on the review screen.

'Okay, what am I looking at?'

Still on bent knee, Cædmon rose to his feet. 'Bear in mind that this Beauséant, or battle standard, is carved in stone. That said, a battle standard was a large cloth banner held aloft on a wooden staff that served as a rallying point for one's army during battle. When it came to the Beauséant, the Templars had a simple code of conduct – as long as it flew, they must fight.'

'I'm guessing that the actual banner would have been brightly coloured so it could easily be seen from a distance.'

'Indeed, the Beauséant was comprised of three armorial colours: red, white and black.'

'A simple but bold fashion statement.'

Cædmon placed his hand on top of the boulder. 'This is a clue, I'm certain of it. No man would go to the trouble of climbing a granite tower to carve this image without a reason.'

'True, but this is what I don't get – if the Knights Templar hid their treasure trove in Arcadia, why leave secret clues as to its whereabouts? They did, after all, know where they'd hidden it.'

'But not everyone in the Templar colony would be privy to the treasure's whereabouts. Only a select few.' He glanced at the silver signet ring on his right hand. 'The Grand Master and his inner circle. There's also the possibility that the clues were left for their Scottish brethren – in the event that calamity struck.'

'Which is *exactly* what happened . . . a tragic calamity befell the colony at Arcadia.' While she hated to play the devil's advocate, Edie knew that Cædmon sometimes suffered from myopic vision when it came to the Knights Templar. 'That being the case, there's a very real possibility that someone, say the Scottish branch of the Templar family, found out about the massacre, sailed to the New World, deciphered the clues and collected the treasure.'

'We will cross that bridge when we come to it. Speaking of which, the Beauséant faces due west.' He removed the GPS device from his pocket. 'According to the GPS receiver, that also happens to be the direction of Yawgoog's stone bridge. There may well be a connection between the Beauséant and the stone bridge.'

Resigned to the fact that Cædmon would not surrender while the Beauséant still figuratively flew, Edie led the way back to the other side of the granite ledge. It was a little past one o'clock; they still had plenty of time to find Yawgoog's bridge and hightail it out of the Arcadia Management Area before sunset.

A few minutes later, having safely navigated their descent, they headed due west.

29

Lifting his head heavenward, Saviour inhaled, savouring the invigorating aroma of cedar and pine.

Head cleared, he readjusted his earphones. He'd been tracking Aisquith and the Miller woman since they left the Hope Valley Inn. An easy enough feat. He simply aimed the parabolic dish on his listening device and he could hear the couple's every utterance. Stalking prey had never been easier.

And the fun part?

The couple were oblivious to the fact that he followed in their wake. Although he'd learned his lesson and would be more careful this time.

Two nights ago, he'd misjudged Edie Miller, thinking her little more than a silly bitch. When she'd thrown the towel out of the car window, she'd proved him wrong. Not only was she tenacious, she possessed an admirable cunning. *Would she fight back?* He hoped so. Without question, the Brit would prove a worthy contender.

Saviour smiled, anxiously anticipating the bout.

Such fun and games.

Hearing the sound of rending fabric, Saviour glanced down, his jacket had snagged on a branch. Shrugging, he yanked the lightweight nylon free. It was the sort of careless mishap that would normally enrage him; he took such care with his wardrobe. But not today. Today, his thoughts, his emotions, were all attuned to the thrill of the hunt.

In truth, a manhunt.

So much better than stalking furry mammals. A deer could not scream. A fox could not beg for mercy. A rabbit could not plead to be put out of its misery. Only one kind of prey could scream and beg and plead.

But the predator had to exercise patience when stalking human prey.

On Thessaloniki, he used to spend an inordinate amount of time studying each and every prospective john, carefully scrutinizing the man's facial expressions, his eye movements. The way he dressed. The aperitif he ordered as he pretended to read the newspaper. Sometimes he would spend hours in the pursuit of one man, waiting and watching instinctive to him.

So, too, killing.

His smile broadened . . . *Let the games begin.*

30

Edie estimated that they'd gone approximately a quarter of a mile when they reached the edge of the swift-moving river.

Worried they'd come to the proverbial dead end, she stared at the stone bridge comprised of gigantic rectangular granite slabs that extended from one side of the river bank to the other.

Frowning, Cædmon's gaze was glued to the gushing, white-capped water that flowed across the middle of the bridge.

'The Indians forgot to mention that a fifteen-foot waterfall flows right down the middle of Yawgoog's stone bridge. Which makes crossing the river next to impossible,' Edie glumly remarked. 'Some bridge.'

'Interesting that Dr Lovett made no mention of the waterfall in his field book. Evidently, he didn't consider it pertinent.'

'Dr Lovett didn't mention a lot of things in his little notebook. Too paranoid that someone would steal his notes and beat him to the treasure. Okay, scoutmaster, now what? As near as I can tell, this is a bridge to nowhere.'

'Quarried and built by man . . . but to what end? As you said, it's impossible to cross to the other side.'

'Are you sure this is even man-made?'

'There's no doubt in my mind. See these rough-hewn

marks –' he pointed to the edge of the nearest block – 'these slabs were obviously cut from the local granite, of which there is an abundance.'

'Using the same tools employed by fourteenth-century stonemasons.'

Cædmon nodded. 'The Indian tales mention that Yawgoog wore a leather apron as he constructed his fabled bridge. European stonemasons similarly garbed themselves in leather aprons.'

'Okay, we've got the "how" of it figured out. Any ideas as to *why* it was built?'

'My gut instinct is that this is related to the carved Beauséant, but . . .' He shrugged, clearly at loss.

'Let's backtrack,' she said, hoping to kick-start a brainstorming session. 'What do we know about the Beauséant? We know it means "glorious" and that the actual banner was red, white and black. We also know that the Templars—'

'Red, white and black . . . of course.' He rubbed his hand over his mouth as he contemplated Yawgoog's bridge. A few moments later, he said, 'Since the Beauséant was carved on to the boulder, the colours were *implied*.'

Even though she had no idea why that was relevant, Edie encouragingly nodded her head. 'I'm with you. Keep rolling.' She made a 'rolling' motion with her hand.

'Mind you, I'm thinking aloud, but it could well be that the oak trees that bracket either side of the bridge are a clue. You may not have noticed, but the grove of trees on one side of the river bank is *white* oak and the grove on the opposite bank is *red*.'

She glanced at the massive old-growth oak trees. 'How do you know? They look identical to me.'

He made no reply. Instead, he picked up a dried oak leaf near his boot tip. Then, bending at the waist, his eyes glued to the ground, he walked several feet before picking up yet another brown, sun-dried leaf. 'The proof is in the foliage,' he said, showing her the two similar, but uniquely different, oak leaves. 'The lobes on the white oak are round.'

'And the lobes on the red oak are pointed. It was probably blown across the river last autumn. But how do you know that these two oak groves were intentionally planted?'

'Had God's hand been involved in the design, one would expect mixed groves on either side of the bank. But, instead, there's one species on each bank. Red and white. Clearly, the oaks relate to the Beauséant.'

'All right, then riddle me this . . . where does the black come into play? Lest you forgot, the Beauséant is comprised of three colours, not two.'

'Indeed.' For several long seconds he stared at the two oak leaves he still held in his hand. 'Medieval battle standards can be thought of as a type of shorthand. Then, as now, each armorial colour had a specific meaning. In heraldry, black symbolizes the virtue of wisdom.'

'Which is another name for knowledge. And the Latin phrase "I am a witness to knowledge" is engraved on the Templar signet.' She pointedly glanced at his ring finger.

'Moreover, the colour black is represented by the numeral eight.' He turned to her, smiling. 'And as anyone familiar with the Knights Templar knows, there are eight points on a Templar cross.'

'So then, the colour black has a strong connection to the Knights Templar.'

'*And* the colour black is symbolic of the grave, underground caves and the primordial void.' He flung the two oak leaves to the ground. 'Riddle solved.'

Without any explanation as to what he was doing, Cædmon stepped out on to Yawgoog's bridge, purposely striding to where stone met water. Turning his back, he slid his knapsack off his shoulders and deposited it on the granite slab. He then removed the GPS receiver from his pocket, placing it on top of the knapsack.

'Cædmon! What are you doing?'

'Preparing to leap into the primordial void.'

With those parting words, he jumped off the granite bridge into the river. Disappearing from sight.

31

'Nail on the head!' Cædmon triumphantly exclaimed as his booted feet made contact with a granite ledge.

Barely able to contain his excitement, he stared at the entrance to the hidden cave, the opening of which was located *behind* the waterfall.

The combination of fast-moving water and strategically placed granite slabs had completely obscured the cave below. Standing above, it was impossible for one to see through the sparkling water to the entrance. He'd taken the plunge because, if his theory proved false, the worst-case scenario would have been a wet trek back to the rental car. As it'd turned out, he was only slightly damp.

His suspicion about an underground vault having been bang-on, he wanted to whoop with joy.

'Cædmon!'

Craning his neck, he peered upward. Edie's voice sounded as though it was coming from some faraway place, muffled by the gush of water falling over the granite slab above him. He squinted as he tried to bring her blurry image into focus.

He cupped his hands around his mouth. 'Edie, I'm perfectly safe!' he shouted through his makeshift megaphone. 'There's a hidden cave behind the waterfall!'

'What!? Get out of town! There's a cave down there?'

Really and truly.

He glanced behind him at the entryway, one that perpetually glistened with a wet sheen.

He suddenly felt lightheaded. Apprehensive. *The strangeness of the place, the refreshing water spray, the dappled play of light passing through the fast-moving water.* All of his senses were fully engaged. He'd had a similar sensation years ago when he sat for his university exams, the years of study reduced to a group of undisclosed questions contained within an official examination booklet. A mystery to be solved. To be conquered.

Testis sum agnitio. I am a witness to knowledge.

'I want you to remove the coil of nylon rope and the pickaxe from my field kit,' he shouted up at Edie, anxious to explore the cave.

'What do you want me to do with 'em?' she called down a few moments later.

'If you would be so kind as to toss them to me.'

The two requested items landed on the granite ledge with a loud clang and a dull thud.

'Excellent.' Cædmon quickly went to work, securing one end of the rope around the metal head of the pickaxe. Satisfied that the knot would hold, he shouted up at Edie, 'Be on your guard, I'm going to toss the pickaxe back to the surface.'

Warning issued, he hurled upward.

'Got it! Now what?'

'Secure the chiselled end of the head on to the nearest granite slab. And do make sure it's a snug fit.'

He had no idea how the Templars had exited their secret lair, but he intended to use the rope to climb to the surface.

'Okay, that ought to hold me,' Edie yelled, having incorrectly guessed at his intention.

'For God's sake, stay put!'

'Hey, time to run with the bulls.'

Bloody hell!

Unable to stop her, Cædmon positioned himself at the edge of the granite ledge, ready to catch Edie should she fall.

To his relief, she very ably rappelled down the stacked granite slabs.

Landing in the bent-knee position, Edie straightened. She then graced him with a toothy grin, the woman clearly pleased with her stunt.

''Ello, luv,' she cooed in an exaggerated Cockney accent.

Cædmon stared at her, watching the strange play of light that flickered across her face, filtered by the nearby gush of water. He was conflicted, wanting to hold her tight *and* to shake her roughly.

'Always thought the proverbial "leap of faith" was just a figure of speech,' she said, oblivious to his tumult. 'But I stand corrected. What? Why are you looking at me like that?'

'I should throttle you,' he hissed between clenched teeth. 'This isn't a summer jolly. It could well prove a dangerous expedition.'

'Said the voice of doom and gloom.' She removed a knotted plastic shopping bag that was looped around her wrist. 'Play nice or you don't get the goody bag. And in case you're wondering, I packed two flashlights and my digital camera. Everything else I left stateside.' Displaying a complete lack of remorse, Edie handed him the bag. 'So, how did you do it, oh great one? How did you figure out that there was a cave *behind* the waterfall?'

His anger dissipated, Cædmon said, 'Knowing from the Narragansett legends that Yawgoog had built a cave, I suddenly recalled how the ancient Visigoths would temporarily divert the course of a river. They did this in order to dig a cave in the exposed river bed. Once the cave was dug out, they then directed the river back to its original flow, their ill-gotten gains cleverly concealed.'

'And Jason Lovett was convinced that the Knights Templar found the Visigoth treasure vault in the south of France. Probably buried under a river. Guess the Templars knew a good idea when they saw it. So let's flip on these flashlights and check out Yawgoog's cave.'

They each took a torch. Walking side by side, they entered the cave. A few feet into their trek, Edie abruptly came to a standstill.

Physically recoiling, she pointed at the nearby wall. 'What in heaven's name is *that*?' she screeched.

His gaze alighted on a horned, winged, claw-footed figure carved in high relief. 'No creature of heaven, I can assure you. That is Asmodeus.'

'*That* is butt ugly!'

'I stand corrected. Grotesque appearance aside, Asmodeus is the king of the demons, customarily invoked to protect buried treasure.'

'Buried treasure?' His companion surprised him by leaning forward and kissing the horny-toed creature. 'Love that.'

'Shall we continue with the tour?' Torch in hand, he illuminated a tunnel that was approximately five feet in height.

'Don't forget to duck,' Edie said over her shoulder, leading the way. 'I have to admit, I feel like one of those kids in the Christmas story with visions of golden plums dancing in my head.'

He ambled close behind in an uncomfortable crouch. 'I believe it was sugar plums prancing about.'

'Not in my vision. We are *so* close to finding the Templar treasure trove!' she excitedly predicted. 'Where do you want to retire to, a Caribbean island or the south of France?'

'I'm not one to spend my pennies before they're earned.'

Cædmon was admittedly relieved when, a few moments later, the tunnel gave way to a small anteroom that better accommodated his six-foot three-inch frame.

He swiped at a low-hanging cobweb. 'I see a crudely fashioned staircase on the opposite side of the chamber. Would you like to wait here while I go downstairs and investigate?'

'Not on your life! We're equal partners, remember?'

'Yes, of course. How could I forget?' he deadpanned. 'But I hope you don't mind if I take the lead. My fragile male ego will be shattered if you fend off the dragon while I'm pulling up the rear.'

With an airy wave of the hand, Edie gestured for him to precede her down the steps.

Like the rest of the cave, the stairway had a dank, tomb-like feel to it, Cædmon grateful that neither of them suffered from claustrophobia. When they reached the bottom step, he directed his torch beam around the sunken chamber.

His breath caught in his throat.

Rendered speechless, he could do little else but gape, stunned to be standing in an octagon-shaped room. The corners of the eight stone walls were each decorated with a life-sized medieval Knights Templar – replete with broadsword and helmet – carved in bas-relief on the smooth rock surface. Directly opposite the entrance there was a stone altar placed upon a low dais. Circular architecture, based on the tenets of sacred geometry, was often executed as the eight-sided octagon.

Eight.

Symbolic of paradise regained. For it was on the eighth day that man, who had been created in the image of God, attained a state of divine grace. No coincidence that the Templar cross had eight points.

Staggered by the find, Cædmon next aimed his torch at the ceiling. The celestial firmament – sun, moon, stars and the seven known planets of the fourteenth century – had been incised into it. It brought to mind King David's awe-struck exaltation in Psalms, '*The Heavens declare the glory of God; and the firmament sheweth his handiwork.*'

'As above, so below . . . how bloody apropos,' he breathlessly uttered. For so long the Templars had been hidden in the shadows, but he was beginning to see more clearly.

If only he'd known about this New World sanctuary when he'd written his dissertation.

Certain that fourteenth-century Templars once stood where he now stood, he closed his eyes, envisioning a group of initiated knights solemnly standing in a circle, heads bowed, flickering candlelight casting a golden hue on to their bearded faces as they enacted a sacred ritual.

But a ritual for which religion?

The moment the question popped into his head, the evocative image vanished.

Barely able to contain his excitement, he turned to Edie, surprised at her crestfallen expression.

'Where are the ingots? The florins? The gold, frankincense and myrrh?' she moaned. There was no mistaking her disappointment. 'It's just a lot of carved stone. Somebody beat us to the treasure. Or maybe there never was a treasure.'

'In and of itself, this sanctuary *is* the treasure. In the mystery rites, it is here, in the symbolic grave, that man is freed from his earthly bondage by accruing divine knowledge.'

'Oh, yeah, whoop-de-do. *Testis sum agnitio*.'

Ignoring her sarcasm, he again marvelled at the beautifully executed design, his gaze alighting on a magnificently carved knight. How many centuries had he kept silent sentry?

So many dark secrets to keep.

'My God, I can't even begin to imagine how long it took them to build this. How many hours of pounding away with hammer and chisel, of hauling in stone and carting out the debris. No doubt it was a project years in the making.'

'Looking on the bright side –' Edie rolled her eyes, clearly an impossible undertaking in her opinion – 'the fact that the sanctuary exists proves that the fugitive Knights Templar journeyed to the undiscovered New World.'

'Bringing with them a treasure so valuable, so sacred, they built this subterranean chapel to house it.'

'*Hel-lo*,' she chirped in a sing-songy voice. 'Mission control to Cædmon. The chapel is empty.'

He shook his head. 'The Templars wouldn't have carved Asmodeus if there had been no treasure. Something of great value was safeguarded here. And may be here still,' he impetuously added, hit with a sudden burst of hope. 'Hidden away.'

'Why didn't you say so in the first place? Let's case the joint.' Edie's glum mood instantly improving, she frenetically shone her torch around the chapel.

Cædmon also flashed his torch around the chapel, turning in a slow, deliberate circle.

'Stop right there!' Edie shouted. 'I just saw something. Behind the altar.' She charged on to the dais.

Cædmon followed, the beam of light illuminating a shallow niche, some eighteen inches square and approximately four inches deep, carved into the wall. The niche was five feet above the ground.

'Given its placement in the room, centred behind the altar, this niche may well have housed a holy reliquary or devotional object.' As he spoke, it belatedly occurred to Cædmon that in a Christian church this was the space customarily reserved for a crucifix. Ironically, the Templars had been accused by their inquisitors of denigrating and spitting on the holy cross. And while he'd always considered that a baseless accusation, it was curious to note that there were no crosses anywhere in the sanctuary.

'Ohmygod!' Like a yanked window shade, Edie's eyes instantly opened wide. 'What if this is where the Knights Templar kept the Holy Grail?'

He disavowed her of the notion with a terse shake of the head. 'The niche isn't deep enough to hold a chalice.' He glanced at the signet ring on his right hand.

Testis sum agnitio.

Suddenly, he was struck with an idea.

'The niche may have been used to display a sacred text. Before their mass arrest in 1307, the Templars were rumoured to have an incredible library that contained works by, among others, the Gnostics, the Egyptian adepts and the Jewish Kabbalists.' He shrugged, wishing he had more to go on.

'The not knowing is frustrating, huh?'

'Actually, I'm more intrigued than frustrated. It's a mystery, is it not? Is there enough torch light for you to take a few digital photos?'

'I think it's do-able. Since I don't have a tripod, I'm going to set the camera on the altar to take the picture.' She passed her torch to him. 'Hold this, will ya?'

'Where should I stand?'

She glanced around then pointed to a spot to the left of her. 'Over there will be just fine.' Lifting the strap over her head, she set the camera on the altar, leaning her torso on the granite slab as she determined the best position. 'I'm going to first take a photo with the built-in flash. If we get too much light bouncing off the background, I can fiddle around with the aperture. Okay, lights, camera – Oh, I almost forgot, don't move. And don't let the kiddies try this at home.' She winked at him, her mood noticeably improved.

Cædmon obediently stood still as a flashpoint of bright light emanated from the camera.

Removing the camera from the altar, Edie walked towards him. 'Let's see what we've got.'

Leaning over her shoulder, Cædmon peered at the small LCD screen, pleased.

‘I think a Templar photo album is in order.’ Edie slipped the strap over her head. Digital camera in hand, she slowly walked backward, stopping and starting as she peered into the viewfinder.

She snapped several photos, each accompanied by a flash of light.

‘At Rosslyn Chapel in Scotland, the twenty St Clair knights interred in the underground tombs are rumoured to glow with an otherworldly light,’ he conversationally mentioned.

‘Thanks for the spooky sidebar.’ Camera still pressed to her face, she took another backward step. ‘Like I wasn’t unnerved enough already, now I’m envisioning a bunch of dead guys glowing in the—’

Without warning, the ground beneath Edie’s feet suddenly gave way, the earth opening up to swallow her whole.

32

Unnerved, Saviour peered over the edge of the stone slab, into the frothy, white-capped river below. Catching sight of the pickaxe hooked on to a jagged rock, he frowned. Baffled.

'*Den katalaveno*,' he muttered. 'Where did they go?'

It made no sense. None whatsoever. How could they have vanished into thin air?

Noticing the abandoned knapsacks in plain view, he walked over to them. The packs suggested that the pair were planning to return.

But, again, from where?

He squatted on his haunches and rifled through the packs. The first contained a small computer, cell phone, notebook, water bottle and a bag of nuts. The second pack held miscellaneous digging equipment, more water and a flare gun. In case the little lambs got lost in the woods.

Hearing an incoming call on his Bluetooth ear hook, he tapped the TALK button. It'd been thirty minutes since he last checked in with Mercurius, his mentor was understandably curious. Hopefully, he could provide insight into this strange development.

'They've disappeared,' Saviour said without preamble.

'From sight or . . . '

'From the face of the planet,' Saviour interjected, worried that he might be blamed for losing the sheep. For being an inattentive shepherd. 'I am standing on the river bank where they left their knapsacks. The woman mentioned a cave as well as—

'A cave?' There was no mistaking the excitement in Mercurius's voice. 'Are you certain this is what you overheard?'

'With the parabolic dish, I can hear a rabbit fart three hundred meters away. Yes, I am certain. Hooked on to the edge of the stone slab is a pickaxe with a length of rope tied to the end. The entrance to the cave must be hidden beneath the river rocks, but . . . it is invisible to the naked eye.'

There was a pause on the other end of the line. Saviour didn't have to see Mercurius to know that the other man had lightly grasped his chin in his right hand and that he was now slowly tapping his index finger against his lips. Lost in thought.

'Do you want me to follow them into this underwater cave?' Saviour prayed the answer was 'no'.

'Be patient, my love. They will return. Find yourself a suitable hiding place. But I want you to contact me the moment they appear. I want to know if they have retrieved anything from this cave.'

Hearing that, Saviour exhaled a gusty sigh of relief. Although loathe to admit it, he had a dread fear of caves. They were too much like the grave. Or a dark, eerie house.

And he knew all about living in a dark house.

When he had first arrived on Panos Island, he'd been an impressionable eighteen-year-old who couldn't believe the blessing that had been bestowed upon him . . . he'd caught the eye of Greek shipping tycoon Evangelos Danielides. And had literally been whisked off the streets of Thessaloniki to a pampered, luxurious idyll on a sun-kissed private island in the Aegean.

A dream come true.

He'd tried to act cool but, in truth, he'd been utterly dazzled. By the thousand-acre isle with its turquoise lagoons ringed with cedar and wild olive trees. By the opulent marble villa with its cadre of obsequious servants who would draw his bath, clip his fingernails, massage him with sweet-smelling oils. *Was he not a prince among men?* And, of course, most of all, he'd been dazzled by the man himself, Evangelos Danielides.

At the dawn of the twenty-first century, the booming economies of China and India had created a whole new generation of Greek tycoons who made massive fortunes transporting the world's goods. But unlike the more famous young bloods, Evangelos Danielides maintained a low profile, disdaining the jet set. To Saviour's surprise, Evangelos had a casual 'laid-back' style. When not attired in bathing trunks, he wore loose linen trousers paired with a white T-shirt. He drank ouzo rather than champagne. Although he did have one curious affectation – he smoked Sobranie Black Russian cigarettes, which lent a sexy rasp to his already deep voice.

Those first weeks on Panos had been a heady experience, almost too much for Saviour to absorb. Which is why he always looked forward to the end of day when he and Evangelos would lounge beside the infinity pool, the setting sun turning the blue Aegean a fiery red.

And then things turned very ugly, very quickly.

It started one day at archery practice, when Evangelos – justly proud of having been on the 2000 Greek archery team – was instructing him on how to improve his draw. Standing directly behind him, crotch firmly planted against his ass, he'd whispered in his ear, 'Pull with your shoulder.' As he spoke, Evangelos slipped a hand between Saviour's legs. Suddenly uninterested in archery, Saviour turned his head to kiss his beloved. 'I said pull with your shoulder, bitch!' Evangelos hissed in his ear as he roughly squeezed his testicles. Saviour bit back a yelp of pain, tears flooding his eyes, uncertain what he'd done to incur the vicious outburst.

In the days to come, Evangelos took to slapping him. Kicking and shoving. Then punching him in the face. One morning he presented Saviour with a studded metal collar and a leather jockstrap. His new uniform. What had been a life of idle luxury became one of degradation. Pain and humiliation. There was no one he could turn to for help, the servants turning a deaf ear to his screams. Trapped on the private island, Saviour was Evangelos Danielides' chattel. A piece of ass that the shipping tycoon owned. A possession. No different than his yacht. Or his prized Argentine mastiffs. His to do with as he pleased.

Or so he thought. Never imagining that his meek little lamb would turn into a vicious, snarling wolf.

And just as Saviour had dealt with Evangelos Danielides, he would deal with the Brit when he emerged from the cave.

Readjusting the straps on his hiking pack, he headed towards an overgrown patch of land inundated with evergreen shrubs some fifty yards from the river bank. An excellent place to wait for his quarry.

33

'Edie!'

Too terrified to answer, afraid she'd lose her grip, Edie clung to a stone nubbin that protruded from the side of the dark shaft. She frantically moved her dangling feet, hoping, *pleading* –

Yes!

One booted foot found purchase on a minuscule pucker of rock.

'I'm down here,' she called out hoarsely. 'I fell into a shaft.' She didn't dare look up, fearful she'd lose her balance. She also didn't look down, sensing that an inky abyss yawned beneath her.

A beam of light suddenly illuminated the shaft.

'My God, are you all right?' Cædmon's voice echoed off the stone walls, the sound strangely distorted.

'No, I'm hanging on for dear life,' she whimpered. With her hands painfully crimped, her right foot awkwardly splayed and her left foot limply suspended in mid-air, she wondered how long she could maintain her precarious perch.

'Don't panic.'

'You're kidding, right?' She felt a trickle of blood meander down the side of her face, having scraped her cheek when she took the unexpected plunge. Probably scraped a whole lot of body parts.

'I want you to listen very carefully.' Cædmon spoke slowly, precisely, the way one would speak to a terrified child. 'You're about six feet from the surface. Too far of a distance for me to physically reach you.'

'Oh, God, no!'

'Not to fear. I will get you out of the shaft, but it's going to take a minute or two before I can toss a lifeline down to you.' Cædmon pulled the flashlight away from the opening, the shaft instantly cast into darkness.

'Please hurry,' Edie murmured, her cheek pressed against the rusticated stone. 'Any idea what the hell just happened?'

'You fell into a very cleverly designed death trap,' Cædmon's disembodied voice replied. 'My guess is that the opening was concealed with a layer of clay hardpan.'

'Which gave way when I stepped on it.'

'Precisely. The Templars obviously didn't want anyone stealing whatever it was they had safeguarded in the sanctuary. Quite an engineering feat really.'

Edie made no comment. Instead she clamped her jaw together. *Tight.* Trying to stop her teeth from clattering, worried that the slightest motion would upset what had become a delicate balancing act. She knew the chitchat was Cædmon's attempt at keeping her calm. And while she loved him for it, it wasn't doing a damned thing to quell her fear.

The golden beam of light reappeared.

'I want you to listen very carefully to me, Edie. I'm about to lower a lifeline to you. It will pass on your right side. Understood?'

'Yeah, yeah,' she muttered, not altogether certain what he meant by a 'lifeline'.

She had her answer a few moments later when a length

of soft chambray grazed her right hand. She instantly recognized the blue fabric – it was the sleeve from Cædmon's shirt.

'I've tied my anorak and shirt together, contriving a lead for you to grasp. Now, *very carefully*, you are to reach out and take hold of the lead with your right hand.'

Edie visualized the instructions just given to her. Very quickly she realized that to grab hold of the lead, she'd have to let go of the rock that she was clinging to.

'I can't!'

'You *can*,' Cædmon urged. 'It won't take but a second to grab the sleeve. Grasp it and wrap the fabric around your hand. Good and tight. While you do that, you can continue holding on to the rock with your left hand.'

'But I might lose my balance.' Her voice was little more than a terrified croak.

'The key is to *not* to make any sudden movements. Maintain your centre of balance by taking slow, measured breaths. Understood?'

She made no reply, terrified that she was seconds away from plunging to her death.

'Edie, this is the only way to extract you from the shaft. *Please*, love . . . I know you can do this.'

She heard a catch in his voice. That's when she knew the calm tone was all for show. Cædmon was just as terrified as she. For some insane reason, that imbued her with a burst of courage.

Not giving herself time to change her mind, Edie released her hold on the rock, moved her fingers a scant inch to the right. Snatching hold of the dangling length of chambray, she wrapped the fabric around her hand.

She held the shirt in a death grip.

'Okay, I just jumped the first hurdle. Now what?' She still didn't have the courage to crane her neck and look up.

'You now need to grab the lead with your left hand. After which, you can firmly plant the soles of your boots against the shaft wall. While I haul you to the surface, you will carefully climb up the side of the shaft. Similar to rappelling down the side of Yawgoog's bridge,' Cædmon informed her, once again speaking in that surreally calm voice. 'Only in reverse.'

'Are you insane!? It's completely different. If I lose my grip, I'm a goner.' If she'd lost her grip on the bridge, she would have simply gone for a cold dunk.

'Rest assured, I have a firm grip on my end. Believe me, Edie, if I could climb into this hole and carry you on my back, I would. But I can't.'

'I know, Cædmon. I know.' She fought back the tears. At the moment, it was the only battle she had a prayer of winning.

Stay in control.

Stay focused.

It's the only way to get out of the shaft.

To that end, Edie grabbed the length of fabric with her left hand, following through on the rest of Cædmon's instructions. To her surprise, the new position – flat-footed, torso inclined away from the shaft wall – felt far more secure than the old position. She even felt stable enough to peer up to the top of the shaft. She could see that Cædmon's long legs were straddled over the shaft opening, his feet firmly planted on the rim, giving him the necessary leverage to hoist her to the top.

'Set to begin the upward trek?'

'Ready to roll,' she called up to him.

With Cædmon doing all of the heavy lifting, the climb was much easier than she had envisioned. Between his grunts and her groans, Edie slowly and sure-footedly made her way to the top. When Cædmon secured a hand around her wrist, pulling her up and out of the shaft, she collapsed against him.

Still holding her in his arms, Cædmon scooted away from the shaft.

'You're only wearing an undershirt,' she inanely whispered against his chest.

'I was fully prepared to strip naked if need be.'

'Just so you know, that was the ground zero of fear.'

'For us both.' Cædmon jostled her shoulder. 'We need to depart. Before the bloody roof collapses on us. That may not be the only death trap in the sanctuary.' There was no mistaking the urgency in his voice.

'What are you saying? That the entire place is booby-trapped?'

'It's possible.' Shoving himself upright, he extended a hand to her. 'Come on. There's nothing more to investigate. While the sanctuary is proof that the Templars established a colony in the New World, it's obvious that whatever treasure had been housed here disappeared long years ago.'

Edie scrambled to her feet. She belatedly realized that her digital camera hung limply around her neck. 'Hope it still works. It took quite a beating in the fall.'

In the process of putting an arm into a chambray shirt sleeve, Cædmon gazed over at her. Instead of donning the shirt, he used the shirt sleeve to gently wipe her cheek. 'It appears that you took quite a beating as well.'

She shoved his hand aside. 'I can get cleaned up later. Let's get the heck out of it. And I don't know how to tell you this, but your beloved Knights Templar were a devious bunch of bastards.'

'The secret to their success,' he replied as he finished dressing. He handed her the second flashlight. 'I lead, you follow. Do be vigilant.'

As they walked single file across the sanctuary, Edie aimed her flashlight at the floor, scanning for any anomaly that might be a concealed Templar death trap. No sooner did they go into the narrow passageway that led back to the cave entrance than she sighted something out of the ordinary.

'Stop!' she shouted, grabbing the back of Cædmon's jacket with her free hand. 'There's something suspicious-looking on the floor. To the left side of the entryway.'

Slowly pivoting, Cædmon aimed his flashlight at the floor.

'Stay put,' he ordered. 'I'm not certain, but – Good Lord! It's an inscription.' He went down on bent knee. 'It appears to be written in charcoal. Pass me your camera. I want to document this.'

Extending her arm, Edie handed over the camera. Afraid of falling into another shaft, she didn't move her feet so much as an inch. From where she stood, she could see that the inscription was several lines long.

'What does it say?' she asked as Cædmon snapped off a shot.

Frowning, he shook his head. 'No idea. As I recall, you brought your netbook computer.'

‘It’s in my knapsack.’

‘Excellent. I’m hoping we can get a mobile signal from the bridge. That will enable us to search the Internet. I’m not altogether certain, but I think the inscription is written in the Enochian alphabet.’

‘The Enochian alphabet? Never heard of it.’

‘Enochian is an occult language devised by Dr John Dee in the late sixteenth century.’

‘Next question: who’s Dr John Dee?’

Camera in hand, Cædmon walked towards her. ‘Well, that’s what is so damned odd . . . Dr John Dee, in addition to being an alchemist, was a personal advisor to the monarch Queen Elizabeth.’

34

'Okay, let's tackle this Enochian inscription,' Edie said as she booted up her netbook. Since it weighed in at only two pounds, she'd gone ahead and packed it. Using her iPhone as a wireless modem enabled her to hook into the Internet anywhere there was cell-phone service. On the cheap.

Sitting side by side on the sun-kissed granite slab, she and Cædmon were drying out. The ascent out of the hidden cave had been a wet one, their clothes sodden, their boots soggy. All in all, it'd been a helluva day.

Finished cleaning Edie's various scrapes and cuts, Cædmon shoved a small first-aid kit back into his knapsack.

As she waited for the computer to boot up, Edie pulled the memory chip from her digital camera. Hopefully, the chip had survived the plunge in the shaft. 'You said that some guy named Dr John Dee invented the Enochian alphabet.'

'Actually, he invented an entire language. If I recall the story correctly, Dr Dee claimed the Enochian language was transmitted to him by the heavenly host; and that it was the same language spoken by Adam in the Garden of Eden.'

'The heavenly host? What are you saying, that this Dr Dee communicated with angels?'

'It was a popular pastime in the Elizabethan period,' Cædmon replied as he removed his wet jacket. That done, he leaned back on his forearms and tipped his face to the afternoon sun. 'Personally, I have my doubts as to the celestial provenance of the Enochian language. Although, mystical tendencies aside, Dr Dee was the first to apply Euclidean geometry to navigation. A brilliant mathematician, he built navigational tools which enabled an entire generation of English seafarers to sail the high seas and explore the great beyond.'

'Quite the Renaissance guy. Must be something in the English water.' Glancing up from the computer, she winked.

'I think mercurial wizard is a more apt description. Dee was the inspiration for such literary characters as Prospero and Dr Faustus. Not to mention Ian Fleming's 007.'

'So in addition to everything else, Dr Dee was a spy.'

Cædmon nodded. 'The Virgin Queen's *premier* spy at that.'

Edie popped the memory chip into her computer. Pleased to get the Removable Disk menu, she saved the photos on to her hard-drive then opened them for viewing. Despite the dim light in the cave, she'd managed to shoot clean, crisp images.

'Okay, here's the digital photo of the Enochian message.'

Sitting upright, Cædmon stared at the computer screen, his gaze narrowing. Edie figured that he was zeroing in on the very same thing that caught her eye – a Templar Beauséant smack dab in the middle of the inscription.

'While we don't know how to translate the words written in the Enochian script, we do know that the Beauséant means "glorious".' Edie tried to put an upbeat spin on what she feared might be an impossible task – deciphering a message written in angel code.

'Mmmm . . .' Cædmon lightly tapped his chin with his index finger. 'If you would be kind enough to Google the words "Enochian alphabet".'

Edie typed the two words into the Google search engine.

'That one,' Cædmon said, pointing to the image results. 'The chart with the Enochian alphabet juxtaposed with its Latin counterpart. I'm thinking our charcoaled message may be a simple transliteration.'

'Meaning that whoever wrote the message substituted an Enochian letter for its Latin counterpart?'

'That's the working theory. Dr Lovett's notebook is in my field kit.'

Rolling on to her side, Edie opened his knapsack and rummaged through it. When her hand made contact with an object that closely resembled a pistol, she said, 'I cannot believe that you actually brought a flare gun.'

'In case we get lost on the moors.' He took the mechanical pencil and notebook from her, opening the latter to a blank page. 'Right. Let's have a go at it, shall we?'

'Well, it *was* a good idea,' Edie murmured a few moments later as she peered over his shoulder at the translated message. 'Too bad it didn't pan out.'

HGELAR

ENIWS
TRUOC

'You need to come at this particular horse from the arse end.' Cædmon's blue eyes twinkled, the man clearly knowing more than he let on. 'By that I mean you must read the message from right to left.'

'Oh, I get it, like Hebrew.' She made the necessary course correction. 'Okay, I come up with "Ralegh Beauséant Swine Court". Which doesn't tell me a whole heck of a lot.'

'It's pronounced *rawley* not *raleff*,' he informed her, now grinning broadly. 'As in Sir Walter Ralegh, the Elizabethan sea captain and famed explorer.'

'Wait a minute . . . are you saying that this message was written by Walter Ralegh?'

'Possibly,' Cædmon hedged. For several seconds he stared at the deciphered message before saying, 'It could well be that Ralegh left the charcoaled message to inform anyone who might follow in his footsteps that he had discovered the Templars' sanctuary and that he was homeward bound.

In those days, safe passage across the Atlantic was in no way guaranteed. An armed Spanish galleon or a turbulent storm at sea could have sent Sir Walter and his wooden ship to the bottom of the ocean.'

'So you think he left the message just in case he didn't make it back to England?'

'Precisely. But let's put that aside for the moment.' He tapped the Templar battle standard with the pencil tip. 'I suspect that the Beauséant is a pictogram that refers to the Templars' "glorious" relic.'

'Which we presume was kept in the niche inside the sanctuary.'

'That is the working assumption.' He next tapped the last line in the communiqué. 'Now this business about the "swine court" . . . admittedly, I'm baffled.'

Edie stared at the nonsensical phrase. 'Guess it has something to do with pigs.'

Cædmon suddenly slapped his palm against the granite slab. 'Oh, for bollocky's sake! Swine refers to Bacon.'

'Only after you cook it.'

'No, I mean Sir Francis Bacon, the sixteenth-century English philosopher. Elizabethan history has never been my strong suit but, as I recall, Bacon, Ralegh and Dee all ran in the same circle, bound by their shared interest in hermetic philosophy and the occult sciences.'

'The occult sciences being something of an oxymoron, right?'

'To the learned and enlightened men of Elizabeth's court, occult science, or alchemy, was the *first* of the sciences. And, curiously enough, the Knights Templar also had an interest in alchemy, having been exposed to it in the course of their dealings with the Sephardic Jews.' Evidently realizing that he was rambling, he smiled self-deprecatingly. 'But I digress.' Pencil still in hand, he underlined the last line of the translated message. 'Bacon's court can only refer to one place, Gray's Inn.'

'Sorry, but I'm drawing a big fat blank.'

Cædmon crossed his booted feet at the ankle, once more leaning back on his elbows. 'Located in London, Gray's Inn is a professional association for barristers. There are four of these inns, the other three being the Middle Temple, the Inner Temple and Lincoln's Inn. During the Elizabethan period, the inns were boarding houses and social clubs all rolled into one. Sir Francis maintained lodging at Gray's Inn.'

'So then it's possible that Walter Ralegh took whatever it was that he found in the Templar sanctuary to Gray's Inn, whereupon he turned it over to Francis Bacon.'

'According to the Enochian communiqué, that's what Ralegh *intended* to do. We have no way of knowing if he followed through.' Reaching for a water bottle, he twisted the cap and offered the opened bottle to her.

Edie waved it off. 'Perhaps at this juncture I should point out that there's *a lot* we don't know. Particularly since we have no clue as to *what* this "glorious" relic is. Even if we did know what we're looking for, we have no idea *where* to look for it. And, news flash, Sir Walter and Sir Francis died centuries ago.'

'At which time the Templars' "glorious" relic was bequeathed to someone. No doubt, someone in that same circle of men.' Seemingly unperturbed, Cædmon took a swig of water.

'Oh, yeah, a completely unknown "someone" should be easy to track down.' Shaking her head, Edie rolled her eyes.

'There's no need for sarcasm.'

'Hey, one person's sarcasm is another person's reality check,' she countered. 'In my humble opinion, we just smashed headlong into a concrete barrier.'

35

Mercurius sighed heavily. 'It must be done.'

'You have my word.'

Communiqué ended, Saviour turned his attention to the pair lounging on the stone slab beside the river. His mentor had been displeased to learn that the Brit and his woman had emerged from the cave empty-handed. It meant that there was nothing in the cave to retrieve. Whatever treasure had once been safeguarded in the subterranean hideaway had already been confiscated. That being the case, Saviour now had to ensure that no one ever learned of the cave's existence.

Unzipping his canvas carrying case, he first removed a leather quiver that contained two dozen wooden arrows. Unlike an aluminium or fibreglass arrow, a cedar shaft had its own unique personality. The wood grain gave each arrow its own feel. Its own smell.

He fingered several arrows, gauging the spines of each, the stiffness of the arrow determining its flight distance. He settled on a wooden arrow with blue feather fletching. The colour of the Aegean Sea in the early morning light.

On Panos Island he used to feign interest as Evangelos droned on about shear drag, kinetic energy and the laws of physics. When it came to archery, Saviour knew that only one thing mattered – hit the target.

And he was *very* good at that.

Smiling, he lightly touched the steel tip of the selected arrow. 'This will hurt you a great deal, Englishman,' he softly whispered.

Before it kills you.

36

'The car may be dented, but the engine still runs,' Cædmon informed Edie, refusing to acknowledge that they'd hit a roadblock. After all the years of study, this was the closest he'd ever come to deciphering the mystery of the Knights Templar.

Monks. Warriors. Mystics. New World colonists. It was fast becoming a heady brew.

Of one thing he was certain: Sir Walter Ralegh had not only discovered the subterranean sanctuary, but he had removed *something* from it. Meaning Ralegh had succeeded where Giovanni Verrazano had failed. The unwitting Verrazano had most likely led the swashbuckling Englishman to the prize, the Italian sea captain having mentioned the Newport stone tower in his ship's log. Enough of a clue for Ralegh, Bacon and Dee to put the pieces of the Templar puzzle together. After all, it'd been known for centuries that a large contingent of knights had managed to elude the Inquisition, escaping by sea. But until the sixteenth century, nobody knew *where* they'd escaped to.

Now that he knew the *where*, Cædmon was determined to find out *what* precisely Ralegh had found in the Templar sanctuary. Once he knew what he was looking for, he could then begin the hunt in earnest.

'May I borrow your laptop?'

'Be my guest.' Edie popped out the memory chip before

handing over her two-pound dynamo. Reaching into her field kit, she removed a zip-lock plastic bag. 'Mind filling me in?'

'Not in the least. I'm checking for the next available flight to London. I believe there's an airport at Providence. Even with the translated Ralegh communiqué, I'm still very much in the starting blocks.'

'And going to London will change that *how*?' In the process of placing the memory chip into the plastic bag, she stopped in mid-motion. The woman didn't just stare at him, she out-and-out scowled. No doubt thinking him completely bonkers.

'There's a chap in London, name of Rubin Woolf. In addition to being an antiquarian, Rubin is an acknowledged Baconian expert.'

'And you're thinking that this Rubin character can shed some light on Bacon and his esoteric cronies?' Edie ran her thumb and index finger across the top of the zip-lock baggie, sealing the memory chip inside.

'If Francis Bacon came into possession of a "glorious" Templar relic, Rubin might know something about it. The man is quite obsessed.'

Edie chuckled. 'One pod, two peas. Okay, let's do it. Let's go to London.'

'I think you should know that London can be beastly in March, chill wind, driving rain.'

'That's why the umbrella was invented.' She cocked her head to one side, a questioning expression on her face. 'You're sending a mixed message. Do you want me to accompany you or not?'

Cædmon hesitated. Two days ago Jason Lovett had

been executed, the murder weapon emblazoned with an octogram star. Moreover, the man's cottage had been thoroughly ransacked, the intruder leaving a painted star as a parting signature. While he didn't know how the symbol related to those two violent episodes, he had to assume the beautiful bastard was still on the hunt.

'You're taking *way* too long to answer a simple question.'

He stared at her wordlessly, not certain how to reply. *My brave, beautiful Edie.* Although he willed it otherwise, he couldn't erase the image of her perilously clinging to the shaft.

'According to the computer, there's a flight leaving Providence, Rhode Island, at 7:20 this evening. There are two seats still available,' he said finally, deciding the best way to keep her safe was to keep her close. 'And the umbrella was invented by the ancient Egyptians.'

'Well, praise be, the riddle is finally solved.'

Ignoring her smirk, Cædmon booked the flight, keying in names, dates and his credit-card number.

Edie glanced at her watch. 'We have plenty of time to hike out of here, return to our hotel and catch a bite to eat, then drive to Providence. Lucky for you, I packed my passport.'

'How fortunate,' Cædmon deadpanned as he reached for his field kit. The instant he leaned over, he experienced an excruciating burst of pain.

He glanced down, flabbergasted to see an arrow protruding from his upper arm.

37

Skata!

How could he have missed his target? To kill a man, you must strike him in the head or the heart. A lesson learned on Panos Island.

Enraged, Saviour took a deep breath, filling his nostrils with the scent of cedar. Remembering . . .

Evangelos, stunned that Saviour had turned the bow on him, angrily pointed a finger at his boy-toy. 'What are you doing?'

'Defending my honour,' Saviour calmly informed him.

'You're my little pousties. *You have no honour.'*

'As to thialo! *Although hell's too good a place for you,' Saviour hissed, releasing the arrow, striking Evangelos in the upper thigh. The tycoon dropped to his knees, gasping.*

Saviour slowly walked towards him, a second arrow notched. 'Beg.'

'Yes . . . mercy, please.'

Saviour clucked his tongue, disappointed. 'I meant, beg for forgiveness.'

'I adored you . . . worshipped you like the god that you are.'

'Liar.' Saviour calmly released his finger, the arrow flying into Evangelos Danielides' left orbital socket. A perfect bull's eye.

'Calm. Above all else, I must remain calm,' Saviour murmured, the memory imbuing him with newfound strength. If he kept his focus, he could accomplish anything he set his sights upon. Isn't that what Mercurius always told him?

Yes, focus.

I must kill the Brit.

'I *will* kill the Brit.'

38

Christ Almighty!

Grabbing Edie with his uninjured right arm, Cædmon pulled her under him just as several more arrows soared in their direction.

'Cædmon, what's happening?'

'It's raining bloody arrows,' he snarled, the projectiles bouncing off the granite and skittering into the gushing river beside the ledge. 'We have to take cover.'

With Edie tucked against his torso, Cædmon scooted backwards on to the granite shelf that protruded from under their makeshift office, Yawgoog's bridge comprised stacked and staggered granite slabs. While the manoeuvre got them out of the open, it gave them little more than an eighteen-inch bulwark to crouch behind.

'Are you all right?'

Edie bobbed her head, a stunned look on her face. 'If you hadn't . . . hadn't leaned over when you did, the arrow would . . . would have . . .'

Gone straight to his heart.

As it was, the metal tip had burrowed into his bicep. A flesh wound, albeit a painful one.

Cædmon glanced over the top of the stone rampart just in time to see the archer briefly step into the open to launch his next salvo. He ducked. The arrow sailed past, plunging into the opposite bank.

‘Stay as low to the surface as humanly possible,’ he hissed. ‘I’m going to scramble on to the ledge and grab my field kit.’

‘You can’t be serious!?’

‘Dead.’

Edie pointedly stared at the wooden shaft embedded perpendicular to his arm and the bloody circle of fabric that surrounded it. ‘Given that you have an arrow protruding from your body, “yes” or “no” are the two preferred answers.’

‘The first-aid kit and the GPS receiver are—’

‘In your knapsack,’ she said over the top of him. ‘I’ll get them.’ She raised up slightly.

Cædmon shoved his right hand on her shoulder, pushing her back down. ‘No! And the matter isn’t open for debate.’

Not exactly thrilled by the prospect of becoming a human pincushion, he scurried over the granite ledge. The field kit was five feet away. He awkwardly crawled towards it. Just as his hand made contact with the nylon strap, a feather-tipped arrow came flying his way. Raising the kit to his face, he used it to deflect the arrow.

Still holding the makeshift shield in front of him, he grabbed one more item – the zip-lock plastic bag with Edie’s memory chip – before lurching over the side of the granite ledge.

Edie snatched the canvas pack from him. Her normally pale cheeks splotched with uneven colour, she removed the first-aid kit and the GPS receiver.

Taking a deep stabilizing breath, Cædmon grasped the wooden shaft of the arrow.

'Wait!' She grabbed his wrist. 'You can't just pull it out. What if the shaft breaks away from the arrowhead? What if the arrowhead hits an artery?'

'The tip isn't anywhere near my brachial artery. And while it'll make for a nasty puncture wound, I'll live to tell the tale.' Gritting his teeth, he slowly pulled the arrow from his flesh. A small geyser of bright red blood gushed from his arm. He grunted. It hurt like hell. Eyes watering, he flung the bloodied arrow aside.

'I didn't think there'd be so much blood,' Edie gasped.

'Gauze! Hurry!' he hissed, unable to manage a complete sentence.

Another arrow soared in their direction, striking next to the laptop computer. He watched as it bounced towards them. An ominous sign.

Edie, her hands visibly shaking, placed the end of the gauze roll on top of the puncture wound. 'Are you sure it's Lovett's killer who's taking aim?'

'Quite.' The man had a face straight out of a Botticelli canvas; it wasn't one that he would easily forget.

Finished wrapping his wound, Edie tore the gauze from the roll with her teeth and knotted it off. 'Okay. Now what?'

'We take the plunge.'

Her brows instantly shot upward. Eyes saucer-like, she turned towards the river. Flowing at a furiously fast rate, the current frothed and foamed as it pounded against the granite slabs.

'Unfortunately, the river is our only means of escape.' He hurriedly shoved the GPS device into the same zip-lock bag with Edie's memory chip, along with the gauze roll and a tube of antibiotic ointment. He then checked to make sure his shirt-tails were tucked into his denim jeans before placing the watertight parcel inside his shirt, buttoning it to his chin. That done, he cinched his belt another notch.

'So, how do we stop Rico Suave from following us downstream? All he has to do is jog along the river bank and wait for us to get out of the pool.'

'A diversion is required.' Leaning over, he retrieved the flare gun from the field kit. Plan hatched, he verified that a 12-gauge shell was in the barrel.

'We need more than a diversion,' Edie muttered, dubiously glancing at the plastic single-shot gun. 'We need a Sherman tank.'

'Diversions can move mountains.' He caught a flash of motion out of the corner of his eye. 'Here he comes! Ready yourself!'

Heart painfully thumping against his breastbone, Cædmon watched as their assailant slowly moved towards them, bow held in front of him, the string drawn.

Come on, you bloodthirsty bastard, just a few more feet.

The bow dipped slightly, the killer having sighted his prey.

Beside him, Edie drew in a sharp breath.

Every muscle in Cædmon's body tensed. Then, like a jack-in the-box, he sprang up. Took aim. *And fired.*

The discharged shell made a high-pitched whistling sound – the only warning the archer had before the flare lodged in the V of his armpit. The sleeve of his nylon windbreaker instantly caught fire. Dropping the bow, the beautiful young man began to flap his arm wildly as he spun around in circles. An enraged rooster desperately trying to extinguish the flame.

'Hurry! There's no time to lose!'

Offering up a quick prayer that they wouldn't be dashed on the rocks, Cædmon grabbed hold of Edie's hand and leaped.

Colder. Deeper.

Those were the first two thoughts that Cædmon processed as his body hit the water, plunging feet first into a river that was much colder and far deeper than he'd expected. Keeping his arms locked at his sides, he furiously kicked his feet as the raging current shot him back to the surface like an ocean buoy.

'Edie!'

He turned his head just in time to see her break the surface, her arms flailing as she pitched and rolled in the river current. She opened her mouth, hacking, coughing, gasping for air.

'Cædmon!'

'I'm here! To your left!' he yelled over the crescendo of thundering whitecaps. He tried to swim towards her, but the current was too strong. Already carrying him down river, as though he'd been shot through a water chute. 'Go with it! Don't fight the current!'

Cædmon took his own advice; going with the flow, using his legs as propellers, he concentrated on keeping his head above water. Glancing behind him, he could see that Edie was now swimming with stronger, more confident strokes. *Thank God.*

About fifty yards ahead of them the river curved, the current smoothing out into a more manageable course. In the bend of the curve was a toppled tree, the fallen hardwood extending into the river. *A perfect place to dock.*

'I see it!' Edie shouted, having read his thoughts. 'I'm headed that way!'

'Right!' He deepened his strokes. Grunting, he furiously kicked his arms and legs, putting every ounce of effort into –

Yes! He grabbed hold of the rough-hewn bark. Fortuitously, a large boulder was wedged beneath the tree. Using it as a launch pad, he pulled himself out of the water and on to the limb. A throbbing corona of pain radiated from the arrow wound. He wanted very much to bellow.

'I'm right behind you!' Edie called out.

Cædmon leaned over the side of the tree and wrapped his uninjured arm around her torso, hauling her out of the river. They both awkwardly straddled the limb. Huffing from her exertions, Edie's head dropped to her chest.

'I know that you're exhausted, Edie, but it's imperative that we make a hasty departure. Can you manage the tree trunk?'

Raising her head, Edie nodded. 'I've got a good sense of balance and it's a pretty thick trunk.'

'Right.' Testing his own sense of balance, he stood up.

With his arms held perpendicular to his body, Cædmon gracelessly ambled to the river bank, doing a fair impersonation of an inebriated tight-rope walker. Leaping to the ground, he turned and, with outstretched arms, caught Edie as she jumped from the tree trunk.

For several long moments they clung to one another. That is until Edie began to violently shiver. Worried, he pulled away.

'We need to get you to the car before hypothermia—'

'Cædmon, look down!'

A stricken expression on her face, Edie pointed to a spot some eighteen inches from his boot tip. There, coiled in a pile of rotting humus beside the fallen hardwood, was a mottled brown snake. Beautifully camouflaged as nature had intended. Cædmon took its measure at three to four feet.

'I think it's a copperhead,' Edie whispered. 'No sudden moves. They're very sensitive to vibration.'

In a lowered voice, he asked the obvious. 'Is it poisonous?'

'Oh, yeah. And they can strike as fast as you can move.'

As though to prove that very point, the snake reared its head.

Bloody hell!

About to shove Edie out of striking range, he was flat-out shocked when a single shot rang out, severing the snake's head from its coiled body.

Cædmon spun on his heel, brought up short when he saw a dark-skinned man standing twenty feet away. The scowling stranger had a face like a closed fist. He also had a bolt-action rifle raised to his shoulder . . . the muzzle pointed directly at them.

39

'Do you want to live?' the rifleman enquired.

Edie's jaw slackened, disbelief trumping fear. 'That's a rhetorical question, right?'

'Yes, we want to live,' Cædmon answered. He stepped forward, his right hand extended. 'Tonto Sinclair, I presume?'

'Well, I sure as hell ain't Dr Livingstone.' The pony-tailed Native American, who Edie placed in his early sixties, tipped the rifle skyward. To her relief, he flipped on the safety. Still scowling, he stared at Cædmon's proffered hand. Rather than take it, he shrugged out of his brown flannel jacket and flung it at Cædmon's chest. 'Leech the lead from your asses. He'll soon be on the hunt.'

Edie assumed that their 'guide' referred to Rico Suave.

'Put out the flame, did he?' Cædmon handed her the jacket, silently mouthing the words '*Put it on.*'

The other man shrugged. 'You only singed him. He'll live.'

'Pity.' Cædmon gallantly swept his arm, drops of water plopping to the ground as he did so. 'By all means, lead the way.'

Grateful, Edie donned the jacket, toasty warm from Tonto Sinclair's body heat. Peering at their guide, she noticed the faded tattoo that ran across the knuckles of both his hands – *red blooded.* That's how Cædmon had correctly deduced Sinclair's identity; Jason Lovett had mentioned the tattoo in his digital voice recording.

The three of them, Sinclair on point, she and Cædmon pulling up the rear, headed due east, the pace brisk. Edie kept her eyes glued on the rifle.

They hadn't gone far when Sinclair veered to the right, heading towards a path bordered by towering trees. She realized they were traipsing along an abandoned logging road, the parallel ruts discernible through the overgrown foliage. The afternoon sun, shining through the leafless hardwoods, cast filigree shadows.

'How does your arm feel?' Edie asked in concern; Cædmon had yet to utter a single complaint.

'Not quite in the pink, but I shall soldier on.'

'No stiff upper lip clichés. How do you *really* feel?'

'Hurts like hell.' Cædmon glanced at the makeshift bandage, grimacing. 'If I could, I'd trade my whole kingdom for a handful of aspirin.'

'Maybe we can get –' she glanced at their guide's backside, not exactly sure what to call him – 'Mr Sinclair to take us to the nearest emergency room. You really should have your arm examined by a doctor.'

'Rather difficult injury to explain away.'

'Tell 'em you were accidentally shot by an off-season bow hunter,' Tonto Sinclair said. The remark was issued without so much as backward glance.

'Inventive but believable,' Edie seconded, thinking it was a pretty good lie. 'And while we're at it, maybe we should contact the police. To inform them that a lunatic armed with a bow and arrow is on the loose.'

'Bad idea.' This time Sinclair turned his head a few inches, *almost* acknowledging them.

'Are you aware of the fact that two days ago the lunatic in question killed Jason Lovett?'

'Lovett knew the risks when he uncovered that mass grave.' Sinclair punctuated the callous remark with an unconcerned shrug. 'What can I say? A fool and his gold.'

Are soon parted. Or dearly departed as the case may be.

Lengthening his stride, Cædmon came abreast of their guide. 'According to Dr Lovett, the treasure consists of a fortune in gold bullion. Covetous, he might have been, but the man was no fool.'

This time, Tonto Sinclair actually swivelled his head in their direction. For what seemed like an interminable length of time, he silently scrutinized them. While Edie knew it was impossible, it felt like the Indian was peering into her very soul.

'There is no gold bullion.'

Hearing that, Edie's jaw dropped. 'So why did you *purposefully* mislead Jason Lovett into thinking there was a monetary treasure trove buried in Arcadia?'

The question got their guide's attention, Sinclair coming to a complete standstill.

'For five hundred years the white man has fucked my people.' The Indian's voice lowered to a guttural rumble. 'I needed the scrawny shit to help me find Yawgoog's treasure. It's called payback.'

There was no gold, but there was a treasure.

Edie turned to Cædmon, bewildered. 'Am I missing something?'

'Indeed, Mr Sinclair's remark begs the question: what exactly is Yawgoog's treasure?'

The begged question elicited another drawn-out silence.

'Yawgoog entrusted my people with his sacred stone,' Sinclair said at last. 'That's the treasure.'

What!? Edie shook her head, wondering if she had heard correctly.

'A stone . . . how curious.' Cædmon didn't seem the least bit surprised. Or even disappointed for that matter.

'Earlier today we found a carved stone with a Templar Beauséant,' Edie said, still grappling with the notion that someone had just tried to kill them because of a rock. 'I thought *that* was Yawgoog's Stone.'

Sinclair shook his head. 'That's what I told Jason Lovett, but that's not Yawgoog's sacred stone. Before Yawgoog died, he entrusted his sacred stone to the Narragansett. And we did a pretty damned good job of minding the store . . . until the white man showed up and stole it from us.'

Given the way Tonto glared at them, Edie had the unnerving feeling that he was holding them personally accountable for the centuries-old theft.

'You know, a description of this stone would be nice,' she shot back, peeved. 'Are we talking about your garden-variety rock? Or some kind of polished pebble?'

'According to the legends of my people, the sacred stone is the size of a flat grinding mortar.' Moving his hands slightly, Tonto indicated dimensions comparable to a large dictionary.

Which meant that Yawgoog's Stone would have fitted perfectly into the empty niche that she and Cædmon had discovered in the Templar sanctuary.

'Because we failed to keep our promise to Yawgoog, the Narragansett paid with their blood. And will continue to pay until the sacred stone is returned to us.' Sinclair took a menacing step in their direction, his scowl deepening. 'So I'm only going to ask you this one time . . . did you find the sacred stone?'

The air fairly crackled with hostile intent. Edie fearfully glanced at Cædmon, wondering if he was aware that the finger emblazoned with a blue 'O' now hovered over the trigger.

'We did not find the sacred stone. Although you may be interested to know that we discovered Yawgoog's cave, the entrance of which is located behind the falls that course over the stone bridge. The cave, however, was empty,' Cædmon quickly clarified. 'That said, do exercise caution if you're of a mind to explore. There are deadly traps concealed throughout.'

'Thanks for the update. Guess that means I won't be shooting the two of you in the head and burying the bodies in a shallow grave.' One side of Sinclair's mouth twitched. The ghost of a very sick smile. Turning his back on them, he continued walking.

'Disappointed does not even begin to explain how I feel right now,' Edie hissed in a lowered voice. 'In the last two minutes, we've gone from a treasure worth a hundred billion dollars to a simple stone.'

'A *sacred* stone,' Cædmon quietly emphasized. 'And I doubt there is anything simple about it. Several hundred Templar descendants were massacred on account of this stone. Moreover, the sacred stone may have led to their forbears' demise at the hands of the Inquisition.'

'Do you think Rico Suave knows that the fabled Templar treasure trove is just an old stone?'

'A *sacred* stone,' he again reiterated. 'And I have no idea what our assailant knows or doesn't know.'

'You keep using the word "sacred". Do you mean sacred like the Ten Commandments?' she asked, wondering why he kept harping on that particular attribute.

'Possibly.' No sooner did he say it than Cædmon shook his head. 'While the Ten Commandments were carved on to stone tablets, Sinclair is adamant that Yawgoog had only one stone, not two.'

'And what about Sir Walter Ralegh, still convinced he took Yawgoog's Stone to London?'

'Oh, yes,' he quietly avowed, blue eyes glimmering.

'I noticed you didn't volunteer *that* titbit to our gun-toting guide.'

'While the purpose of Yawgoog's sacred stone is still a mystery, any number of men have killed to possess it.'

A dire thought. One that she preferred *not* to dwell on. Luckily, they had strict gun laws in the UK.

Up ahead, Edie caught sight of a beaten-up truck. The blue jalopy had to have been at least thirty years old. And, no surprise, there was a gun rack mounted to the back window.

Cædmon caught up to their guide. 'Our vehicle is parked near the eastern border of the wilderness area,' he said, diplomatically requesting a lift.

'Somebody slashed the tyres on your little piece of Japanese crap.'

Edie groaned; she had a pretty good idea who had wielded the knife.

'Not entirely unexpected,' Cædmon said calmly, taking the news in his stride. 'I'll need to get some items out of the boot.' He cleared his throat, giving Sinclair ample opportunity to offer them a ride. When no invitation was forthcoming, Cædmon, a tight smile on his lips, said, 'Would it be too much of an inconvenience to drive Miss Miller and myself to the airport at Providence?'

Sinclair pulled his car keys out of his pocket. 'You paying for the gas?'

40

Kologameio! Butt fuck!

Sobbing, barely able to pull breath into his lungs, Saviour collapsed on the ground, the tinder-dry foliage crunching beneath him.

Deeply humiliated, he hugged his knees and rocked back and forth, still able to smell the smouldering nylon jacket that he'd flung aside. *Uncomprehending.* He'd been on the verge of taking down his quarry when the wounded animal reared up and . . . and the *boutso gliftie*, the cock sucker, nearly set him ablaze. And while he flapped about like a bird on fire, the Brit and his woman had escaped. The two of them jumping into the river.

Angry tears scorching his cheeks, Saviour gave vent to his rage. *Kologameio!* He pounded the leaf-strewn soil with his balled fist. A moment later, he gulped a deep breath. Then another.

Focus.

He needed to 'check his emotions at the door' and focus.

Christos! There was no door! He was in the dark forest. A forest that reeked of cedar and wild olives. *No!* That was another forest. On the island of Panos. He'd been so scared. So certain that once Evangelos Danielides' arrow-riddled body was discovered, the servants would set the Argentine mastiffs loose on him. Terrified, he ran from the archery range and took refuge in the forest that bordered the villa. He'd hiked through the cedar and wild olive groves to the service dock on the far side of the island, where the supplies were delivered weekly on a motor launch from the mainland. Evangelos' Sobranie Black Russian cigarettes. Crates of ouzo. Feta. Tomatoes. Fresh octopus and slabs of tuna. *A godsend!* He could sneak on board. He didn't care where the vessel was headed. It didn't matter. *Somehow* he would find his way to Thessaloniki.

It took a week of sucking cocks and picking pockets on the docks of Piraeus before he could purchase a train ticket.

Afraid he would be hunted for Evangelos Danielides' murder, he'd kept to the shadows, becoming so skittish that he'd physically lurch when he heard a siren or a police whistle. Even a barking dog. To his surprise, there was no mention of the 'murder' in the Greek newspapers. Although he read that an elaborate funeral was held in Athens, the cause of death was officially reported as 'cardiac arrest'. A cover-up. He didn't even shoot the bastard in the heart. Obviously, the powerful Danielides family didn't want their son's predilections made public. Nonetheless, he feared that same powerful family would seek revenge for the murder of their only son.

Like a fugitive on the run, Saviour spent his nights roaming the Leoforos Nikis for quick pick-ups and hiding out in Thessaloniki's churches during the daylight hours. The last place the Danielides' hired guns would look for him. As though it were fated, at the Agía Sophía, the Church of Holy Wisdom, he met *his* saviour, the man who would alter the course of his life in a profound and wondrous way.

A beautiful memory.

Revived somewhat, he used his sweater sleeve to dry his face. He had to get a grip. Another American phrase. Shoving himself upright, he walked over to the stone slab where the English *boutso gliftie* and his bitch had held court before the attack. In a hurry to escape, they had left one of their packs. As well as a small laptop computer.

What were they doing with a computer? he wondered, struck by the oddity of seeing a high-tech device in the middle of the dark forest. He picked up the computer and, with the tap of a finger, took it out of hibernation mode.

Christos!

There on the screen was a reservation confirmation: airline tickets for two to London, including a three-night stay at the St Martin's Lane Hotel.

Overjoyed, he threw back his head and merrily laughed aloud.

Truly a gift from the gods.

41

'"When you have one of the first brains of Europe up against you, and all the powers of darkness at his back, there are infinite possibilities."'

'A first brain! The Englishman is a *vlakas*, I tell you! An *archimalakas*!'

While Mercurius could not say whether Cædmon Aisquith merited the damning praise that Sherlock Holmes had heaped upon his nemesis, Professor Moriarty, it was obvious that the man was no idiot. Far from it.

'Do you want me to go to London?'

'And confront the powers of darkness?' Mercurius countered, injecting a touch of humour into his voice.

'You often tell me to look to the Light.'

'So I do,' he murmured.

'You must always remember, little one, that you were named for the Bringer of the Light.'

'Do not fear the Light, Merkür. For it will lead you to your life's purpose.'

Faced with a conundrum, Mercurius said, 'Let me think on this, *amoretto*. I will call you back in a few minutes.'

Hanging up the telephone, Mercurius wandered into the kitchen.

For sixty years, he'd been haunted by the parting remarks of his father, Osman de Léon, and his milk brother, Moshe Benaroya. And because he'd been haunted, when he was sixty-five years of age he had *finally* returned to the city of his birth, Thessaloniki. To confront the horror of that spring night when the Nazis loaded the two men on to a train bound for Auschwitz.

From the grungy window of the airport taxi, he'd caught his first glimpse of the city, disappointed to see that it had changed greatly in the intervening years. Where once there had been graceful cypress trees, there were now garish billboards that advertised everything from yogurt to motorcycles. And blocks of hideous post-war apartment buildings. To someone who'd grown up with the city's lavish *fin-de-siècle* architecture, it seemed relentlessly dreary.

Once he'd arrived in the city, however, there were familiar sights and sounds. Modiano Market with tables piled high with oranges, figs, tomatoes and fresh-cut flowers. The bouzouki music that emanated from the tavernas. The clusters of men with their newspapers and clacking worry beads.

The first two nights he had stayed at a downtown hotel where he endured the constant roar of traffic outside his window. Needing his sleep, he checked out of the pricey hotel and headed for the old Turkish quarter near the Byzantine walls. There, he rented an unadorned flat in a white-washed building. He slept blissfully that night, awaking the next morning to a breakfast of feta cheese, olives and crusty bread. Refreshed of mind and body, he set off to find the house where he'd lived for the first seven years of his life.

He found it easily enough, taken aback to see a crone mopping the marble stoop. *Black shawl. Black stockings.*

Black shoes. White hair. So much like their old housekeeper Cybele that he nearly called out her name. Instead, he respectfully doffed his beret – an affectation he'd adopted as a much younger man – and introduced himself, explaining that his family had once owned the house.

The crone eyed him suspiciously, then said curtly, 'Did you know the Jew named Moshe Benaroya?'

If she'd asked if he'd known Atatürk, he would not have been more surprised. Now his turn to be suspicious, he warily nodded his head.

'*Perimenete!*' she ordered, gesturing for him to wait outside while she scurried into the house. A few minutes later she appeared, carrying what looked to be a loose-leaf manuscript of several hundred pages bound with string. 'We found this under the floorboards in one of the bedrooms.' She thrust the bundle at him before impatiently shooing him on his way. '*Feeghe!*'

He took no offence at her brusque manner, too stunned to be insulted.

By all that was holy . . . she'd just handed him a treasure trove.

One week later, he went to Agía Sophía, the Church of Holy Wisdom, a magnificent Orthodox church that had been constructed in the eighth century, to photograph the ceiling mosaics. He'd just finished photographing the famous *Ascension* mosaic in the central dome. Not yet acclimatized to the heat, he sat down in a wooden chair.

No more than a few moments had passed when a shadow fell over him.

He glanced up, taken aback to see a young man standing beside his chair. There was a halo of light surrounding the youth's dark head. He blinked several times. Noticed the small details. That the young man wore tight jeans and too much cologne. *But, oh, that face.*

Suddenly, he was very much aware of being a mature man in a tailored wool suit.

Without asking permission, the young man sat in the chair next to him.

Leary, Mercurius clutched his soft-sided attaché case to his chest, afraid that a thief might make off with the incredible manuscript. He'd taken to carrying it with him, having learned his lesson years earlier at the Archaeology Museum in Amman.

Oblivious to the sanctity of the church, the young man said nonchalantly, 'Would you like to fuck me up the ass? For you, I'll give a discount.'

Mercurius didn't know whether to laugh or cry. He relaxed the tight hold on his attaché. 'No, but I would like to take you to the patisserie on the other side of the square.' In truth, he feared a church priest might overhear the profane young man.

The beautiful youth accepted the invitation with a bored shrug. Together, they walked across Agía Sophía Square.

'The Christians held a thanksgiving service in this square when the Allies liberated the city from the Germans,' Mercurius remarked. The comment elicited another bored shrug.

Although it was a hot day, they sat outside at a bistro table, shaded by a colourful umbrella. Possessed of a ravenous appetite, Saviour ate, not one, but two slices of almond cake piled high with chocolate shavings. Mercurius refrained – doctor's orders – and, instead, sipped unsweetened coffee from a demitasse. No sooner did Saviour wipe the plate clean than he suggested they leave. Intrigued by the young man, Mercurius led him to the old section of town.

As they approached the towering Byzantine walls, the streets became narrow, more precipitous, the old district set on a hillside that overlooked the harbour. Inexplicably animated, Mercurius pointed to a waterless fountain. 'When I was a young boy, I once saw the ghost of a whirling dervish twirling in that fountain, arms spread to the heavens as water spewed between his lips.' A moment later, he gestured to a row of shops. 'Before the war, that used to be an olive grove. Until the Italians mistook it for a military target and bombed it.'

'The Italians can't hit porcelain when they piss,' the young man sneered contemptuously.

Standing in the shadow cast by the ancient walls that had once fortified the Byzantine city, he showed Saviour several places in the wall that had been repaired with marble tombstones from the desecrated Sephardi cemetery, removed from the necropolis when the Greeks went on a wild rampage searching for Jewish treasure.

Whether it was the burst of melancholy induced by that sombre reminder of the past or the fact that he'd given up jogging years ago, Mercurius came to a sudden halt. Breathless, his 65-year-old heart raced wildly.

'We must rest,' his companion declared abruptly, taking hold of Mercurius's elbow as he ushered him to a marble doorstep.

They sat side by side on the steps, the air fragranced with the scent of honeysuckle and mimosa.

'Tell me, why did you leave Thessaloniki? I left once. I couldn't wait to return.' As he spoke, Saviour bent down to pet a stray cat that had impudently rubbed against his lower leg. When the cat began to lick the same fingers that Saviour had earlier licked at the patisserie, the young man smiled, clearly enjoying the feline's antics.

Mercurius found himself, again, breathless. This time for a wholly different reason.

Hit with a sudden impulse to make a connection with the youth, he proceeded to tell Saviour about the remarkable friendship between a Muslim *Ma'min* and a Jewish Kabbalist. To his surprise, the youth listened to the tale with rapt attention.

'As soon as the war ended, my family moved to America. None of us knew about the hidden manuscript.'

'Is that what's inside your attaché case?' the youth astutely enquired.

He hesitated only a brief second before unbuckling his leather case and removing the loose-leaf manuscript that had been given to him a few days prior. He noticed the awestruck expression on Saviour's face when he saw the cover sheet with its exquisite illuminated gold star.

'The manuscript, entitled the *Luminarium*, is dedicated to my father.' With the tip of his index finger, Mercurius underscored the handwritten dedication. '*To my dear brother Osman. The courage of a lion, the gentleness of the lamb.*'

'Me, I like to read westerns. What is this *Luminarium* about?'

Mercurius contemplated whether to give the long answer or the abbreviated one. He decided on the latter, not wanting to bore his companion with the history of Judaic mysticism.

'It's a book about Creation and how the world came into being *ex nihilo*.' The young man's brow wrinkled. 'Out of nothing,' he clarified.

What Mercurius didn't tell the young man, at least not then, was that when the crone had unceremoniously shoved Moshe's manuscript into his hands, it was the Third Sign. Validation that he was the chosen one, his destiny intertwined with the stunning revelations contained within the *Luminarium*.

Another seven years would pass before the Fourth and final Sign was revealed to him.

'Why hide it? Maybe if he'd published it, your Moshe could have made some money.'

'Moshe Benaroya had to hide the *Luminarium* to ensure its survival. During the war the Nazis sent the *Sonderkommando Rosenberg* to Thessaloniki to plunder the sacred Jewish texts. While the Nazis loathed the Jews, they were fascinated with their mystical teachings.'

'Like the Nazis who tried to find the Ark of the Covenant in the Indiana Jones movie?'

Mercurius suppressed an amused smile. 'Exactly so. Afraid that the ancient teachings would be confiscated by the Germans, Moshe carefully hid the *Luminarium*.'

Saviour shrugged a shoulder. 'It doesn't look ancient,' he said dismissively.

This time, Mercurius did smile, the young man no fool. 'The *Luminarium* is the first *written* transcription of ancient teachings that had been deemed too holy to ever transcribe. For millennia, these sacred teachings were passed verbally from one Kabbalist to the next. Moshe Benaroya, fearing that no Jewish Kabbalists would survive the war, did the unthinkable . . . he put pen to paper and recorded the *Luminarium.* The manuscript contains many secrets and –' he leaned closer to the youth and lowered his voice to a soft whisper – 'it describes a sacred relic that the Jews of Spain gave to the Knights Templar.'

Hearing that, Saviour's brown eyes opened wide. 'This relic, it's made of gold and silver, *ne*?'

'Something far more valuable than gold and silver. Although when the Inquisition arrested the knights in the fourteenth century, the sacred relic had mysteriously disappeared.' As he spoke, Mercurius realized that the sun had nearly vanished in the western sky, leaving a pink blush in its wake. They'd been conversing for hours.

'So you are the only person in the world who knows the secret.'

'No, Saviour . . . now there are two of us.'

That was seven years ago.

Mercurius feared that someone else might now be privy to the secret.

As he lifted the telephone from its cradle, Mercurius sighed ponderously. '*London, that great cesspool.*'

Or so claimed Dr Watson.

42

'. . . and I happen to think our hotel is ultra hip,' Edie remarked as she passed in front of Cædmon and scooted into a glass turnstile. Mischievously grinning, well aware that he despised modern design, particularly when 'fused' to other styles, she pushed the revolving glass door, exiting the lobby.

'It's hotel as grand theatre,' she continued a few seconds later when he joined her on the pavement in front of the St Martin's Lane Hotel. 'Very energetic. Kinda like this fuchsia trench coat, huh?' Holding her straightened arms in front of her, Edie glanced from one brightly coloured sleeve to the other. As he'd earlier mentioned, there was no risk of losing her in the crowd.

'You're a vision,' he gallantly complimented. 'The hotel, on the other hand, is . . .' He glanced behind him at the stark glass façade.

Given the plain, almost drab exterior, one would never suspect that the interior housed an eye-popping space filled with gold stools shaped like back molars, African art and upholstered baroque armchairs. Catching sight of the two traditional red phone boxes at the edge of the pavement, he thought it all a bit surreal. Surreal but incredibly secure, the real reason he had booked the reservation at the 'energetic' hotel. Catering to celebrities and well-heeled tourists, the hotel management provided a safe sanctuary for its guests.

And security was an issue *whenever* he visited his homeland. Five years ago, he had killed the Real Irish Republican Army ringleader responsible for a deadly terrorist act. Soon thereafter, the RIRA put a bounty on his head. His superiors at MI5, concerned for his safety, spirited him out of the UK. To this day, he maintained a residence in Paris rather than London.

He shook off the bad memory. It was an unsavoury chapter that he preferred not to think about. God knows how Edie would react if she ever discovered his dark secret.

'Shall we nip across the street for a coffee? Our appointment with Rubin Woolf isn't until three.' He glanced at his wristwatch. 'There's still twenty minutes before the clock strikes the hour.'

'How far is it to Rubin's bookstore?'

Cædmon jutted his chin at the pedestrian passageway on the other side of the street. 'His shop is located at the far end of Cecil Court. No more than a few yards away.' Yet another reason he'd booked the room at the St Martin's. The less time he spent gadding about in public, the better.

'Since I'm about to succumb to a bad case of jetlag, I think a cup of coffee is definitely in order.' As she spoke, Edie took hold of his upper arm and leaned her head companionably against his shoulder.

'Right. Starbucks it is.' He ushered her across the street to the coffee bar opposite, the American franchise nearly as ubiquitous in London as red double-decker buses and black hackney cabs.

'If you don't mind, I'm going to plop on the bench while you go inside and contend with the bean and the blend and the nonsensical cup sizes.' Edie gestured to a wood garden bench beneath the familiar green and white signage.

'Probably best if you join me inside.' Cædmon held open the front door. 'Since we're clearly dealing with a man one step ahead of the game, we should be on our guard,' he said in a lowered voice, not wanting to give false comfort.

'Don't know about you, but I can't get a handle on this Rico Suave guy.' Edie took her place in the queue. 'Go it alone whack jobs like our Unibomber or your Jack the Ripper are pull-out-the-garlic, lock-the-car-doors creepy. But we're dealing with someone who's drop-dead *GQ* gorgeous. Emphasis on the drop dead.'

'A comely face does not connote a virtuous heart. That said, in the post 9-11 world, it's impossible to smuggle a nail file let alone a stiletto into an international airport.'

'But everyone boards the plane with their bare hands,' Edie countered. 'Weapon enough for some men.'

'Let's not get ahead of ourselves. A cappuccino?'

'Better make it a grande. And it's kinda hard *not* to get ahead of myself. I mean, we don't even know the kil—' realizing that she was in a public place, she quickly back-peddled. 'This guy's name.'

'Or his *modus operandi*.' Leaning over Edie's shoulder, he gave their order to a glum-faced, lip-studded barista.

Order placed, they obediently shuffled to the end of the counter to wait for their beverages.

'Of course, we know his motive: Rico Suave wants the Templar treasure, i.e. Yawgoog's Stone.'

'Undoubtedly, but there may be more to the stew than that.'

'You're thinking about the fact that our pretty boy likes to brand his handiwork with an eight-pointed star.'

Cædmon nodded wordlessly, still unable to fit the bizarre puzzle piece.

'How's your arm doing?'

He smiled. 'Still attached to my shoulder.'

Yesterday Tonto Sinclair had grudgingly taken him to an emergency-care facility near the Providence airport where the wound had been cleaned and bandaged. The harried physician had also put him on a twice daily regimen of antibiotics to ward off infection along with a prescription for a painkiller which he declined to take. The dull ache kept his mind sharp. And given all that had transpired in the last four days, he needed to keep his wits about him.

A different barista, this one tattooed rather than studded, placed two covered paper cups on the counter in front of them. Cædmon passed the larger of the two cups to Edie. They then stepped over to a different counter. Without asking, he handed his companion a stirrer and two packets of sugar.

Cups in hand, they headed for the door.

A few moments later, catching his first glimpse of Cecil Court, known locally as Booksellers' Row, Cædmon came to a standstill. To his surprise, his heartbeat accelerated. Shocked by the reaction, he took a deep breath. He'd once managed an antiquarian bookshop in Cecil Court. Part of a carefully constructed MI5 legend. For nearly a year he'd taken on the identity of an unassuming bibliophile. Until that balmy summer night when the whole operation, quite literally, blew up.

'You okay? You seem, I don't know, agitated.'

'I'm fine,' he lied glibly as he forced himself to put one foot in front of the other.

Edie strolled over to an outdoor cart full of second-hand books. 'Wow, what a great place to shop. This place is like its own little world, isn't it?'

As he could attest, Cecil Court was its 'own little world', seemingly immune from London's hustle-bustle.

Joining her at the cart, Cædmon glanced at the charming Victorian storefronts, taking in the familiar row of antiquarian and second-hand bookshops interspersed with the odd philately and antique dealer. While each shop sold uniquely different merchandise, each boasted a subdued green exterior and a tastefully lettered hanging sign. Long years ago one of those signs had read '*Peter Willoughby-Jones. Rare books and prints*'.

'Ahem.' Raising a balled fist to his mouth, he cleared his throat. 'There's something that I need to caution you about before we enter Rubin's bookshop.'

Edie returned a musty volume to the cart. Given the awkward lead-in, it was no surprise that her brows drew together in the middle.

'I met Rubin Woolf during an undercover operation,' he said matter-of-factly.

'You mean he's a spy?'

'Er, no. What I'm trying to say is that Rubin knows me by the alias Peter Willoughby-Jones.' A rush of blood heated his cheeks. 'At the time, I was posing as an antiquarian book dealer.'

Her shoulders shook with a barely contained mirth. 'Not very James Bond of you.'

'The spooks at Five are a more staid lot than the chaps at Six. With my academic background, it was a believable cover. And another thing before we go in –' he guided her to the other side of the lane – 'Rubin can be difficult at times. A bit of a temperamental genius, I'm afraid.'

'An English antiquarian who comes with a warning label.' Edie reassuringly patted his chest. 'Don't worry, Big Red. Now that I'm properly caffeinated, I'm up for the challenge.' To prove her point, she pitched her coffee cup some four feet into the air, the cup landing squarely in the nearby waste bin.

Cædmon, not feeling nearly as athletic, disposed of his half-empty coffee cup from a more sedate distance.

'When the bombs drop, please remember that the alarm was duly sounded.' Warning issued, he stepped in front of Edie and opened a plate-glass door.

A tinny bell announced their entry into the small shop lined floor to ceiling with dark espresso-stained bookcases. In the middle of the shop were three glass display cabinets showcasing valuable prints and maps.

'Peter Willoughby-Jones!' a cultured female voice hailed him. 'At long last you've deigned to visit your old chums at Cecil Court.'

A chicly dressed blonde got up from an Edwardian desk and walked over to greet them.

Taking Marnie Pritchard's outstretched hand, Cædmon leaned forward and kissed her on the cheek. At one time they'd been well acquainted. The Cecil Court crowd frequently met for drinkies and he'd been friendly with more than a few of his fellow dealers.

As they stood before each other, slowly shaking their

respective heads, the way people do when they run into someone they haven't seen in some time, he realized that the passing years had not put so much as a dent in Marnie's confident posh-girl persona.

'The place hasn't changed one bit. *You* haven't changed one bit,' he said.

'"Thank God! Cecil Court remains Cecil Court,"' she retorted, the Graham Greene quote a familiar refrain amongst the close-knit booksellers.

'Marnie Pritchard, allow me to introduce you to Edie Miller.'

'So very pleased to meet you,' Marnie said warmly as she took Edie's hand.

'Likewise.' Edie's brown eyes crinkled at the corners; a sure sign of mischief in the making. 'So, you and Peter have known each other a long time, I take it?'

'Too many years to count.' Marnie airily waved her hand, the light catching on a very expensive Baume & Mercier watch.

As Cædmon recalled, Marnie came from a moneyed background. Why she continued to work for the tetchy Rubin Woolf was a mystery.

'Rubin is still angry at you, Peter, for unceremoniously leaving the fold,' Marnie remarked, having intuited his thoughts. 'Not a day goes by that he doesn't gripe about the dodgy Moscow émigré who took over your shop. Oleg Rostov specializes in Russian literature. Although I understand that, for a price, he'll be happy to show you the religious icons that he keeps in the back room. *Very* black market,' she added in a conspiratorial whisper.

'Sounds like a case for MI5.'

Hearing that, Cædmon inwardly groaned, suspecting that Edie intended to have a bit of fun at his expense.

'Maybe you could go undercover and help take down the Russian smuggling ring,' she added a split second later, pushing the envelope right out of the plate-glass door.

'How utterly exciting,' Marnie trilled with a deep-throated chuckle. 'I've always wanted to be a *femme fatale*.' Still chuckling, she gestured to the staircase at the back of the shop. 'Rubin's upstairs in his boudoir anxiously awaiting your arrival. And it was very nice to make your acquaintance, Miss Miller.'

'Please call me Edie.'

Cædmon waited until he and his companion were halfway up the stairs, and out of earshot, before laying in to her. 'I will have a great deal of explaining to do to a great many people if you continue in this vein. So please tone it down,' he hissed. Then, realizing he'd come at her like a boulder on a butterfly, he softened the rhetoric. 'This is an awkward situation for me. I never thought I'd see these people again.'

'And you feel guilty because you lied to them,' Edie deduced astutely.

'Yes, I do feel guilty.'

'Sorry, Peter.' Rising up on her tiptoes, Edie gave him a quick peck on the lips. 'Won't happen again.'

A shadow suddenly fell across the two of them. Glancing up, Cædmon saw a rotund, bespectacled man garbed in a bespoke three-piece Nevis tweed suit, the conservative attire completely at odds with the gelled spiky white hair and royal-blue polka-dot bow tie.

'A bit old for shagging in the shadows, aren't you?'

'One is never too old for stolen pleasures,' Cædmon called out. Taking Edie by the hand, he led the way upstairs.

When they reached the top, Rubin had already retreated to the 'boudoir'.

'Where's Tweedy Bird?' Edie whispered in his ear.

'Shhh.'

Admonishment given, he ushered her through an open doorway; Rubin stood inside the small foyer beside a heavily carved court cupboard. Beyond his tweed-clad shoulder, Cædmon glimpsed their host's pride and joy – an authentic sixteenth-century panelled bedroom that had been painstakingly deconstructed and reassembled on site. The room included a massive Tudor four-poster bed that doubled as Rubin's desk, the top covered with books. The only two things that stood out as *not* belonging in the historically accurate recreation were the framed photographs on top of the court cupboard and the nineteenth-century German cuckoo clock that hung above it.

'Rubin Woolf, may I present Miss Edie Miller.'

'Nice to meet you.' Edie held out her right hand.

Pulling a long face, Rubin shook hands with her. 'An American? Well, well. Haven't met one yet who didn't consider the Bible the only book worth reading. "Get thee to a nunnery",' he quoted, pointing to the open doorway behind them.

Proving that she could ably roll with Rubin's well-aimed punches, Edie stepped over to the court cupboard. 'Wow. Are these people who I think they are?' She pointed to a framed group photograph. The leather, chains and general dishevelled appearance of all four people in the grainy shot instantly dated the picture. Vintage punk rock. Rubin, thin to the point of emaciation, sported the same spiky coif, the only difference being that three decades ago it was platinum blond.

Wearing a bored expression, Rubin nodded. 'Sid Vicious, Nancy Spungen and Johnny Rotten.' He jutted his chin at the shirtless pixie who defiantly glared at the camera. 'And, of course, yours truly. Back in '77 we were all vying to get into Nancy's pantsies.' He chortled nastily. 'She was an American you know, so no coaxing required. God, what a frightful night.' Shuddering, he glanced heavenward. 'She had the smelliest feet imaginable.'

'Didn't you guys in the seventies ever eat?' Still studying the photograph, Edie glanced over her shoulder at Rubin.

'"There is no excellent beauty that hath not some strangeness in the proportions."'

Cædmon put a hand on Edie's shoulder. 'Our host has a marked proclivity for bardolatry. And how is Regina?' he politely enquired.

'The cow left me for a younger man.' Rubin turned to Edie. Wearing a practised punk-rock sneer, he said, '"Unsex me here", faithless woman.'

'Sorry about the break-up. Unrequited love sucks.'

Hearing that, Cædmon bit back a smile, punk-rock swagger checked by Gen X candour.

'Now that the pleasantries are out of the way, we've come to enquire about the Right Honourable Sir Francis Bacon. Without question, Rubin, you are London's foremost Baconian scholar.'

'You flatter me, Peter.'

'The truth and you know it.'

'And what has brought on this sudden fascination with—'

Just then the hand-carved bird that nested within the German cuckoo clock popped through a pair of wooden shutters, alerting them to the new hour.

'Ah! Three o'clock,' Rubin theatrically announced. 'A most portentous hour of the day. For it was at three o'clock in the afternoon that your saviour died for your sins. And, worthless lot, how did you repay the sacrifice? By slaughtering defenceless Jews and heretics in his good name.'

43

'A bit difficult.'

Personally, Edie thought that Cædmon's earlier description of their mercurial host had been watered down. Without a doubt, Rubin Woolf was a punk-rock pain in the ass.

Keeping that assessment very much to herself, she pasted a bland expression on her face as she examined Tweedy Bird's 'boudoir'. Floor, walls and even the ceiling were covered in dark, stained wood, most of it heavily carved. The bed, which took centre stage in the room, was unlike anything she'd ever seen. The four-poster and attached canopy were massive. At the foot of the bed was a raised wooden cradle. Like the bed's mattress, it was stacked with books. On the walls were gilt-framed oil paintings. All that was missing was Henry VIII holding a big, greasy drumstick.

'I think the axe men felled an entire forest to build this room.' No sooner was the observation made than Edie winced, realizing, too late, that she'd spoken aloud. Worried that she may have inadvertently insulted their prickly host, she apologetically smiled.

'Oak is a hard wood resistant to woodworm.' Rubin gestured to the intricately carved panel insets on the bed's headboard. 'The flamboyant carving on these magnificent panels is a true and accurate reflection of late sixteenth-century England, the Golden Age of Elizabeth ushering in the glorious Age of Exploration. Do be seated.'

Command issued, Rubin parked his tweed-covered bottom in a pretentious oak armchair with a decorative motif painted on the back; Cædmon took the folding Tudor X chair, the entire thing, including the wooden legs, upholstered in mauve velvet. That left a backless wooden stool with a tasselled cushion for Edie. For some reason she felt like the odd man out in musical chairs.

'You've yet to disclose the reason for your sudden interest in Sir Francis Bacon.'

Knowing the remark wasn't directed to her, Edie sat silent, wondering how much Cædmon would divulge. When she'd earlier quizzed him on the same topic, he'd evasively said that it would all depend on Rubin.

For several seconds Cædmon stared at his hands, neatly folded in his lap. Then, raising his head, he looked their host directly in the eye. 'I need to know that what we say here today will be held in the strictest confidence.'

Rubin solemnly pointed an index finger to the ceiling, directing their attention to the carved Tudor rose above them. 'As you no doubt know, the ancient symbol of the rose traces its parentage to Eros, the god of love, who created the first rose which he presented to Harpocrates, the god of silence. *Sub rosa*, my friend. You have my word.'

'Very good. That said, I wish to hold off a bit on the disclosure. Probably better if you first put flesh to bone so that I have a proper frame on which to pose my query.'

'My curiosity is piqued. *That said*, I'll chuck the both of you through the window if you don't come clean.' Rubin emphasized the threat by jutting his double-chin at the double-hung window on the other side of the room. 'My own interest in Sir Francis stems from the fact that he was, above all else, a man of mystery.'

'Not to mention a Jack of all trades,' Cædmon commented. 'As I recall, he was a barrister, a philosopher, a playwright, a courtier and a high-ranking statesman, having served as James the First's Lord Chancellor.'

Rubin crossed one tweed-clad knee over the other, flicking a piece of lint from his trouser leg. 'Indeed, Sir Francis devoted the whole of his life to exploring and investigating the universe's hidden stream of knowledge.'

Hearing that, Edie's head jerked, her gaze involuntarily dropping to the silver ring on Cædmon's right hand.

Testis sum agnitio. 'I am a witness to knowledge.'

She and Cædmon shared a quick, furtive glance. *Was there a connection between Francis Bacon and the Knights Templar?*

'Furthermore, Sir Francis founded several fraternal societies,' Rubin continued, oblivious to the bombshell he had just dropped, 'that served as clearing houses for the advancement of the hidden stream of knowledge. The most interesting, by far, being a secret society known as the Knights of the Helmet. The group met at Gray's Inn in London.'

Gray's Inn. Where Walter Ralegh took the Templar relic, aka Yawgoog's Stone.

'Comprised of writers, poets and philosophers, it was an inspired gathering of the intelligentsia and literati of Elizabethan England,' Rubin continued. 'To aid in the dissemination of the hidden stream of knowledge, the Knights of the Helmet owned and operated their own printing press which enabled them to anonymously publish some of their more provocative ideas.'

'It's a strange name, isn't it, the Knights of the Helmet?'

'A tongue-in-cheek reference to the goddess of wisdom,' Cædmon explained. 'Pallas Athena was usually depicted wearing a helmet and carrying a spear. The helmet symbolized secrecy and the spear represented a ray of light. Which, in turn, symbolized divine wisdom.'

'And shaking her ray of divine wisdom, Pallas Athena would slay the dragon of ignorance,' Rubin said as he raised his right arm and shook it high above his head. Point made, he lowered his arm, taking a moment to fuss with his jacket sleeve. 'If you have not yet guessed at the correct answer, Pallas Athena was an ancient spear-shaker. Intellect and wisdom incarnate. Residing at Parnassus, the Mount of Inspiration, she was *the* divine muse.'

'"Be thou the tenth Muse, ten times more in worth than those old nine,"' Cædmon quoted, Edie presumed from the great man himself, Sir Francis Bacon.

'Of course, Bacon wasn't the only notable luminary in the Knights of the Helmet.' Rubin folded his arms over his chest, clearly warming to the topic. 'Two other members, deserving of praise, should be singled out. I'm referring to Sir Walter Ralegh who, in addition to being a mariner, was a talented poet and first-rate historian, and the famous mathematician and magician, Dr John Dee.'

Sir Francis Bacon, Sir Walter Ralegh and Dr John Dee. The Philosopher, the Explorer and the Magus. The three men involved, either directly or indirectly, with Yawgoog's sacred stone. The Elizabethan Trinity.

'You mentioned "intellect" and "wisdom", but what about this so-called "hidden stream of knowledge"?' Edie asked. 'I still don't have a clue what you mean by that.'

A slow Cheshire cat-like smile worked its way on to Rubin's face. 'Ah, time to delve into the murky realm of *alchymia*, *kabbalah* and *magia*.'

'Otherwise known as the magical mystery tour,' Edie quipped. Seeing the instant glower on Rubin's face, she chuckled. 'Okay. Sorry. I forgot that as a former punk-rock roadie, you *despise* the Beatles.'

Turning away from her with a noticeable huff, Rubin tugged his waistcoat over his midsection, as though re-arranging his personal dignity. 'The occult practices of alchemy, Kabbalah and magic comprised the three branches of the hidden stream of knowledge.'

'Are you saying that Bacon and the other members of the Knights of the Helmet were occult practitioners?'

When Rubin nodded, Cædmon said, 'That being the case, they were heretics of the first order.'

'And in the early seventeenth century, accusations of heresy were treated with the solemnity and intrusiveness of a proctology exam. King James had a dread fear of the so-called dark arts and had more than one heretic condemned to death.'

Shuddering, Edie murmured that most horrific of chants. 'Burn, witch.'

'And they very nearly did. Dee, an antiquarian, maintained a magnificent library at Mortlake, his country estate. Unfortunately the passion of a lifetime was not only ransacked by a vigilante mob, but very nearly went up in flames.' Shaking his head, Rubin intoned, 'God save us from the ignorant in our midst. Their hatred knows no bounds.'

'Unfortunately, every century has its *Kristallnacht*,' Cædmon said quietly, the mood in the room having turned decidedly maudlin.

Suddenly, like a spiky-haired jack-in-the-box, Rubin shot to his feet. 'I think refreshments are in order.' He took several steps towards the door, only to abruptly stop in his tracks. He turned towards Cædmon. 'I know this is a few years late, Peter, but I never had an opportunity to express my condolences for your loss. It was a grievous day when Juliana left us.'

'Quite. Thank you. Very kind,' Cædmon mumbled.

'Yes, well, won't be but a moment.' With that, Rubin headed for the door.

Not exactly sure what had just transpired between 'Peter' and Rubin, Edie stared at the man sitting next to her. The man she thought she knew.

Who the hell was Juliana?

Cædmon, his cheeks stained a vivid shade of red, cleared his throat. 'Given the awkward silence, I'd say that went over like a lead balloon.'

'Try plutonium. It weighs more.'

44

'Was Juliana your wife?'

'Good God! No!'

Caught off his stride, well aware that he'd overreacted to Edie's question, Cædmon cleared his throat.

He began again, calmer this time. 'No, Juliana was not my wife.'

'Okay, we've cleared that hurdle. So, who was she?'

Hit with a barrage of painful memories, Cædmon got up from his chair and walked over to the bed. His memories were more violent, more brutal, than most. He tried to block the horrific images of charred, mutilated flesh. Tried and failed miserably. He wrapped his hand around the elaborately carved post. Holding on for dear life.

In a carefully measured voice, he replied, 'Juliana Howe was the woman that I loved.'

'I see,' Edie replied in an equally measured tone.

'No, you don't. Because the truth of the matter is that Juliana died a horrible death that I could have prevented had I only—' He stopped abruptly. Although no longer in MI5's employ, he was duty-bound to keep silent.

Lies and deception. It was happening all over again.

The silence between them lengthened, Edie wordlessly stared at him with her sad, beautiful brown eyes.

To hell with his duty. Edie had a right to know. Although there was a very good chance that once she found out about his sordid past, she'd want nothing more to do with him.

Uncertain how to begin, he picked up a leather-bound volume from the bed. An eighteenth-century edition of Samuel Johnson's *A Dictionary of the English Language*. He absently thumbed through it. Belatedly realizing that he was stalling, he put it back on the bed.

'As you already know, when I left Oxford I was recruited by MI5. Juliana Howe was a rising star at the BBC. Five learned that she had extensive contacts in the North African community here in London and decided to insert an officer. I went undercover as Peter Willoughby-Jones specifically so I could meet Jules, establish a rapport and, once I gained her trust, find out everything I could about an Algerian arms-smuggling ring.'

'"Establish a rapport" . . . is that spy lingo for sleeping with the enemy?'

'She wasn't the enemy,' he replied, quick to come to Jules's defence. 'She was a brilliant investigative reporter who had a *very* low opinion of Her Majesty's Secret Service. That said, yes, I did sleep with her. I then made the grievous mistake of falling in love with her. Grievous because I was forced to keep Five's dirty little secret. The charade *must* be maintained. National security depended upon it.' He laughed caustically.

Getting up from her stool, Edie walked towards him. 'If it caused you so much distress, why didn't you just tell her the truth?'

'I couldn't . . . she wasn't vetted by Five. And, even if she had been, I would have lost her had I ever confessed that the absent-minded man who kept the antiquarian bookshop in Cecil Court was a spook in Her Majesty's Secret Service. Although, in the end, that's exactly what happened . . . I lost her. And all because of my damned spook job.'

Her brow furrowed. 'I don't understand.'

'I had a last-minute briefing at Thames House which caused me to be an hour late picking up Juliana.' As he spoke, the muscles in his belly began to tighten painfully. 'In those sixty minutes, Juliana Howe became the random victim of a well-planned bomb attack. Had I put Jules before my bloody job—' He stopped in midstream, the memory no easier to bear now than it had been five years ago.

'It wasn't your fault, Cædmon.' Then, no doubt thinking him a dense bloke, she again said, this time more forcefully, 'The bomb blast wasn't your fault.'

'Intellectually, I know that. But here –' he put his hand over his heart – 'in this visceral place that obeys no law of reason, I am very much to blame. And knowing that I was to blame, I used the resources of British Intelligence to track down the ringleader who ordered the bomb blast. And then I killed the Irish bastard. In cold blood. Old Testament vengeance.'

'Wh-what happened next?'

Cædmon heard the hitch in her voice. Saw the tears in her eyes. He feared it was the beginning of the end.

'Inundated with New Testament guilt, I sought solace in a gin bottle. Dived right in. Stayed in a pickled state until the boys at Five dried me out. I was then sent packing, seconded to MI6. It was quite a demotion. I spent the next few years operating a safe house in Paris before Five finally decommissioned me. Booted me right out of the door.' *Free to grapple with my demons.*

'How's your scar tissue?'

It was a strange question, but he knew what Edie meant.

'It took a while, but I managed to exorcise the grief. Even the blind rage. Although I have yet to rid myself of the memories. Even now, after all these years, they cling to me like a guilty conscience.' A self-deprecating laugh escaped him. 'Yes, I know, it's a boringly tragic tale.'

'No, it's not. Although it explains why you never have more than two drinks. Why you're so secretive. Why you take such *care* with your emotions.'

And why their long-distance relationship suited him so well. The quiet comforts of his Paris flat provided an emotional safety net.

'While I learned to live after love died, the transition didn't come easy.' Extending a hand, he smoothed a flyaway curl from Edie's face. 'Am I in danger of losing you?'

'I don't scare easily.'

He smiled, relieved. Although he revelled in the solitude of living alone, he frequently missed Edie's cheery companionship and irreverent humour. Those were the times when he ardently yearned for the pleasure of her company. He just needed more time.

'Come here.' Taking her by the hand, he pulled Edie into his arms. Bending his head, he kissed her, leisurely exploring the soft swell of her lower lip before thrusting his tongue inside her warm, sweet-tasting mouth.

Two packets of sugar, indeed.

Edie moaned softly and swayed towards him.

'Good God!' Rubin bellowed from the open doorway, where he stood holding a tray. 'You're at it again!'

They instantly broke apart, Edie's shoulders shaking with barely suppressed mirth.

Cædmon glanced at the Martini pitcher and three iced cocktail glasses on Rubin's tray. 'A bit early for that, don't you think?'

'Nonsense. Never too early to celebrate renewed friendships.' Pronouncement made, their host proceeded to fill their glasses from the sleek Waterford pitcher.

Edie also seemed surprised by the choice of 'refreshments'. 'Silly me. I was expecting tea and crumpets.'

'Of course you were. No doubt served by Miss Moppet.' Rubin handed Edie a cocktail garnished with a sliver of lemon. 'No maraschino cherries, no ridiculous paper umbrellas. The dry martini is a civilized drink, "the only American invention as perfect as the sonnet".'

45

'So this is what Shakespeare meant by "masking the business from the common eye",' Marnie Pritchard complained aloud, frustrated. Squinting, she tried to bring the computerized spreadsheet into clearer focus.

Still blurry.

Expediency trumping vanity, she opened the top drawer on the inlaid mahogany desk and snatched her prescription reading glasses. While Botox injections, monthly highlights at Daniel Galvin's to cover the grey, and daily workouts at Gymbox kept Father Time somewhat at bay, there wasn't much she could do about her deteriorating eyesight.

Oh, the vagaries of middle age.

Since Rubin was hopeless with numbers, she handled all of the financial accounts. Recently she'd computerized their outdated record system, Woolf's Antiquarian Books having officially gone green. No more filing cabinets full of dog-eared vouchers and yellowing slips of paper. The boxed records were currently stacked in the upstairs stockroom awaiting pick-up by one of those data-storage companies.

Once again, she'd proved herself a model of professional efficiency.

Although in the nearly forty years that she'd known Rubin Woolf, she'd never had to prove herself to him. He'd always accepted her 'as is'. No impossible expectations. No buyer's remorse.

So different from her adoptive parents, Rex and Lynda Pritchard.

When the pricey fertility treatments at the Swedish clinic failed to bring about the desired result, the barren couple had returned to their native England. Whereupon they opted for the next best thing – adopting a blonde-haired, blue-eyed four-year-old orphan named Marnie. A ready-made daughter. Old enough so Lynda didn't have to bother with soiled nappies, but young enough to still mould in their own image.

Or so they thought.

Imagine their surprise, and keen disappointment, when little Marnie turned out to be an introverted child, afraid of the dark, prone to screaming fits and only able to speak in monosyllabic, barely intelligible phrases. Hardly the sort of child to make one beam. '*Well, Lynda, darling, what did you expect? The child* was *named after a character in a Hitchcock film.*' Fortunately for the Pritchards, they proved the fertility doctors wrong, Lynda giving birth to a scrunch-faced baby girl two years after the lamentable adoption. Soon thereafter the Pritchards began referring to Marnie as their 'adopted daughter'. Presumably to distinguish her from their biological pride and joy, the aptly named Felicity.

Relegated to second best, Marnie withdrew even more. Until she met her next-door neighbour, Rubin Woolf. Five years older, he had funny hair that stuck straight up from his scalp at odd angles and wore thick Coke-bottle glasses that magnified his brown eyes, making him appear as though he were in a perpetual state of wide-eyed wonder. Like her, Rubin had a less than perfect family life. Without the buffers of adulthood to contend with, they immediately recognized each other for what they were, kindred spirits. Rubin, who had a precocious love of books, taught her to read. Soon they were performing Shakespeare plays in the back garden, complete with costumes and painted scenery. Her parents were delighted that 'the little Jew boy' had managed the impossible, although it didn't escape Marnie's notice that Mummy and Daddy still referred to her as their 'adopted daughter'.

For the next five years, with her playmate Rubin at her side, Marnie continued to blossom. Until her parents realized that 'the little Jew boy' had become a teenager who, they feared, had an unnatural attraction to their eleven-year-old 'adopted daughter'. In short order, calls were made, bags were packed and, before Marnie realized what was happening, she was shipped off to Cheltenham Ladies' College. Where she spent the next seven years imprisoned at one of England's finest boarding schools.

By the time she was paroled from college, she'd acquired a haughty manner and a biting sense of humour – the best armour a girl could have. Particularly a girl making her way in London. Five feet ten inches tall and blessed with a fashionably thin frame, Marnie soon found work as a fitting model for the avant-garde designer Vivienne Westwood. The uninhibited excess of eighties London – couture, clubbing and cocaine – nurtured her inner wild child, Marnie ran with a *very* fast crowd. But as the bright lights around her began to extinguish – an anorexic model friend dying from a sudden heart attack, a flatmate tragically discovering what happens to bad boys who share needles – Marnie became disenchanted with the glam life.

And, just like that, she packed it all in.

Steering a new course, she finagled a position with a charity events planner. It was at a fund-raiser for the St Stephen's AIDS Trust that she ran into her long-lost friend Rubin Woolf. The rapport was immediate. And strong. As though the decade just passed had come and gone in the proverbial blink. Except Rubin's hair was now spiky all over and he'd traded the Coke-bottles for an ultra-hip pair of I. M. Pei-style glasses. He mentioned that, having inherited the family house in Stanmore, he'd promptly sold it, using the proceeds to open an antiquarian bookshop in Cecil Court. *Would she like to work for him?* He needed an educated assistant with a bit of flash to chat up the male clientele. Some of the more valuable volumes could fetch upward of £30,000.

If he'd asked her to set sail on HMS *Bounty*, she would have readily agreed.

Rubin's estranged lover Regina had always been a tad jealous of their relationship, mistakenly thinking it was a sexual attraction. Simply put, it wasn't an attraction. It was a bond. Different kettle altogether. And the reason why they'd never once slept together.

Over the years she and Rubin had weathered many a summer storm – his prostate cancer, her decade-long affair with a married man. Weight gains. Lost friends. Shaky finances. Lost faith. He'd held her hand when she'd had the abortion. She was at his side for the annual PET scan. They cried for the one and celebrated the other.

She and Rubin had now been together longer than most spouses stay married.

Admittedly there were times – usually when she saw a couple like Peter Willoughby-Jones and Edie Miller who, if not bound for happily ever after, were on track for a few good years – that she regretted the path not taken. She'd never married. She had no children. Had never even owned a dog.

From Blitz kid to woman of a certain age. Proverbial blink.

'You're not to brood. It's not allowed,' she chastised herself.

Hearing the shop bell merrily tinkle, Marnie yanked off her reading glasses, stowing them in the desk drawer. Her movements well-practised, she stood up and smoothed a hand over her chin-length blonde bob. She then checked her Jil Sander sheath for any stray pieces of lint, Rubin's bit of flash ready to take the stage.

The customer stood at a bookcase, his back to her. She quickly sized him up. Hugo Boss jacket. Black leather messenger bag. John Varvatos calfskin boots. Not their typical customer.

'Good afternoon. Just browsing or are you looking for something specific?'

He slowly turned in her direction. 'I'm looking for a volume of love poems.'

My God, he's beautiful. Like a young Johnny Depp. And that accent. To die for.

'Perhaps you should try the public library,' she retorted. Uncharacteristically snippy, she suspected it had something to do with the fact that she was old enough to be the beautiful young man's mother.

And that realization incited a tumult, the kind she hadn't experienced since childhood, suddenly hit with a burst of gut-twisting insecurity. Twenty years ago she would have taken great delight in making this beautiful young man beg for her phone number. *On your knees, boy.* Proverbial blink.

The beautiful man took several steps in her direction. He came to a standstill less than an arm's span from where she stood. Blatantly invading her personal space.

He smiled winsomely. 'I'm too transparent, I fear.'

'Absolutely see-through.' Even as she said it, Marnie wondered at his game. He'd just transmitted a sonar-strength vibe wrapped in a come-hither smile. *But why?*

Could it be that he was one of those men who actually preferred older women?

At that thought, she felt a small dribble of confidence.

'You do know that you're an angel?'

'Ah, yes. "May she grow in Heavenly light,"' Marnie replied flippantly.

His smile broadened. 'You took the words right out of my mouth.'

'I very much doubt *that*.' Particularly given the fact that she'd quoted the Cheltenham school motto.

'Dine with me this evening.' He stepped even closer. '*Please*.'

Marnie finally deigned to return the smile, her confidence fully restored.

'Perhaps.'

46

'Now that I have plied you with strong spirits, perhaps you will reveal the true purpose of this delightful, but unexpected, visit.'

'Right.' Cocktail glass in hand, Cædmon strolled over to the window. Peering down at Cecil Court, he sighted a few late-afternoon shoppers browsing at the book carts. *All Quiet on the Western Front.* 'Do you happen to have a laptop computer handy?' he asked over his shoulder.

If Rubin was surprised by the request, he gave no indication, wordlessly trudging to the court cupboard in the foyer. From where he stood at the window, Cædmon could hear a cabinet door squeak on its hinge. A few moments later, Rubin returned with a computer in tow. Shoving several volumes aside, he made room for it on the bed.

'I assume you want me to boot up?'

'If you would be so kind.' Deciding to plough right into it, Cædmon unceremoniously said, 'In the year 1307 the Knights Templar, fleeing the *auto-da-fé*, sailed to the undiscovered New World where they established a colony in Arcadia, Rhode Island.'

Rubin snorted derisively. 'An utterly outlandish claim.'

'*Nullius in verba.*' As he spoke, Cædmon tugged at the silver signet that he wore on his right ring finger.

About to take a sip of her Martini, Edie instead lowered

her cocktail glass. 'Translation please. The only Latin I know is the pig variety.'

'Take no one's word,' he obligingly translated. 'Or, put another way, seeing is believing.' Cædmon walked over to where their host now held court in his outrageously carved Tudor chair. Hit with a childish impulse, he dropped the signet ring into Rubin's cocktail glass. '*That* was found buried at the Templar colony in Rhode Island.'

His brows drawn together in an annoyed frown, Rubin fished the bauble out of his cocktail glass. Bringing the ring up to his face, he carefully examined it. A moment later, the frown re-worked itself into an awestruck expression. 'There's an inscription that I can't quite make out.' He peered over the top of his round tortoiseshell glasses as he brought the ring closer to his face.

'*Testis sum agnitio*,' Cædmon informed him. 'In addition to the signet ring, a number of other artefacts were uncovered at the site including several gold coins that predate the *auto-da-fé*.'

At hearing that, Rubin gasped aloud, nearly dropping the ring back into his cocktail glass. 'And where are these gold coins and other—'

'Safely secured,' Cædmon interjected. Before leaving the US, he'd taken the precaution of renting a long-term airport locker, not about to risk losing the valuable artefacts to a London pickpocket. 'The archaeological evidence strongly suggests that sometime in the early sixteenth century, a massacre took place, the colony completely destroyed by the Knights of Malta. After carefully sifting through the evidence, the two of us –' he pointedly glanced at Edie, indicating that she was very much a full and equal partner in the venture – 'came to the conclusion that the Templars had constructed a hidden vault a few miles from the settlement site.'

'My God! Did the two of you actually find this vault?'

'We did. However, I must inform you that the archaeologist who provided us with the necessary research was murdered.'

Rubin's brows noticeably lifted. 'Not exactly a disclosure for the weak-kneed. Fortunately, I'm made of sterner stuff. You've issued your warning, Peter, pray continue.'

'Very well.' Reaching into his trouser pocket, Cædmon removed a computer memory chip. He handed his full Martini glass to Rubin before walking over to the laptop computer on the bed. 'I should clarify at the onset that while we did find the Templar vault, it was empty,' he stated, not wanting to raise false hopes. He pulled up the first of the digital photos that Edie had taken inside the Templar sanctuary.

Both Edie and Rubin joined him at the four-poster bed.

Holding a Martini glass in each hand, Rubin leaned over the mattress to view the photos. 'This is stunning. Truly magnificent. The plot has indeed thickened.' Raising the Martini in his right hand, he completely drained it. 'These photos are absolutely—' He stopped in mid-stream. Long moments passed as he stared intently at the digital photo of the Enochian message written by Walter Ralegh. ''Tis the handwriting on the wall.'

'Or, in this case, the floor,' Edie quipped. 'We deciphered the message to read "Ralegh took the Templar relic to swine's court."'

'And while we can't be completely certain, we believe the relic in question is some sort of sacred stone.'

Rubin raised the full glass in his left hand and quaffed it down in three swallows. A few moments passed before he muttered, 'That bastard Ralegh actually found the Templar vault.'

'We did an Internet search, but couldn't find any information pertaining to Walter Ralegh sailing to Rhode Island. Leading me to conclude that the Rhode Island voyage was covertly undertaken. Very much a hush-hush operation.'

'Ah! I can help you there,' Rubin said as he deposited his two empty cocktail glasses on the refreshment tray. 'In 1584, Ralegh sailed to America to scout for locations suitable for colonization. And you are quite correct; there was an ulterior motive to the voyage. A motive hidden from history. With good reason given that the true purpose of the expedition was to locate the seventy-seventh meridian. *That's* what Walter Ralegh was doing in Rhode Island.'

'Okay, I'm sure this is *really* significant, but I'm not following,' Edie confessed, never bashful about asking questions. 'What's the seventy-seventh meridian? And why was searching for it such a big secret?'

'The seventy-seventh meridian is a line of longitude. Longitude, as you know, is an east–west measurement taken from a known starting point referred to as the prime meridian. Mystics have long believed the seventy-seventh meridian sits on top of the world's most powerful ley line,' Cædmon explained.

'Ley lines are power conduits that resonate with magnetic energy, right?'

Cædmon nodded. 'The pyramids in Egypt, Stonehenge in England, the Mayan Temples in Central America and even Rosslyn Chapel in Scotland are all built on top of ley lines.'

'Deemed sacred, the Knights of the Helmet referred to the seventy-seventh meridian as "God's Longitude",' Rubin said, rejoining the conversation.

'And why was Sir Walter Ralegh searching for this sacred meridian?'

Cædmon tilted his head in Rubin's direction, politely deferring to their host.

'If you want to build a utopian society, what better place to do so than on a sacred parcel of land. And the Knights of the Helmet were *keenly* intent on establishing a New Atlantis far from the tyrannical grip of the English monarchy. The well-connected politician Sir Francis Bacon worked tirelessly to secure permission to colonize. The mathematical genius Dr Dee created detailed nautical charts. And the bold adventurer Sir Walter Ralegh readied his ships. Unfortunately time and tyranny were against them, the endeavour never getting past the planning stage.'

'In that, their goal was no different from the Knights Templar who attempted to establish a New Jerusalem far from a brutal regime.' Cædmon turned and walked over to a floor-standing globe situated on the other side of the room. Eyes narrowing, he moved the orb slightly with his finger. 'My God, the Templar colony was situated at approximately seventy-two degrees longitude. Just a few degrees off the mark. Given the fact that their only navigational tools were a crude compass and a sheepskin portolan map, the Templars came remarkably close to finding the seventy-seventh meridian.'

'Unfortunately, the dashing Ralegh's navigational tools were not up to the task either.' Rubin slyly smiled. 'That said, I may be able to provide some insight as to what it was that Ralegh discovered in the Templar vault.'

Cædmon stared at Rubin Woolf. *Had the antiquarian been playing him for a fool?* 'I'd say you'd better come clean,' he warned, losing patience. 'And be quick about it.'

'Since you so obligingly showed me yours, I shall now show mine.' Pronouncement made, Rubin strode to the foyer. When he reached the open doorway, he craned his neck in their direction. 'Well, don't just stand there gawking. I want you two to follow me to the other room. Do leave your cocktail glass. Beverages are not permitted.'

Edie obediently set her cocktail glass on the tray. Hands freed, she grabbed hold of Cædmon's arm. Leaning in close, she whispered, 'What's this all about?'

'I have no idea,' he replied in an equally hushed voice.

They followed Rubin down the hall to a closed door. Reaching into his pocket, Rubin removed a skeleton key which he fitted into the old-fashioned lock. It took a bit of jiggling for him to get the antiquated lock open.

Chuckling, he said, 'Marnie calls this my "man cave", but I prefer to think of it as my therapy room.' Stepping inside, he switched on the light.

'Therapy, indeed,' Cædmon murmured as he entered the windowless, climate-controlled room that was illuminated with incandescent lights fitted with UV filters. All of which was necessary to protect what appeared to be an incredible collection of rare books, oil paintings, antique maps and various other ephemera.

'You might want to invest in a better lock,' Edie remarked

as she examined an ornately framed painting of a Madonna and Child.

'While I'd love to show off some of my more prized possessions, I know that you're anxious to see the *pièce de résistance.*' Rubin stepped over to a large map cabinet. With his index finger he counted down five drawers. His movements slow, he opened the drawer and removed a single sheet of yellowed paper encased in a Mylar sleeve.

With reverential care, he carried the protected sheet to the work table in the middle of the room and set it down for them to view.

'My God,' Cædmon whispered, stunned. *How the bloody hell did Rubin come by this?*

Edie shrugged, clearly unimpressed. 'Am I missing something? I'm no expert, but even I know *that* isn't the Templar treasure.'

'You are correct.' Rubin inclined his head slightly. 'Shall I tell her or do you want the honours?'

Cædmon gestured to the protected sheet of paper on the table. 'What Rubin has in his possession is something that, by all accounts, *doesn't* exist.'

47

Edie was the first to break the silence.

'It's the title page for an old book, right?'

'What *do* they teach in American schools? *That* is the frontispiece for Francis Bacon's opus magnum, the *New Atlantis*,' Rubin huffed.

The instant he glanced away, Edie, exasperated, stuck out her tongue. A juvenile response. No doubt the result of being cooped up in what amounted to a claustrophobic windowless vault.

Cædmon put a staying hand on her shoulder, lessening the sting. 'In a printed book, the frontispiece is the illustration opposite the title page. Taken from the Latin word *frontispicium*, meaning façade, it's a word seldom used in the modern lexicon. Highly ornate engravings, these prints are artistic masterpieces in their own right.'

'A fact that incites avaricious art collectors to take sharp razorblades to priceless antiquarian books.' Rubin's unkind tone made it clear what he thought of the practice.

Still confused, Edie said to Cædmon, 'Why did you say that this particular frontispiece shouldn't exist? I mean, we're looking at it so obviously it, um, you know, exists.' Too late, she realized how garbled that sounded. She immediately braced for a Rubin on wry.

Their host tapped a manicured finger against the Mylar-encased print. '"Thy end is truth's and beauty's doom and date."'

Still clueless, Edie apologetically shrugged.

'The date, woman! Look at the publishing date!'

She did, but the date *1614* meant absolutely nothing to her. 'Sorry, not ringing a single bell.'

'Francis Bacon died in the year 1626,' Rubin informed her. 'Among his papers was discovered an unfinished, unpublished manuscript entitled *New Atlantis*. Bacon's long-time secretary, a man by the name of William Rawley, had the unfinished manuscript posthumously published in 1627. With a completely different frontispiece to the one that's on the table. Publication of the *New Atlantis*, a parable outlining Bacon's plan for a utopian society, sparked a heated public debate. One that continues to this very day.'

Cædmon picked up the print. His gaze narrowed as he examined it intently. 'This 1614 frontispiece implies two things: first, Bacon actually completed the *New Atlantis* manuscript, and, second, he intended to publish it in 1614. For whatever reason, Sir Francis had a change of heart. Since there are no known copies of the 1614 frontispiece, other than the one before us, we must presume that Bacon had the engraved prints destroyed. Save for the one.' As he spoke, Cædmon pulled a stool out from under the sturdy work table where they stood. He offered the vacant seat to Edie. 'What I want to know, Rubin, is how in God's name did you come by this?'

'Since you're a member of the Antiquarian Booksellers' Association, I probably shouldn't say.'

'I take that to mean he got it off the back of a truck,' Edie snickered.

'Of all the cheek!' Rubin turned to Cædmon, an unctuous smile on his lips. 'Credit me with a bit of honour; I paid a fair price.'

'Although I warrant it was an undocumented sale,' Cædmon said with a knowing glance.

'Yes, well . . . needs must.' Their host pulled a second stool out from the table.

'Have you shown this frontispiece to anyone else?'

Rubin's eyes opened wide. 'Surely you jest? Aside from Marnie, you and your American sidekick are the only ones privy to the secret. And I wouldn't have been so hospitable except we have a mutual interest.'

'Speaking of which, what connection does your rare

frontispiece have with the Templar relic discovered by Walter Ralegh?' Cædmon took the last vacant stool, brushing shoulders with Edie as he sat down.

'Before I answer: how familiar are you with the *New Atlantis*?' Rubin glanced first at Cædmon, then at Edie.

'It's been more than twenty-five years since I read it last.'

'Still on my "Things to read before I die" list,' Edie fibbed.

'Then we must bring you up to speed. The *New Atlantis* begins with a ship lost at sea "in the greatest wilderness of the waters of the world",' Rubin began in one of those strident voices that people reserve for public recitation. 'A new day dawns and land is sighted, the crew's fervent prayers having been answered. But the hapless Europeans soon discover that the uncharted island of Bensalem is a country unlike any other. While it is a Christian realm, Bensalem practises a form of pure Christianity based entirely on the precept of brotherly love. Additionally, Bensalem is reminiscent of the legendary Atlantis.'

'Plato's dialogues *Timaeus* and *Critias* are the only ancient source that specifically mention Atlantis,' Cædmon said, elaborating on Rubin's narration. 'Technologically advanced, as well as being a great naval power, the continent of Atlantis mysteriously sank into the ocean after a failed attempt to conquer Athens. Or so claimed Plato. However, Bacon's new, improved Atlantis, renamed Bensalem, is a place of peace not war.'

'From the outset the Europeans are impressed with the Bensalemites' advanced society,' their host continued, picking up the plotline. 'Bringing us to the focal point of the tale: and that is the island's premier institute, a college of higher learning called Solomon's House.'

'The name "Solomon's House" is an obvious nod to the biblical King Solomon who was famous for his wisdom,' Cædmon elaborated.

'But with a Baconian twist. In the *New Atlantis*, the scholars of Solomon's House have at their disposal sacred relics as well as the ancient texts that inspired King Solomon's much-vaunted wisdom. These ancient texts are unknown to European Christians and, supposedly, contain the very secret of creation.'

'Let me guess . . . this secret has something to do with the hidden stream of knowledge, aka alchemy, Kabbalah and magic.'

Rubin acknowledged her remark with a nod. 'Revered by the citizenry, the scholars tirelessly conduct their research, always with an eye to improving and bettering society. Bacon alludes to the fact that their research is magically inspired by heavenly angels.'

Still trying to make sense of Bacon's utopia, Edie said, 'If I'm hearing this right, the entire population of Bensalem was communicating with angels and practising alchemy and Kabbalah.'

'Good God, no!' Rubin exclaimed, quite emphatically. 'Francis Bacon was wise enough to know that the common man, or *woman* –' he peered at her from over the top of his tortoiseshell glasses – 'could not grasp the esoteric nature of the scholar's research. The common man, or *woman*, is far too consumed with the material world to fully comprehend the spiritual realm. It is for that reason that Bensalem maintained an enlightened division of labour based on one's abilities.'

Smelling an elitist rat, Edie pointed an accusing finger

at the Mylar-covered frontispiece. 'Peace and justice in Bensalem came at a steep price, that being the loss of individual liberty.'

Rubin placed his right hand over his heart, assuming a theatrical pose. '"Give me liberty or give me death!"' Mocking oration delivered, he dropped his hand to his side. 'I, for one, would gladly concede a few liberties in order to live in a virtuous, peaceful, just society.'

Well, what do you know? Even an aged punk rocker will cheerfully dip his cup in the Kool-Aid vat, Edie thought irreverently.

'All of which explains why Walter Ralegh was searching for the seventy-seventh meridian.' She figured that was as good a segue as any. 'The Knights of the Helmet wanted to place their utopian colony on top of the world's most powerful ley line.'

Rubin turned on a magnifying lamp mounted on the edge of the table. He placed the print directly underneath it. 'I earlier mentioned that King James had a dread fear of the occult. I suspect that was a contributing factor in Sir Francis's decision *not* to publish his masterpiece.' He wordlessly motioned for Edie to take a gander.

'Ohmygosh!' she exclaimed a moment later, recognizing a *very* familiar occult symbol. 'Peter, look.'

Cædmon peered at the frontispiece through the magnifying glass. 'The All-Seeing Eye,' he murmured. 'Signifying divine enlightenment, the symbol can trace its lineage all the way back to ancient Egypt.'

'The symbol is also on the Great Seal of the United States. Which is printed on the American dollar bill,' Edie informed them. She turned to their host. 'Does the

All-Seeing Eye have anything to do with the Templar treasure?'

'The answer to that may well be hidden within the imagery that adorns this magnificent rendering.'

'Do you mean to say that the print has an encrypted message?'

'I believe so,' Rubin said in reply to Cædmon's query. 'Sir Francis was an amateur cryptologist who frequently hid secret communiqués within his published works. The iconography on the print is highly symbolic of the hidden stream of knowledge and the seventy-seventh meridian. Given what you've told me today, one may reasonably conjecture that the Templars' sacred relic is part of that esoteric mix.'

Cædmon slowly tapped his finger against his chin, his gaze fixed on the print. 'Have you had any luck deciphering the encrypted message?'

'I'm an antiquarian, not a blasted code-breaker.'

'I'll take that as a "no". May I have a go at it?'

'Why in God's name do you think I had you examine the print?' Rubin irritably retorted. 'Since the frontispiece cannot leave the premises, I'll ring the St Martin's Lane Hotel and have your things sent around. You and your lady love may stay upstairs in the guest bedroom.'

'So much for a fabulous night on the town,' Edie groused.

Reaching under the table, Rubin opened a drawer. From it he extracted a hand-held magnifying glass which he passed to Cædmon. 'You may have need of this. The devil's in the details, as they say.'

48

To kill or not to kill . . . always the question.

Standing beside the unkempt bed, Saviour rubbed a hand over his bare chest as he stared at the sleeping woman. At the bony backside. Softly rounded buttocks. Tousled blonde hair. A first for him. The fact that she was a woman, not that she was a blonde. It'd been rather amusing, the way she'd gasped in surprise when he took her from behind. But gasps soon turned to whimpers and moans. Then a climactic cry. *Anemostruvilos.* The Greek word for cyclone. So similar to the Greek word for sodomy.

In no hurry, he took his fill of the somnolent Jocasta. Although Marnie Pritchard claimed to be thirty-five years of age, he placed her closer to fifty. Old enough to be his mother. It'd been a long time since he'd given that bitch even a passing thought. Five years after leaving the flat in Vardalis Square, he'd caught sight of his mother at the Apokries Festival before Lenten Monday. By then, the anger had mutated into a bland indifference; he'd turned and walked away from Iphigenia Argyros without so much as a wave of the hand. A free man.

Tilting his head to one side, Saviour noticed that Marnie had a mole on her upper left back. And a small pucker of cellulite under the curve of her ass. While she hadn't been a fount, Marnie had given him some valuable information. For starters, he'd learned that Cædmon Aisquith was impersonating someone named Peter Willoughby-Jones. Making him think that Aisquith/Willoughby-Jones might be a fugitive from the law. He'd changed his own last name from Argyros to Panos after he had killed Evangelos Danielides. He chose the new surname in memory of Panos Island. So he would never forget the degradation that he'd suffered and how he'd bested the dragon.

He'd also learned that Rubin Woolf was an expert on Francis Bacon. While he'd never heard of Francis Bacon himself, Mercurius was well-acquainted with the name and had been greatly interested to learn of this. Throughout the evening, he'd slyly probed and prodded, but Marnie Pritchard clearly had no knowledge of the treasure. *A pity that.*

His evening's work unfinished, Saviour left the bed and padded to the dresser where he snatched up Marnie's expensive leather handbag. Bag in hand, he headed for the en suite bathroom, a luxurious room boasting a claw-footed bathtub and gas fireplace. Taking care not to make any noise, he closed the door. Sitting on the toilet lid, he rifled through the bag, commandeering a cherry-red mobile phone and a key ring. He muted the ringer before shoving the mobile into his trouser pocket. Fingering through the keys – the organized Marnie having labelled them for him – he removed the silver key marked 'shop'.

About to exit the bathroom, he instead stepped over to the gilt mirror that hung above the vanity unit. Frowning, he leaned closer to the glass, annoyed to see two long scratch marks etched into his smooth skin. Mercurius often admired his muscled physique – the reason why Saviour took such care with his appearance, wanting his mentor to find him physically desirable.

Together, he and Mercurius made a perfect whole. Wisdom wedded to youth. Mind and body united. A fact that Saviour had realized not long after Mercurius had found him hiding in the Agía Sophía. That was when Mercurius had offered him the opportunity to be reborn, his beloved bestowing upon him a gift that could never be repaid. Saviour happily made the effort, Mercurius the only man, other than Ari, who he had ever trusted. Distrust a trait bred in the womb.

As he left the bathroom, Saviour saw a length of fabric hanging from the back of a chair. A Fendi silk jacquard scarf. *Perfect.* He plucked the scarf from the back of the chair and walked over to the bed.

As he stared at the sleeping woman, he wrinkled his nose. *Patchouli.* A certain Düsseldorf banker had also doused himself with the sickening fragrance, the fused aroma of patchouli and sauerkraut having triggered a murderous rage.

Saviour wrapped one end of the silk scarf around his palm. Just as he was about to perform the same motion with his other hand, Marnie opened her eyes and smiled drowsily at him.

'Don't go . . . sweet sorrow and all that.'

Dangling the length of silk, Saviour slowly trailed it over her bare breasts.

To kill or not to kill . . . always the question.

49

'God is in the details . . . who said that, Flaubert or Mies Van der Rohe?' Edie, propped against a menagerie of flounced pillows in the middle of the bed, peered over the top of an art magazine.

'No bloody idea.' Cædmon sat on the other side of the guest bedroom at a large oak desk, his arse planted on another of Rubin's unbearably uncomfortable chairs, this one a Gothic revival fit for a feudal baron. 'On second thoughts, didn't Michelangelo first coin the phrase?'

'Well, whoever said it, I agree with Gloria Steinem –' Edie wickedly grinned – '"the goddess is in the questions."'

'Well put.'

Craning his neck, Cædmon glanced at the clock on the night table. *10:05 p.m.* Time to set out on his quest, smash his nose to the grindstone and decipher the rare 1614 frontispiece.

'Still convinced that the Muses have something to do with Bacon's secret message?'

'Mmmm . . . er, yes.' Elbows on the table, he rubbed his eyes. 'In Greek mythology the Nine Muses, offspring of Zeus and Mnemosyne, the goddess of memory, divinely inspired the arts. But more importantly than that, in a time before the printing press was invented, the Nine Muses were the source of oral knowledge.'

Tossing her magazine aside, Edie got off the bed. Silk,

satin and tasselled pillows tumbled in her wake. Unlike Rubin's 'boudoir', the guest suite was a veritable explosion of clashing Victorian patterns, the colour green being the only common denominator.

Edie stood behind his chair. Wrapping one hand around a spiny Gothic chair post, she reached over the top of him and snatched the Mylar-covered print. 'Okay, we've got nine muses with Pallas Athena, the tenth muse, in the twelve o'clock position. We can only hope that a picture isn't really worth a thousand words. Otherwise it's going to be a *very* long message.'

'And that's a mere sampling of the mythological objects. We mustn't overlook the occult symbols – the two columns, the ladder, the tree, the mulberry and, of course, the All-Seeing Eye.'

Lifting her wool skirt, she hitched a hip on to the edge of the table. 'Yeah, I noticed the ladder, the tree and the piece of fruit in each of the muse panels, but I thought that was just a decorative element.'

'Trust me, *nothing* in this frontispiece is purely decorative. In fact, the ladder, the tree and the mulberry represent the three branches of the hidden stream of knowledge.'

'As in alchemy, Kabbalah and magic, right?' She scooted closer, her outer thigh pressing against his forearm.

'Correct. The ladder symbolizes magic, specifically the type of celestial divination practised by John Dee. Since one can climb up *and* down the rungs of a ladder, it represents direct two-way communication between heaven and earth.' With his index finger, he lightly circled a medallion with a leafy tree. 'This is the Kabbalah Tree of Life which symbolizes the process by which the universe came into being. It's more familiarly depicted as a diagram with the ten Sephiroth that represent the ten attributes of God.'

'Ten seems to be a popular number. There are, after all, ten muses illustrated on the frontispiece.'

He wearily nodded, having already tried, unsuccessfully, to use it in a numeric cipher.

'And finally there's the mulberry which changes in colour from white to red to black during the ripening process. The change in colour symbolizes the three stages of the alchemical process, known by their Latin names: *albedo*, *rubedo* and *nigredo*.'

'White, red and black. The same three colours that comprise the Templar Beauséant.' Using her arm to support her upper body, Edie reclined back. 'Coincidence or do you think the Knights Templar were practising alchemy in their secret sanctuary?'

'I won't know the answer to that until I decipher the frontispiece. That's the nature of the esoteric beast, the creature too often leads one into a bloody labyrinth,' he uncharitably grumbled. Framing either side of his face with the palms of his hands, he again stared at the engraved illustration. 'The secret of the Templar relic could well be hidden in this frontispiece and I'm determined to break the code.'

'You do know that your interest in the Knights Templar borders on idolatry,' Edie chided, pointedly glancing at his silver ring.

Cædmon let his hands drop to the tabletop. 'The first person to launch that accusation was my Aunt Winifred, a sharp-tongued spinster with whom I spent the summers of my youth. She lived and died in the hillside village of

Garway in far-flung Herefordshire. The only noteworthy attraction in the village was St Michael's where, in the twelfth century, the Knights Templar constructed a circular church.'

'Is the circular church still standing?'

'Alas, no, but the foundation of the Templar church is visible.'

'I'm guessing that's all it took to fuel your youthful imagination.'

'The vicar, something of an amateur historian, was quite knowledgeable about the Templars.' He smiled, the memory a pleasant one. 'That first summer I haunted the local library, reading everything related to the Knights Templar. The more I learned about their heroic exploits in the Holy Land, the more enamoured I became. Aunt Winnie put her foot down when she caught me creeping about in the garden dressed in a white bed sheet, clutching a brolly in one hand and a butter knife in the other as I re-enacted the Siege of Acre.'

Chuckling, Edie reached over and smoothed a lock of hair from his brow. 'As an adult, do you ever, you know, fantasize about being a Knights Templar?'

'You mean do I still imagine myself swinging a broadsword at Acre? No, never,' he retorted, emphatically shaking his head. 'The fact that the Templars didn't shave, rarely bathed, and that they took a vow of celibacy doesn't make for a lusty male fantasy.'

'Oooh, I want to hear more about the lusty stuff.' As she spoke, Edie provocatively shimmied her shoulders.

'There's a reason why St Bernard of Clairvaux famously wrote that "the company of women is a dangerous thing, for by it the devil has led many from the straight path to Paradise".' He gestured to the small stack of books on the tabletop. 'Since I'm on this blasted quest, I must refrain from the pleasures of the flesh.'

She scooted her bum off the edge of the table . . . landing squarely in his lap.

Unable to help himself, Cædmon slid a hand under her skirt.

Wrapping her arms around his neck, Edie leaned in close and whispered, 'If you don't tell St Bernard, *I* won't tell St Bernard.'

50

'Your dressing gown, milady.'

Edie languorously rolled on to her back and peered up at Cædmon, a red silk kimono dangling from his fingertips. Sprawled on the rumpled bed, she felt like a castaway who'd washed up on to a warm, welcoming beach. Surrounded by a sea of colourful pillows.

'Thank you, Sir Peter.' She took the kimono from him. Their hands brushed. She loved Cædmon's hands. Loved the fact that they were lean and strong. That his fingers were sprinkled with sun-bleached hair. She even loved the smattering of ginger-coloured freckles. And she'd yet to tire of seeing his hands on her body.

She swung her bare legs over the side of the mattress. 'Now that I'm rejuvenated, I'm ready to hit the books.'

Smiling, Cædmon brushed several damp curls from her face. 'Would have taken you to bed hours ago had I known the restorative effect.'

'Magic elixir, what can I say?' She rose to her feet and slipped on the kimono.

'Actually, the seventeenth-century alchemists thought the very same thing, semen was used as an ingredient in quite a few alchemical concoctions.'

'Now *that* is pushing the esoteric envelope. And not in

a good way.' Belting her kimono, she peered over her shoulder. 'Come on, Big Red. You need to get dressed. It's time to burn the midnight oil.'

'Right.'

He padded, naked, to the other side of the room. Edie's gaze zeroed in on the deep groove of his spine, the play of muscles in his back as he lifted his robe off a hook on the bathroom door. Donning the blue-checked robe, he winced slightly, his left arm still bandaged.

Seating herself in a wooden chair with a carved quatrefoil back, Edie clapped her hands together. 'Okay, ready to get to it.'

Cædmon handed her a blank sheet of paper and a sharpened pencil with an eraser. The Mylar-covered print was set between them. 'As I said earlier, Bacon's frontispiece is a damned labyrinth.'

She stared at the engraving. Struck with a sudden idea, she reached across the table and grabbed the magnifying glass, holding it within inches of her face as she examined the frontispiece. Noticing something odd, she handed the magnifying glass to Cædmon. 'Take a look at the ladders, trees and mulberries.'

Wearing a quizzical expression, he viewed the illustration through the magnifying lens.

A split-second later, raising his head, he grinned. Einstein figuring out E, M and C.

'It's a numeric cipher! In the Athena box, the mulberry has thirteen drupelets, but next door in the Calliope box, the mulberry has five drupelets.'

'Same with the tree and the ladder.' She snatched the

magnifier out of his hand. 'As you move from box to box, the number of drupelets, leaves and rungs changes.'

'Let's diagram the frontispiece and see what we get.' Snatching a clean sheet of paper, Cædmon quickly drew a blank frontispiece – ten squares around the perimeter of the sheet with a blank square in the middle. He neatly wrote the name of each muse in the appropriate box. 'Now we fill in the blanks,' he said, his pencil tip hovering over the Athena box. 'You count, I'll notate. Let's start with the spear-shaker herself.'

For the next few minutes, they see-sawed back and forth until all the ladders, trees and mulberries had been counted.

'Okay, now what?' Although pleased with their progress, Edie had no idea where they were headed.

As he silently stared at their diagram, Cædmon rubbed a hand over his bristled cheek. 'I found evidence in the historic record of Bacon using a twenty-four-letter simple replacement cipher. I suggest we begin with that.' He quickly scrawled a cipher chart on a sheet of blank paper.

A	B	C	D	E	F	G	H	I	J	K	L	M	N	O	P	Q	R	S	T	U	V	W	X	Y	Z
1	2	3	4	5	6	7	8	9	10	11	12	13	14	15	16	17	18	19	20	21	22	23	24	25	26

'I'm guessing that we now work backward and assign a letter to each number.' When he nodded, she began assigning letters to numbers.

Cædmon examined her handiwork.

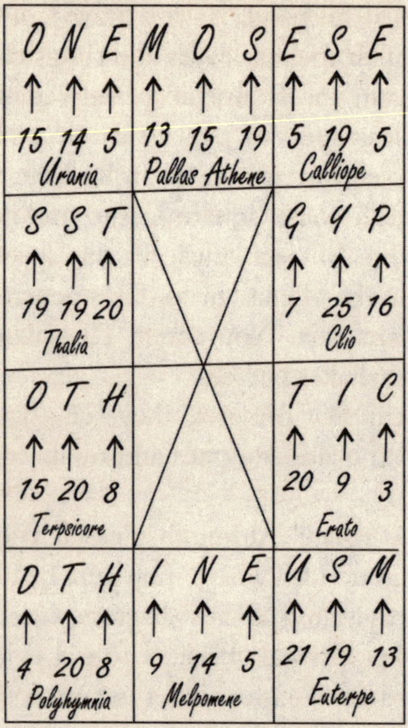

'Excellent. All we have to do is figure out the correct order in which to read the letters. I suggest we go clockwise, using Pallas Athena as our starting point.'

Edie watched, her excitement mounting, as Cædmon next wrote out a long string of letters, thirty in total. She noticed that his hand quivered slightly, his excitement mounting.

'We must now determine where the word breaks occur.' His gaze narrowed as he stared at the string of thirty letters. Then, lips pursed, head cocked to one side, he made four slash marks. That done, he carefully placed his pencil on the table. A student finishing the exam.

'My God . . . it all makes sense now. The *auto-da-fé* of the fourteenth century. The witch hunts of the seventeenth century.' Lurching to his feet, Cædmon snatched the deciphered message off the table and strode to the other side of the room. With the sheet of paper clutched in his right hand, he furiously paced back and forth across the Aubusson carpet. 'This is an absolutely astounding revelation and it certainly explains why the Church and the monarchs of the day slaughtered anyone and everyone who had knowledge of the Templar secret. Even in our day and age, *this* could ignite a religious conflagration.'

Edie scooted back her chair and headed to where Cædmon stood at the window. Curious, she plucked the sheet of paper out of his hand.

moses | egypticus | mined | thoths | stone

'The only three words I completely comprehend are "moses mined stone",' she said, wondering what all the hullabaloo was about. 'I assume that refers to the fact that Moses carved the Ten Commandments on the stone tablets. Of which there were *two*, not one. That's straight out of the Book of Exodus, so no shocker there.'

'Well and good. However, the addition of the other two words radically alters the cipher's meaning. The full message reads "Moses Egypticus mined Thoth's stone". Same Moses, but different stone altogether.'

'And why is that significant? Or even shocking?'

'"Thoth's stone" is a figure of speech, a metaphor for the Emerald Tablet. In his encrypted frontispiece, Francis Bacon is boldly claiming that not only was Moses, the patriarch of the Old Testament, an Egyptian, but he had the fabled Emerald Tablet in his possession.'

Cædmon walked over to the table and gracelessly plunked down on the Gothic monstrosity. Hunkering forward, he braced his elbows on top of his thighs as he held his head in his hands.

'It's truly astonishing. Breathtaking, in fact. My God . . . the Emerald Tablet . . . the Templars' *modus vivendi*,' he whispered. 'Not only did the Knights Templar have the Emerald Tablet, but Moses may actually have possessed the bloody thing . . . *the* most sacred relic in the whole of ancient Egypt.'

Edie rejoined him at the table. 'The Emerald Tablet. Um, sounds familiar. Just having a little trouble accessing the correct memory bank.'

'In a nutshell, the mystery religion of ancient Egypt adheres to the premise that our physical reality is created by a Divine Mind. What you and I call "God". Through an extensive process of spiritual transformation, mankind can have direct knowledge of God and in so doing alter or recreate the material world.'

'Emphasis on the word *knowledge*.' She was finally beginning to understand the centuries-long hullabaloo. 'And the "knowledge" that we're talking about is the secret of creation. Wonder if Tonto Sinclair knows that Yawgoog's Stone is really the Emerald Tablet.'

Cædmon snatched his mobile phone off the table.

'Who are you calling?'

'I'm ringing Rubin.' Their host maintained a private residence two floors above the bookshop. The guest suite was one floor above Rubin's apartment.

Edie glanced at the bedside clock. 'It's kinda late for—'

'Wakey, wakey,' Cædmon boomed in an obnoxiously loud voice. Activating the speaker feature, he put his phone back on the table.

'Who the hell is ringing at this hour?' a very irritable Rubin barked back.

'It's the town crier.' Cædmon grinned. 'Put on the kettle. We've deciphered the frontispiece.'

51

Garbed in dressing gowns and bedroom slippers, Cædmon and Edie trudged down the steps to Rubin's private residence on the second floor. Cædmon had the Mylar-encased frontispiece and the decoded encryption clutched in his right hand.

As they approached Rubin's flat, the door flung wide open.

'Comrades! The battle is joined. Time to gin up the troops.' Rubin, wearing a black velvet smoking jacket, complete with monogrammed breast pocket and silk ascot, handed each of them a full Martini glass. If one ignored the spiky punk coif, he looked like the lead character in a Noël Coward play. Seeing Cædmon's askance expression, Rubin sheepishly smiled. 'I couldn't locate the tea kettle.'

'It's usually found on top of the Aga.' Cædmon ushered Edie through the doorway. Stepping inside the ultra-modern flat, he pointedly directed his gaze towards the kitchen, a sleek chrome kettle in plain sight.

Rubin walked over to the built-in bar and retrieved a third cocktail glass. Raising his glass in their direction, he cheerfully said, 'I'm absolutely over the moon that you've deciphered the frontispiece. Well done, Sir Peter. And kudos to the lovely Edie as well. *Mazel tov.*'

Edie's eyes opened wide. 'Boy, he *is* in good spirits,' she murmured under her breath.

'Dear Peter, I'm about to collapse with anticipation. Do tell! What is the encrypted message that Sir Francis left for posterity?'

Barely able to contain a triumphant smirk, Cædmon handed Rubin the sheet of paper with the decoded encryption.

'Moses Egypticus mined Thoth's stone.'

The other man's eyes narrowed. 'You're certain?'

Cædmon nodded wordlessly.

'Unbelievable. Francis Bacon actually had the sacred Emerald Tablet in his possession.' Rubin's left hand noticeably shook, gin and vermouth sloshing over the side of his Martini glass. 'I am utterly staggered.'

Yes, it is staggering, Cædmon thought, still marvelling at the revelation. Sought after by pharaohs. Confiscated by Moses. Uncovered by the Knights Templar. And rediscovered by Walter Ralegh. The damned thing had been secretly bandied about for centuries.

The Emerald Tablet.

Nearly fourteen years after the disgrace at Oxford, he'd discovered a 'missing link' actually existed that connected the Knights Templar to ancient Egypt. A 'missing link' that would validate his derided dissertation.

He had only to find the relic.

Visibly agog, their host motioned them towards a low-slung white divan. Mounted on the wall directly behind the settee was a triptych by the twentieth-century abstract painter Francis Bacon. A ghoulishly ironic homage to the famed artist's namesake. In the near corner a white baby-grand piano stood prominently.

Bustling over to the kitchen, Rubin retrieved a cerulean-blue serving plate piled high with coconut macaroons. 'A celebration is in order.' All smiles, he gallantly extended the plate in Edie's direction.

'Gosh, thanks.' If she thought Martinis and macaroons a curious pairing, she hid it well. 'And one for the road,' she added, plucking a second macaroon off the plate.

'The only pleasant memory that I have from childhood,' Rubin confided as he set the plate of confections on the glass-topped Noguchi cocktail table, 'is Aunt Tovah's Passover macaroons. Being a smart lad with a voracious sweet tooth, I charmed the recipe out of her before she met her just desserts.' As he sat down on the armchair opposite, he giggled at the tactless pun.

Seating herself on the divan, Edie tucked one leg under her bum, the silk kimono a splash of colour against the white leather. A vibrant red poppy in impish full bloom. 'I'm still confused as to why the Emerald Tablet is considered a sacred object. If it's a big emerald, then, yeah, I can see why it's priceless. But that's not the same thing as being *sacred*.'

'According to legend, the Emerald Tablet isn't made of emeralds, but was instead fashioned from a green crystalline substance. Thus the confusing moniker.' Cædmon crossed his legs at the knee. Noticing a hairy shin, he frowned. While Edie and Rubin both seemed perfectly at ease, he felt slightly ridiculous gadding about in his nightclothes.

'Which doesn't answer the lady's query,' Rubin said around a chewy mouthful, the man already on his third macaroon. 'The Emerald Tablet is not *considered* sacred; it *is* sacred. One does not have to believe in a god to respect the sanctity of creation. Oh, for God's sake! Drink up!' He jutted his chin at their untouched Martini glasses. 'You're acting like a pair of Calvinists at a prayer meeting.'

Edie obediently raised her glass. 'Earlier, when we were upstairs, Peter also mentioned something about the secret of creation. Do you guys mean *the* Creation with a capital "C"?'

Rubin spread his arms wide as he gazed at the ceiling, his expression theatrically pious. '"In the beginning, God created the heavens and the earth." Yes, my dear, *capital* "C".' He lowered his arms and smiled. As pleased as Punchinello after he'd committed a truly heinous act. 'The Emerald Tablet contains the code to set the whole of Creation into motion.'

'Unlock the code and one can create the primeval atom from which the fabric of time and space comes into existence,' Cædmon explained.

At hearing that, Edie's jaw nearly came unhinged. 'Whoa! You're talking about the Big Bang, right? Admittedly, quantum physics isn't my strong suit, but according to the theory, the universe was created when one incredibly dense atom exploded.' No sooner were the words spoken than her brow furrowed. 'Now I'm really confused. Is the Emerald Tablet a device of some sort?'

'No, it's not a device. It is a relic. And as Rubin so aptly put it, the relic contains the code for Creation. Sequenced steps to put the process into motion.' Cædmon raised the Martini glass to his lips. 'A Genesis code, if you will.'

'Okay, we know from the frontispiece that Moses *mined* the Emerald Tablet, but who *made* it? How did it become, well, the Emerald Tablet?' Edie's gaze ricocheted between

Cædmon and Rubin, signalling she'd take an answer from either court.

Rubin was the first to hit the ball. 'References to the Emerald Tablet have turned up in several Egyptian source materials, most notably the Book of the Dead which dates to 1500 BC. And while it's true that the relic's authorship is unknown, the honour is most often accorded to the Egyptian god Thoth whom the ancients considered the originator of all forms of knowledge, hidden and seen.'

Edie's eyes opened wide. 'Thoth? How can that be? I thought that Thoth had the body of a man and the head of an ibis. How could a Bird Man have created the Emerald Tablet?'

Lurching to his feet, Rubin strode across the room to the baby-grand piano and seated himself at the keyboard. 'The aforementioned Book of the Dead records that in the *Zep Tepi*, that being the epoch before the Great Flood, some twelve thousand years ago, mysterious visitors appeared in Egypt, the sole survivors of Atlantis. These visitors, who were deemed *gods* by the more primitive Egyptians, introduced the hidden stream of knowledge to the Nile Valley. Thoth, the pre-eminent visitor of the group, became known as the vehicle of all knowledge, the word made manifest. For it was Thoth who created language, science and medicine. Thus he was deified as Thoth the Thrice Great.'

Pronouncement made, Rubin wiggled all ten fingers . . . just before he launched into a Schubert piano lied. 'Winterreise' unless he was greatly mistaken. Cædmon wondered at the musical selection, one of those dreary pieces that harkened to the pain of love lost.

As abruptly as it began, the recital ended.

'There are numerous ancient writers who claim that Thoth hid a number of sacred relics and esoteric texts inside a massive pair of magnificently crafted columns,' Cædmon said, untangling a few more strands. 'The cache, which included the Emerald Tablet, remained concealed for centuries.'

Still seated at the piano bench, Rubin swivelled in their direction. 'Which brings us to the great Egyptian heretic, the Pharaoh Akhenaton, who ruled during the Amenhotep Dynasty.'

'The charge of heresy was levelled when Akhenaton insisted that there was not a central god in the Egyptian pantheon; there was only *one* god, the Aten,' Cædmon informed Edie, the conversation having veered to a topic that had long fascinated him. 'Aten was declared the Supreme Being of Radiant Light, his divine essence embodied in the rays of the sun disc and manifested in the creative process.'

Edie set her empty Martini glass on top of the cocktail table. 'If Aten was declared the *only* god, what happened to the Bird Man, Thoth?'

Rubin graced her with his trademark Cheshire-cat smile. 'Absolutely nothing. The creator of knowledge, Thoth preceded and transcended the entire Egyptian pantheon. During Akhenaton's reign, the Sacred Eye of Thoth was transformed into the Radiant Disc of Aten.'

Edie's brows drew together. 'Sorry. Not following.'

Rubin got up from the piano bench and walked over to the built-in bookcase where he retrieved a sheet of paper and a pencil. Reseating himself in the Le Corbusier knock-off, he quickly drew three images. When finished, he shoved the sheet of paper in Edie's direction.

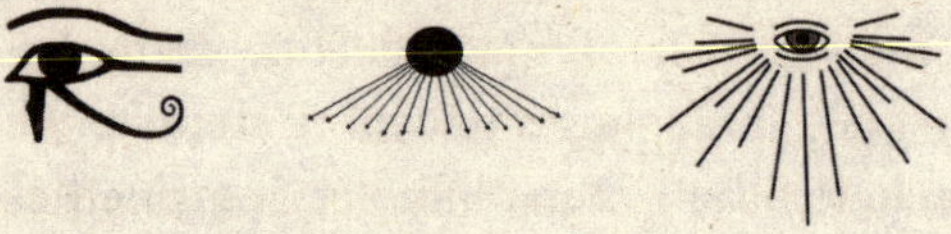

'A thousand words, as they say. The Eye of Thoth symbolizes knowledge.' Rubin tapped the drawing on the left. Then he tapped the sketch in the middle. 'The Radiant Disc of Aten symbolizes the divine creation. And, finally, we have the All-Seeing Eye which embodies and combines the attributes of both Thoth and Aten. Knowledge wedded to creation. Each builds upon the previous one. But at the core of each symbol, you will find Thoth, who designed and fashioned the Emerald Tablet. Which contains the secret of all knowledge and all creation.'

'And *that* is the reason why the Pharaoh Akhenaton searched the whole of Egypt, desperate to find the Emerald Tablet that had been hidden away by Thoth centuries before.' Cædmon leaned forward, the conversation about to get *very* interesting. 'The task of finding the Emerald Tablet fell to Akhenaton's most trusted magician and fellow Aten devotee, the aptly named Tuthmose.'

'Aptly named because Tuthmose means "son of Thoth".' Rubin's eyes twinkled with delight, the man well aware of where the conversation was headed.

'And though Tuthmose located the Emerald Tablet in a pillar at Hermopolis, the discovery came too late to save Akhenaton's empire.' Cædmon reached for a macaroon, his first of the evening. 'When the heretical pharaoh died, a rebel army led by the ousted temple priests descended on Akhenaton's capitol city of Armana. It fell to Tuthmose to save the royal court from the impending slaughter.'

'Tuthmose and his entourage fled Egypt in the dead of night, their trusty Hebrew slaves in tow. A mass exodus unlike any other in history,' their host said airily, waving his right hand in the air to punctuate the remark. 'And the only reason the venture succeeded is because Tuthmose had the Emerald Tablet. An Egyptian grimoire, the inscriptions carved on to the Emerald Tablet enabled Tuthmose to create the Ark of the Covenant, that legendary weapon of mass destruction.'

'Let me guess . . .' Edie paused for dramatic effect. 'It was right around this time that Tuthmose, the Egyptian magician, changed his name to Moses.'

'And while he was at it, created a new religion for the Hebrew slaves. As the Old Testament so vividly recounts, the Hebrews were a belligerent lot in dire need of a calming opiate. To that end, Moses wrote the first five books of the Bible, what we Jews call the Torah. In it, Moses spells out the belief system of the new religion. Then, to keep the Hebrew rabble in line, Moses bequeathed to them ten iron-clad rules carved on to two stone tablets. And thus Judaism, the religion of my forebears, was born.' With a clap of his hands, Rubin bounced to his feet. 'Another round of Martinis?'

52

Standing in a darkened doorway on Cecil Court, Saviour Panos aimed the parabolic dish at the second-storey window on the opposite building. A few seconds later, he wrinkled his nose, the aroma of cardamom and turmeric wafting through the air from the curry house on the next block. *Too many vile stenches.* First patchouli, now Indian spices. *What next?* A stray dog taking a crap.

After leaving Marnie Pritchard's flat, he'd returned to his hotel and retrieved the case containing his surveillance equipment. From there, he'd gone straightaway to Cecil Court on the off-chance that the lovebirds might still be awake. To his delight, it sounded as though he would get three for the price of two, able to detect a third voice in his headset. He double-checked the jack on the recording device so he could later replay the conversation for Mercurius.

He'd been sent to London to act as Mercurius's eyes and ears. A task that he'd undertaken with a glad heart. Willing to do *anything* for the man who had rescued him, protected him, *loved* him. And who had entrusted him with a great and glorious secret. One that involved a 'paradigm shift' as Mercurius liked to call it. The details of which were too arcane, too elusive, for Saviour to grasp. Having had only seven years of schooling, he didn't possess the intellectual breadth to comprehend.

Bored by the conversation taking place in the flat across the way, Saviour slipped a hand inside his jacket and removed a box of cigarettes. *Thoth. Akhenaton. Tuthmose.* So much silly gibberish. He much preferred eavesdropping on the Brit and his woman when they were fucking each other. Still a lot of gibberish, but more exciting.

Wondering how much longer the droning threesome would continue, he flipped open a silver cigarette lighter, his gaze alighting on the eight-pointed star engraved on one side.

The Creator's Star.

How many times had he seen Mercurius staring at the Creator's Star, transfixed? Too many times to count. Usually in an altered state of mind, so far gone that he was unaware of the sights and sounds of *this* world.

Saviour revered the Creator's Star because Mercurius revered the Creator's Star.

Exhaling a plume of smoke, he glanced upward, noticing the shimmering crescent moon. Like a curved Arabian knife blade in the night sky.

According to Mercurius, men contemplated the night sky to discern the eternal mystery of the heavens. Better than contemplating the eternal agonies of hell, he supposed. Although, personally, he thought heaven and hell co-existed here on earth. Eternity was merely the instantaneous burst of nothingness, the pitiless void known as death.

As the Brit and his woman would soon discover.

53

'Wise man that he was, Moses knew that the average Hebrew slave, prone to wild brawling and even wilder fornication, was incapable of the requisite piety required in a truly spiritual society. And so the shrewd patriarch gave the Hebrews a religion they could fully embrace as their own.'

Hearing that, Edie extended a slipper-clad foot in Rubin's direction. 'Why don't you pull the other one while you're at it? Because if you're implying that the Hebrew slaves were practising one religion and that Tuthmose and his Egyptian compatriots were practising an entirely different one, *you* are full of it. I've read the Old Testament.'

'You fail to grasp that while there were two separate religions, there was only the one god. The newly minted Yahweh and the radiant Aten were simply two sides of the one coin,' Rubin testily countered. 'So, too, the Ten Commandments and the Emerald Tablet. One exoteric, one esoteric. Every religion under the heavens has a set of exoteric beliefs for the common man and a secret set of esoteric beliefs known only to a privileged inner circle. While Christian mystics, Jewish Kabbalists and Muslim Sufis actively pursue an individual relationship with the Divine through spiritual transformation, the rest of us poor smucks are saddled with endless rituals and a convoluted hierarchy.'

Edie took a moment to digest what she'd just heard. The esoteric and the exoteric. *The sacred and the profane.* How did a person go about figuring out which was which?

'The Ark of the Covenant, exoteric or esoteric?' She tossed the query over to Cædmon.

To her surprise, the man with all the answers shrugged. 'Perhaps a little of both. Since it was the sacred duty of the hereditary Levite priests to safeguard the Emerald Tablet as well as the Ten Commandments, presumably both relics were kept inside the Ark.'

'So how did we get from the Emerald Tablet being hidden inside the Ark of the Covenant during the forty years in the Wilderness to the Knights Templar getting a hold of it during the Middle Ages?'

Their host gallantly gestured in Cædmon's direction. 'A history lesson is in order. Sir Peter, will you do the honours?'

'Right.' Cædmon planted his elbows on his thighs, his chin resting on top of his steepled fingers. 'As you know, Moses led the masses to the Promised Land, but he died before the final conquest of Israel. Upon his death, the Levite priests, trained by Moses and his brother Aaron, assumed responsibility for the Ark of the Covenant and its sacred relics. The Levis were one of the twelve tribes of Israel.

'And, more importantly for our tale, the Levis were the *only* tribe that could ascend to the priesthood. They, and they alone, had access to the Emerald Tablet.

'Let us now leap over centuries of Hebrew internecine rivalries to the first century AD when a contingent of the Levite priests fled to the Iberian Peninsula in advance of the Roman army.' Cædmon reached for his Martini glass. Only to abruptly retract his extended arm. A change of heart at the last. 'Deeply steeped in Jewish mysticism, the Levite priesthood, who by now were called Kabbalists, were hailed throughout Europe as practitioners of the hidden stream of knowledge. This was the period known as the Golden Age of Sephardi Jewry. And it was during this period that the Eight Precepts were made public.'

'What the heck are the Eight Precepts?'

'They are the eight maxims inscribed on the front of the Emerald Tablet,' Cædmon said in reply to Edie's query. 'Conversely, on the backside of the relic there is an elaborately complex pictograph.'

Removing his eyeglasses, Rubin cleaned them with the hem of his smoking jacket. 'If the ancient rumours are to be believed, the secret of creation was encrypted into this pictograph.'

'Wow. Does a picture of the pictograph exist?'

'No one knows what the pictograph looks like. That's why it's called the *secret* of creation,' their host cheekily retorted. 'However, as Peter mentioned, the Eight Precepts were widely circulated in Europe during the Middle Ages.' Rubin got up and walked over to the bookcase. Tapping a finger against his pursed lips, he scanned the jam-packed shelves. 'Ah! Here she be.' He plucked a thin volume from the top shelf. 'A copy of the Eight Precepts for the kimono-clad Edie to peruse.'

As below, so above; and as above so below.

And since all things exist in and emanate from the One who is the ultimate Cause, so all things are born after their kind from the One.

The Sun is the father, the Moon is the mother.

Earth must be separated from Fire, the subtle from the dense, with gentle heat and good judgement.

This ascends from the earth into the sky. Again, it descends to earth, and takes back the power of the above and the below.

By this means you will receive the Light of the whole world, and Darkness will fly from thee.

This is the strength of all power, for it will penetrate all mysteries and dispel all ignorance.

By it the world was created.

Edie quickly read the list. 'Hey, I actually know this one.' She underlined the first line with her finger. '"As above, so below." It's a famous saying. Although I didn't know until just now that it was carved on to the Emerald Tablet.'

'During the Middle Ages, Thoth the Thrice Great, also known by his Greek name, Hermes Trismegistus, was always depicted in the garb of an Egyptian high priest holding an armillary sphere aloft. A pictorial representation of that very precept.'

'What's an armillary?'

'An armillary is a skeletal sphere comprised of metal bands which represent the heavens, the equator, the ecliptic, meridians and latitude,' Cædmon replied. 'Thoth holds the armillary aloft to convey the idea that a connection to the heavens is a requisite for the creative process to take place on the earthly plane.'

'"The creative process." A quaint way of saying the Big Bang. Got it. But to get back to my original question –' she placed her palm over the top of the opened book with the Eight Precepts – 'how did the Knights Templar get a hold of the Emerald Tablet?'

Cædmon, frowning, tugged at his blue plaid robe, pulling it more securely over his kneecaps. Edie had the distinct impression that he regretted not having dressed before heading downstairs. 'During the twelfth and thirteenth centuries, the Knights Templar were instrumental in liberating Spain from the Moors. Grateful for their military assistance, various Christian monarchs bequeathed large Spanish land tracts to the Templars.'

'Which is how the Knights Templar made contact with the Spanish Kabbalists,' Edie said, the story beginning to make sense.

'The Templars, deservedly famed for their religious tolerance, were the only Christian order that maintained strong relations with European Jews and were known to come to their aid during times of duress.' As he spoke, Cædmon reached for another macaroon.

'If there really is a Genesis code encrypted within the pictograph, why didn't the Knights Templar, you know, take the Emerald Tablet out for a test drive? Or why didn't Francis Bacon try to *create* something?'

'For the simple reason that neither the Templars nor Sir Francis possessed the encryption key,' Cædmon replied. Then, elaborating, he said, 'As with any code or cipher, an encryption key is required in order to correctly decode the hidden message. In cryptography, there is a famous axiom, the Kerckhoff Principle, which states that "only secrecy of the key provides security". Without the encryption key, the Genesis code can't be deciphered. Be that as it may, the Emerald Tablet is still a highly desirable relic.'

Edie shot both of them a meaningful glance. 'Okay, guys. When do we take the scavenger hunt to the next level?'

'*You*, Edie Miller, are a woman after my own heart.' Placing an arm around her shoulders, Cædmon pulled her close.

Rubin dolefully shook his spiky white head. 'I wouldn't pop the corks just yet. We have no idea where to begin the hunt.'

Cædmon picked up the Mylar-encased frontispiece. 'You never did say, Rubin, how you came by this.'

'And with good reason.'

Looking decidedly guilty, their host walked back over to the piano, retaking his seat at the upholstered bench. A few moments later, Edie suppressed a smile, recognizing the dirge-like opening to the punk-rock anthem 'London Calling'.

Banging out the final note, Rubin removed his hands from the keyboard and turned towards the divan. 'Oh, very well. I bought it from a young chit who clearly had no idea as to the engraving's true value. She sent me an unsolicited email in which she alluded to having something that I might be interested in purchasing.' He cackled mirthlessly. 'She'd invented some outlandish story about finding it behind a wall panel at her place of employment.'

'And why, may I ask, was that an "outlandish" claim?' Cædmon stared intently at the antiquarian.

'Well, because of *where* she is employed,' Rubin churlishly retorted. 'Good God, the chit works at Craven House.'

'Get out of town! That's right here in London.'

Turning to Edie, Cædmon raised a questioning brow. 'You're familiar with this Craven House?'

'Oh, I've never been there,' Edie was quick to clarify. 'But a few years back I read a Franklin biography. Most people don't know this, but he lived in London for nearly thirty years. As I recall, Craven House was his last residence in Merry Olde.'

Clearly stunned by the revelation, Cædmon's eyes opened wide. 'As in *Dr Benjamin Franklin*?'

'None other.'

54

Craning his neck, Mercurius gazed upon the night sky, dazzled by the glittering array. Like a beacon fire, the stars, the planets and the celestial bodies beckoned. *The Lost Heaven*. That luminous place that gave birth to the divine spark – the soul – that resided within each living creature. And where each soul yearned to return.

He pulled his robe tighter across his chest as he strolled to the other side of the slate terrace. Through the limbs of his neighbour's towering oak, Mercurius easily sighted the Orion constellation. The most conspicuous of all the starry configurations, it was known to the ancient Egyptians as Unas. So named for the pharaoh who rose to military greatness by eating the flesh of his mortal enemies. A ghoulish custom that married the Egyptians' lurid fascination with death to the art of war. 'The business of barbarians' as Napoleon so adroitly referred to it.

But the Egyptians were not the first civilization obsessed with warfare.

Before Egypt came to the forefront of the ancient world, there was the mighty Atlantis. *The fabled island of Atlas*. The continent rose to prominence twelve thousand years ago. Even then, its culture, medical arts and highly advanced technology were legendary. It was this highly advanced technology that enabled the Atlanteans to rule the ancient world with an iron fist.

Intolerant. Bloodthirsty. Merciless.

Plato, in his two dialogues, *Timaeus* and *Critias*, wrote at length about the war-mongering Atlanteans. Determined to conquer Athens, an unforeseen calamity befell the mighty Atlanteans prior to the final sea battle, their entire continent destroyed in a cataclysmic explosion. In one fiery instant, Atlantis was no more.

The antiquarian Rubin Woolf had been correct in his assertions; there were survivors from Atlantis who made their way to Egypt. Pre-eminent among them was Thoth, the High Priest. Thoth bequeathed the Emerald Tablet to the Egyptians and instructed them in the sacred knowledge of the universe. He taught the Egyptians about the sacred Light, that limitless well of energy that could be accessed, tapped into and used for the greater good. But like the Atlanteans before them, the Egyptians abused and corrupted the sacred knowledge, using it to create a vast militaristic empire. Sad-hearted, the wise Thoth realized the evil still lurked, having slithered forth from the smouldering ashes of Atlantis. Fearful of how the sacred knowledge would be exploited after his death, Thoth concealed the Emerald Tablet.

For thousands of years, the Emerald Tablet remained hidden; until an ambitious upstart named Tuthmose discovered the sacred relic hidden inside a temple column at Hermopolis. A high-ranking member of Pharaoh Akhenaton's court, Tuthmose was an adherent of monotheism, holding firm to the belief that Aten was the *only* god in the heavens. It was this ardent belief in the one god that led Tuthmose to slay the temple priests who still believed in the divine pantheon. It was this ardent belief in the one god that led Tuthmose to command the Pharaoh's armies and crush all dissenters. And it was this same ardent belief that inspired Tuthmose to lead the Egyptian royal court and all of its Hebrew slaves out of Egypt.

To secure and consolidate his power, the ambitious Tuthmose, now called Moses, wielded the Emerald Tablet like a weapon. He further strengthened his dominion by creating a *new* monotheistic religion that heralded Yahweh as the one god. A capricious divinity, Yahweh demanded blind obedience, capable of unimaginable bloodlust if his divine will was thwarted.

Yahweh's *divine* will became the basis for Moses' innumerable laws; violations of the law were punishable by death. To record these draconian strictures, Moses invented the Hebrew alphabet. He then wrote the Torah, the first five books of the Old Testament, to reinforce the laws, and he instituted a hereditary priesthood to safeguard the mystical secrets that enabled his totalitarian rule. Gifts from the patriarch.

But Moses was not content to stop there. The ruthless leader next taught the Hebrews how to kill in the name of the one god. To wage 'holy' war. And with the sacred relic in his arsenal, no one could stop Moses.

None did. In fact, the first recorded genocides in history were those of the Old Testament. All committed in the name of the one god, the newly minted Yahweh. One brutal account, in particular, speaks to Moses' infamy. When the Hebrew army returned from their conquest of Midian, it was not enough that the enemy army had been put to the sword and their entire adult male population slaughtered. Moses, infuriated by this act of 'leniency', commanded his soldiers to kill the adult women, butcher every male child and debauch every virgin girl. Regardless of her age. According to the account in Numbers, thousands of children were raped.

Oh, the horror of it!

An atrocity like none other. Glorified for time immemorial in the biblical text.

A villain for the ages. Moses was a maniacal leader who used the sacred knowledge to further his dark ambitions. Even those close to Moses dared not oppose him. When his sister Miriam questioned her brother's authority, taking issue that he was the only one permitted to communicate with Yahweh, Moses used the sacred knowledge to afflict her with leprosy. When the leaders of the Reuben tribe accused Moses of using his sacred knowledge to promote himself above the rest of the Hebrews, his accusers met an untimely death. When a large contingent of Hebrews expressed outrage after the incident, Moses again used the sacred power to inflict a plague that killed fourteen thousand of the dissenters.

Is it any wonder that the political theorist Niccolò Machiavelli greatly admired the biblical patriarch?

But Mercurius knew, as did Osman de Léon and Moshe Benaroya, that the man immortalized as the Patriarch of the three religions of the Book distorted and corrupted the Light; profaned the sanctity of life; and abused the sacred knowledge to further his own megalomaniacal ambitions. And by so doing, Moses unleashed a dark energy that permeates the world still. In the *Luminarium*, Osman and Moshe explained how this dark energy was an ancient curse. One that must be reversed.

Chilled, Mercurius walked to the patio door. Despite the cool temperature, a palpable heaviness hung in the air. As though each airborne molecule had been drenched in a thick syrup. He entered the house and walked down the hallway towards his study. As was his custom, he stopped in front of the row of framed photographs and with respectful silence gazed at each horrific image.

Eyes welling with tears, he lightly rested his forehead on the photograph in the middle. *Auschwitz.* That sadistic death camp where Osman and Moshe drew their last breaths.

Oh, the horror of it!

Knowing it will happen again. And again . . .

The Crusades. The Wars of Religion. The World Wars.

Not only did Moses glorify war, he claimed that those horrific atrocities were sanctioned by God. But that was a lie. A hoax. A cruel deception that perpetuated the evil by wrapping it in hallowed vestments. The 'holy wars' were simply a bloodthirsty exercise of power. No different to the bloodthirsty exercise of power that forced Thoth, the Atlantean High Priest, to use the sacred relic to *create* a single catastrophic burst of energy that destroyed the entire continent of Atlantis.

For the greater good.

55

'It was the light that led me to the Bacon frontispiece.' As she spoke, the young woman in the farthingale and mop cap nervously eyed Cædmon and Edie.

The Light? Surely the costumed museum guide wasn't referring to Aten, the god of radiant light. Or was she?

Cædmon didn't know what to make of the woman's enigmatic statement.

He peered over his shoulder, verifying that they still had the first-floor drawing room to themselves, the next tour group due to traipse through a few minutes hence. A living history museum, 36 Craven Street was a popular tourist destination. Benjamin Franklin had resided at the modest Georgian townhouse in the decades immediately preceding the revolution. As he understood it, the house had fallen into a derelict state and had only recently been resuscitated, having undergone a complete restoration.

Luckily, he and Edie had had no difficulty tracking down 'the chit' who'd sold Rubin the frontispiece. The introductions had been simple and straightforward:

'Miss Beatrice Stanley, I'm Chief Inspector Peter Willoughby-Jones, Metropolitan Police. This is Special Agent Elizabeth Ross, my counterpart at the FBI. *We have a few questions regarding a recent transaction that you made with one Rubin Woolf.'*

On hearing that, the slack-jawed guide in the farthingale had immediately capitulated, no doubt terrified that she would be arrested on the spot and hauled to jail in handcuffs.

The heavy artillery unlimbered, the interrogation had proceeded in a straightforward manner. Now they were in the process of establishing how precisely Miss Stanley came to be in possession of the Francis Bacon frontispiece.

'The Light?' Edie parroted, her thoughts running a parallel course. 'Do you mean to say that it was divine inspiration that—'

'Are you daft?! I mean the *light!*' Having unexpectedly turned belligerent, the guide gestured to the bank of floor-to-ceiling windows that lined one wall of the first-floor drawing room. Although grey storm clouds cast a dismal hue, daylight flooded the empty room. 'I was leading a tour group through the drawing room when an obnoxious Yank, who claimed he was a restoration expert, pointed out that because of the way the sunlight was streaming through the windows, he could see that the dado railing had slightly buckled away from the wall. I commended the fat bastard for his keen eye and promised him that I would report the defect to the appropriate personnel.'

'And did you make good on the promise?'

'If I had, we wouldn't be standing here, would we?'

'Can the attitude,' Edie snarled, having assumed the role of 'bad cop' to Cædmon's 'good'. 'And do me another favour, just stick to the facts.'

Cædmon wasn't altogether certain, but he thought Edie's last remark had been lifted from the script of a vintage police drama.

'Curious bitch that I am –' the costumed guide defiantly

glared at Edie – 'I wedged my house keys behind the railing and pried off a small section of woodwork. Imagine my surprise at discovering a cavity with a bunch of old papers hidden behind the wainscoting.'

Papers! But he thought there was just the one engraved frontispiece.

'Ohmygosh!' Edie exclaimed, also surprised by the revelation. 'Do you mean to say there were other Bacon documents hidden behind the panel?'

Cædmon cast Edie a stern glance, the sudden outburst not in keeping with her FBI cover.

Miss Stanley's eyes narrowed suspiciously. 'I assumed that you already knew about the hidden recess. And the papers weren't written by Francis Bacon. They were composed by the great man himself, Dr Benjamin Franklin.'

'We were unaware of the concealed niche,' Cædmon informed her, thinking the onion might be better peeled with the truth.

Pacified, the costumed attendant gestured to the nearby corner. 'The recess is behind that section of woodwork between the window and the fireplace.'

The three of them trooped over to the corner to inspect the woodwork. The drawing room, with its taupe-coloured walls, was not only drab, but sparse, the only furnishing in the entire room a lone tea table.

Standing in front of the railing, Cædmon slowly ran his hand over the milled dado, able to feel a slight crevice between the rail and the wall. *What prompted Franklin to go to such lengths?*

Hoping the truculent guide wouldn't object to what he was about to do, he removed a stainless-steel door key from his trouser pocket. To ensure the young woman's cooperation, Edie assumed a confrontational stance. No doubt, she'd seen that tactic on the telly, as well.

The eighteen-inch section of dado rail was easily pried from the wall.

That, in turn, caused a piece of wooden wainscoting to angle forward, secured to the wall with an old metal hinge. Inside the shallow wall cavity was a leather pouch that measured approximately twelve inches by ten inches, the front flap secured with two leather thongs. He removed the pouch and handed it to his 'partner'.

'You can't take that!' the guide practically screeched.

'Did I just hear you say that two *authorized* agents can't seize valuable evidence to aid in a Scotland Yard investigation?' Edie's scowl deepened.

The young woman quickly backpedalled. 'I never said anything of the sort. I'm just worried that . . . that I'm going to be arrested and charged with—'

'As I informed you at the onset, Miss Stanley, we will turn a blind eye to the original theft provided you cooperate with our investigation,' Cædmon reassured the skittish woman.

'I knew I couldn't trust that fancy-pants bugger who bought the engraving. And just so we're clear, I'm not returning the money. It's already spent.'

'We have no intention of demanding recompense.' Afraid of an inopportune intrusion, Cædmon quickly replaced all of the woodwork, hammering the dado into place with his balled fist.

'Speaking of money, I'm curious . . . why did you only sell the frontispiece? Why not sell the whole kit'n'kaboodle?'

This from Edie, his partner seemingly unaware that a trained investigator would have phrased the question differently.

'Thought it best to put some distance between the sales. And the market for Franklin letters is kind of soft right now.' The guide's blasé attitude indicated a remarkable lack of guilt.

'Special Agent Ross and I have everything that we need for our investigation. Thank you for your assistance.' Hoping the farthingaled thief didn't capitulate to latent regret – and sound the alarm – he motioned Edie towards the door.

As they hurriedly made their way down the staircase, he surreptitiously slid the pouch inside his anorak.

A few moments later, a smiling museum worker, this one in street clothes, opened the door, bidding them, 'Good day.'

'Indeed, it is,' Cædmon replied, pleased by the outcome. While the contents of the pouch might prove valueless, the fact that they had finagled the prize with such ease was nothing less than astonishing. A pair of glib-tongued thespians, the both of them.

They stepped through the panelled eighteenth-century door, returning to the twenty-first-century world of speeding cars and the ubiquitous mobile phone. The rain was coming down in sheets. With the push of a plastic button, Edie extended and opened her umbrella, the waterproof fabric emblazoned with a bold leopard pattern. Cædmon instantly wished that she'd made a more decorous choice. He took the brolly from her, holding it aloft.

Grabbing hold of his arm, Edie leaned in close. 'Don't

know about you, but I'm glad that Rubin stood us up. A three-piece tweed suit doesn't exactly say "badass copper".'

'And a leopard print umbrella does?' A last-minute appointment had kept the Third Musketeer at the bookshop. A potential client who'd just inherited a rare collection wanted an appraisal. 'Once Rubin catches the scent of a rare-book cache, there's no pulling him off the hunt. Indeed, he has always maintained that it's more advantageous –'

'By that you mean profitable.'

'– to meet with the heirs while they're still in a grieved state.'

'Just a simple man earning his thirty pieces of silver,' Edie breezily remarked.

'Rubin is a businessman. The heirs on the other hand . . .' Having been in the same business, he knowingly shook his head. 'I suspect the dirt is still fresh on the dearly beloved's grave.'

'Well, ol' Ben has been a'mouldering in his grave for more than two hundred years. That said, I don't want to wait until we get back to Scotland Yard. Let's look inside the pouch.'

'Wasn't it Chaucer who coined the phrase "Patience is a high virtue"?'

'To which I say, virtue ain't what it's cracked up to be. Just ask any fallen woman.' Edie tilted her head and seductively smiled at him. A curly-haired temptress. 'Come on. Just one teensy little peek.'

'Given that I'm so enamoured—'

He broke off, impolitely jostled by a harried passer-by carrying an oversized black umbrella.

'Out of the way, old man,' the ill-mannered pedestrian muttered as he scurried past in the opposite direction.

Sorely tempted to bark out his own rude refrain, Cædmon craned his head, glaring. 'Cheeky bastard,' he muttered under his breath, the chap already out of barking range.

'Lucky for you, I happen to like older men.' As she spoke, Edie pulled him towards a narrow passageway that bisected Craven Street, little more than a paved alley between two buildings.

Their backs turned to street traffic, they huddled close together, giving every appearance of being two lovers sharing an intimate moment.

Reaching inside his anorak, he removed the pouch. Edie, barely able to contain her excitement, tugged on the leather thong that fastened it, releasing the loose knot. Holding his breath, his companion's excitement contagious, he lifted the flap and scanned the contents. It contained what appeared to be a dozen sheaths of yellowing paper. Well aware that they were irresponsibly handling rare ephemera – viewing the documents in the rain, no less! – he slid the pages several inches out of the pouch. Just far enough to read the elegantly penned title at the top of the first page.

Edie was the first to break the silence. 'Coincidence? I think not.'

'Nor I,' he murmured.

Like Edie, he was taken aback that Franklin had titled his work *The Book of Moses*.

56

Softly humming, Saviour Panos turned on to St Martin's Lane, the pouring rain coating everything in a wet patina. Amused at how easy it had been to jostle the Brit, he twirled his big black umbrella. All was going according to plan.

As he strolled past a shoe shop, a sales clerk arranging leather footwear in the window silently appraised him. Saviour lifted his chin to acknowledge the admiring glance.

After listening to the surveillance tapes from last night's conversation, Mercurius had initially expressed delight upon learning the Emerald Tablet had been brought to England. But delight soon turned to alarm. And though Saviour didn't have the intellect to fully grasp the connection, he knew that the Creator's Star was the symbolic embodiment of the Emerald Tablet. Mercurius feared what would happen if the threesome actually *found* the sacred relic, claiming it would be an unthinkable sacrilege.

'*Rest assured, that won't happen*,' he had fervently promised his mentor.

'*You are well and truly loved, Saviour.*'

About to turn on to Cecil Court, he glanced in a plate-glass window . . . and smiled. Feeling very much like the conquering hero.

An instant later, recalling the infuriated expression on Aisquith's face, he chuckled.

'Soon, Englishman, your goose will be thoroughly cooked.'

Burnt to a crisp.

57

'Moses supposes his toes are roses, but Moses supposes erroneously . . .'

Alone in the flat, Rubin Woolf sang the silly ditty in a booming voice. Old Hollywood musicals were a secret obsession, *Singing in the Rain* one of his favourites.

Still annoyed that he couldn't accompany Peter Willoughby-Jones to Craven Street, he trudged upstairs. He preferred to await the eleven o'clock appointment in the comfort of his boudoir. Opening the door at the top of the landing, he entered the foyer.

Almost immediately, his gaze went to one of the photographs displayed on top of the court cabinet. Hit with an inexplicable burst of nostalgia, he walked over and picked up the framed picture. Long moments passed as he stared at the scowling, bare-chested punk rocker who had glared at the camera that memorable night. *1977. The Pegasus.* As he recalled, one had to scowl just to get past the bouncer.

He carefully replaced the photograph. Then, lost in thought, he idly watched the slow-moving minute hand on the German-made cuckoo clock, counting the seconds until . . . the little shutters on the clock flew open, the nesting chick shrilly announcing the hour.

He should have chucked the gaudy old-fashioned clock years ago. Should have. But could never summon the courage to toss it on the rubbish heap. A glutton for punishment, he kept the annoying cuckoo clock because it was the only memento he had of his long-dead father.

And, as fate would have it, the clock was the only memento that Chaim Woolf had had of that violent night in 1938 when the Jewish community in Berlin was rudely awakened in the middle of the night by the sound of smashing glass and raucous jeers, the SS banging at their doors.

Kristallnacht.

The spark that ignited the Holocaust.

Chaim had been a lad of eight, forced to witness an unspeakable atrocity – his father, Menachem Woolf, a veteran of the Great War, foolishly standing his ground with a rusty firearm. As the windows of Menachem's antiquarian shop had been smashed with a sledgehammer. As the books and volumes that lined his antiquarian shop were tossed on to a fiery bonfire. The SS officer in charge acted with the detached efficiency for which the German people pride themselves – he put a single bullet in Menachem Woolf's head, killing him on the spot. Then, to show he was not the monster that the screaming Chaim accused him of being, he removed the handcrafted Bavarian cuckoo clock from the wall, the only item in the room that had not yet been smashed. Handing it to the tearful child, he patted Chaim's head and said, 'Never resist . . . and never forget.'

Indeed, that night stayed with Chaim Woolf for the rest of his life. Even after his mother, two young children in tow, paid a small fortune for the three British visas that secured them safe passage out of Berlin. They arrived in England just in time for the *blitzkrieg* of German bombs that nightly rained down on the scurrying, frightened denizens of London.

Rubin learned of these things from his Aunt Tovah. She'd not been given a cuckoo clock on that long-ago night. Instead, she'd been bequeathed a badly scarred face from having been shoved into the bonfire by a gang of local boys intent on 'joining the fun'. It was his Aunt Tovah who told Rubin about that monstrous episode, hoping he'd understand why, each year on 10 November, his father would sit for hours on end, in the dark, sobbing uncontrollably. Rubin only understood that living with his father was akin to living with a ghost. Chaim Woolf walked and talked and took meals with his family, but he had no ties or bonds with the living.

Rubin had always asserted, rather strenuously, in fact, that he didn't care. *What use did he have for a father who lacked the emotional fortitude to overcome his inner demons?* Chaim Woolf's retreat from the world bespoke a weakness that made his son cringe.

'Daddy, Daddy, you bastard, I'm through.'

As the line of poetry popped into his head, Rubin snorted derisively. Sylvia Plath. *Really*. How pathetic. Besides, what need did he have for a father? What need did anyone have?

'I have my books. I am content,' he reassured himself as he entered the boudoir. Originally a staid Victorian parlour, ten years ago he'd completely transformed the space, paying a small fortune to have a room in a half-timbered Winchester abode completely dismantled, the woodwork shipped to Cecil Court and reassembled. The panelled walls exemplified the very best of the era, masculine exuberance wedded to feminine civility.

He suspected that his father had never known an exuberant day in his life.

No doubt that was the reason why Rubin had been drawn to the scowling anarchists who'd invaded the London club scene in the 1970s. But, like the punk-rock movement itself, the love affair had been short-lived. Rubin had always required an intellectual challenge to maintain a long-term interest.

Enter Sir Francis Bacon.

He'd often wondered if his family history didn't have something to do with his fascination with Sir Francis. A Renaissance man *extraordinaire*, Sir Francis was at once philosopher, courtier and esoteric adept. But, more importantly, Sir Francis Bacon was a tolerant and benevolent man of God.

Walking over to the bed, he picked up the Mylar-covered frontispiece. In the *New Atlantis*, Jews played a prominent role in society and lived harmoniously side-by-side with their Christian neighbours. The children of the Old Covenant united with those of the New. A paradise not seen since Adam and Eve blithely strolled their earthly garden. And the adhesive that bound the residents of Bacon's utopian realm was the hidden stream of knowledge.

Knowledge is power.

I am a witness to knowledge.

Heady sentiments made manifest by the alchemical power inherent in the Emerald Tablet. Sacred teachings whose roots extended to the time before the pharaohs. To the time when Thoth and his fellow refugees fled the destruction of Atlantis.

No different to when the German Jews fled from the Nazi thugs.

Rubin chortled, cynical enough to be amused by the comparison.

In the foyer, the cuckoo annoyingly announced the quarter hour. *Fifteen minutes late.* Royally pissed off, he strode over to the window and stared at the gloomy montage below. A few shops kept Sunday hours. Most were closed. Christians were not as rigid as Jews when it came to keeping their Sabbath.

As if on cue, the downstairs bell rang.

'About time,' he muttered as he turned away from the window.

Annoyed at being made to wait, he took his time descending the steps. *Let the bastard stand in the rain a bit longer.* Time was a valuable commodity, tardiness a tiresome character flaw.

Again, the bell rang.

Reaching the ground floor, he stormed across the dimly lit bookshop, in high dudgeon.

'Ask not for whom the bell tolls, you bloody impatient bastard, it tolls for . . .'

Unbolting the lock, Rubin swung open the shop door.

On the other side of the threshold stood a dark-haired man. Six feet in height, he had about him a classical beauty that harkened back to the ancient world. A marble *kouros* come to life. Carved by the hand of the master sculptor Phidias.

Admittedly taken aback, Rubin could see that, like the *kouroi* of ancient Greece, his beautiful visitor was the living, breathing embodiment of the ideal male form.

For several moments they stared mutely at one another.

The beautiful stranger smiled. 'I'm Saviour Panos. We

have an eleven o'clock appointment. Please accept my apology for being a few minutes later. I hope that you weren't inconvenienced.'

'Not in the least,' Rubin assured him. He tugged at the bottom of his waistcoat, self-consciously aware of his middle-aged paunch.

'May I come inside?'

'Where are my manners? Of course, please come in,' Rubin invited. Then, as an afterthought, 'I trust that you like Martinis.'

58

'. . . and Benjamin Franklin's code name was Moses.'

'Indeed?'

'Yeah, no kidding.' Edie scooted her chair closer to the flat-screened monitor.

To get out of the rain, she and Cædmon had ducked into an Internet café called Pie-Ro-Mania. Owned and operated by an American expat, the joint billed itself as a 'No Latte Zone' that served dark-roast coffee and home-made pie by the slice. The décor was equally bare-boned, with several rows of conference tables lined with monitors and keyboards. The music – Muddy Waters – and the incredibly flaky piecrust more than compensated for the spartan design. She'd ordered pecan with a big dollop of whipped cream.

'The whole time that he was living at the townhouse on Craven Street, ol' Ben was engaged in high-level espionage activities,' Edie continued. She hurriedly ripped open a cellophane package with plastic cutlery, anxious for a sugar fix. 'Those were the turbulent years leading up to the Revolution. And, according to the biography that I read a few years back, Franklin used the secret code name "Moses".'

'Which explains why he titled the hidden pages *The Book of Moses*. It's a tongue-in-cheek reference to his espionage activities.'

'Okay, book title explained. But what I want to know is how did Franklin get a hold of the Bacon frontispiece? Ohmygosh! This is to die for,' she exclaimed around a mouthful of pie. 'You sure you don't want some?' She extended her plastic fork in Cædmon's direction.

He politely shook his head, clearly spooked by the idea of so much corn syrup having gone into a single slice of pie. 'Perhaps Franklin's enigmatically titled missive will shed some light.' Cædmon opened the leather pouch and carefully removed the dozen or so sheets of thick old-fashioned paper. 'Let's have a go at it, shall we?'

'Since we have no idea as to the contents, I think we should read this quietly at our desks rather than reciting it aloud.'

Cædmon inched his chair closer to hers. 'I agree. *Sub rosa.*'

The Book of Moses

London
March 17, 1775

I write this missive in haste, fearful that the bloody backs will barge through the entry at any moment, an arrest warrant in one hand and a length of rope in the other. Lest I be accused of fraudulent alienations, a principal offender of the Crown, in word and deed, I am transcribing an account of my actions during the years 1724 to 1775.

The particulars of my life story are familiar enough to readers of my scribblings. While I wrote naught but the truth in my Autobiography, I am guilty of having spun a lie of omission. The lapse involves my arrival in London in 1724. A penniless lad, a mere eighteen winters upon my head, I apprenticed myself to one John Watts, a printer by trade. My lodgings, though sparse, did accommodate most comfortably, youth more accepting of privation. Endowed with a prying nature, I spent my evenings combing through the stacks of printed material housed in the shop storeroom. Which is how I happened upon an incised plate which I recognized as a frontispiece. Curious, I inked the plate and drew a print, surprised to find myself holding a frontispiece for the New Atlantis by Sir Francis Bacon. My attention was immediately drawn to a glaring inaccuracy: the date incised on to the plate. I had more than a passing familiarity with the work in question, having read the volume the year prior. Therefore, I knew that it had been published in 1627, not 1614 as indicated on the frontispiece. Surely the graver made grave error.

Thinking the illustration a fine work of art nonetheless, I tacked it on to the wall beside my cot. Innumerable nights I stared upon those muses before I realized that the date was not the engraving's only error. Indeed, there *seemed to be a glaring number of mistakes. Which led me to deduce that a message was hidden within those inconsistencies. Soon enough, I discovered a numeric cipher that, when translated into the Latin alphabet, read 'Moses Egypticus mined Thoths stone.' I did not know it at the time, but that curious message would one day change the course of my life.*

In truth, 'twas a strange riddle, one I could not penetrate. Though I did strenuously attempt the feat, burning my betty lamp into the wee hours, books a lonely man's steadfast companion. From my reading, I ascertained that 'Thoths stone' referred to an ancient relic known as the Emerald Tablet and that this relic had been much coveted during the Middle Ages. Particularly in alchemical circles. I also knew from my reading of the Bible that Moses, the Hebrew patriarch, was trained in all the arts of Egypt. Was it possible that during ancient times, no less a personage than Moses had this relic in his possession and that centuries later it had been bequeathed to Sir Francis Bacon? If so, what happened to the sacred relic upon Sir Francis's death?

While those questions bedevilled me, I grew desirous of more animated companions than my growing collection of leather-bound volumes and soon began to patronize the coffee houses of London. At each week's end, meagre earnings in hand, I traded my black bib and apron for beggar's velvet, and made straightway for St Paul's coffee house where, for a modest admission, I could enjoy the exalted company of poets, writers and the like.

The ease with which the coffee house habitués bandied ideas, both scientific and arcane, astounded me. One night, hoping to impress, I mentioned the Bacon frontispiece and the hidden cipher to a newly formed acquaintance. Aghast, the man informed me that I would be wise not to make mention of this in so public a place. Rather than dampen, this ominous warning aroused my curiosity. Over the course of many months, I gently probed the clientele of St Paul's. While a strong brew heightened a man's faculties, I discovered that, inundated with spirituous drink, that same man's faculties fled for higher ground. Indeed, I was privy to many a drunken murmuring, the common thread being the Freemasons. One saturated fellow did let slip that the Freemasons were the guardians of a sacred relic which they inherited from a well-known English nobleman. A lofty claim. One I would have rejected outright had it not been for the encryption on the frontispiece. I gently pressed the matter, but my drunken companion refused to give up the prize. Struck by divine inspiration, I vowed to join the ranks of the Freemasons. What better way to siphon from that well-guarded well of knowledge?

In 1726, I returned to Philadelphia and

eventually secured an invitation to join the Grand Lodge of Free and Accepted Masons. The secret proceedings were carried out with an air of constipated gravitas and I was forced to swallow many an amused guffaw. What man would not be struck by the patent absurdity of a Philadelphia merchant claiming descent from sun-worshipping Egyptians? Not content to stop there, my brethren did maintain that the mysticism of the Nile had a guiding hand in the construction of Solomon's Temple. Even going so far as to claim that behind each of history's great achievements, there beamed the illuminating rays of the Light, the name they bestowed upon God Almighty. Who but an itinerant simpleton would proclaim as truth such outlandish assertions? Or spout incomprehensible drivel and pass it off as 'knowledge'. To my great disappointment, I soon came to realize that the members of the Philadelphia Lodge had no knowledge of Francis Bacon or his sacred relic. However, the inane rituals and silly natterings did serve a purpose, namely to open the doors of Philadelphia's most exclusive drawing rooms, providing me with the entrée denied by birth. Where men of high standing once turned a blind eye, they now greeted me with open arms.

As the years passed, I never forgot the unsolved puzzle of the Bacon frontispiece. From time to time, I would make the acquaintance of a man who intimated that he had knowledge of the sacred relic. More than a few of my esteemed Royal Society fellows implied as much. While I have never profaned the name of God nor purposefully set my sights on Perdition's pathway, in this one instance, those endowed with a less charitable bent may claim that I did well succeed at both endeavours.

'Astounding. I've always thought of Franklin as a brilliant boffin, but I must now add Machiavellian schemer to the list.' There was no mistaking the admiration in Cædmon's voice. 'Care for another slice of pie?'

About to put in an order for lemon meringue, Edie reluctantly shook her head at the last. 'I'm a little confused. What do the Freemasons and the Royal Society have to do with Francis Bacon?'

'Given his slavish devotion to Bacon and the Bard, Rubin could better answer the question. He is, after all, the resident expert on the Knights of the Helmet. That said, I'll take a stab.' As he spoke, Cædmon slowly twisted the silver signet ring, as though he was channelling the Templar Grand Master who wore it last. 'During the mid seventeenth century, there was a resurgent interest in Bacon and his utopian vision for creating a society dedicated to the principles of the hidden stream of knowledge.'

'I've heard this tune before.' Edie moved her hands through the air like a symphony conductor. 'Alchemy, Kabbalah and magic. The Unholy Trinity.'

'While the Royal Society promoted the advancement

of philosophical, mathematical and scientific learning, a good many fellows were secretly engaged in the occult. In fact, the most famous member of the Royal Society, Sir Isaac Newton, was utterly obsessed with alchemy.'

Hearing that, Edie nearly gagged on her coffee. 'Isaac Newton was an alchemist!?'

'The aim of alchemy is to glean the secret of creation, the Genesis code a tempting lure for any man.'

'And the Freemasons? Where do they fit into the picture?'

'Despite their outrageous claims of an ancient pedigree, the Freemasons were founded in 1717. And it's no coincidence that the founding members were all fellows in the Royal Society.'

'So, it makes perfect sense for Benjamin Franklin to join the Philadelphia Lodge. He figured the Freemasons might have the low-down on the Emerald Tablet, given their interest in the occult.'

'And, while he was at it, Franklin could climb the social ladder and gain entrée into the charmed circles of English society. Armed with wit, charisma and innate intelligence, Dr Franklin ascended to the top rung, that of Grand Master. A brilliant move, really. Given the rigid class structure of the eighteenth century, becoming a Freemason enabled Franklin, an autodidact of humble birth, to hobnob with the crème de la crème.'

'Do you think there's any chance he actually found the Emerald Tablet?'

Blue eyes gleaming, Cædmon handed her the next page of Franklin's handwritten missive. 'I am keen to find out.'

59

In 1765, I returned to London a loyal supporter of the king. I leave ten years later an embittered traitor to the Crown. Continually I did urge harmonious accord between parent and child, my efforts for naught. May Providence prove me wrong, but I fear the relationship is now strained beyond repair. My actions this night will further weaken the fragile bond. As fate would have it, the object that has long held my fascination is at the heart of the severance. I speak, of course, of the Emerald Tablet.

Unlike my first youthful sojourn, I arrived in London a Freemason grand master and Royal Society fellow. Soon after my arrival, a fellow Mason, his tongue loosened with drink, let slip that Sir Francis Dashwood had been entrusted with the Brothers' most sacred relic. The man's name was familiar enough to me, Dashwood being a known confidant of the king. Having caught the scent, I immediately set about to make Dashwood's acquaintance. As those in the upper echelons will attest, Dashwood is a charming fellow, possessed of a courtier's manners and the morals of a whore. Indeed, he lived his life ad libitum, always at pleasure's beck and call.

Furthermore, he surrounded himself with a hand-picked circle, a privileged gathering of free-thinkers, libertines and artists, all members of the aristocratic class who held to the shared belief that they were exempt from the rules that bound the lower castes.

I secured an invitation to join Dashwood and his compatriots for an evening's revel. Laughter being the most expedient means to gain a man's confidence, I liberally peppered my speech with bawdy jests and risqué witticisms. Over the years, I had perfected the art of playing the fool, the jester often the wisest man at court, privy to all manner of intrigue. To my surprise, I discovered that Dashwood and his inner circle, Freemasons all, spent a goodly amount of time plotting the course of king and empire. Their political discourse exposed a surprising undercurrent, the king's confidant not as enamoured of the royal personage as he did profess in public. In truth, Dashwood held a low opinion of the monarch and expressed disdain for the monarchy in general. With the conceit of the high-born, Dashwood claimed that society would be better served if educated men of high rank served as overseers for a new world order. Having read the New Atlantis, I recognized the scheme, Dashwood and his associates taking upon themselves the role played by the scholars who resided at Solomon's House. Dashwood ardently maintained that society's salvation is entirely dependent upon men of noble birth, the 'anointed ones' who will implement Bacon's utopian vision. Because of their superior intellect, they would decide each man's lot in life, be he yeoman or tinsmith or printer. And as the most exalted members of society, Dashwood and his inner circle would also be the guardians of the sacred teachings. The common man, dumb as dirt, must content himself with ploughing the field and printing the page while the intellectual elites busied themselves creating a new religion that would merge the three people of the Book. In Dashwood's utopia, Christians, Hebrews and Moslems would all worship the Light, as man did in the days when the pharaohs ruled, occultism woven into the very warp and woof of their Masonic scheme. Privately, I took issue with all of this. Indeed, a benevolent tyrant is still a tyrant.

As the months passed, I proved myself an amiable companion, Dashwood confiding all manner of secret to me. Indeed, he once boasted that he could ride ten whores in a single night. While I applauded his stamina, I questioned the veracity of the claim. To validate the allegation, Dashwood invited me to join his 'monks' on their next unholy pilgrimage. My curiosity piqued, I readily accepted the invitation.

Several nights later, our pilgrimage illuminated by a ponderous full moon, we travelled by gondola up the Thames to a ruined abbey in the vicinity of West Wycombe, known to the locals as Medmenham Abbey. Our arrival was announced with the sombre toll of the cloister bell. As we disembarked, a manservant handed each 'monk' a brown cowl to don. Properly attired, we made our way in single-file procession. One of our party, a deep baritone, took up a popish chant. We entered a subterranean sanctuary beneath the abbey and were ushered to the chapter room. The sanctuary contained a stone altar and a painted mural of Harpocrates, finger to lips, cautioning the assembled adherents to silence. We were soon greeted by a timorous nun attired in a Capuchin habit and a stern-faced priest in dark cassock. To my utter astonishment, the priest raised his robe, shoved the nun on to the altar, and proceeded to roger her in full view of the friars. Clearly enjoying themselves, the pair sang bestial hosannas. The priest brayed like a he-ass; the nun cooed like David's turtle dove. My host turned to me and said slyly, 'Nothing quite as inspiring as a holy man performing his officium divinum. *'His sacred duty made all the more pleasurable by having such a delectable vessel beneath him,' I replied, beginning to suspect that sacrilegious amusements were commonplace at Medmenham. Indeed, a horde of nuns soon entered the sanctuary, their appearance setting off a blazing* feu de joie.

Had there ever been a more impious gathering? Later I was informed that the 'pilgrimage' had been my initiation into the club's inner circle. A sinner circle, God help me.

In the ensuing months, I was a frequent guest at the abbey and can attest that costumed amusements and bawdy entertainments were routinely performed in the subterranean sanctuary, the monks' motto being 'Do you what you will.' Where you will and when you will, no space too public for a monk to slake his lust with an obliging nun.

One evening I arrived at the abbey keenly disappointed that the gay gaggle of whores was absent. Indeed, the gathered company seemed strangely solemn. I was informed that the 'monks' had decided to bestow upon me a high honour; I was to participate in a sacred ritual. A metal case had been placed upon the stone altar. My heart beat a rapid tattoo against my breast. Dashwood, attired in Egyptian garb, opened the case and revealed a green tablet of unaccountable beauty. I stood transfixed. After half a century, I finally laid my eyes upon the Emerald Tablet. The high priest then mixed several powdered substances, heating them over a flame. Soon a noxious smoke filled the room. A few moments later, I was given a draught of a vile-tasting potion that caused my bowels to painfully cramp. Libations administered, Dashwood next attempted to penetrate the *supernatural realm and rouse a demon to do his bidding. Any man with a passing knowledge of biblical text knows that governance over the devil is a risky venture. And a potentially dangerous pursuit. Intoning an ungodly chant, Dashwood held the Emerald Tablet aloft and displayed the relic's ornate emblem, proclaiming that the secret of creation was contained within its arcane symbolism and that a man had only to decipher the symbols to commune directly with the heavenly sphere. As I am an avowed Deist, my mind did baulk at this assertion.*

Francis Dashwood, by his own admission, is a libertine bar none. But, as with all of the men in his inner circle, he was first and foremost an adherent to the hidden stream of knowledge. Not only did he practise alchemy, but he studied the Conjecture Cabalistica, and embraced the dark arts, particularly those that evoked the mysticism of ancient Egypt. In truth, Dashwood's inner circle was a superstitious coven of sun-worshipping Atenists and bewigged magi.

Appalled and fascinated by their rituals, I feared the beautiful relic might indeed possess some mysterious power. Unlike my Brothers at the Philadelphia Lodge, Dashwood and his Masonic coven are a determined group of well-connected aristocrats with an ambitious bill of sale. Moreover, they contend that the relic was the true power behind the British Empire. They prefix this claim by declaring that no sooner did Ralegh secure the relic than England's global ascendancy began. Not unlike the ascendancy of the Hebrew tribes in the Old Testament, Thoth's stone the beating heart of each empire's rise. I decided then and there that delenda est Carthago. Carthage must be destroyed. And to ensure that the phoenix cannot open its beak, let alone rise from the ashes, their most sacred relic must be seized. The felicity and well-being of the colonies depends upon it. My plan was simple, but brazen. I would appropriate the relic at the monks' next gathering, a wild bacchanal the perfect diversion.

Several weeks later, an opportunity presented itself, a buxom nun in a state of déshabillé my unwitting accomplice. Attired in cowl and robe, I ushered the nun to the monk's cell where I knew the relic to be safeguarded by an armed grenadier. Assuming an intoxicated demeanour, made all the more believable by an unsteady weaving to-and-fro, I approached the guard. Grinning like a jack-a-napes, I informed the fellow that I was too far along in my cups to enjoy a good gallop and would he like to ride the flanking mare in my stead. 'Indeed, I would be happy to oblige the request,' he assured me, making haste to unbutton his breeches, perhaps fearful that I might retract the offer if he did not thrum the good sister in swift order. Flourishing his weapon, he paid me no mind.

Suspecting his stamina would prove of short duration, I hurriedly made my way to the adjoining room. The holy of holies. There I did find the relic housed in a metal case set inside a stone niche. I snatched the prize and, securing it beneath my voluminous garment, escaped to London in a waiting carriage.

That was four hours ago. I am soon to depart Craven Street in yet another carriage, this one headed to Portsmouth where I will board a packet ship bound for the colonies. This night I have crossed the Rubicon, the bridge in flames behind me. As for the sacred relic, I propose to take Thoth's stone to the city nearest the Centre to that place where men strive to improve the common stock of knowledge so that all may prosper in mind as well as spirit.

Though tempted to delve into the relic's supernatural mystery, I shall refrain. Enlightened man, empowered with intellect and reason, need not fall victim to the counterfeit claims of medieval occultism. I do believe that Francis Bacon was a gifted man who straddled two universes, one foot firmly planted in the enlightened world and the other firmly planted in the medieval age, a man of science with occult inclinations. But a man cannot be so divided, his very nature torn asunder. He must commit to one or the other. An enlightened man, a man burnished in the fire of science, knows that the mind is the most powerful weapon of all. God did not intend for man to take his sustenance from the meagre larder of alchemy and magic, false sciences the both of them. Rather the Creator, the Supreme Deity, desired that man eat from the Tree of Knowledge.

To safeguard the relic, I intend to create a Triad of like-minded men who will ensure that Thoth's stone is hidden away. As I am not entirely oblivious to the relic's import, I shall propose to my fellow Triad members that we leave signposts lest a future age, unencumbered by the superstitions of this age, would find some scholastic merit in archiving the relic. If that day should come to pass, I suspect it will be long centuries from now. Since the dawn of time, man has been burdened with a superstitious nature which is not likely to dissipate in the near decades. In this, as with a good many things, there is a fine line between the sacred and the profane. Yea, for every Francis Bacon there are ten Francis Dashwoods who would leap at the chance to exploit the relic's supposed power.

Given that these are dangerous times, I further propose that each member of the Triad select his successor. Should a Triad member meet an untimely end, another shall assume his responsibilities. In this way, the Triad can germinate itself indefinitely. My task is now made clear. I must find the catheti to my hypotenuse. Men of good moral character but not given to public piety. Men possessed of intellect but not lacking in compassion. And, most importantly, I seek honourable men who will not be seduced by the relic's potential power. Alas, there are no men in my current circle who I feel sufficiently capable of discharging this monumental duty. However, in two months' time, the Second Continental Congress will convene in Philadelphia and I will have the pick of the bushel.

The looming storm clouds portend a crisis that must be met. The Creator bequeathed to Adam's progeny the gift of reason so he may safely navigate through this dark night. If, long years from now, my actions come to light, posterity may harshly judge me. But it is to safeguard posterity that I now steer my course, knowing that I have done all that I can do, certain in the conviction that Rebellion to Tyrants is obedience to God. Thus I do God's will.

60

'"Morning has broken,"' Mercurius murmured, luxuriating in the sun's rays shining through the bedroom window.

As he stretched the kinks out of his 72-year-old back, he slid his bare feet into a pair of ornately beaded Moroccan slippers. Ali Baba slippers – his *amoretto* liked to tease. The frivolous footwear was a colourful reminder of the deprivations suffered during the war years. Those years when he had no shoes, climbed garden walls to pilfer oranges and wore mended clothing.

He snatched his silk robe from the hook on the back of the door and slipped his bare arms into the sleeves, tying the garment at his waist.

Before retiring last evening, he'd listened to the recordings that his *amoretto* had made, distressed to learn how much Aisquith and his two cohorts had pieced together. Not only did they know about the three streams of hidden knowledge – alchemy, Kabbalah and magic – they knew the Emerald Tablet contained a pictograph in which the secret of creation had been encoded.

He took a small measure of comfort in the fact that, even if they uncovered the relic, without the encryption key they could not access the sacred power. Not even the brilliant Sir Francis Bacon had been able to decipher the encryption. Long millennia ago, Thoth had devised an ingeniously complex code.

Entering his study, Mercurius walked over to the built-in bookcase and rolled the floor-to-ceiling ladder several feet to one side. Hit with a twinge of arthritis in his right hip, he gingerly climbed the rungs. It took a moment to locate a slender volume: *New Atlantis.*

One could not help but admire the utopian thinkers who attempted to fashion a better world. One without war. Without hunger. Without misery. But every utopian colony ever founded had collapsed, besieged, the dark energy from the outside world too great a force to withstand. The inhabitants beaten down and demoralized because they dared to remake the world anew. While their aspirations were commendable, there was a flaw in the very concept of an earthly utopia. Simply put, it was *impossible* to remake or rehabilitate this dark planet.

For ours was a cursed world.

Which is not to say that a better world doesn't exist. It did, on a plane of existence where the Light permeates every thought and every action of every man. Contained within each living creature, there was a divine spark. *The soul.* Our individual piece of eternity. Imprisoned within a physical body, from the very moment of conception, our souls long to be reunited with the Light. To return to the Lost Heaven.

Mercurius glanced down at his own withered body. How could anyone possibly accept the ridiculous notion that this belching, farting, perspiring vessel was made in God's image? Physical existence was proof positive that this dark world was a failed experiment created by a malevolent demiurge.

To be free of this dark world, a soul must wrench itself

from the physical prison of the body. Once liberated, the soul could return to the Lost Heaven and dwell in a state of luminous grace, that being the only *true* utopia.

He idly flipped through the pages of the slender volume that he held in his hands, the *New Atlantis* less than fifty pages in length. He stopped on page thirteen, a sentence in the text capturing his attention. '*Thou hast vouchsafed of thy grace to those of our order to know thy works of creation, and true secrets of them.*'

In the *New Atlantis*, the scholars of Solomon's House possess the secret of creation. Moreover, the esteemed scholars know that there's a link between creation and the hidden stream of knowledge. While the brilliant Sir Francis was correct in postulating that the hidden stream of knowledge was the key, he was unaware that there were *four* streams of hidden knowledge. Not three. And that the fourth stream was the key to unlock the mystery of the Emerald Tablet.

As fate would have it, Mercurius had the key.

61

Finished reading *The Book of Moses*, Edie released a gusty breath. 'Whew! Those Monks of Medmenham were *very* bad boys.'

'A *nom de plume* for London's notorious Hellfire Club,' Cædmon informed her. 'Rakes, lechers and pornographers, the lot of them.'

'Talk about the secret life of Benjamin Franklin. Although we're still very much in the dark as to the relic's whereabouts.'

'According to his confession, Franklin whisked the Emerald Tablet off to the colonies.' He banged the table with a balled fist. 'Damn the man!'

'Being a Freemason, Benjamin Franklin knew all about Francis Bacon's scheme to use the Emerald Tablet to create a utopian society. A hundred and fifty years after Bacon's death, the plot was still very much on the front burner.' Edie lowered her voice to a conspiratorial whisper, as though suddenly aware that they were discussing a centuries-old mystery in the middle of an Internet café. 'Franklin knew that the English aristocracy had plans to create a benevolent tyranny run by intellectual elites. Moreover, they intended to use the Emerald Tablet to achieve their despotic ends. Deny it all you want, but that *is* the beating heart of Bacon's *New Atlantis*.'

Cædmon placed his right hand over his heart and gazed

heavenward. 'Thank God for Dr Franklin! The great American hero who fought the evil English elites with a kite in one hand and the Emerald Tablet in the other.'

'Make mock if you will, but Benjamin Franklin believed that "Rebellion to tyrants is obedience to God." '

Well aware that Americans tended to be a tetchy lot when it came to their civil liberties, *Sic Semper Tyrannis* and all that, he altered course. 'Given that Franklin was an avowed Deist, I'm not the least bit surprised that he's so disdainful of the occult rituals observed at Medmenham Abbey.'

Edie snapped two sugar packets to and fro before tearing them open and pouring the contents into a cup of coffee, her third of the day. 'I seem to recall that quite a few of the American Founding Fathers were Deists. Wasn't it a religious movement that came about in the seventeenth and eighteenth centuries?'

'The Deists were spawned during the Enlightenment,' he verified with a nod. 'Nominally Christian, the Deists were convinced that God not only created the universe, but at the same time devised the laws of nature. Indeed, one can *only* know God through reason and observation of the natural world. Not through miracles or prophecy or other-worldly voices emanating from the Ark of the Covenant.'

About to raise her coffee cup to her lips, Edie instead lowered it to the table. 'Makes perfect sense that a dyed-in-the-wool Deist like Benjamin Franklin would be horrified by the notion of using the Emerald Tablet to tap into the mind of God in order to create the perfect society. Given everything he'd heard and witnessed, he suspected the relic contained the so-called Genesis code. And it scared the hell out of him.'

'Franklin came of age during the Enlightenment and like his Deist brethren, he was convinced that God graced mankind with intellect,' Cædmon said, a deep-held belief of his own as well. 'By employing our God-given intellect, we can create and fashion a world based upon the tenets of reason and natural law. A whole different type of creation altogether.'

'Yeah, the safe kind. As in, no Big Bang.' Edie pointedly glanced at the yellow sheaths of paper. 'Last night, Rubin mentioned that Thoth brought the Emerald Tablet to Egypt from Atlantis. Do you think the Emerald Tablet had something to do with the destruction of Atlantis?'

'Mmmm . . . an interesting question. The few references to Atlantis in the ancient records claim that the entire continent was obliterated from the earth. That said, it is possible that the Genesis code contained within the Emerald Tablet triggered the catastrophe.'

'It would only take one exploding atom to do the trick.' Edie shuddered. 'Franklin was afraid of what would happen if the Freemasons found the encryption key and decoded the pictograph.'

'Indeed.' He drummed his fingers on the tabletop. 'Your Benjamin Franklin is proving a difficult circle to square.'

'Might have been nice if he'd left a clue as to where he intended to take the Emerald Tablet once he left London.'

'I believe that he did.' With his index finger, Cædmon drew Edie's attention to several lines of text. 'Franklin writes, "I propose to take Thoth's stone to the city nearest the Centre to that place where men strive to improve the common stock of Knowledge so that all may prosper in mind as well as spirit." Without question, it's a clue as to where Dr Franklin intended to take the Emerald Tablet.'

Edie rolled her eyes. 'Good luck finding *that* location on a Rand McNally map.'

He studied the last page of Franklin's missive. Selection made, he said, 'These two phrases look promising: "the city nearest the Centre" and "the common stock of Knowledge".' He quickly typed both phrases into the Internet search engine.

'In one way or another, it always comes back to "knowledge", doesn't it?'

'The glue that binds one century to the next. Well, well. We have a hit,' he announced. At seeing the two phrases pop up in the same online document, he experienced a surge of optimism. 'It seems that the wise sage used those same phrases in a written proposal dated 1743.' He quickly skimmed the text that had come up on the screen. 'In this document Franklin states his intention to found an organization in Philadelphia, that "being the City nearest the Centre of the Continent-Colonies", to be known as the American Philosophical Society.'

Edie picked up where he left off. 'The aim of which was to "cultivate the finer Arts, and improve the common Stock of Knowledge".' She glanced at him. 'Sounds like the American Philosophical Society was supposed to be the colonial counterpart of the Royal Society.'

He quickly typed 'American Philosophical Society' into the search engine. 'And still is,' he informed her, grinning. *One step closer.*

Scooting her metal folding chair nearer to the table, Edie excitedly pointed to the web page he'd just pulled up. 'Ohmygosh! You're right. The American Philosophical Society, founded by Benjamin Franklin in 1743, is *still* a going concern with a library, archives *and* a very extensive Franklin Collection. Oh, and get this . . . it's located in the old historic district of Philadelphia right next to Independence Hall.' When he raised a quizzical brow, she elaborated. 'That's where the Second Continental Congress convened in May, 1775, and where, fourteen months later, Ben Franklin and the rest of the American Founding Fathers signed the Declaration of Independence on the fourth of July, 1776.'

'Mmmm . . . interesting.' For several seconds he pondered the significance of the Emerald Tablet being hidden in the same colonial city where the American rebels so famously put pen to paper, formalizing their break with Great Britain. 'According to *The Book of Moses*, Franklin intended to establish a protectorate, "The Triad" as he called it, to ensure that the Emerald Tablet never fell into the hands of those who would exploit it for personal gain.'

'So, when do we leave for Philly?'

He smiled. *How well she knew him.*

'I'll check the online travel agency to see when the next flight—' He stopped in mid-sentence, suddenly hearing the refrain from the 1980s song 'Karma Chameleon'. The offending sound was emanating from his anorak pocket.

'I never took you for being a Boy George fan.'

'I'm not.' Rummaging in his pocket, he removed an unfamiliar mobile phone, belatedly realizing that what they were hearing was the ring tone. Wondering how the bright red mobile had found its way into his pocket, he took the call. Except it wasn't a call. It was an incoming video.

'Hey, that looks exactly like Rubin's boudoir,' Edie said, leaning over his shoulder. 'In fact, there's Rubin's big four-poster bed with – oh, my God!'

'What the bloody—' His heart slammed against his chest as he saw Rubin, stark naked, standing on a Tudor stool beside an ornately carved wooden post. A long black cord was looped around his neck, the other end wrapped around the top of the four-poster bed.

Tears streaming down his face, Rubin stared directly at the camera. '*Vater, ich liebe dich.*'

A split-second later, a second person, seen only from behind walked over and kicked the stool out from under Rubin's feet. He dropped nearly a foot. Body convulsing. Feet dangling.

Edie screamed.

Cædmon forcefully shoved the mobile into her hand. 'Dial 999. Tell the police to go to Woolf's Antiquarian Books in Cecil Court. And for God's sake, don't leave the café!' he yelled over his shoulder as he ran towards the door.

62

Cædmon burst on to the pavement outside the Internet café, brusquely shoving several patrons aside in his haste to exit the building.

Shocked by the video he'd just seen – well aware that he had no time to lose – he sprinted in the direction of Cecil Court. The café was only two blocks from the bookshop. There might still be time to rescue Rubin.

Storefronts and eateries passed in a blur of plate glass and shuttered entryways. His heart pounding against his breastbone, he darted across the road. Horns blared. The driver of a black cab hollered a rude insult. He kept on running.

He had two minutes. Three if he was lucky. Probably closer to two since Rubin had a roly-poly build which would put more pressure on his trachea.

Don't struggle, Rubin! For God's sake, don't fight it. You'll only hasten the end. Death by hanging. In reality, death by strangulation, the victim's own body weight causing the noose to tighten, which induced asphyxiation.

He refrained from glancing at his watch. Instead, he pumped his legs that much harder, grateful the earlier rain had stopped, although the pavement was slick with moisture. As he found out a few moments later when he skidded into a lamp post.

His energy flagging, he turned the corner on to Cecil

Court, immediately assaulted by the pungent scent of garam masala. The curry house on the corner was open for business. Breathless, he quickly surveyed the pedestrian-only thoroughfare searching for a dark-haired man with the face of an angel. *The heart of a demon.*

The beautiful bastard was nowhere in sight. In fact, Cecil Court seemed surreally calm. A peaceful tableau.

At a glance he saw the usual smattering of tourists and Sunday shoppers leisurely strolling the walkway and huddled in front of book carousels. Time always seemed to move at a slower pace on Booksellers' Row. Which is why heads turned as he sprinted towards the bookshop in the middle of the court. He paid the curious no mind. A man had just been brutally accosted in their midst and they were serenely oblivious. He didn't have that luxury.

Reaching the front door of the bookshop, he turned the knob. *Locked. Damn!* Rubin's assailant had a key to the shop! And had actually gone to the trouble of locking up as he departed the premises. Cædmon shoved his hand into his trouser pocket and removed the silver key that Rubin had earlier given him, his fingers trembling slightly as he jammed it in the lock. He cursed under his breath.

The instant the lock clicked, he turned the knob and flung the door wide open, the entry bell ringing wildly. He didn't bother to close the door, in far more of a hurry than Rubin's assailant. As he dashed across the shop, he bumped his shoulder against a bookcase, his vision impaired by the dim light. Again, he cursed, this time louder.

Reaching the back staircase that led upstairs to Rubin's boudoir, he grabbed the newel post and lunged upward . . . only to gracelessly stumble. Stopped in this tracks by a small barricade of cardboard boxes. He stepped on top of one of the boxes, his shoe promptly plunging through the crack in the cardboard top.

'Damn!' Holding on to the banister, he yanked his foot out of the box. Awkwardly scrambling over the obstacle, he took the steps two at a time.

'Rubin!' he shouted as he neared the top step. Although he didn't expect an answer, the eerie silence filled him with dread.

A moment later, he charged through the foyer with its massive court cabinet and hideous cuckoo clock into the flamboyantly panelled room. He came to a shuddering halt.

He was too late.

Rubin Woolf hung lifelessly from the ornate four-poster bed. Snow-white hair. Pale spindly limbs and rotund belly. Bulging tongue. A blue-tinged icicle suspended a foot above the floor. A 'gallows bird' dangling from an oak perch.

He fought the instinctive urge to recoil from the macabre sight. Instead, he closed his eyes, giving his mind a much-needed respite to take it all in. To process the horror of it all.

This was not the Rubin he knew. This was not the animated man who, less than twelve hours ago, had merrily quaffed a Martini while banging out 'London Calling' on the piano.

Opening his eyes, he glanced around the room. There was no blood. Not a single drop. Only a puddle of piss on the floor. He swallowed a mouthful of bile, nauseated. Unable to recall the last time he'd felt so powerless.

Horrified, he turned his head. Then he saw it . . . an

eight-pointed star neatly incised into the oak panel directly opposite. The same octogram star that had adorned the dagger hilt used to kill Jason Lovett.

Think, man! The bastard was obviously sending a message.

His shoulders slumped, grief, horror and bewilderment assaulting him in equal measure. *Why kill Rubin Woolf?* Since the Mylar-encased Bacon frontispiece was on the bed, in plain sight, he must assume that the killer knew about the Knights of the Helmet. And, quite possibly, the Emerald Tablet – although the bastard was probably in the dark about Benjamin Franklin. Meaning they were one step ahead. Still in the game.

He rubbed a hand over his cheek. *Good God, did I really just think that?* With Rubin's lifeless body dangling from the . . .

Cædmon tensed.

He felt rather than heard the vibration of a repeated footfall. *Someone was coming up the stairs.* The bastard had returned to claim another victim.

He turned his head from side to side, searching for a weapon. His gaze alighted on the upturned stool. The same stool that Rubin had stood upon in the moments before his death. Determined to smash the bastard's skull, Cædmon grabbed the stool by one of its spindle legs.

A split-second later, seeing a pink blur and a mass of curly dark hair, he immediately flung the stool aside, catching Edie in his arms as she burst into the room. Trying as best he could to shield her from the ghoulish scene.

'Don't look, love.'

The admonition came too late.

'No!' Edie gasped, violently shuddering in his arms.

Uncertain what to say, he said nothing. There was no flowery platitude that could erase so violent an image.

Long moments later, Edie pulled away from him, a shell-shocked expression on her face. 'There was no reason to kill . . .' She swung her head towards the foyer. 'Do you hear that?'

He listened. Then he heard it. A faint, but unmistakable, crackling sound. Accompanied by an unmistakable smell. *Smoke.*

He dashed to the foyer and out to the stairwell just beyond.

'I can see flames!' Edie screeched.

Indeed, a sprightly fire crackled and danced at the bottom of the steps, flames darting upward. *A fire-breathing dragon come to life!*

'We're trapped, aren't we?' Edie gestured wildly to the stairwell, pointing out the obvious – that the flames were quickly advancing, the wooden steps the perfect kindling.

'Get back in the room!' he ordered, grabbing Edie by the arm and forcibly pulling her away from the stairwell.

'We'll never get out of here alive! This is a bookshop. Meaning it's a tinder box ready to blow!'

Well aware that a raging inferno would soon engulf them unless they could put out the fire, he scanned the wood-panelled room. He needed something with which to smother the flames. Charging towards the window, he reached up and yanked the heavy velvet drapes off the wall, rod and all.

Ignoring Edie's wild-eyed stare, he dashed back to the stairwell. In the short time since he'd been gone, the flames had travelled nearly to the top of the stairs. Quickly he pulled the metal rod through the fabric. He then unfurled the fabric and laid the heavy swathe on top of the roaring flames.

Like humans, fire required oxygen to breathe. Cut the oxygen flow, kill the fire.

'Damn it,' he swore as the flames consumed the velvet drapery in a fiery burst. The soft crackle they'd heard a few moments ago was now a deadly roar.

His lungs filling with smoke, he hacked noisily. Reflexively crooking his elbow, he placed his bent arm over his mouth and nose as he backed away from the fire. *There were more flames in the stairwell than London during the Blitz.* The funeral pyre had been carefully planned to the last detail, the jumble of boxes at the foot of the steps having been set on fire. Probably soon after Edie ran up the stairs. For all he knew, the bastard had been in the bookshop the entire time. Waiting. Watching.

'Cædmon!'

'Window!' he hollered back at her. 'Quickly!'

Knowing it was their last line of retreat, he rushed towards the window, relieved to see a narrow ledge on the other side of the glass.

'We're a full storey above ground. We'll break our necks if we try to jump.'

'And we'll meet a fiery end if we don't,' he told Edie as he hurriedly unlatched the window. Legs straddled wide, he put a hand on either side of the wood rail and shoved upward.

'Bloody hell! It's painted shut!'

Edie began to cough. 'Fire . . . in the . . . foyer!' she gasped.

'Right.' Knowing they only had a few seconds before the menacing flames devoured the wood-panelled room – an incinerator in the making – he hurriedly shrugged out of his anorak. He then wrapped it around his right forearm and hand. 'Stand back!'

Order issued, he smashed through the glass with his heavily padded arm. It took a few seconds of determined bashing before he'd cleared all the jagged pieces out of the frame. As he unravelled the coat from his arm, he glanced over his shoulder. The fire was now lapping at Rubin's bare legs.

Grabbing Edie by the hand, he pulled her towards the opening. 'Out you go!'

A stricken expression on her face, Edie ducked her head through the window. Carefully holding on to the frame, she bent at the waist and swung a jean-clad leg through the opening. Seconds later, she was on the ledge.

In the near distance, Cædmon heard the blare of sirens.

'Probably best if you don't look down,' he warned her as he made his way through the window, hoping she didn't suffer from acrophobia. A few seconds later, hugging the painted brick exterior wall, he carefully sidled next to Edie. 'You all right, love?'

Brown eyes fearfully opened wide, she nodded. 'All things considered.' She attempted a brave smile. One that fell woefully shy of the mark.

A few feet from where they stood, tangerine flames darted through the open window.

Taking Edie gently by the wrist, he wordlessly coaxed her to side-step as far away from the window as possible.

They got no more than four feet before they were stopped by a chunky bit of architectural ornamentation. A coved bulwark that protruded from the exterior façade. There was no way to straddle the bloody thing without falling off the ledge.

Edie turned to him with a stricken expression. 'Now what?'

Excellent question.

He scanned Cecil Court. Pure pandemonium reigned in both directions. Several frantic book dealers ran towards Charing Cross, presumably to direct the fire brigade that had just pulled up at the end of the block and ensure they didn't lose their precious inventories. A cluster of gawking pedestrians had gathered near Rubin's shop, several of them holding up their mobiles, capturing the fire on video. Beneath them, the plate-glass window on the ground floor violently shattered, inciting several of the gawkers to scream.

'Wouldn't you know . . . not a ladder in sight,' Edie muttered.

'Although I see something that will do in a pinch.' About fifteen feet from the entrance to Rubin's bookshop, Cædmon sighted a sturdy waste bin.

'You there! Drag that waste receptacle under the ledge!' he shouted to a burly fellow who stood in the crowd. He gestured, first to the receptacle, then to a spot directly beneath the ledge. 'And be quick about it!' *Before our bloody arses catch fire.*

Beside him, Edie tensed, evidently sensing what he had in mind. 'The trash can only shaves off three feet. A fire truck's just pulled up at the end of the block. Let's wait.'

'Waiting isn't an option.' Already he could see that the flames shooting through the window had ignited the elaborate woodwork around the opening. A goodly amount of the exterior trim was made of wood and covered in oil-based paint. He feared that, all too soon, it would erupt in a fiery blaze. 'Don't worry, love. I'll go first.'

Normally, ladies would go first, but he knew that Edie didn't have the requisite upper body strength to maintain her grip while she lowered herself off the ledge. He had the strength and he was nine inches taller. With those advantages in his favour, he would be able to lower himself to the waste bin, then reach up and pluck Edie off the ledge. *Piece of cake*, as the Americans were fond of saying.

It ended up taking two men to roll the heavy receptacle in place.

Cædmon carefully pivoted so that he faced the painted brick wall behind him. Then, squatting, he grasped the edge of the ledge as he swung, first one leg, then the other, over the edge. For several seconds, he dangled, suspended in mid-air. An intense bolt of pain radiated out from the puncture wound on his left bicep. *Bloody hell.* Glancing down, he could see that the waste bin was directly beneath him. No more than a two-foot drop. The lid was made of metal with a round ten-inch opening in the middle. His plan was to land on the solid metal rim.

'Cædmon, be careful!' Edie called out. There was no mistaking the panic in her voice.

Hoping his aim was true, he let go of the ledge.

The two obliging chaps reached out just as he landed on top of the receptacle. Their steadying hands prevented him from toppling over the side.

There being no time to congratulate himself on a safe landing, he planted his feet squarely on either side of the sturdy bin. 'Edie, you need to lower yourself over the edge,' he instructed in a calm, measured tone. Hoping that would quell her fear.

Edie peered down at him, a determined gleam in her eyes.

That's my girl.

His heart in his throat, Cædmon watched as Edie slowly removed the oversized leather bag that was draped, bandolier-style, across her chest and let it drop to the ground. She then turned towards the brick wall directly behind her, keeping the flat of both hands in contact with the brick, as though that ephemeral connection would somehow hold her in place should she lose her balance.

The two stalwart bystanders who'd just aided his plunge stood at the ready.

Suddenly a blast shook the bookshop; the glass in the upper panes of the window shattered.

'Jump! Now!' Cædmon hollered.

'Oh, God!'

With that panic-stricken yell, Edie was airborne.

Three pairs of hands reached out for her.

Cædmon won the prize, snatching her at mid-waist. Relieved, he awkwardly held her tight, one hand splayed on her hip, the other wrapped around her backside. Behind him he heard hoarse cheers and exuberant clapping.

Glancing up, he saw that the ledge above was now consumed in fire.

He handed Edie to the hefty bloke standing to the left of him. As he leapt off the waste bin, he winced, the pain in his arm unbearable.

Shuffling over to Edie, he plastered a cocky grin on his face. If for no other reason than to mask the pain. 'A trial by fire, eh?'

The muscles in Edie's jaw clenched. Then, eyes narrowing, she raised her right hand. Catching him completely off guard, she slapped him across the face. *Hard.*

'You bastard!'

63

Manna from heaven, Mercurius thought as he watched a delicate swarm of cherry blossoms from his study window, haphazardly tossed in the morning breeze.

But, as he knew all too well, such splendours were suspect, both blossom and breeze animated with a dark fire.

His heart heavy, Mercurius turned away from the window. Because of Cædmon Aisquith's expansive breadth of knowledge, he'd had to make a painful decision. *For the greater good.* Although, *mercifully*, the Englishman had been unaware that there was a fourth stream of hidden knowledge; a disclosure contained within the pages of the *Luminarium*.

As he left the study and walked down the hall, he glanced at the grandfather clock in the foyer. *7:07*. The deed had been done. The secret was still safe.

When he'd been unceremoniously given the *Luminarium* seven years ago by the Greek crone, he'd quickly realized that Moshe Benaroya's handwritten manuscript was more than a fascinating text; it was a revelation of the secrets of the universe. Secrets that had been safeguarded by the Sephardic Kabbalists and, before them, the Levite priesthood. Those secrets had never been transcribed for fear they would fall into the wrong hands. Not until Moshe Benaroya put pen to paper in 1943.

Like many academics, Mercurius had been a card-carrying

secular humanist, firmly believing that morality was rooted in reason and justice, not supernatural mumbo-jumbo. But all that changed when he read the *Luminarium*. Comprised of three separate parts, the first, entitled *The Great Work*, was a lengthy commentary on the four streams of hidden knowledge.

According to Moshe Benaroya, the first stream was alchemy, a word derived from the phrase *al-khem* meaning 'from the land of Egypt'. The goal was to find the *Prima Materia* and to affect its physical alteration by transforming it into a different material substance. In the next stream, Kabbalah, the adherent calculated the numeric equivalences of the individual words and phrases of the Torah. And in the third stream, magic, the novice mastered the art of crafting protective amulets and seals based on the Mogen David hexagram.

In actuality, it was a misnomer to refer to these three streams of knowledge as 'hidden' since seers, soothsayers and students of the arcane had been practising the proscribed rituals for centuries. But as Moshe Benaroya tellingly revealed, these three streams were merely a smokescreen. A carefully contrived decoy. Indeed, a man could devote a lifetime to studying alchemy, Kabbalah and magic – and many did – blissfully unaware that there was a fourth stream. Well hidden from the uninitiated, and with good cause, the fourth stream contained the secret of creation.

Moshe Benaroya named this fourth stream of sacred knowledge the Divine Harmonic.

The sacred sounds intrinsic to the letters of the Hebrew alphabet are at the heart of the mystery, each of the twenty-two letters of the *Otiyot Yesod* animated with its own unique vibration. This was the reason why the Hebrew word for 'letter', *ot*, also meant pulse or vibration. When the letters were sounded out in a prescribed sequence, these sacred utterances initiated a flow of vibrational energy. Not only is sound a fundamental element of the universe, but everything in the universe vibrates. And it was vibrating clusters of energy bound together that created mass.

This vibrational energy was the basis for creation.

According to the *Luminarium*, our world came into existence through the Divine Harmonic, the entire creation dependent upon a sequence of non-verbal utterances or *kol*. Before God ever recited the words 'Let there be light', he made a series of inarticulate sounds that created the vibrational energy that *created* 'the light'. This was why 'In the beginning, God created the heavens and the earth' transpired *before* the Almighty uttered a single coherent word. Furthermore, the Hebrew word for that phrase 'In the beginning', *Bereshit*, can also be translated as 'He created six'. Sound moves outward in a spherical wave. And the wave *always* travels simultaneously in *six* different directions.

Adept at using the fourth stream, the patriarch Moses knew that by changing the energy vibration through sound, mass is either altered or destroyed. Moses used the Divine Harmonic to perform every single one of his so-called 'miracles'.

In Exodus 14, the famous story of the parting of the Red Sea is recounted. Students of the Bible, and fans of old Charlton Heston movies, know that 600,000 Hebrew slaves stood stranded on the banks of the mighty sea, the

Pharaoh's army in pursuit. Suddenly, a pillar of cloud appeared near the Hebrews' flank, casting a dark shadow that the Egyptians could not penetrate. In that instant, Moses extended his hand over the waters, causing a gale-force wind to drive back the sea, enabling the Hebrews to cross the exposed seabed.

What the story fails to mention is that it wasn't God who parted the sea; it was Moses.

And Moses, who authored the Book of Exodus, arrogantly gave the secret away in the biblical text. The tale is told in three verses, 19–21, each verse containing *exactly* seventy-two letters – the actual code! Albeit cleverly scrambled. The story also failed to mention that while Moses stood on the banks of the Red Sea, he chanted the sequenced code of seventy-two letters. The change in the vibrational energy current was what parted the Red Sea. *The Divine Harmonic.* An ancient technology whose roots extended back to Atlantis.

As the Hebrew tribes began their conquest of the Sinai, Moses used this ancient technology repeatedly, enabling the 'Chosen People' to crush every army that came between them and the Promised Land. Nine thousand years before that, Thoth used the same technology to destroy the continent of Atlantis.

Create. Transform. Destroy.

All of which proved that the process of creation, or an act of cataclysmic destruction, could be put into motion by a mere mortal. No omnipotent god required. A man had only to utter the correct sound sequence to alter the vibrational energy that permeated the entire universe. Any man could do it. Provided he had the encryption key to unlock the sequenced code contained on the Emerald Tablet, the relic encoded with a complex pictograph comprised of symbols, letters and glyphs.

Not only did Moses possess the encryption key, but he taught it to the Levis, the hereditary Hebrew priesthood. Committing the key to memory, for generations the Levis passed the secret from father to son. Because of the inherent power contained within the sound vibration, they were expressly forbidden from transcribing the key. The Levite priests and, later, the Sephardic Kabbalists, didn't dare cross the line that the patriarch had drawn in the Sinai sands more than three thousand years earlier.

Until Moshe Benaroya valiantly defied the patriarch and transcribed the key in the *Luminarium.*

Part Two of his courageous manuscript, entitled *The Key*, contained a detailed formulary for the Emerald Tablet – a sequential equation that, if correctly applied, would alter the vibrational energy of the universe. But the undertaking wasn't for the faint-hearted. It had taken Mercurius years to master the correct tone for each letter of the Hebrew alphabet. Years of laborious practice before he could move effortlessly through the *Otiyot Yesod.*

Opening a door at the end of the hallway, Mercurius entered a windowless room. Ten cubits by ten cubits. A faithful recreation of the Holy of Holies, the Kodesh Kodashim. Painted gold, the letters of the Hebrew alphabet were stencilled on the wall. Here, each morning, he practised the sacred chant. Over and over.

Barukh hamelamed et yadi lesapper et ha'otiyot.

'Blessed is the One who has taught my hand to scribe the letters!' he softly murmured.

Removing his red babouche slippers, he seated himself on the room's only piece of furniture, a hardback chair, bare feet firmly planted on the floor. As he stared at the twenty-two stencilled letters, he tightened his abdominal muscles, preparing his diaphragm. He breathed deeply, filling his lungs with air before pushing the exhalation through his nostrils. Controlled breathing was vital to the correct execution of the chant.

In Part Three of the *Luminarium*, entitled *The Deception*, Moshe Benaroya revealed how the patriarch Moses profaned and corrupted the sacred knowledge, using the Divine Harmonic to commit heinous acts of unimaginable brutality. The dark energy created during Moses' bloodthirsty rule had yet to dissipate. That dark energy was a curse suffered anew by each generation of innocent victims. *This* was the reason why Moshe Benaroya violated the ancient restriction.

That long ago day when the Greek crone unexpectedly gave him the *Luminarium*, Mercurius had had an epiphany. After nearly seven decades, he *finally* knew his life's purpose. Moshe Benaroya had written a magnificent sacred text, but had been killed before he could use the ancient knowledge for the greater good.

His life purpose, *his mission*, was to find the Emerald Tablet and use the encryption key to extinguish the dark fire that permeated the earth.

Like his forebears, Mercurius was fearless.

He'd lived long enough to know that evil could not be contained; it had to be destroyed. Only then could the Bringer of Light illuminate the way back to the Lost Heaven where all souls originated and where we all yearned to return. That luminous place where the Light dwelt.

Where there was no hatred or brutality.

Where children weren't raped or women murdered.

Where no one had to live in dread fear of being dragged away in the middle of the night. Of having a gun put to his head. Or a noose slipped around the neck.

If he had the Emerald Tablet, he could activate the harmonic sequence that would end all suffering. For all time.

That was the message that Osman de Léon and his milk brother Moshe Beneroya had imparted to him before the SS officer forcibly led them to the train station on that fateful night in 1943.

'You must always remember, little one, that you were named for the Bringer of the Light.'

'Do not fear the Light, Merkür. For it will lead you to your life's purpose.'

About to begin the sacred ritual, Mercurius stopped in mid-breath, his revelries disturbed by a ringing telephone. Given the early hour, it could only be one person calling – his *amoretto*, Saviour.

Hurriedly, he padded, barefoot, to the nearest telephone, the one on the hallway credenza.

Moments later, he listened intently as Saviour, in a highly agitated state, briefed him about what had transpired in the last few hours.

The well-laid plan that they had concocted the previous night had only been partially successful.

'A moment, please,' he told his *amoretto*, his heart painfully thumping against his chest. He placed the phone on the credenza.

Bending at the waist, he placed his hands on his thighs, gripped with a sudden case of vertigo. He closed his eyes.

Took several deep breaths. *Dear Lord.* He could *hear* the pain-wracked screams of all the victims. Too innumerable to count.

The shrieks. The sobs. The agonized bellows. A hideous cacophony of suffering.

The persecuted masses.

Oh, the horror of it!

Mercurius put his hands over his ears, trying to block out the anguished dissonance. To no avail. The screams and shrieks only got that much louder.

Building towards an unbearable crescendo.

'Deliver us from evil!'

'Yes! Yes! I intend to do just that,' he gasped aloud. To deliver the world from the evil energy that was all-pervasive. To shepherd the pain-wracked souls of mankind *home* to the Lost Heaven.

It had been done once before. In Atlantis, millenniums ago. It could be done again. It *had* to be done again.

Yes! Fearless.

Determined to fulfil his sacred purpose, the Light Bringer grabbed the cordless phone.

64

'I deserved that.'

Edie stared at the red imprint of her hand on Cædmon's left cheek. 'You deserve a lot worse than that. An innocent man is dead because—' Choking back a sob, she placed her hand over her mouth. A few feet away, firefighters decked out in maroon and yellow held a long hose as they blasted the exterior of Woolf's Antiquarian Books with water.

'I'm sorry, love.' Cædmon put a comforting hand on her shoulder.

'Not good enough. You should have warned Rubin that there's a killer on the loose who will do *anything* to get his hands on the Emerald Tablet.' Shaking her head, she gasped, still horrified by what she'd seen in Rubin's boudoir. 'God! Why didn't you tell him about Rico Suave?'

'I had no way of knowing that the bastard followed us to London. So, yes, *mea maxima culpa*.'

Hearing his apology – *in Latin!* – made her livid. 'Go to hell!' she retorted, shrugging off his hand.

'At the moment, neither of us is going anywhere.' Cædmon jutted his chin at the quartet of police officers who were busy cordoning off the area near the bookshop. 'No doubt, the quiz masters at the London Fire Brigade and Scotland Yard will want to interrogate us thoroughly.' Taking her by the elbow, he steered her away from the frantic flow of pedestrians, firefighters and paramedics.

Edie stooped to pick up the shoulder bag that she'd earlier flung to the ground. 'Any idea what we should tell the authorities?'

'As little as possible.' Cædmon shepherded her into the doorway of a print and map shop, closed for business on account of it being a Sunday. 'Best to keep answers to a minimum. We were visiting an old friend. Yes, he had many valuable books on the premises. Since we barely survived the inferno, there should be no finger pointing in our direction.'

'What if we're grilled?' She stopped herself from saying 'over the fire'.

'My old group leader at MI5 will see to it that we're cleared in short order.'

Friends in high places. Must be nice.

'And I don't advise mentioning the video,' Cædmon continued, his eyes glued to the devastated bookshop across the way. 'A bit too much spice in the ragout. Especially if Scotland Yard discovers we were present at Jason Lovett's murder five days ago. Thames House will cover for me on this side of the Atlantic but that's as far as they'll go. And they won't be happy about traversing that distance.'

'So we tell them that we found Rubin hanging from – oh, my God!' Edie raised her arm and pointed to the stylishly dressed blonde woman running down Cecil Court. 'It's Marnie!' Putting a hand on his back, she shoved Cædmon out of the doorway. 'Don't let her see this!'

No one should have to witness so horrific a scene of death.

No, not death – *murder.*

Cædmon ran towards Marnie, catching her in his arms.

Standing in the doorway, Edie watched as Marnie, frantically trying to escape, began to scream hysterically. Tears welled in her eyes, the other woman's pain so tangible, so gut-wrenching, she could feel it from a distance.

Not wishing to be an intruder to Marnie's grief, she turned her head and examined the wares in the shop window, feigning an interest in a rare and exorbitantly expensive cartoon from *Punch* magazine. Out of the corner of her eye she saw Cædmon turn Marnie over to the rescue workers who, in turn, wrapped a blanket around her shoulders before leading her to an ambulance parked at the end of the court.

'The bastard ought to be strung up by his entrails,' Cædmon muttered a few moments later, rejoining her. 'Such a waste of blood and treasure.' He sighed wearily. 'My God, what a gruelling day.'

'Like so many of your countrymen, you have a gift for understatement.'

Rather than reply, Cædmon turned his head, presenting his face in profile.

'What are you doing?'

'It's called turning the other cheek,' he informed her.

Belatedly realizing that she'd behaved like a teenage drama queen, Edie smoothed her hand over the proffered cheek. 'So how did Rico Suave find us?' Suddenly cold, she sidled closer to him.

'Obviously, he's been tracking us since we arrived. Probably followed us from Rhode Island.'

'It's crazy . . . we don't even know his name. He's just a pretty face with a big murky question mark superimposed over his forehead.'

'According to Marnie, yesterday she met a beautiful young man who hails from Thessaloniki, of all places. Do you have the mobile?'

She reached into the pocket of her trench coat and removed the cell phone, handing it to him.

As he examined the cherry-red phone, a crease materialized between his brows. 'Marnie's, I believe. She mentioned that it was pinched yesterday evening. She noticed it missing after she spent the night with the aforementioned young man.'

'You're kidding me! Marnie actually slept with Rico Suave? But he's . . . he's a cold-blooded killer,' she sputtered, stunned by the revelation.

'A fact of which she is blissfully ignorant. Moreover, she has no idea that her Greek lover was involved with Rubin's murder. I'm assuming that in addition to lifting her mobile, the bastard also nicked the key to the bookshop.' He flipped open the cell phone. Manoeuvring through the NAV keys, he replayed the video. He turned slightly, preventing her from viewing the ghoulish imagery. A few moments later, he snapped the phone shut. 'I don't know if you noticed, but there was an eight-pointed star incised in one of the wooden panels.'

'That's the same symbol that was on the knife used to kill Jason Lovett.'

'The eight-pointed octogram is a Judeo-Christian pictogram of the Creation. Composed of two interlacing squares, it symbolizes the seven days of Genesis followed by the eighth day of regeneration in the newly created Paradise.' As he spoke, Cædmon absently rubbed his hand over his reddened cheek. 'The fact that the killer uses the octogram so freely implies that he is aware of the so-called Genesis code that's encrypted on the Emerald Tablet.'

'Please don't tell me that after all of *this* –' Edie gestured to the chaotic crush of rescue workers and spectators – 'we're still going to Philly.'

'If I don't go, Rubin will have died in vain.'

'Time out.' She made a T with her hands. 'I think we're getting *way* ahead of ourselves. We don't know if the Emerald Tablet actually contains a Genesis code. That has yet to be verified. Meaning it's still very much a speculative premise.'

'I can't take the chance that Rubin's killer will find the relic,' Cædmon countered, a determined look on his face. 'Twelve thousand years ago, an entire continent *vanished* from the face of the planet. Obliterated. The Genesis code that's embedded on the Emerald Tablet may have triggered the catastrophe.'

'But you said it yourself, without the encryption key the Emerald Tablet has no power.' No sooner did she utter those words than Edie was hit with a horrifying thought. '*Oh, God!* You're worried that Rico Suave has the encryption key.'

'Or the group that he's working for is in possession of it . . . yes, the thought has crossed my mind.'

'So, who is Rico Suave's employer?'

Cædmon shrugged. 'A rogue nation. Or perhaps a terrorist cell. Even a lone madman is a terrifying prospect if the madman has the motive and the means to *create* the primeval atom.'

'Because the Big Bang only needs one exploding atom,' she quietly murmured, the dread escalating.

'Surely, you understand why I must fly to Philadelphia?'

'Telling me there are six universes parallel to this one doesn't mean that I understand quantum physics. Not to mention you used the singular "I" instead of the plural "we".'

'When I call Thames House, I'll arrange to have you taken to—'

She put a silencing hand over his mouth. 'Don't waste your breath. I'm going with you.' Point made, she lowered the makeshift gag.

'Right.' He acquiesced with a grim nod. 'In all honesty, I don't know where the clues contained within *The Book of Moses* will take us. If anywhere. After two hundred and thirty-five years, the trail is a bit cold. Our search may very well begin and end at the American Philosophical Society. What we do know is that Franklin intended to conscript two accomplices to help him safeguard the Emerald Tablet. The Triad, as he called it.'

'And he planned to use the Second Continental Congress as his recruiting office.' Suddenly realizing the significance of that, she gasped. 'Meaning that all of the members of the Triad were signatories to the Declaration of Independence.'

65

'... we mutually pledge to each other our lives, our fortunes and our sacred honor.'

On the sheet of parchment, beneath those immortal words, were penned fifty-six signatures beginning with the most flamboyant, that of John Hancock, the president of the Second Continental Congress. Several of the names were famous, others known only to students of American history. All were considered 'Founding Fathers' of the fledging nation that on 4 July, 1776, officially took its place on the world stage.

'A daunting task, eh?'

Tell me something I don't already know, Edie despondently thought, making no reply to Cædmon's wry observation.

Sitting side by side at the library table, an open book placed squarely between them, they stared at a copy of the Declaration of Independence. Next to the library book was a new Dell netbook computer, a small stack of plain white paper and four sharpened lead pencils – the only supplies permitted in the reading room at Philadelphia's Library Hall. Located around the corner from Independence Hall – where the Second Continental Congress met in 1776 – Library Hall was owned by the American Philosophical Society. As with the parent, the library had been founded by Benjamin Franklin.

Edie's gaze alighted on the top sheet of paper which was noticeably blank. If a picture was worth a thousand words, that blank sheet of paper did not bode well.

Not quite ready to throw in the towel, she said, 'We're looking at the signatures of the best and brightest men the colonies had to offer. A list that includes men from all walks: lawyers, farmers, businessmen and professional politicians. We know that Benjamin Franklin intended to recruit two men from this group to help him safeguard the Emerald Tablet.'

'The Triad,' Cædmon said in a lowered voice. The floor-to-ceiling bookcases, Georgian windows and colonial-style chandeliers invited reverential tones.

'Any idea how to whittle down the list?' She pasted a chipper smile on her face, hoping the non-stop flight from London to Philly wouldn't prove a colossal waste of time, energy and money.

Cædmon thoughtfully stared at the open book. 'I suspect that Franklin's Triad would not have included any Freemasons,' he said after a lengthy pause. Then, smiling slightly, 'Aside from the wise sage of Craven Street himself.'

'I agree. It would defeat his purpose to have an initiated fox stand sentry. And Franklin made it very clear in *The Book of Moses* that he considered the Freemasons "a superstitious coven of sun-worshipping Atenists and bewigged magi".'

'His own membership in the group was simply a means to an end. A way to get his leather-shod foot in the drawing-room door.'

'The old coot was wily, I'll give him that,' Edie said with a chuckle, still amused at how Franklin pilfered the

Emerald Tablet. 'We should be able to find an online list of signatories to the Declaration of Independence who were also Freemasons.'

'Right.' Cædmon deftly pecked away on the computer keyboard. Because of his publishing credentials, he'd managed to secure a researcher's pass for the both of them, the library being open only to academics. 'There you have it, the rogue's gallery,' he announced a few moments later, jutting his chin at the roster of names on the computer screen.

William Whipple	William Ellery	William Hooper
John Hancock	Richard Stockton	Joseph Hewes
Robert Treat Paine	Benjamin Franklin	George Walton

'Our task has been rendered slightly less daunting.'

Edie examined the list of Freemason-slash-Founding Fathers. 'Just so you know, there's no doubt in my mind that every one of these guys was a loyal patriot,' she avowed, refusing to sling mud. Even at a 'sun-worshipping Atenist'.

'What you reckon as patriotism, King George and his ministers deemed treason.'

Not wanting to fight another revolution, Edie decided a change of subject was in order. 'Okay, we've reduced the roll-call to forty-seven signatories. Which is still a far cry from Franklin's two-man tag team.'

'Not to fear, I have another trick up my sleeve.' Blue eyes mischievously twinkling, Cædmon's fingers furiously pecked away at the keyboard.

'What are you doing?'

'Accessing the member database for the American Philosophical Society. In those turbulent months leading up to the final break with Britain, loyalties were shifting and uncertain. Franklin couldn't be too careful in his selection.'

'I seem to recall from a long-ago history lesson that Franklin's own son William, who happened to be the governor of New Jersey, remained loyal to the Crown. So, what are you thinking? That Franklin would have recruited the other two members of the Triad in-house?' Raising her arms, Edie gestured to the four walls of the reading room. 'Specifically, *this* house.'

Still typing, Cædmon nodded. 'Franklin was searching for two trustworthy, like-minded men possessed of "a keen intellect and a stalwart heart".'

'Given that the American Philosophical Society was Franklin's homegrown answer to the Royal Society, all of the members would have satisfied the first criteria.'

'However, unlike its English template, Franklin was determined that his society would be free of the elitist taint associated with the Royal Society. Ah! I give you the American Philosophical Society circa 1776.' Cædmon gestured expansively to the monitor.

John Adams	Benjamin Rush	Francis Lightfoot Lee
Stephen Hopkins	Benjamin Franklin	Thomas Jefferson
John Witherspoon	George Clymer	John Penn
Francis Hopkinson	James Wilson	Thomas Heyward, Jr
Robert Morris	Thomas McKean	

'At least, all the members who signed the Declaration of Independence.' Edie quickly took a head count. 'Including

Franklin, I get fourteen fellas.' She grabbed a pencil and jotted all fourteen names on to a sheet of paper. Then she opened *The Book of Moses* file on the laptop. Since they couldn't bring any outside materials into the library, except for the computer, she'd taken digital photos and downloaded them on to the Dell. She quickly scrolled to the last page. Gnawing on her lower lip, she ruminated on Franklin's checklist of 'suitable' criteria. 'We're trying to unravel a 235-year-old mystery, but coming at it backward.'

'I admit we have scant clues to go on. And the few crumbs that Franklin drops are interspersed with political sound bites. Take this, for example –' using his fingertip, he underscored the last line of handwritten text – '"Rebellion to tyrants is obedience to God." Makes me want to dress up like an Indian and toss a crate of tea into Boston Harbour.'

Edie absently folded a sheet of blank paper. 'Okay, let's suppose for argument's sake that Ben *did* invite two fellow members of the American Philosophical Society to join his Triad. There's a very good chance the guys simply hid the darned thing right here at Library Hall, concealed within the bowels of the building.' Which, according to the pamphlet she'd picked up in the lobby, housed over 350,000 volumes and bound periodicals, eleven million manuscripts and nearly a quarter of a million images including a massive collection of Franklin's papers, as well as his personal library. The proverbial haystack.

'You'll be disappointed to know that Library Hall was constructed in the mid-twentieth century,' Cædmon informed her.

'You're kidding! I would've sworn this was a colonial-era building.'

'A very convincing reproduction, I'm afraid. And the building across the street, which is the official headquarters for the American Philosophical Society, was constructed in 1789. Twelve years *after* the Second Continental Congress disbanded. So while Dr Franklin may have transported the Emerald Tablet to Philadelphia, I suspect the City of Brotherly Love was merely a way station.'

'Great.' Edie glanced down, bemused to see that she'd made a paper airplane. Hit with a childish impulse to send it sailing across the room, she instead shoved back her chair and rose to her feet. 'I need a time-out.'

'I'm not about to let you gallivant on your own. I'll accompany you.'

'To the ladies' room? I think not.' She put a staying hand on his shoulder. 'Besides, I don't intend to gallivant any farther than the lobby.'

'The bastard followed us to London. He could have followed us to—'

'But he *didn't*. We were *very* careful,' she said over the top of him, hoping to nip his concern in the bud. While endearing, she didn't need a bodyguard. She was a big girl and they were in a public building. 'Now excuse me while I go to the loo.'

Not giving Cædmon a chance to protest, she did a military-style turn and headed for the exit.

In the lobby – the only area of the library open to the public – a group of school-age children were being ushered past an exhibit entitled 'Franklin: Man of Many Words'. As near as she could tell, the exhibit consisted of various pieces of ephemera displayed in glass cases. A generation acclimatized to the visual overload of the Digital Age, the kiddies were clearly bored out of their bonkers. She suppressed a chuckle.

Moments later, about to ask the attendant for directions to the restroom, Edie stopped in her tracks. Out of the corner of her eye, she caught sight of a blown-up excerpt mounted inside one of the display cases.

She did a double-take, stunned at seeing a very recognizable phrase . . . '*Rebellion to tyrants is obedience to God.*'

66

'I think I know the names of the other two Triad members,' Edie blurted without preamble, setting a large leather-bound book on the library table.

Cædmon glanced up from the computer. 'Indeed?'

'Yes, indeedy. But first a quick American history lesson.' Cheeks flushed with impassioned colour, she shoved her hand into her jeans pocket and removed a crumpled one-dollar bill which she slapped on to the tabletop, backside on display. '*This* is the Great Seal of the United States that was approved by Congress in the year 1782.' With her index finger, she indicated the two circular medallions that adorned the left and right side of the note.

His curiosity piqued, Cædmon examined the familiar green-and-white bill; American currency was famous the world over. 'I've always been fascinated with the blatant esoteric symbolism engraved on your paper money,' he remarked, his attentive gaze landing on the unfinished pyramid, the Latin mottoes and the All-Seeing Eye. The last had become something of a perennial bloom, the ancient symbol popping up with disturbing frequency.

'According to the library attendant, between the years 1776 and 1782, three separate congressional committees submitted design ideas for the Great Seal of the United States. Congress rejected all three designs.'

'And what does this have to do with our signatories?'

Next to the laptop was the list of prime suspects: the thirteen members of the American Philosophical Society, all of whom were signatories to the Declaration of Independence.

'Well, it just so happens that the first of the three Great Seal committees was formed on fourth July, 1776, the very day that the Declaration of Independence was signed. And guess what? The 1776 committee recommended that the country's new motto should be "Rebellion to tyrants is obedience to God".'

Hearing that, his heart rate spiked, Edie having just spilled a bag of gilded beans. Again, he glanced at the list that they'd compiled, wondering if any of the members of the American Philosophical Society had been on the 1776 Great Seal committee.

'Now this is where the story gets *really* interesting.' Opening the volume she'd brought with her, Edie quickly flipped through the pages. 'This book contains the minutes of the Continental Congress for the year 1776. The librarian was kind enough to pull it from the stacks.' A few moments later, excitedly tapping an open page, she drew his attention to two printed lines of text. 'Look! There it is! The official congressional entry: "Resolved, that Dr Franklin, Mr J. Adams and Mr Jefferson, be a committee, to bring in a device for a seal for the United States of America."'

'My God . . . I don't bloody believe it.'

Edie turned to him, beaming. 'Unless I'm greatly mistaken, we have our three Triad members.' Grabbing a pencil, she circled three names on their handwritten list: Benjamin Franklin, John Adams and Thomas Jefferson.

'As you can see, all three men were members of the American Philosophical Society.'

'Adams and Jefferson . . . the catheti to Franklin's hypotenuse,' he murmured, recalling a line from *The Book of Moses*: '*I must find the catheti to my hypotenuse.*'

'In 1776, Franklin became a septuagenarian. Old by any man's measure. In youthful contrast, Adams was forty-one years of age, Jefferson a mere thirty-three,' Edie remarked, fast proving herself a fount. 'Both men were young enough to do the physical legwork to safeguard the Emerald Tablet.'

'Without question, Franklin snared the best of a very fine lot.'

'While I can't lay claim to being an expert in American history, I do know that Franklin, Jefferson and Adams also served on the committee that wrote the Declaration of Independence, the famous document having the input of all three men. *And*, here's the real kicker –' she paused dramatically to ensure his full attention – 'to a man, they were dyed-in-the-wool Deists.'

'Advocating the light of reason, the hidden stream of knowledge consigned to history's rubbish heap.' Hit with a guilty twinge, he glanced at the silver signet on his right ring finger. 'Franklin's committee must have submitted a design for the Great Seal. Do you by any chance know if there's a record of it?'

Broadly grinning, she pulled a single sheet of loose paper from the volume's inside cover. 'One step ahead of you, Big Red. I had the librarian photocopy this and –' she slapped the sheet in front of him – 'guess what? The Triad put the All-Seeing Eye on the design!'

Astounded, his jaw slackened.

As with the emblems on the back of the dollar bill, there were two separate drawings, comprising the front and the back of the proposed Great Seal. On the face side were Lady Liberty and Lady Justice crowned with the All-Seeing Eye. On the reverse, a detailed drawing of Moses parting the Red Sea emblazoned with Franklin's catch-phrase, 'Rebellion to tyrants is obedience to God.' The *gratin* on the casserole.

'Do you think the Moses reference has anything to do with Franklin's espionage activity in London?' Edie asked, her attention also drawn to the biblical scene. 'After all, Moses was his code name.'

'Rather tongue-in-cheek, don't you think? I suspect the biblical scene has more to do with the ragtag American colonies severing their ties with the English monarch. This design was, after all, conceived shortly after the Declaration had been signed. Shackles shucked, the Americans will now venture forth to find the Promised Land.'

'I don't know about you, but there's no doubt in *my* mind that the 1776 Great Seal is one of Franklin's "sign-posts".'

'Mmmm . . . an intriguing notion.' Transfixed, he stared at the photocopied seal as he wrapped his mind around the various pieces of the puzzle.

'What I don't get is this business about the All-Seeing Eye. As Deists, Franklin, Jefferson and Adams spurned the superstition and ritual of the ancient religions. So why include a symbol on the Great Seal that so brazenly harkens to Thoth, the Radiant Light of Aten and the hidden stream of knowledge?'

'It does add "a precious seeing to the eye". Perhaps the All-Seeing Eye is a red herring,' he suggested.

Edie nodded. 'For nearly fifty years, Franklin had the Bacon frontispiece in his possession. Not to mention that he was the Grand Master of the Philadelphia Lodge. Knowing the All-Seeing Eye was highly symbolic within esoteric circles, he could have used the symbol as a smoke-screen. He knew the Freemasons would be searching high and low for the stolen relic so he cloaked himself in the magi's mantle. "Don't look at me. I didn't steal it. I'm a Freemason in good standing."' She chuckled. 'You're right. Benjamin Franklin *was* a brilliant boffin.'

'And, as I recall, something of an amateur cryptologist.'

Edie grabbed a sharpened pencil and a blank sheet of paper. 'Okay, where do we start?'

'Given that Dr Franklin purposely hid *The Book of Moses*, we must assume *that* is the first signpost. What connects the secret missive to the proposal for the 1776 Great Seal is—'

'"Rebellion to tyrants is obedience to God,"' she interjected, transcribing the motto on to the sheet of paper. 'Making it the *second* signpost.'

'Perhaps.' Unlike Edie – who tended to hurl herself at a conclusion – Cædmon preferred a more circumspect approach. 'There's a possibility that the phrase is an anagram.'

'Oh, I get it. You think the letters of the motto can be rearranged to make another phrase.'

He grabbed a pencil and began scribbling several word combinations. 'We'll need to shake the tree and see if any fruit falls from the limb.'

'I like "God" and "stone",' Edie said, leaning over his shoulder to examine the list.

'As do I.' He stared at the remaining twenty-six letters, wondering if they'd undertaken an impossible task. 'This may take some time.'

It did. Three hours and fourteen minutes, to be precise. As well as four sharpened pencils and ten sheets of paper.

Physically exhausted and mentally drained, Cædmon turned to Edie. 'Well, what do you think? I know, it's not perfect.'

REBELLION TO TYRANTS IS OBEDIENCE TO GOD

=

BIBLICIL ATEN STONE TO GODS EYE DO NOT ERR

Cædmon underscored the first word with his finger. 'This may be an archaic or variant spelling of the word "biblical".'

Edie chuckled. 'Personally? I think it's a colonial typo.'

'Whether it's a typo or a variant spelling, I think we've found our second "signpost".'

'I agree,' his partner enthused. 'The "biblicil aten stone" obviously refers to the Emerald Tablet, which *used* to be kept in the Ark of the Covenant. And "Gods eye" is clearly a reference to the All-Seeing Eye. Together, they form a flashing neon signpost that leads to . . .' Edie frowned, her voice trailing into silence.

'As you have just surmised, we've reached an impasse.'

Because without a bloody map, the newly discovered signpost was meaningless.

67

'"The pale ghost escapes from the vanquished pyre,"' Cædmon murmured, glancing about the Christ Church burial grounds.

Standing beside him at the gravesite, Edie shuddered. 'The joint definitely feels haunted. As in "Who ya gonna call?"'

Having left Library Hall, they'd been en route to their hotel when Cædmon had espied a placard publicizing the great one's gravesite. Of like mind, they'd nipped inside the cemetery, hoping to find a 'signpost' inscribed on Dr Franklin's last resting place. Perhaps a cleverly worded epitaph. Or an ingeniously designed emblem.

Instead they discovered the humble inscription: '*Benjamin Franklin and Deborah. 1790.*' Husband and wife buried side by side, each grave marked with a simple stone slab, no mention of Franklin's brilliant achievements. *Ashes to ashes.*

Digital camera in hand, Edie snapped several photos of the conjoined slabs. 'A teensy clue would have been nice.'

'I, too, had hoped for a snippet,' he admitted, well aware that while they'd deciphered the Great Seal anagram, they had no idea how to parlay the secret message into something concrete.

Moses. The Knights Templar. Sir Francis Bacon. And

Benjamin Franklin. *The magus. The warrior monks. The alchemist. The Deist.* Separated by the centuries, they were bound, one to the other, through a complex web of symbols and secrets.

'*Biblicil aten stone to Gods eye do not err.*' What the bloody hell did it mean?

Glancing at the burial slab, he plaintively sighed.

Pivoting in his direction, Edie took his photo. 'I'm going to label that pic "Cædmon in pensive mode". Since there's no All-Seeing Eye on the tombstone, we can assume that ol' Ben didn't take the Emerald Tablet to the grave.'

'Damn. I shall have to scratch that possibility off the list,' he good-naturedly grumbled.

As Edie continued to take photos, Cædmon took a moment to survey the grounds. Serene in the way that old cemeteries often are, the two-acre brick-walled enclave was also curiously surreal. On the near horizon, looming office buildings cast dark shadows on to the marble yard and in the near distance the erratic rumble of car engines lulled the dead to sleep. The pungent odour from a hot-dog vendor's cart combined with exhaust fumes, the fused scents wafting over the brick enclosure.

'This is going to sound strange, but I have no idea where my mother is buried. Somewhere in Orlando, I suppose.' Edie lowered the camera from her face, enabling him to see that she had a deep pucker between her brows. 'Is there still such a thing as a pauper's grave?'

Startled by the candid remarks followed by the unexpected query, he fumbled a bit. 'Er, yes, no doubt cemeteries still maintain a paupers' section.' '*For the poor always ye have with you*,' he thought, but didn't say, not wanting to unintentionally cause offence. Then, inspired, he said, 'I could help you locate the gravesite.'

The pucker deepened. 'Why? She's not there. She was never there. You know, high on arrival.'

Cædmon presumed the odd remark referred to her mother's heroin overdose.

'The here and now, that's all we have,' Edie continued as she stowed the digital camera in her shoulder satchel. 'Take your pleasures where you can because tomorrow the sheriff's deputy might slap an eviction notice on the trailer door. Although don't get me wrong, there were times when my mother and I were very tight. Just two little hamsters on the wheel of life.' Smiling wistfully, she made a twirling motion with her fingers.

He placed a hand on her shoulder and pulled her towards him, wrapping his arms around her fuchsia-clad torso. His Edie. *So beautiful. So intrepid.* And at times so incredibly fragile.

'I didn't say that to elicit your sympathy.'

'I know.' He rested his chin on top of her head.

'Change of subject: is it just me, or is there something weirdly seductive about being in a graveyard?' Tilting her head, Edie peered up at him as she slid her hands under his wool blazer. 'No need to answer. Your heartbeat just accelerated a notch.'

'Close contact has that effect.'

She affected a disappointed moué. 'Here I thought we had something special, but it seems that a close encounter with *any* woman can—'

'Not true,' he interjected, pulling her even closer. 'And

you're the only woman of my acquaintance who can do *this* to me.' He purposefully pressed himself against her mid-section.

'Oh, my. Now *my* pulse just quickened.'

Throwing back his head, he laughed.

'Hel-lo! That remark was supposed to turn you on, not make you laugh uproariously.'

'My apologies.' He softly nuzzled the corner of her mouth before moving to a flushed cheek, then a shell-coloured lobe, all the while breathing in her scent, a heady vanilla. Raising a hand, he smoothed a flyaway curl from her face.

Quite brazenly, Edie pushed her breasts against his chest, bringing the two of them into even closer contact. '*Now* you may kiss me.'

'Thy will be done.'

However, not as she may have intended. For what began as a sweetly romantic kiss quickly snowballed into something decidedly carnal. A passionate kaleidoscope of twisting mouths, grasping hands and muffled whimpers.

Aware of their surroundings, he reluctantly brought it to a breathless close.

An impassioned silence vibrated between them, accentuated by the strains of Spanish flamenco from a street musician giving an impromptu concert on the other side of the brick wall.

Edie heaved a lusty sigh. 'Wow . . . almost like a mariachi band playing under my balcony window.'

His mood greatly improved, Caedmon took Edie by the elbow and steered her away from the great man's gravesite. 'Fancy a stroll?'

'Think we should risk it?' She glanced heavenward, the skies inundated with swollen clouds saturated with unshed rain. 'Maybe we should scurry back to the hotel.'

'Live dangerously, I say. One can't always have a brolly at the ready.'

'I've got a better idea.' Pulling away from him, she stepped over to a raised funerary slab, the surface pitted by acid rain. Without a care for the dearly departed, she unceremoniously parked her arse. 'Let's do some cyber sleuthing.'

'*Here?* In the middle of the Christ Church burial grounds?'

'Don't look so aghast.' Opening the leather satchel, she removed the netbook. 'Just think of this as an open-air office. Makes me wonder how folks managed before the Information Age. A laptop computer with 3G wireless service sure beats a quill pen and messenger pigeon, huh?'

Curiosity trumping decorum, he sat down on the weathered stone. Like Edie, he very much wanted to cobble together the disparate pieces of the puzzle. 'I suggest that we begin with the deciphered anagram "biblicil aten stone to gods eye do not err".'

Although she raised a dubious brow, Edie obliged the request. 'Aha! Just as I thought,' she exclaimed a split second later. 'Not a single result.'

'An inauspicious start.'

'Okay, we know that the motto "Rebellion to tyrants is obedience to God" was significant to Benjamin Franklin, but what about the other two members of the Triad?' As she spoke, Edie typed out the phrase plus the name 'Thomas Jefferson'.

'The first entry, I think.' Cædmon quickly scanned the selected page. 'Fascinating . . . Not only did Thomas Jefferson adopt the phrase as his personal motto, but he had it cast on to a signet to seal his correspondence.'

'Let's see if we get any hits with John Adams . . . hmm, looks like Adams mentioned the phrase in passing to his wife Abigail, but that's about the extent of it.'

'Fuel for an historian perhaps, but unless I'm greatly mistaken, we've just run out of petrol.'

'You are such a naysayer. New search.' Undaunted, Edie flexed her fingers above the keyboard. 'Earlier today you hypothesized that the All-Seeing Eye is a red herring. With that in mind, let's key in "All-Seeing Eye" plus the names of the three Triad members.' An instant later, she shielded her face with her arm. As though protecting herself from flying debris. 'Whoa! Talk about a conspiracy theory bomb blast. I think I just got nicked by a hurtling wing nut. Or was that a flying whack-a-doo?'

Cædmon scanned the list of results. 'Good God! Given the surfeit of entries that contain the word "satanic", it may take hours to find an intelligible kernel in all that dross.'

'Online hysteria over secret cabals has become all the rage. Evidently, we wandered into the eye of the storm.'

He smiled, amused by the pun. 'We need to refine our search.'

Edie tapped a finger against her chin. 'When we were in London, Rubin spoke at length about the Eye of Thoth, the Radiant Light of Aten and the All-Seeing Eye. As I recall, he was convinced that they were variant expressions derived from the same stream of hidden knowledge.'

'That's because Thoth, the author of the Emerald Tablet, was at the root of each of those symbols. Ergo, those three iconic images each conveyed the essence of creation made manifest in the material world.'

'Yada, yada, yada. Let's see if we can find a connection between Thoth and any of our Triad members.' Edie Googled 'Benjamin Franklin + Thoth'. 'Nada on the yada,' she muttered when 'No results found' popped up on the computer. 'Ditto for Jefferson. Who, by the way, happens to be my *second* favourite red-head.' She punctuated the playful addendum with a wink. 'And, lastly, the portly man from Quincy.' A moment later, slack-jawed, her brown eyes open wide, she turned to him. 'Ohmygod . . . we got a hit.'

Squinting, he leaned closer to the computer. 'Are you certain?'

'Oh, yeah. Look, it's a bronze bas-relief sculpture of *Thoth* on an exterior door. The door in question is hinged on to the John Adams Building in Washington, DC. Which, in case you don't know, is an annex building for the Library of Congress.'

He stared, dumbfounded. *Thoth, the ibis-headed Egyptian god, depicted, not in a temple on the Nile, but in the American capital on the Potomac.*

Washington, the city of secrets. Past and present.

'And did you happen to notice what the bird man is holding aloft in his right hand?'

'I do believe that our Egyptian friend is clutching the Emerald Tablet.' Amazed by the startling image, he could do little more than shake his head and gawk.

'Ruh-roh.' Edie pointed to a section of text that accompanied the online image. 'According to this, the Adams

Annex was constructed in 1938. One hundred and twelve years *after* John Adams died.'

'It doesn't matter.' Unconcerned by the incongruous date, he elaborated. 'Dr Franklin indicated in *The Book of Moses* that he intended for the Triad to germinate itself, each member responsible for selecting his own successor. In that way, the Triad would continue in perpetuity. Blooming anew each generation.'

'If that's true, then at some point the Emerald Tablet was transported from Philadelphia to Washington.'

'A bas-relief sculpture is hardly proof positive.'

'"Biblicil aten stone to Gods eye do not err",' she iterated, an exasperated edge to her voice. 'Not only do we have an image of Thoth holding the Emerald Tablet, but I think I know who was responsible for moving the relic to the capital city.'

'Indeed?' He wondered how, *sans* a crystal ball, she could know such a thing.

'Guess who first broached the idea of turning a swampy parcel on the Potomac into the nation's capital?'

'Admittedly, my grasp of American history is sketchy, but I thought that George Washington was the culprit, aided by the French-born city planner Pierre Charles L'Enfant. Both of whom were Freemasons.'

'That's the story the Freemasons would like you to believe,' Edie informed him. 'The truth of the matter is that Thomas Jefferson strenuously lobbied Congress to purchase land along the Potomac River to serve as the site for the new capital. And he did this *before* the Revolution ended in 1781. An amateur architect, he even drew up a plan for the city layout.'

'Did Franklin have anything to do with the design of Washington?' he asked, admittedly intrigued.

'Not according to the history books. Benjamin Franklin died the same year that Washington was founded in 1790. But given that it was Jefferson who chose the site, Jefferson who oversaw the city survey and Jefferson who managed the entire construction project when he was Secretary of State, I'm wondering if the three members of the Triad – Franklin, Adams and Jefferson – didn't hatch the plan to build the new capital on the Potomac long before it became a reality. Because, *yes*, you guessed it, *that's* where they all along intended to hide the Emerald Tablet.'

Her supposition certainly had merit. Curious – Edie's wealth of knowledge impressive – he enquired, 'How is it that you're so well-informed on these matters?'

Grabbing the netbook, she set it on her lap. 'The summer between junior and senior year in college, I worked as a guide for the Washington Tourmobile company making me a walking encyclopaedia when it comes to DC history and lore.'

'And have you seen this bronze bas-relief sculpture of Thoth in situ?'

'I've seen the building, but not the bronze doors. Do you think the Emerald Tablet could *possibly* be hidden in the Adams Annex?' she asked as she shut down the computer.

'It's possible. We won't know until we examine the bas-relief sculpture on the Adams Annex.'

'Then it's homeward bound. Kinda ironic that we're going full circle, huh?' Closing the lid on the computer,

Edie shoved it into her satchel. 'Ever give any thought to what you want on *your* epitaph?'

'I've given little thought to departing the mortal coil. Although, like Dr Franklin, perhaps something pithy and—'

'Oh, my God!' Edie gasped, grabbing his arm. 'I just saw Rico Suave!'

68

'At least I think I saw him,' Edie amended, having caught sight of a dark-haired, well-dressed blur out of the corner of her eye. 'Whatever I saw, we need to get out of here!' Particularly since the cemetery was noticeably deserted.

Outwardly calm, Cædmon leaned in close; a man about to whisper sweet nothings into his lover's ear. 'Keep your voice down. We don't want to alert our foe.'

A command easier said than done, her nerves were like vibrating guitar strings. A frenzied flamenco come to life.

'I need to know where precisely you saw the bastard.'

'To my left, about fifty yards back.' Although tempted to turn and point, she didn't.

'Do you by any chance have a mirror in your satchel?'

'Um, yeah . . . I think so.' Opening her shoulder bag, she hurriedly ransacked the contents. A few seconds later, she removed an old cosmetic compact. Fumbling a bit with the latch, she opened it, wordlessly passing it to him.

The mirror enabled Cædmon to scan the cemetery without turning his head. 'Damn. The bastard's too far away to identify. Although he appears to be manning the front gate. Since the cemetery is enclosed by a seven-foot-high brick wall and that gate is the *only* way out of here, I suspect he's waiting for us to come to him.'

At which time Rico Suave could shoot them, stab them

or even hit them on the head with a metal pipe. And there wasn't anything they could do to stop him.

'Admittedly, our options are limited.' Closing the compact, Cædmon returned it to her.

'God, I'm *so* stupid! I've got a cell phone. I can dial 9-1-1,' she exclaimed, riding a big Waikiki wave of relief. 'One call and the cops will be here in a jiff.'

'*If* they show up.'

'Why wouldn't they?'

Cædmon raised a dubious brow. 'What exactly do you plan on telling the police? That a lone man, who has done nothing untoward or threatening, is milling about, minding his own business. No crime in that.'

'He's murdered two men!' Edie hissed. Being cool under pressure was one thing. Being blasé in the face of danger another matter altogether. 'In this country, that's an electric-chair offence.'

'For which we have no proof.' Cædmon stood up. Grabbing the satchel, he wrapped his other hand around her upper arm, pulling her upright. He gave her a tight smile. 'Time to put on your jolly face.'

'And this is going to help us *how*?'

He made no reply. Instead, he slung a companionable arm around her shoulder as he shepherded her along the crushed-stone walkway. In the complete opposite direction to the cemetery gate. While relieved to be moving away from Rico Suave, she didn't like putting so much distance between themselves and the gate – that being the only means of escape from the walled enclosure.

As they *leisurely* strolled, Edie could feel the tensed muscles in Cædmon's arm. And though he smiled and attentively and bent his head in her direction, his eyes kept darting from side to side. Plotting. Planning.

A few moments later, plan evidently hatched, he veered away from the walkway on to a dirt path that ribboned off at a scraggly angle, the grass beaten from years of pedestrian traffic. The arm instantly dropped from her shoulder as Cædmon snatched hold of her hand, accelerating the pace as they hurried past stone crosses, carved sarcophagi, funerary urns and tilted headstones.

'This is as good a bulwark as any,' he muttered, dodging behind a massive granite plinth surmounted by a carved memorial obelisk. 'And completely out of the bastard's line of sight.'

Edie nestled close, well aware that they were playing a potentially deadly game of hide-and-seek.

Pressed against her backside, Cædmon peered around the granite pedestal. 'Perfect . . . our gatekeeper is on the move.'

He's on the move! A garbled sound – midway between a gasp and a whimper – passed between her lips. Cædmon chastened her with a cautionary glance.

'You mean that you actually *want* him to follow us?' she whispered.

'How else to lure him away from the exit? Which brings me to the matter of your coat. If you would be so kind as to hand it over.'

'Why do you want my trench coat?'

'It will make the perfect *capote de brega*. Bullfighter's cape,' he translated.

All thumbs, Edie clumsily untied the belt and removed her coat. Clueless as to what exactly he intended to do with the fuchsia-coloured garment, she handed it to him.

The last thing she expected was Cædmon to roll it into a ball and shove it *under* his wool sports jacket.

'Off to set the trap.'

Edie grabbed his wrist. 'Please don't tell me this is where we go our separate ways and meet up later in Prague.'

'If all goes well, I'll only be gone a few minutes.' A determined look on his face, Cædmon squeezed her hand reassuringly. 'If the bastard shows up before I return, kick him in the cubes and scream like a banshee.'

Battle orders given, he took off running, tucking his tall frame into a low crouch as he zigzagged from monument to obelisk to tree trunk. The dark clouds overhead washed the cemetery in muted shades of grey and granite. She soon lost sight of Cædmon, inciting a barrage of graphic, gory images to flash across her mind's eye. *Worst case scenarios.*

In her peripheral vision, Edie saw a blaze of fuchsia. And though she knew it was an illusion, it *appeared* that someone decked out in a bright pink coat was crouched behind a tombstone.

The trap had been set.

Anxiously peering around the corner of the granite plinth, she searched for Cædmon, still unable to locate him amidst the stone jumble. Just then, a large hand snaked in front of her, covering her mouth. In the next instant, she was yanked against a male torso. Completely immobilized.

'Shhh! It's me.'

Cædmon!

Relieved, Edie slumped against his chest.

'No time to chat!' he whispered, removing his hand from her mouth. 'He took the bait.'

'I don't think so! Look over there!' She pointed to a fast-moving blur. 'He's headed this way!'

That being their cue, they sprinted towards the front gate. Their pounding footfalls made a loud crunching sound on the stone walkway. Up ahead, Edie could see that the double gate was closed.

Please, please, don't be locked!

Cædmon charged ahead of her to the gate. With a mighty tug, he swung it wide open, metal hinges loudly squeaking. Seconds later, they charged through the opened gateway, emerging on to a city pavement teeming with tourists and office workers.

Always thinking two moves ahead, Cædmon manoeuvred them into the middle of a large crowd headed in the direction of the US Mint.

'I don't know about you, but I stupidly thought Rico's "sell by" date had expired,' she wheezed, her breath noticeably uneven.

'Still very much on the shelf.' Breaking away from the crowd, Cædmon stepped off the kerb and raised his right hand. 'Taxi!'

69

Softly chuckling, Saviour Panos watched the fleeing pair get into a taxi.

'Where you go, I will go. And where you stay, I will stay.'

He didn't know what that was from, but Mercurius often quoted it. Apropos given the circumstances.

Back in London, he'd followed the pair to Heathrow where an obliging ticket clerk had informed him that they'd purchased nonstop tickets to Philadelphia. When their flight landed nine hours later, Mercurius had followed them from Philadelphia International Airport to Library Hall. When Saviour arrived shortly thereafter, having caught a different flight, Mercurius had had the wise foresight to purchase a tracking device from a downtown spy shop. The sort of establishment that caters to men anxious to catch their cheating wives in the act of copulation. Giving him the tracking device, Mercurius had hugged him tight before taking his leave.

'Take heart, my beloved. You are not to blame for what happened in London.'

Maybe so, but Saviour was determined to make amends.

And the Creator was doing all in his power to assist him – knapsacks, purses and briefcases were expressly forbidden inside the Reading Room. Because of the regulation, the Brit and his woman had been forced to check their satchel at the Library Hall front desk. Saviour simply had to wait for the attendant to leave her post. It'd taken but a moment to insert the small tracking device – embedded on an adhesive strip – inside the Miller woman's bag.

He'd enjoyed the romp in the cemetery. Had enjoyed the fear that he'd seen on the bitch's face. With the tracking device in place, the pair had become his unwitting pawns. Saviour glanced at the display screen on his PDA Smartphone, able to track their every move on the interactive map.

And that meant he *would* be able to make amends, wanting only to please Mercurius. Particularly since he could not pleasure his beloved sexually. At least, not to climax. That was never permitted, his mentor a celibate.

'In the self-same point where the soul is made sensual, in the self-same point is the city of God.'

Another of his mentor's favourite sayings. Although Saviour could not comprehend the logic. According to Mercurius, a man could communicate with the Creator by manipulating the flow of sexual energy as it traversed his spine. A mystical fire that burnt its way to the third eye. The one that was all-seeing. When that point was flooded with sacred energy, the life force of creation, a gateway was opened between heaven and earth.

As above, so below.

Saviour was too coarse by far. He lacked the spiritual awareness to harness his own sexual energy. For him, the point of arousal was to come. Not to go. Once the blood pumped into his cock, there was but one outcome. And it did not involve the Creator.

But Mercurius was a man of deep and abiding spiritual

beliefs who daily attempted to open the sacred gate. To master the lower self so he could communicate with the Creator. Saviour considered it a great honour to assist him in this endeavour.

'Fire and flowing water are contraries. Happy thou if thou canst unite them.'

And how happy Mercurius would be when he presented him with the Emerald Tablet. Because his mentor would then be able to apply his sacred knowledge to that most ecstatic of all labours . . . the act of creation. Making something out of nothing.

His mentor was fond of reading aloud from the Old Testament. Saviour particularly enjoyed the tales of valiant men engaged in violent conflict. According to Mercurius, the Emerald Tablet enabled Moses to perform all of his miraculous feats – parting the Red Sea, producing manna in the desert, making the sun and the moon to stand still and causing the walls of Jericho to come tumbling down. *Creating something out of nothing.*

Saviour again glanced at the PDA. The pair was headed to the train station. He smiled.

Where you go, I will go . . .

70

Side by side, they stood in front of three sets of double bronze doors that marked the entrance to the Adams Annex.

Shielding her eyes from the early-morning light, Edie could see that each door contained six bas-relief figures. A veritable rogue's gallery – Odin, Nabu, Brahma, Quetzalcoatl – to name a few. However, Cædmon's attention was focused on the figure depicted on the upper tier of the centre door. *Thoth*. Egyptian god of wisdom. The ibis-headed god was garbed in an Egyptian kilt. In his right hand, Thoth did indeed hold the fabled Emerald Tablet.

'All-in-all, a rather brazen depiction,' Cædmon remarked after a lengthy silence. 'Not only is it a public declaration that Thoth authored the Emerald Tablet, but the sculpture intimates that he gave the relic to mankind, conferring upon them the gift of divine knowledge.'

'And that divine knowledge, aka the hidden stream of knowledge, is at the heart of creation.' Edie wasn't so much surprised by the image as the fact that it'd been placed in the open for everyone to see. 'Brazen is right. Nothing *sub rosa* about this.'

'Indeed.' Cædmon reverently moved his hand over the raised bronze surface. Aladdin polishing the oil lamp. 'While the inclusion of the Emerald Tablet on the bas-relief is notable, the sculpture is even more remarkable for what *isn't* depicted.'

Her head jerked. 'You mean something's missing?'

'Thoth is almost always depicted with an *ankh* grasped in one hand and a *was* held in the other,' he informed her. 'In ancient Egypt, the *ankh*, sometimes referred to as the key of the Nile, symbolized life. While the *was*, a type of wand or rod, symbolized power. I'm troubled by the fact that those two attributes are missing. They *should* be here.'

'So, what are you saying, that we need to find the AWOL attributes?'

'Possibly.' Frowning, he cocked his head to one side, as though trying to come at the problem from a different angle.

Now it was Edie's turn to be baffled. 'But I thought we were searching for the All-Seeing Eye, not an *ankh* or *was*. The deciphered anagram read "Biblicil aten stone to Gods eye do not err,"' she reminded him, wondering if the Thoth sculpture was a fluke rather than a bona fide signpost.

'These doors face due west.' Cædmon executed a slow one-eighty, turning away from the austerity of the annex to face the Library of Congress across the street. A massive and ornate edifice that resembled an elaborate wedding cake. 'Blast. I can't see a thing. The colossus completely obscures the western horizon.'

'Not to worry. I can tell you *exactly* what's on the other side of the building. First, there's the Capitol grounds where you have trolling police and politicos. And, beyond that, you have the Mall. Or museum alley, as we used to call it in the tourist industry. And having once been an industry insider, I know there isn't an *ankh* or *was* to be had.'

Cædmon made no reply. Instead, he grabbed her hand and set off in the direction of East Capitol Street. Making her think that he hadn't heard a word she'd just said. When they reached the corner, he came to a halt. Morning rush-hour traffic was hectic, the streets congested, the sidewalks packed with worker bees late for the hive.

Releasing her hand, he raised his arm and pointed due west; to a familiar object at the far end of the Mall, more than a mile and a half away. 'I just located one of Thoth's missing attributes. Behold the *was*!'

Edie stared at the western horizon. 'You're kidding, right? That's the Washington Monument.' At 555 feet, the white marble spire was the tallest structure in Washington. And, as she knew from her tour-guide stint, it had the distinction of being the tallest stone structure in the world. Most locals took the odd edifice for granted. Herself, included.

'*That* is an Egyptian obelisk,' Cædmon informed her, blue eyes excitedly gleaming. 'A petrified ray of the god Aten made manifest in stone. Moreover, the obelisk is where the Radiant Aten dwells as he illuminates his creation.'

She glanced back at the doors on the Adams Annex, trying to make the connection between the bronze bas-relief and the white marble monument. 'And Thoth's true power, symbolized by the *was*, is the illumination gained through the knowledge inscribed on the Emerald Tablet, which describes the secret of Aten's creation.' She shook her head, worried that Cædmon had veered off course. 'I don't mean to harp, but what does the Washington Monument have to do with the All-Seeing Eye?'

'Fix your gaze upon the top of the monument. What do you see?'

Edie obediently slid her gaze up the tall, gently tapered structure. 'I see . . . ohmygosh! I see a triangle! Just like the triangle that encloses the All-Seeing Eye,' she exclaimed, the pyramidal top of the monument triangular in shape. 'The Washington Monument *does* symbolize the All-Seeing Eye of Aten who dwells within the obelisk!'

'Thus the obelisk harkens to the power of the Radiant Aten who, in turn, bestows his power upon Thoth the Thrice Great.'

'Behold the *was*.' Realizing the implication of that, her enthusiasm instantly waned, Edie wishing she *hadn't* made the connection. 'So, what are you saying, that the Emerald Tablet is hidden *inside* the Washington Monument?'

71

Unnerved, Edie glanced over her shoulder.

'We're perfectly safe,' Cædmon said reassuringly, taking hold of her elbow as he steered her around a boisterous tour group.

The Yoshino cherry trees around the Tidal Basin were in graceful full bloom, which meant the Mall was jam-packed with the spill-over crowds. A grand expanse of manicured grass framed with impressive shade trees, the Mall was arguably one of the most famous pedestrian thoroughfares in the world.

Despite Cædmon's assurance, Edie couldn't belay the niggling fear that something malevolent lurked in the shadows. Watching their every move.

'Need I remind you that we spent last night at the Willard Hotel because you didn't think it was safe to sleep at the house?'

'It's not safe.' Pronouncement made, Cædmon gestured to the gleaming spire at the end of the Mall. 'You mentioned that Thomas Jefferson was instrumental in selecting the site for the new capital city and overseeing the early construction. Did he have a hand in erecting the Washington Monument?'

Given the overly phallic monument, the question begged a bawdy retort. Instead, Edie played it straight and said, 'While Jefferson selected the location for the monument, the actual construction didn't begin until 1848. I'm guessing that Franklin, Jefferson and Adams, the original three members of the Triad, figured out *where* they wanted to leave their signposts, but left the installation to later generations. That would explain how two of the signposts, the Washington Monument and the Adams Annex, were constructed *after* the original Triad members had died.'

'While there's a direct link between Thoth and the obelisk, we still don't know if the Washington Monument is actually a signpost,' Cædmon said, taking a more measured approach. 'What about John Adams? Other than the fact that the Library of Congress annex building is named after him, he seems rather periphery to the tale.'

'Hardly.' Coming to a momentary stop, Edie removed her new cotton pea coat and slung it over her shoulder, the late-morning sun surprisingly warm. 'John Adams was the first president to take up residence in the new capital city of Washington. In fact, he served the first half of his term in the *old* capital at Philadelphia and the second half in Washington.'

'Mmmm . . .' Hands clasped behind his back, Cædmon struck a professorial pose. 'It's conceivable that John Adams transported the Emerald Tablet from one city to the other.'

'That alone makes him a player in all of this. Although Jefferson gets top billing by virtue of the fact that he participated in almost every phase of the project. From planning the Mall to the precise placement of the Capitol and White House.' And though Jefferson never envisioned that the Mall would be lined with world-class museums,

Edie suspected he'd be pleased. As she recalled, the red-headed Virginian had proudly displayed mastodon bones in the entry hall at Monticello.

Cædmon jutted his chin at the Washington Monument, still several blocks away. 'I've decided the bloody thing resembles a lone stalk of marble asparagus.'

Edie chuckled; the description humorously apt. 'Once they broke ground, it took decades to complete the monument. When the Civil War erupted in 1861, it was still an unfinished stump. And you'll find this next factoid *real* interesting –' she paused, ensuring she had his undivided attention – 'after the war, the Freemasons donated a huge chunk of cash to the construction project.'

'How ironic that a trio of Deists conceive of the idea for the monument, yet it's the very group they wish to circumvent who finance the project.'

'Moral of the story? If you're trying to hide a tree, put it in a forest overgrown with esoteric symbols, obelisks and images of Thoth. That way, the Masons will *never* find it.'

'Indeed, they have eyes, but they cannot see,' Cædmon mused.

'Strange to think that two hundred years after Francis Bacon put an All-Seeing Eye on his unpublished frontispiece, the symbols of ancient Egypt would be placed in plain sight for all to see.'

'The "sun-worshipping Atenists" and "bewigged magus" no longer had to fear a monarch overreacting to their occult beliefs,' Cædmon commented, quoting from *The Book of Moses*. 'For the first time since the pharaohs ruled, those who revered the hidden stream of knowledge were in power.'

'But without Thoth's stone, there ain't much hocus to the Freemasons' pocus.'

'The very reason why the wise sage of Craven Street committed his grand larceny, to drain the Freemasons' energy source.'

At the 14th Street traffic light, they came to a standstill. Straight ahead, one block away, Edie sighted the fifty undulating American flags that encircled the base of the Washington Monument. As they stepped off the kerb, the enormity of their task suddenly hit her with gale-force intensity.

They didn't even know what they were looking for!

'It's gigantic,' she muttered, seeing the Washington Monument as though for the very first time.

From her tour-guide stint, she knew a good many of the facts: there were 897 steps to the top; the exterior blocks were quarried marble, the interior commemorative stones a varied mix, including a few jade stones from the Orient; nearly 37,000 blocks had been used in the construction and the tip of the monument was aluminium, making it an excellent lightning rod.

And she knew one other thing . . . if the Emerald Tablet was hidden amongst all those thousands of stones, they were screwed. Plain and simple.

Given the stupefied expression on Cædmon's face, he'd just come to the same conclusion.

'I'm awestruck,' he murmured, his head tilted as he gazed upward. 'It's quite the *tour de force*.'

'In order to tour the *tour de force*, we need to get some tickets. This way.' Grabbing his hand, Edie pulled Cædmon towards the National Park kiosk.

A few minutes later, supplied with tickets and a map, they set off. As they neared the entrance, Edie groaned, the line to get inside the monument snaking halfway around the base.

Unfolding the map, Cædmon held it in front of him. 'I see a marker for something called the Jefferson Pier. Any idea what that is?'

'I've lived in DC eighteen years, laboured an entire summer for the Tourmobile Company, and I have *never* heard of the Jefferson Pier.' Coming to a full stop, Edie examined the map.

'Right there.' Leaning over her shoulder, Cædmon pointed to a small speck on the north-west quadrant of the monument grounds, approximately three hundred yards from their current position.

Glancing at the line of waiting tourists, Edie made a suggestion. 'Let's temporarily bypass the monument and head over to the Jefferson Pier. I suspect the line will shrink the closer we get to the lunch hour.'

'Lead the way.'

She did, veering away from the pavement. Several minutes into the hike, shading her eyes with her hand, Edie scanned the monument grounds. When she caught sight of a familiar Smoky the Bear hat, she exuberantly waved her arm.

'What are you doing?'

'Flagging a Park Service Ranger. We have no idea what we're looking for. These guys know *everything* about the Mall.'

Returning her wave, the uniformed ranger adjusted course and headed in their direction.

Edie read the gold-plated name badge affixed to the right side of the ranger's shirt. *Jermaine Walker.*

'Hi, Ranger Walker! We're lost,' she blurted, cutting right to the chase. 'Could you please tell us where the Jefferson Pier is located?'

The ranger, a moustachioed black man who wore his drab green and grey uniform with surprising panache, good-naturedly smiled. 'Had you'd gotten any closer, you might have stumbled over top of it. The Jefferson Pier is right over there.' He pointed to a stubby granite block situated some thirty feet from where they stood.

'*That?*' Edie didn't even try to mask her keen disappointment. She glanced at Cædmon who, in turn, shrugged his shoulders.

'So sorry to have bothered you,' Cædmon apologized to the ranger. 'We thought the Jefferson Pier might be something of more, er, historic significance.'

'I know. It bewilders a lot of folks who see it on the map and mistakenly head this way searching for the Jefferson Memorial.' Ranger Walker started to walk towards the granite lump; Cædmon and Edie had no choice but to tag along. 'What they don't know is that the pier *is* highly significant.'

Standing in front of the two-foot high post capped with a pyramidal top, Edie had her doubts. It looked like someone had inadvertently plunked a parking barrier in the middle of the expansive monument grounds.

'If you're interested in Washington lore, there's an inscription on the other side.'

'Indeed?' Cædmon had to bend at the waist in order to read the chiselled lettering. '"Position of Jefferson Pier erected December 18, 1804." Fascinating,' he deadpanned, straightening to his full height.

'Actually, it is,' the ranger was quick to inform them. 'In 1793, President Washington appointed Thomas Jefferson, then Secretary of State, as point man for the capital construction project. Very much a micro-manager, Jefferson surveyed a north–south meridian through the new city, personally driving a wooden stake on this very spot to mark the newly surveyed meridian.' Ranger Walker spoke in the kind of sing-songy voice reserved for rote recitation. 'In 1804, *President* Jefferson replaced the wooden post with a stone pier.'

'The inscription on the pier has obviously been defaced.' Cædmon pointed to a gouged-out trench beneath the date. 'As though someone purposefully chiselled away part of the inscription.'

The ranger shrugged. 'Vandals and graffiti artists, what can I say?'

Edie squinted her eyes to tighten her long-distance vision. 'If you head due north from this pier, the meridian passes right through the middle of the White House.'

'That's correct,' Ranger Walker verified with a nod. 'The meridian runs parallel to 16th Street from one end of the city to the other. And –' he leaned close, as though imparting a great secret – 'I hear tell the Freemasons call it "the Corridor of Light". Not exactly sure why. Might have something to do with the House of the Temple that they built up there on 16th Street.'

Neither Cædmon nor Edie responded to Ranger Walker's last remark, both of them well aware that six days ago a brutal murder had taken place at that very location.

'As you no doubt recall, Edie, a meridian is a line of longitude.'

'And it just so happens that Jefferson's meridian is *exactly* at seventy-seven degrees longitude,' Ranger Walker chimed in.

Hearing that, Edie and Cædmon simultaneously swung their heads towards the innocuous granite pier.

The 77th Meridian!

God's line of longitude.

72

Christos!

They were doing nothing but *walking*. Endless blocks of walking, trudging, trekking. Moving from one location to another with nothing to show for the effort.

Standing at the souvenir kiosk on the edge of the monument grounds, Saviour watched as the Brit and his woman began walking towards Constitution Avenue. *Here we go again.* Mercurius said that Aisquith had embarked on a sacred quest. *A sacred quest my ass.*

In no hurry to set off – with the tracking device, he could follow at his leisure – Saviour examined the array of souvenirs being sold at outrageously inflated prices. His gaze alighted on a 10-inch high metal replica of the Washington Monument. Welded on to the front of the miniature obelisk was an outdoor thermostat.

'How much for these two?' he brusquely asked the vendor, picking up a blue baseball cap in his other hand.

'Twenty-four ninety-five.'

Christos! For a baseball cap and a shitty souvenir!

He wordlessly handed over a twenty and a five. Furious that the *malaka* had just swindled him, he barely refrained from throwing the nickel change at the other man's chest.

Slapping the baseball cap on his head, Saviour tucked his souvenir under his arm and strode across the neatly trimmed expanse of lawn towards the stubby stone ballast.

The granite monolith had garnered Aisquith and the woman's attention. In fact, they'd been so interested, they'd consulted with a third party. A third party who presently stood a few feet away from the squat stone.

Saviour affixed a guileless expression on to his face and approached. His gaze immediately alighted on the gleaming gold badge pinned above the black man's left shirt pocket. US *Park Ranger*. Then he glanced at the gold name tag pinned above the right pocket. *Jermaine Walker*. Although he wore a uniform, the ranger carried no weapon.

'Please could you help me?' Saviour entreated with a smile.

The ranger, in the process of wiping the back of his neck with a handkerchief, turned to him. 'Be happy to help, if I can.'

'I was supposed to meet my friends at the monument, but –' still smiling, he lifted his shoulders in a shrug – 'apparently we missed each other in the crowd. Perhaps you saw them: a tall red-headed Brit and a curly—'

'Just missed 'em. Not too many folks ask about the Jefferson Pier.'

Saviour presumed he meant the hunk of granite a few feet away. 'The Jefferson Pier? Why would they be interested in *this*? The Washington Monument is what everyone comes to see, no?'

'By the busloads. But for whatever reason, your friends seemed more interested in the pier. Like I told 'em, this marker was set in place by Thomas Jefferson when he surveyed the 77th Meridian.'

Head tipped to one side, Saviour feigned interest. *Why would the Brit be interested in a rock?* It made no sense.

‘Will you excuse me for a moment?’ Stepping several feet away, Saviour turned his back on Ranger Walker as he tapped the Bluetooth device clipped to his ear. Without preamble, he relayed the conversation to Mercurius, hoping his mentor could provide some context to the strange episode.

‘And you’re quite certain that he said the *77th* Meridian?’

Saviour glanced over his shoulder at the ranger who had resumed mopping the sweat on the back of his neck. ‘Yes, positive.’

‘I am deeply troubled that this man, the ranger, has spoken with Aisquith about the sacred meridian. He may even suspect the reason for the Englishman’s interest. That alone makes him a dangerous impediment.’

‘I understand.’ Saviour tapped the device, disconnecting the phone call.

He walked back to where the ranger stood waiting. ‘The information about the Jefferson Pier has been most helpful.’

Amiably grinning, the ranger jutted his chin at the tacky souvenir nestled under Saviour’s arm. ‘So, what’s the temperature?’

For several seconds, Saviour stared at the black man’s face, noticing the perspiration that dotted his brow. The neatly trimmed moustache. The dark nubbins of ingrown facial hair. Then, very slowly, and very deliberately, his gaze dropped to the slim hips garbed in a pair of dark green trousers. ‘It’s extremely hot.’

The ranger held his hands up, palms facing out. ‘Hey, I don’t swing that way.’

‘Pity.’ Saviour removed the souvenir from under his

arm and held it in his hand like a stake. A makeshift weapon.

Sensing his intention, the other man recoiled.

Too late.

Saviour plunged the pointed tip of the metal obelisk into Jermaine Walker's left breast. Straight to the heart. The ranger's eyes immediately widened. Lips quivered. In that infinitesimal second between life and death, he yanked violently. A terrified animal in its death throes.

In the next second, Ranger Walker went limp.

Throwing his left arm around the ranger's shoulders, Saviour grabbed him before he collapsed in an ungainly heap. Gently, he eased the uniformed man to the ground, propping him against the stone pier. Anyone seeing him from a distance would simply think he was sitting on the grassy lawn.

'You gave up the ghost too quickly, my friend.'

He readjusted the baseball cap on his head as he examined the expanding blood stain that encircled the metal obelisk protruding from Ranger Walker's chest. When he bought the souvenir, he had intended it for a different victim.

'Oh, I almost forgot . . . it's seventy-two degrees Fahrenheit.' Saviour softly cackled, the joke lost on his dead companion.

73

'. . . and as we just recently learned, the Washington Monument was supposed to have been erected at the Jefferson Pier.' Cædmon gave the grove of holly and elm a cursory glance. 'Lovely site for a brainstorming session.'

'According to Ranger Walker, the Corps of Army Engineers didn't think the soil around the Jefferson Pier would support so massive a weight. That's why the Washington Monument ended up, not on the 77th Meridian as originally planned, but four hundred feet away.' Edie sighed. 'And you're right. I can't think of a better place to contemplate God's line of longitude than on Uncle Albert's lap.'

Cædmon stared at the 12-foot-high bronze figure that dominated the grove. At Edie's suggestion, they'd decided to break for lunch and dine al fresco at the Albert Einstein Memorial, the outdoor monument located on Constitution Avenue at the National Academy of Science. To his surprise, the memorial consisted of a charming, almost child-like statue of Einstein seated on a marble step. A secluded and peaceful oasis.

'Did you know that Albert Einstein was a member of the American Philosophical Society? Which is not the reason why I suggested the spot for our picnic.' Edie distractedly waved in the direction of the Jefferson Pier, some eight blocks away. 'I just wanted to get off the beaten path. The Mall is an esoteric free-for-all.'

'Which Jefferson and Adams used to advantage, taking great care in hiding their emerald tree in Washington's esoteric forest. Even going so far as to survey the 77th Meridian.' Placing a hand on Edie's elbow, he guided her towards the marble steps.

'Check out a DC map and you'll see that the city was designed as a perfect ten-mile square.' Edie sat down next to 'Uncle Albert'. 'Sixteenth Street, aka the 77th Meridian, runs right through the middle of the north–south axis of that square, completely dividing the city in half. The next signpost could be *anywhere* along the 77th Meridian.' Opening a plain brown bag, she removed a hotdog wrapped in foil and a can of cola, handing both to him. 'Lunch is served.'

Cædmon sat next to her. Not particularly enthused, he gingerly peeled back the foil on the hotdog. Catching a whiff of onions and relish, he wrinkled his nose. 'Bit of an acquired taste, eh?'

In the process of ripping open a small packet of mustard with her teeth, Edie raised a quizzical brow. 'And black pudding isn't?'

'Point taken.' Following suit, he opened a packet of mustard. *When in Rome.* 'I'm certain that the Jefferson Pier *is* a signpost. As you'll recall, an entire line of inscription had been chiselled from the granite block.'

'And you think the missing inscription may have been important?'

'The pier was erected by one of the original Triad members. No coincidence in that, I'll warrant.'

'If that's the case, we've come to the end of our journey. There's no way we can recover something that's been chiselled out of existence, erased for all eternity.'

At hearing Edie's blunt appraisal, his stomach painfully tightened. What initially started as a crusade for academic vindication – to find the missing link between the Knights Templar and ancient Egypt – had become a deadly quest to find an ancient relic of unimaginable power. The secret of creation. Or the secret of obliteration in the case of the ill-fated Atlantis.

After centuries of being surreptitiously bandied about, the Emerald Tablet had been brought to the new capital city and promptly hidden by a trio of men to prevent it from falling into the hands of a despot. Now, more than two hundred years later, that dire scenario was very much front-burner. *He had to find it.* Only then could he be certain that a rogue nation or terrorist organization didn't use the relic to engineer a catastrophic event.

The sense of urgency real, Cædmon reached into his jacket pocket and removed the DC map that he'd earlier purchased, along with an ink pen. Unfolding the map, he drew solid dots on two locations: the Adams Annex and the Jefferson Pier, connecting the points with a straight line. *But where does the line go from there?*

'It's here, somewhere in this blasted ten-mile square plot of land,' he muttered, angered that they'd lost the scent.

'While the inscription on the Jefferson Pier has been obliterated, maybe there's a record of it elsewhere.' Idea proffered, Edie sank her teeth into the hotdog, making him wait until she'd chewed, swallowed and washed it down with several sips of cola. 'I'm guessing that Jefferson and Adams would have sent one another progress reports. When Jefferson surveyed the meridian, he would have written to Adams to inform him of what he'd done. Conversely, when Adams transported the Emerald Tablet from Philly to Washington, he would have sent a letter to Jefferson letting him know that the transport went off without a hitch.'

'And, in the days before cell phones and email, this information would have been relayed via letters sent in the post.'

'It's possible that one or the other may have mentioned the 77th Meridian in a letter. And I'm fairly certain that the written correspondence between Jefferson and Adams is archived online.' Putting aside her lunch, Edie opened her leather satchel and removed the netbook computer.

'A valid theory worth investigating.' Particularly since they'd reached a roadblock.

'Okay, I've got the complete set of Jefferson–Adams letters,' Edie informed him once the computer had booted up. 'Lordy. Between the two of 'em, there's more than three hundred letters. Any suggestions as to the keyword search?'

'The obvious first choice is "meridian".' He dabbed at the corner of his mouth with a paper napkin before setting aside his half-eaten hotdog, grateful for a reason to do so.

'I don't believe it . . . we got a hit.' Edie silently read the text, her lips moving as she did so. 'Not that it makes a whole lot of sense,' she muttered a few moments later, handing him the netbook.

Cædmon skimmed over the first page of the missive which seemed to be little more than inconsequential musings on the weather and an eloquent passage about the harvesting of English peas. When he reached the last paragraph on the second page, his breath caught in his throat.

By paragraph's end, he'd reached a startling conclusion.

'The Great Seal anagram is embedded within this last paragraph.'

'Really! Are you sure?'

'Beyond a shadow.' To prove the point, he copied the paragraph and pasted it on to a blank page. He then selected ten words out of the text, which he highlighted. Finished, he handed the netbook back to Edie.

> Mister Adams, be assured that **God's eye** will each day be blinded when the noon day sun falls upon our meridian. That is true illumination. Not the superstition and rituals carved on the **biblical ten stone**. I **do** not care that those who dabble in the dark arts will be displeased **to** learn of my deed. I will take my heavenly rest knowing **I** did **not err**. For 'I will stand on the top of the hill with the rod of God in mine hand.'

'Biblicil aten stone to gods eye do not err.' Edie stare at the computer screen, lower lip tucked behind her upper row of teeth. Then, frowning, 'We still don't have a clue what it means.'

'True, but we know that the original Triad members, Franklin, Jefferson and Adams, devised the anagram in July 1776. That, undoubtedly, was when they formulated their long-term plan to safeguard the Emerald Tablet,' he said, thinking that the most likely premise. 'And, clever trio that they were, they knew that if there was a *new* capital city constructed from the ground up, no one would take notice of a man putting spade to dirt and placing something in a hole.'

'Because in 1800 when John Adams transported the Emerald Tablet to Washington, the whole city was one big construction zone,' Edie pointed out.

'From the informative chat with Ranger Walker, we learned that in 1793 Thomas Jefferson surveyed the 77th Meridian. Which, in all likelihood, is when he selected the site where the Triad would hide the Emerald Tablet once it was conveyed to the new capital city.' He paused, taking a moment to flesh out the scheme. 'My best guess is that "biblicil aten stone to gods eye do not err" refers to the exact spot, here in Washington, where the Emerald Tablet was hidden. The three original Triad members knew all along that they would eventually hide the bloody thing on the 77th Meridian.'

'But – and I hate to rain on our picnic – we need a signpost to point us in the right direction. The message originally inscribed on the Jefferson Pier no longer exists.'

He pointed to the last sentence in the paragraph. 'Unless I'm greatly mistaken, *this* is the phrase that was inscribed on Mister Jefferson's pier.'

'"I will stand on the top of the hill with the rod of God in mine hand,"' she read aloud. 'That's from the Old Testament, isn't it?'

'The Book of Exodus, to be precise. And it's a line of scripture rife with layered meaning. The "rod of God" was the wand that Moses used to work his miracles. According to the Bible, it was kept in the Ark of the Covenant.'

'Along with the Ten Commandments and the Emerald Stone.' Edie snapped her fingers, making the next connection. 'And you mentioned earlier that one of Thoth's attributes was an Egyptian *was*. Which was a type of rod, right?'

He nodded. 'Additionally, in the eighteenth century, a "rod" was a unit of measure used by surveyors. An instrument that Thomas Jefferson undoubtedly used in his survey of the 77th Meridian. Rather tongue-in-cheek, don't you think?'

'Yeah, but we were just at the pier and, well, there isn't a hill in sight. If the scripture is supposed to be read literally, it means Jefferson was standing on a hill located somewhere on the 77th – I got it! Hand me that map!' Holding out her hand, Edie wiggled her fingers. The classic 'Gimme' gesture.

Cædmon quickly passed the map and pen to her. Anxious, hoping this truly proved a *Eureka!* moment, he watched as Edie confidently drew two lines on the map, making a right-angled triangle.

'Head due north from the Jefferson Pier along God's line of longitude approximately two miles and you come to –' she handed the map back to him – '*Meridian Hill Park*. As you can see, the Adams Annex, the Jefferson Pier and Meridian Hill Park are the three vertices on the triangle.'

Bowled over, he stared at the map.

'"I must find the catheti to my hypotenuse,"' he murmured, the disparate pieces falling into place. 'That's what

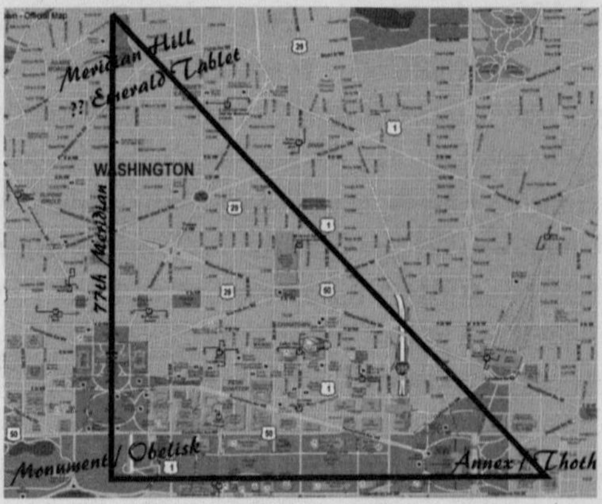

the wily bastard Franklin wrote in *The Book of Moses*. And, in geometry, the catheti are the two shorter sides of a right-angled triangle.'

'The hypotenuse being the longest of the three sides.'

'At the time, I thought it a figurative turn of phrase, Franklin wanting to find two younger men to do his leg-work.' He waved away the flawed deduction.

Overhead, a dark flock of birds flew across the sky in perfect avian formation. Of one mind, they suddenly swung to the left, not an errant one among them.

He summoned a smile. 'Triad. Triangle. Thoth the Thrice Great. Perfect symmetry.'

'Okay. Try this on . . . suppose we actually find the Emerald Tablet. What happens then?'

Mmmm . . . an excellent question. For which there were two distinctly different answers.

He could keep the sacred artefact for himself, hidden from the scholars, schemers and occult fanatics who would descend like vultures. Or he could share his discovery with the world and let fate sort the clean laundry from the soiled sheets. Each of the scenarios had merit, Cædmon undecided.

'I seek neither fame nor fortune. That said, the quest for the Emerald Tablet is a search for wisdom, the ancient relic reputed to contain the Knowledge of the Ages. The secret of creation itself.'

'The secret of creation?' Clearly put off by his reply, Edie pointed to an inscribed equation on the bronze statue. 'E=MC². As you no doubt know, *that* is often referred to as the mathematical equation for Genesis. It boggles the mind, well, *my* mind anyway, to think that a teensy amount of mass can produce a huge amount of destructive energy. Poor Uncle Albert.'

'Indeed, Einstein discovered first-hand the horrific destruction that can ensue when man takes on the mantle of God.'

'Did you know that in the blast at Hiroshima one hundred thousand people were killed?' Edie paused, giving him sufficient time to ponder that particular instance of 'horrific destruction'. 'Create or annihilate . . . why do I have this dreadful feeling that the Genesis code contained within the Emerald Tablet can do either?'

'Benjamin Franklin went to great lengths to keep his powerful discovery out of the hands of men who would misuse it.'

Her movements slow and deliberate, Edie returned her gaze to the bronze statute. 'And Albert Einstein went to his grave regretting the fact that he didn't.'

74

'According to this plaque, there *used* to be a granite pier at Meridian Hill Park just like the one that's on the Washington Monument grounds.' Edie turned towards the busy thoroughfare behind them. 'With all the congestion, it's hard to envision 16th Street as God's line of longitude.'

Cædmon re-read the bronze plate affixed to the tall concrete wall that bordered the park. 'It states that the pier marking the 77th Meridian was situated precisely fifty-two feet and nine inches from where we're currently standing.' Placing it in the centre of what was now four lanes of fast-moving traffic. *Damn.* First a defaced pier, now one that had gone missing. While his hopes weren't dashed, they were dented.

'Back in the day, that being the year 1800 when Adams and Jefferson stashed their cache, this was nothing but a wild hinterland. In fact, the original L'Enfant plan for the new capital city never included the remote bluffs north of the downtown area.'

'And the park, when was it constructed?'

'Sometime in the 1920s. That's when the area became a residential hub, folks moving up here in droves to escape the heat and humidity.' If Edie was disappointed by the missing pier, she gave no indication.

'Shall we?' Cædmon motioned to the covered stairway that led into the park.

An impressive bit of workmanship, the entry was reminiscent of a European citadel. But with a decidedly occult aspect, a flight of steps the age-old symbol of spiritual ascension. Moreover, the darkened passageway bespoke of the primordial chaos from which mankind evolved. *The stairs inside Solomon's Temple that led to the Middle Chamber.*

When he heard the echo of tom-tom drums in the distance, he glanced at the sunlit street behind them, wondering from where the sound emanated.

'I've been to Meridian Hill Park numerous times and every time I walk up these steps, I feel like a devotee making a spiritual pilgrimage.'

'A spot-on observation,' he murmured, the sound of beating drums becoming louder.

No sooner did they exit the enclosed staircase than they had to shield their eyes with their hands. Afternoon sunlight bounced off the pebbles and bits of mica embedded in the concrete aggregate pavement, the shimmery effect too intense to be happenstance. Someone had purposely designed the enclosed passageway so that the initiate would ascend through the dark void into a state of illumination.

Wondering who that someone might be, he turned slightly . . . and gasped.

In the distance, perfectly framed between a majestic avenue of Linden trees, was the most famous Egyptian obelisk in the world, the Washington Monument. Like the glittering effect at the top of the stairs, the dramatic vista was too contrived not to be intentional.

'Guess you figured out, Toto, that we're not in Kansas any more.' Chuckling, Edie gave him a companionable nudge. 'Your reaction, by the way, was priceless. Well, what do you think?' She gestured expansively to the acres of surrounding parkland.

In truth, he didn't know what to think, surprised to be standing at one end of a neoclassical promenade flanked by two monumental fountains that had the look and feel of an Old World pleasure park. But not the sound, the New World version hosting a raucous percussion performance attended by an eclectic crowd of bobbing, dancing, whirling attendees. He estimated there were at least forty drummers playing every type of percussion instrument imaginable. A wood djembe, conga drums, an old-school drum set with crash symbol and hi-hat. There was even a bloke on the end playing a xylophone. Add to that the odd cowbell, whistle and tambourine and it made for a cacophonous fusion of sight and sound.

Beginning to think that he really had been plunked down in Oz, he turned to Edie, hoping she could supply an explanation for the frenzy.

'What can I say? I just want to bang on the drum all day.' Swaying slightly, Edie bobbed her head with the thunderous beat. 'The drum circle is something of a neighbourhood institution.'

And a perfect diversion. At least a hundred people giving uninhibited expression to their inner child. No one would pay him and Edie any mind as they traipsed through the park and peered under statuary and stone.

Needing to focus his thoughts, he turned his back on the drum circle. 'Tell me everything that you know about the layout and design of Meridian Hill Park.' Not only did Edie hail from Washington, but she lived only eight blocks away.

His companion immediately stopped swaying. Assuming

the classic tour guide pose, right arm raised to point out places of interest, she said, 'Basically, it's two separate parks. We're currently standing on the upper level which, as you can see, is a flat escarpment with lots of trees, benches and walkways. Very French. Think Tuileries in Paris.' Arm still raised, she gestured to the right. 'This way, please.'

He walked with Edie to the edge of the escarpment. Bordered by a sturdy balustrade, it afforded one a magnificent view of the city below, the white dome of the Capitol and the skyscrapers of K Street visible from where they stood.

'From here, you can view the lower terrace of the park which is set into a tiered hillside,' Edie said, still in tour-guide mode. 'Of special interest is the cascading fountain flanked on either side by wide steps with a long reflecting pool in the plaza below. Very Italian. Think Villa Medici.' Falling out of character, Edie chuckled. 'All in all, very schizophrenic. Although, oddly enough, it works.'

Cædmon's attention was drawn to the oversized concrete bowls of water set into the hillside, each one positioned beneath the other. As one basin filled, it overflowed into the one beneath it. And so on and so on. All the way down the hillside. Thirteen basins of cascading water that flowed into the glassy reflecting pool at the bottom.

Thirteen.

'I'm guessing the basins represent the original thirteen colonies,' Edie remarked, having intuited the direction of his thoughts.

'For me, it harkens to that most infamous date in medieval history, October the thirteenth, 1307. The day that the royal arrest warrants were issued for the Knights Templar.'

Edie playfully slapped her forehead. 'Silly me! I should have guessed.' Resuming the tour, she gestured to the eastern side of the tiered hillside. 'To the left of the cascade fountain, there's a path that meanders through a lovely grove with a full-length statue of Dante in the clearing. A *sacro bosso*, as they say in the old country. And at the bottom of the hill, across from the reflecting pool, there's a seated marble statue of President James Buchanan. Don't ask me why.'

Cædmon hitched a hip on to the balustrade. As he did, he was taken aback by what he saw in the 'Tuileries' section of the park. 'Good Lord, is that an equestrian statue of Joan of Arc?'

'Keeping a vigilant eye over the city below. A gift from the women of France to the women of America. Girl power at its best. Although, as you can see, somebody stole her thunder.'

He assumed that Edie referred to the fact that the armoured saint was missing the requisite sword, her right arm held aloft, leading the charge against the English army with nothing but thin air.

'If there is a signpost hidden amongst all of these bronze and marble chotchkies, it was put here by a later generation of the Triad.'

'Mmmm . . .' He didn't want to consider the possibility that the granite meridian pier, removed decades ago to make way for the park construction, may have been the signpost they sought.

Edie clapped her hands together. 'So, where do we begin?'

Folding his arms over his chest, a general previewing

the parade ground, Cædmon glanced at the female saint astride a horse, the oversized urns, the bubbling fountains, the *sacro bosso*. 'Safe to say that the signpost will not be in plain sight. At the first vertex of our triangle, we discovered Thoth. At the second, an obelisk. Yet here, at the third and final vertex, someone went to great lengths to recreate a European pleasure garden.' Purposefully confounding the hunt.

'Well, we know that Thoth was missing his two attributes, the *was* and the *ankh*. Since we suspect a reference to the *was* inscribed on the Jefferson Pier, perhaps we need to search for the other attribute.'

'Possibly.' He recalled the anagram that the original Triad members had cleverly concealed within their Great Seal motto, the meaning of which was still unclear. 'Or perhaps an All-Seeing Eye. It has been popping up with annoying frequency.' Stepping away from the balustrade, he slowly turned full circle. 'I say, the park is much larger than I expected.'

'Twelve acres of statuary, fountains, urns and ferns.' For the first time since entering the park, Edie's perky optimism dimmed, as evidenced by the incised lines that suddenly appeared between her brows. 'Yeah, I know, a Herculean task.'

75

Saviour tugged on the baseball cap peak, pulling it lower, obscuring his features. That done, he turned to the muscular Jamaican beside him. Together they swayed and bobbed to the hypnotic percussion beat. Nearly a hundred bystanders swayed and bobbed along with them.

Without a doubt, Meridian Hill was a mystical and magical place.

Utterly seduced by the pulse of the drums and the teeming bodies that moved as one glorious, undulating beast, Saviour put a hand on the other man's shoulder to steady himself. Afraid his legs might actually collapse beneath him. Both sensual *and* martial, this was the rhythm of the sex act fused to the soldiers' call to arms.

He glanced at the nearby statue of an armoured woman astride a bronze horse, charging into battle. Arm raised, leg muscles clenched. Exuberantly riding into the face of danger.

The Brit liked to court danger. To charge into battle. That's why Mercurius wanted Aisquith to take all the risk in this hunt. Let the Brit do all the tedious legwork and backbreaking exertion. Saviour was simply to follow in the Brit's shadow and collect the prize. Then, when the Brit and his woman no longer served a purpose, they would find themselves faced with a danger they could not escape.

As Saviour moved his body to the rhythmic percussion, he felt the sexual energy move up his spine, the pulsating beat animating his entire body. His entire being. The fierce pounding created a jubilant, primal sound that had but one purpose – to incite a man's bloodlust.

Exhilarated, he smiled at the dark-skinned man in front of him.

Returning the smile, the swaying Jamaican grasped him by the wrist. 'See di blood, mon?' He raised Saviour's hand a few inches to show him the crimson smear on the base of his thumb. *Ranger Walker's blood.* 'Me think yah a hot stepper.'

Excited by the contact, Saviour glanced at the red smudge. 'A hot stepper? What is that?'

'Yah is a bad boy, I think.'

Hearing that, he envisioned Ranger Walker propped against the Jefferson Pier, stabbed straight through the heart. A similar fate awaited the Brit and his woman. Soon enough he would have *their* blood on his hands.

Saviour stepped closer to the Jamaican. 'Yes . . . I'm *very* bad.'

76

'Okay, here's the plan –' exhausted, Edie slumped against the balustrade – 'we come back in the morning, *when we're rested*, and search the park with fresh eyes, full bellies and maybe even a metal detector. There's a place in town that rents them by the day.' Having read every inscription on every statue, examined the fountains at close wet range and walked the entire circumference of the park three times, they hadn't found anything even remotely promising.

Cædmon, who showed no sign of calling retreat, grasped the concrete balustrade and stared moodily at the terrace below. *Last man standing*. Twilight fast approaching, the drummers and their colourful entourage had already left the premises, the park nearly deserted.

Feet aching from all the walking, Edie closed her eyes and concentrated on the serene twitter of birdsong rather than the sonorous rumble of city buses.

'Serene and urban don't usually go together in the same sentence, but I've always thought that Meridian Hill Park managed to strike the perfect balance.'

The chatty remark met with silence.

Edie glanced at the notebook she'd earlier set on top of the balustrade. The open page had a hand-drawn park design, the schematic inundated with checkmarks and dashes and circled Xs. 'Look, Cædmon, I know that you're frustrated, but, hey, we fought the good fight. And in the words of my favourite southern belle, "Tomorrow *is* another day." '

'Spare me.'

'Fine,' she retorted, shrugging away his ill humour.

Trying to revive herself with a bit of forced blood flow, Edie vigorously shook her hands. When that didn't work, she took half a dozen slow, deep breaths.

'Two hundred years ago, the view from the escarpment must have been spectacular.' Glancing at her tall, red-headed companion, she could easily envision the tall, red-headed Thomas Jefferson standing in the same spot as he cast his gaze along the 77th Meridian, all the way to the Potomac River. 'Wonder if Jefferson felt it?'

'I beg your pardon?'

'The vibe. We've been here for hours. Surely you've sensed the vibratory energy of the place?'

'Otherwise engaged, I did not sense the, er, vibe.'

'Before the incursion of white settlers, this was a sacred spot for Native Americans,' she remarked, choosing to ignore his sarcasm. 'They used to gather here and—'

'Bang the drum all day?'

'Funny. But there is a reason why people are drawn to this place. And, quite frankly, I'm surprised you can't feel it.'

'The "vibe", as you call it, is the energy generated by the ley line that runs beneath the 77th Meridian,' Cædmon informed her *sans* the sarcasm. 'While it's true that such energy can incite a positive response, as we saw earlier today with the drum circle, Dr Franklin witnessed first-hand how that same occult energy could be perverted in a most demoralizing fashion. That's why the wily bastard and his cunning minions hid the Emerald Tablet.' He angrily slapped the palm of his right hand against the top of the balustrade. 'Damn them!'

'The Triad had no choice in the matter,' Edie argued, quick to come to her countrymen's defence. 'Nine Freemasons signed the Declaration of Independence. Who knows how many more signed the Constitution. And the namesake of this occult Wonderland was, yes, that's right, a Freemason.' As if that weren't enough, from where they stood they could see the stepped pyramid that adorned the top of the House of the Temple and the Washington Monument beyond. One Egyptian-styled structure juxtaposed in front of the other. 'You read *The Book of Moses*. Benjamin Franklin's dark premonition had merit.'

'Still does, I'm afraid, the Emerald Tablet containing a secret worth killing for.'

A thought she preferred not thinking about. At least not at the moment. 'The irony is that the fellas at the House of the Temple have no idea the Emerald Tablet is hidden in their own backyard.'

'Yes, bloody brilliant of the Triad,' Cædmon muttered, back to being crotchety.

A strained silence ensued.

Deciding the time had come to acknowledge the elephant in the park, Edie said, 'You're not going to like hearing this, but it's entirely possible that the Triad decided *not* to leave the last signpost. Or if there was one, it was intentionally removed. Someone went to a lot of trouble to chisel out the inscription on the Jefferson Pier. It could be that at some point in time, the Freemasons got too close for— Cædmon, are you all right?'

Cheeks flushed red, knuckles drained white, Cædmon stood trembling. Then, to her utter surprise, he grinned from ear to ear.

'I've just found the bloody signpost.'

77

'You're kidding, right?'

Wide-eyed, Edie gaped as though he'd just gone bonkers.

Of sound mind, Cædmon stared at the Italianate garden clearly visible from their elevated position at the edge of the escarpment. Raising his right hand, he quoted from the Jefferson letter: '"For I will stand on the top of the hill with the rod of God in mine hand."' Then, raising his left hand, he turned to her and said triumphantly, 'And an *ankh* in mine other.'

'An *ankh*?' Edie peered down the hill, her head swivelling from side to side. '*Where?*'

'It's embedded in the landscape architecture, part of the original park design. Clever bastards,' he grudgingly muttered under his breath, impressed with the masterful subterfuge. Assuming a later generation of the Triad was responsible for the optical illusion, he went on to say, 'They put the *ankh* in plain sight. Yet one can stand in this spot and stare upon that scene –' he gestured to the cascading fountain, the reflecting pool and the adjacent exedra – 'and never see the blasted signpost.'

He snatched the open notebook from the top of the balustrade. Pencil in hand, he quickly drew the hidden *ankh*.

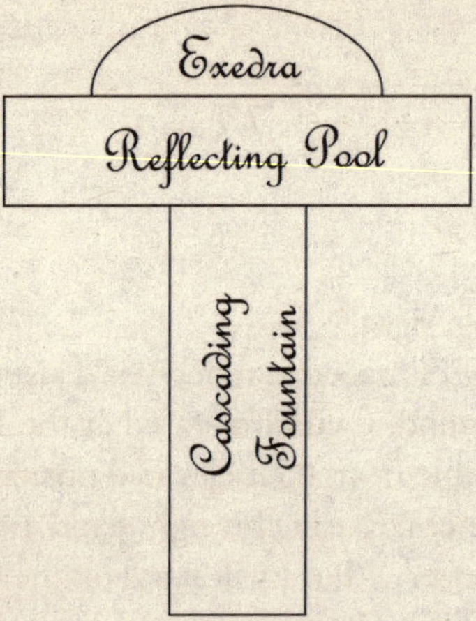

'Ohmygosh! I see it!' Ecstatic, Edie threw herself at his chest. 'One small step for mankind.'

'God willing, we can channel this knowledge to brilliant effect.'

Assuming a more sedate demeanour, his companion stepped back. 'Any ideas where on this gigantic ankh we should look for the Emerald Tablet?'

'Haven't a clue, love.' In a jovial mood, he examined the hastily drawn image. 'In ancient Egypt, the *ankh* symbolized life.'

'And we know that it was one of Thoth's two attributes.'

'Interestingly enough, during the Middle Ages, astrologists used the *ankh* to symbolize the planet Venus and their esoteric compatriots, the alchemists, used the *ankh* as a shorthand symbol for the element copper.'

'Yeah, damned shame about that copper sphere being stolen. Got a light?'

Cædmon spun on his heel, taken aback to find an older dreadlocked gentleman with a Brazilian atabaque drum slung over his shoulder standing directly behind them. Tucked behind his ear was an unlit cigarette.

'Sorry, neither of us smoke,' Edie said with an apologetic shrug.

The stranger turned to leave.

'Sir, a moment of your time, if you would be so kind. You mentioned a copper sphere.'

The drummer jutted his chin at the Italianate garden. 'Used to be a big copper sphere mounted at the bottom of the hill.' He pointed to the concrete exedra adjacent to the reflecting pool. 'An armillary, I think they call it. Disappeared during the '68 riots.' He mirthlessly snorted. 'Course, a lot of things disappeared that week; folks were riled over them murdering Martin down in Memphis. Long since broken up and sold for scrap. But I expect that was before either of you were born.'

'In nappies, actually. And you're absolutely certain there was once an armillary mounted on the exedra?'

'Shit, yeah, I'm sure. I grew up just east of here. Used to play in this park when I was a kid. Back then, DC was a segregated city and Meridian Hill was the only place where whites and blacks could peaceably share space. Black kids from Cardoza, white kids from Adams Morgan.' He laughed, a rich sound that came from deep in his chest. 'Always been hallowed ground. Damned shame that the powers that be can't see fit to replace it.'

Knowing that their informant referred to the pilfered armillary, Cædmon commiserated with a nod. 'Yes, a shame that. By the by, do you recall the approximate size of the sphere?'

Cocking his head to one side, the older man gave the question a moment's thought before saying, 'It was a big sucker, I remember that. Circumference of maybe fifteen or sixteen feet.'

A copper armillary! He could barely contain his excitement.

Cædmon extended his right hand. 'Thank you so much for the fascinating bit of local lore.' *You, sir, are a godsend*, he thought as he shook the other man's hand.

The moment the dreadlocked drummer was out of earshot, Edie excitedly turned to him. 'Didn't Rubin tell us that during the Middle Ages Thoth was often depicted with an armillary?'

'He did indeed.' *Unbloodybelievable.* Thoth the Thrice Great, with a copper armillary held aloft. 'A familiar image in the medieval iconography, the armillary was a skeletal sphere comprised of concentric bands representing the equator, the ecliptic, parallels and meridians.'

'And you mentioned that during the Middle Ages, the *ankh* symbolized copper. So no coincidence that the armillary was fashioned from that same metal.'

Cædmon glanced at the truncated pyramid and white obelisk visible on the horizon. He next gazed at the well-concealed *ankh*. 'They purposefully marked the site with a scientific apparatus. The voice of reason amidst an esoteric cacophony.'

'In essence saying, *science* rules, not the Radiant Light of Aten. From where we're standing, it looks like the looted armillary was replaced with a large decorative shrub.'

'We must assume that a latter-day Triad oversaw the

planting of the gargantuan plant.' A wise move, there being little incentive for anyone to steal a shrub.

'Of course, we're just speculating about the armillary. It could be that the Emerald Tablet is hidden under the cascading fountain or maybe even in the reflecting pool.'

Hit with an inspired thought, Cædmon slapped his hand against the balustrade. '"Biblicil aten stone to gods eye do not err." I think I know what it means. The oversized shrub which replaced the armillary is situated in the centre of the exedra –' he tapped the schematic drawing of the *ankh* – 'the exedra being the *eye* of the *ankh*.'

Edie merrily clapped her hands. 'By George, I think he's got it!'

'We need to go down there and investigate. It's difficult to ascertain the plant species from this distance. Hemlock or perhaps arborvitae. Can't be certain.'

Her smile instantly faded. 'I know exactly what it is . . . off-limits. *That* is a huge shrub or hedge or *whatever* it is. In case you haven't noticed, the circumference on that sucker is as large as the armillary it replaced. Probably weighs a ton. What are you planning to do, call a landscaping company to remove it?'

He made no reply, his attention focused on the exedra at the bottom of the hill. The eye of the *ankh*. A scheme concocted in 1776 and executed in 1926. A plan one hundred and fifty years in the making. How appropriate that the ancient Egyptian symbol for life would lead them to the sacred relic that reputedly contained the secret of creation.

'If the Emerald Tablet is buried in the middle of the exedra, under that big, bushy shrub, there's no way we can get to it,' Edie said, reiterating the objection.

He tuned her out.

Visually scanning the area, he saw a cordoned-off section of the lower park that he'd noticed during their prior search. There were several small earth-moving vehicles parked behind a flimsy barricade. He assumed they were being used for a landscaping project. Like steel to a magnet, he zeroed in on the yellow JCB. What the Yanks called a backhoe.

What price the secret of creation?

'Rather steep, I daresay.'

Edie eyed him suspiciously. 'What are you talking about?'

Mmmm . . . should be easy enough. No different to hotwiring a car. Detach the ignition switch connector. Red wire. White wire. If all goes well, the engine should turn.

Earlier in the day, en route to the park, they'd stopped by Edie's house and retrieved her Mini Cooper, the automobile was parked on 16th Street. Hopefully, the boot was well stocked.

'By any chance, do you have a tool kit in the Mini?'

'No, I don't have a tool kit, but I do have a pair of pliers, a lug wrench and some jumper cables.'

He smiled beseechingly.

'Might I borrow your pliers?'

78

While she'd dearly love to find the Emerald Tablet, Edie drew the line at grand larceny.

Which is why she stood at the edge of the concrete exedra, arms folded over her chest. Fuming. So angry, she could scream. The only reason she didn't holler at Cædmon was that it might alert the police to the fact that he had just hotwired a backhoe and was in the process of digging up a gigantic, beautifully manicured shrub. A federal offence given the fact that Meridian Hill was under the jurisdiction of the National Park Service.

Cædmon, exhibiting a dismaying lack of scruples, was working the backhoe controls like a pro. A neat little trick he undoubtedly learned during his tenure at MI5. Never know when you might have to move several tons of dirt.

In the distance, Edie heard the familiar wail of a police siren. A reminder that the big, bad city, and the police who patrolled the city, were just outside the garden walls.

'Hopefully, the local constabulary won't catch us beavering around. Be rather difficult to explain the JCB.*'*

'You think? If you hotwire that backhoe, Cædmon, you will be in violation of God knows how many laws.'

'Needs must.'

'And you need to seriously consider the ramifications of stealing US *government property.'*

'Quite frankly, Edie, I'm surprised by your reticence. You exercised

no remorse at pinching The Book of Moses *from Craven House.'*

'We didn't steal it!'

'Didn't we?'

Spooked, Edie nervously glanced around the Italianate garden. To her consternation, the park was eerily deserted. *The perfect place for the denizens of the night to lurk in the shadows.* Pulling up the sleeve on her pea coat, she checked the time. They had fifteen, maybe twenty minutes of daylight left. Like any city park, things could get dicey once the sun set.

From her vantage point, it appeared that Cædmon had dug a hole at least six feet deep. The depth of a burial plot. 'Doesn't the man know the meaning of the word "fear"?' she muttered. *Or was he so fixated on the object of his desire that the obsession eclipsed his fear?* 'Yes, indeed, Cædmon, you *really* know how to push the boundaries of a relationship.'

Not for the first time, she wondered if Cædmon was aware of the hold that the Templars had over him. The outlawed order of warrior monks caused him to be ousted from Oxford. Which, in turn, led to his MI5 recruitment. '*The chaps at Thames House purposefully seek out disgraced academics. Such men are malleable.*' But as Cædmon brazenly demonstrated when he hotwired the backhoe, he was anything but malleable.

The shadows lengthening with each passing minute, Edie made a big to-do of pointing to her watch. Cædmon vehemently shook his head. Refusing to back down, she held up her right hand, fingers splayed wide. '*Five more minutes!*' Ultimatum issued. She straightened her shoulders, prepared to put the kibosh on the excavation if Cædmon refused to . . .

Ohmygod!

Seeing something other than dirt drop from the backhoe claw, Edie charged forward.

'I just saw something,' she breathlessly uttered, gesturing to the large earthen pile.

Blue eyes glittering, Cædmon leaped off the excavator. 'Where?'

'In that big pile of dirt.'

Using his hands, Cædmon brushed away the top layer of dirt, exposing a metal case that was about the size of a hefty dictionary. On the front of the case was an old-fashioned lock. One that presumably required an old-fashioned skeleton key to open. Caked with dirt and grime, the case appeared to have been buried in its grave for a very long time.

'There's a rag on the floor of the JCB.'

Edie rushed over to the excavator and grabbed the rag as well as the pliers and lug wrench that Cædmon had commandeered from the Mini Cooper.

Snatching the rag, Cædmon furiously rubbed at the clotted dirt. Fear giving way to excitement, Edie retrieved the digital camera from her shoulder bag. She sidled close.

'Do you see what was hidden beneath the grime?' Cædmon turned the case in her direction, allowing Edie to see that there was a circle of thirteen stars etched on the lid. Beneath the circle, in a fancy, curly-Q script, was a single line of engraved text: 'Rebellion to tyrants is obedience to God.'

Her heart thudded against her breastbone. *Certain.*

'Open it!' she whispered, handing him the lug wrench.

'Right.'

Placing a steadying hand on the back of the case, he jammed the wedged end under the lid and forcefully shoved down on the wrench. The lock popped with a dull *pong!* Cædmon immediately flung the lug wrench aside.

Anxious, Edie raised the camera to her face and peered through the viewfinder. The interior of the metal case was lined with several layers of folded sheepskin.

She snapped off a photo.

His hand visibly shaking, Cædmon grabbed a corner of the dun-coloured hide and pulled it aside. An instant later, Edie heard an audible gasp, uncertain who it came from. Operating on auto-pilot, she depressed the shutter button on top of the camera.

It's stunning. Absolutely breathtakingly stunning.

Nestled in the folded animal skin was a relic unlike anything she'd ever seen. And she'd stood in line to see both the King Tut and the Hidden Treasures of Kabul exhibits. True to its name, it was a tablet that measured some eight by ten inches and was nearly half an inch thick. Made of a milky-green crystalline substance, it was inlaid with gold. *Lots of gold.* Beautiful, gleaming, glittering gold, the workmanship exquisite. On the front were lines of golden text inscribed in a primitive-looking script.

Quickly, she tallied the number of lines. 'There's eight of them,' she murmured. *The Eight Precepts.*

'Perfect symmetry, the Emerald Tablet the esoteric embodiment of creation.'

'Yin and yang,' she murmured. *Male and female.* Mind and blowing.

Cædmon lightly grazed his fingers over the incised text. 'More valuable than rubies.'

'Or big emeralds.' Although she didn't think it was an emerald, despite the tablet being an unusual shade of green.

Hand still shaking, Cædmon lifted the tablet out of the folded sheepskin and turned it over.

The back was even more spectacular than the front, with an inlaid circle of gold comprised of intertwined symbols that completely encircled an eight-pointed star. Each point of the star contained what looked to be a glyph. Within the centre of the star was an elaborate maze. Beneath the design was a character that she instantly recognized – a small Egyptian ibis. Not exactly sure what she was gazing at, Edie thought the pictograph might be some sort of mandala.

'It kinda looks like ancient runes that have been interlaced to create an elaborate ring around an octogram star.'

'It beggars description.' Eyes glistening with unshed tears, Cædmon slowly, reverentially, raised the tablet to his lips. 'This is "ocular proof" that the sacred relic which precipitated the Templars' doom *does* exist.'

Edie made no reply. *What was there to say?*

The Emerald Tablet. *The secret of creation.* Over the course of centuries, men had looted, lied and died for it.

Now Cædmon Aisquith was one of those men.

79

Standing in the shadows of the *sacro bosso*, Saviour gasped. In a state of near ecstasy, he clutched his left breast, palm to heart, and swayed slightly. On the verge of swooning.

The Brit had just uncovered the sacred relic!

His beloved mentor would be overjoyed. And for that reason, he wanted to cry aloud. To leap with joy. To twirl and dance and even hug the stern-faced Dante. Instead, he surreptitiously peered around the marble pedestal that supported the full-length bronze statue, verifying that no one else lurked in the vicinity. The discovery was too important for—

Christos!

A Park Service police officer was walking down the path that meandered through the *sacro bosso* . . . heading straight for the reflecting pool and the adjacent exedra. Where he would *happen* upon the Brit, the stolen digger and the Emerald Tablet. Aisquith and the woman would be arrested on the spot for wanton destruction of public property. Not that he cared about the pair's fate. But he knew that, if arrested, the authorities would confiscate the sacred relic.

He had to prevent the unthinkable from happening!

Stepping away from his hiding place behind the marble pedestal, Saviour strode to the middle of the pathway. He staggered a bit. A split second later, he jerked. Just before he collapsed to the ground, writhing. Moaning insensibly. Spittle flying from his lips. Doing a spot-on impersonation of a childhood friend who'd suffered from epilepsy, prone to sudden uncontrollable seizures. As though possessed by a demon.

Just as Saviour hoped, the police officer charged towards him and knelt at his side.

'Hey, buddy! It's okay! Whatever you do, don't swallow your tongue! I'm gonna call an ambulance, all right?'

Still twitching, Saviour saw the cop turn his head towards the communication device strapped on to his shoulder. About to place a call for medical assistance.

Knowing all would be lost should that happen, Saviour shoved himself upright. Using his elbow like a battering ram, he smashed it into the other man's jaw.

'Mother fucker!' the cop snarled, reaching for the holstered gun at his waist.

Saviour immediately lashed his left hand around the cop's wrist, wrenching it away from the leather holster. He then grasped his adversary's thumb and forcefully yanked it back, the bone loudly popping. The cop bleated like a cow. Seizing the momentum, Saviour toppled him to the ground.

In the next instant, he was on the cop, jabbing a knee into his testicles. Swift as a shadow, he shoved a hand into his jacket pocket, his fingers wrapping around the hilt of a sleek Italian switchblade. He pushed the raised nubbin on the handle. The blade gleamed dully in the dim light. Excited by the struggle, Saviour plunged the blade into the side of the cop's neck. A spurt of warm blood hit him on the cheek.

At that moment, their eyes met. *Such beautiful green eyes.*

Saviour smiled. Shoved the blade deeper. Then, in one quick, vicious motion, he yanked as hard as he could to the right, the honed steel slicing through pale white skin, severing the carotid artery.

Owl-eyed, the other man gurgled, shuddered, pushed one last breath between his lips before he went limp. Rudely and unexpectedly sent to the eternal black void.

Saviour scurried to his feet. Grabbing the dead cop under the arms, he dragged him behind the statue of Dante. *Out of sight.* He bit back a grunt, the uniformed cop no lightweight.

This is my eighth kill, it suddenly occurred to him. Eight. The number of creation. Like the eight points on the Creator's Star. For some inexplicable reason, that thought made him feel whole.

Quickly, he removed the pair of handcuffs clipped on to the waistband of the cop's blue-striped pants. Then he slipped the cop's gun out of the holster. Mimicking the Brit, he raised the gun to his lips and reverentially kissed it. Glancing up, he noticed that the stern-faced Dante held a copy of *La Divina Commedia* between his hands.

Yes, it was funny, wasn't it?

Having disarmed the cop and stowed him out of sight, Saviour moved to the edge of the small clearing and peered down at the exedra. He was only able to see a humungous pile of dirt and the abandoned JCB.

The Brit and his woman were gone!

Enraged, he ran towards the exedra, the cop's gun clutched in his hand. A few moments later, standing at the earthen pile, he turned full circle, hoping to catch a glimpse. A blurred bit of motion.

He could see nothing but lengthening shadows. In every direction.

Christos!

He removed the PDA Smartphone from his pocket and checked the GPS map. *Relieved.* They could not escape him. He had a gun. He had a knife. And he had the vial that Mercurius had given to him in Philadelphia.

There were any number of ways that he could send the Brit and his woman to the eternal black void.

80

'One hazelnut, one Swiss almond, right?'

Not waiting for a confirmation, the gangly waiter placed two chipped mugs on the Formica tabletop, hot coffee sloshing over the rims. Given the soiled apron tied around the young man's waist, Cædmon assumed that spilled coffee was a regular occurrence.

'And heavy on the whipped cream,' Edie implored with a winsome smile as she snatched the sugar dispenser from the end of the table.

'No problem. I'll have your waffle out in a jiff,' the amiable, if maladroit, waiter assured her before departing for the kitchen.

'People come from miles away to eat at Chow Hounds, waffles the specialty of the house.' She measured out two teaspoons of sugar, stirring the granules into her Swiss almond coffee. 'Trust me, you *will* regret not ordering one.'

In the process of reviewing the digital photos that Edie had taken of the Emerald Tablet, Cædmon stopped what he was doing and glanced across the table. 'I doubt it.' Particularly since she'd ordered something called a Belgian S'more. Billed as a '*variation on a campfire favourite*' – whatever *that* meant – the outrageous concoction included chocolate ice cream, gooey marshmallow, graham cracker crumbs and whipped cream. '*Sure to please the hungry camper.*'

Edie deeply inhaled the coffee's aroma before taking a

sip of the sweetened brew. 'After what we just went through, I'm in dire need of a fix and Chow Hounds is my favourite sugar shack. I love eating here. Plus, it's only a mile or so from the house.'

His gaze moved across the crowded dining room, astonished that anyone could enjoy dining in a restaurant with tangerine and turquoise-coloured walls. The boisterous atmosphere was not to his liking either, patrons having to raise their voices to be heard over the rockabilly music blaring from the sound system. However, a conversation held in a crowded eatery was always the safest. A lesson learned at the hands of his old MI5 taskmasters.

'While you're understandably anxious to return home, I think we should spend one more night at the Willard.' When Edie opened her mouth to protest, he raised a hand, forestalling the objection. 'Since we can't put the Emerald Tablet in your safe-deposit box until the bank opens in the morning, I will secure it in the hotel safe.'

At the mention of the relic, Edie's gaze went to the leather satchel that he wore bandolier-style around his chest for safekeeping. 'That's gotta be uncomfortable.'

Cædmon assumed she referred to the fact that the metal case containing the Emerald Tablet was stuffed inside the satchel. 'I'll manage.' He shifted slightly on the cane-bottomed chair, allowing more room on his lap before returning his attention to the digital camera.

'Here. It'll be easier to view the photos on the netbook,' Edie said, sliding the portable laptop across the table.

Anxious to examine the photos, he popped the memory chip out of one slot and into another, hoping the photographs would do the relic justice.

They did, '*magnificent*' the word that instantly came to mind. Without a doubt, the Emerald Tablet was a beautifully crafted, stunning relic with a jaw-dropping provenance. *Although* . . .

'You're frowning.'

'Am I? My apologies. I'm bewildered by the inlaid lettering on the tablet. Quite honestly, I had expected to see more Egyptian hieroglyphs. There's only the one ibis glyph on the backside underneath the entwined circle.'

'Well, the ibis is the symbol for Thoth and since the ibis-headed Thoth supposedly authored the Emerald Tablet maybe it's some sort of signature.'

He stared at the inlaid glyph positioned at the bottom of the tablet. 'As a shore-dwelling bird, the ibis lives in that nebulous realm between land and water. More importantly, it's symbolic of Thoth's ability to straddle the unconscious and the conscious mind, that being the gateway to enlightenment.'

'Okay, but you're still frowning.'

He rearranged his facial muscles into what he hoped was a more congenial expression. 'I'm irked by the fact that while the script is clearly of ancient origin, I've never seen this alphabet before.'

'I have.'

His head jerked, surprised by the revelation.

'You've seen it too.' Shoving her coffee mug aside, Edie slid the netbook to her side of the table.

Craning his neck, Cædmon watched as Edie deftly accessed the computer file that contained her archived photos.

'When we were at Jason Lovett's cottage in Arcadia, we found a sheet of paper in the fax machine with some funky writing on it. Remember?'

He thought back to that day: the ransacked rooms, the octogram star brazenly scrawled on the wall, the hidden artefacts and, yes, an overlooked sheet of paper still in the fax machine. 'As I recall, Dr Lovett sent a fax to a professor at Catholic University. At the time, I didn't think it significant since Lovett mentioned on his digital voice recorder that he'd discovered an inscription on a foundation stone.'

'Look familiar?' Edie turned the computer in his direction.

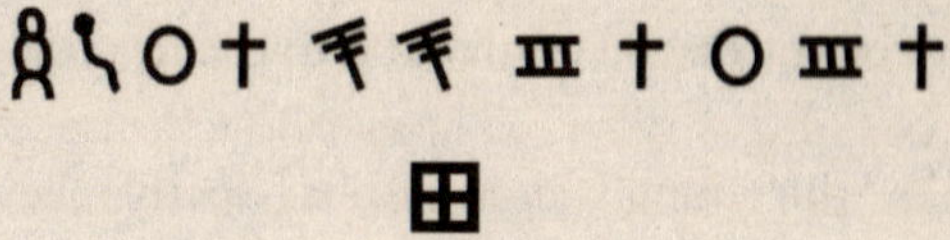

'My God . . . you're absolutely correct. It *is* the same alphabet that's inscribed on the Emerald Tablet.' He shook his head, staggered by the discovery. The Knights Templar had used the same ancient alphabet to inscribe the foundation stone at the Arcadia settlement.

'*This* is the person on the receiving end of Jason Lovett's fax.' Edie tapped on the keyboard, bringing up the next photo in the archive: a facsimile cover sheet addressed to Dr Lyon at Catholic University. 'Do you want me to go to the Catholic—'

'Yes, by all means go to the university site,' he interjected.

Out of the corner of his eye, he saw the gangly waiter approach with a laden tray.

'A Belgian S'more, right?' As with the coffee, the young man didn't wait for a reply before setting the plate on the table.

'Waiter!' a portly man at the next table loudly bellowed. 'That's *my* Belgian S'more! I've been waiting twenty minutes!'

Faced with a thorny dilemma, the waiter nervously glanced from table to table.

Edie stopped typing long enough to turn her head and peer across the aisle. At seeing a florid-faced man built like a sumo wrestler straddling not one, but two rickety cane chairs, she picked up the plate and passed the whipped-cream-topped confection to the next table. 'Bon appétit.'

'Thanks!' the young waiter gushed, clearly relieved that he didn't have to battle the hefty dragon. 'I'll put a rush on your waffle.'

'No hurry.' Edie turned her attention to the computer screen. 'According to the university site, Dr Lyon is Professor Emeritus in the Department of Semitic and Egyptian Languages. Here's a picture of him.' Edie cocked her head to one side. 'For an older man, he's quite handsome. One of those frail, aristocratic Ian McKellen types.'

Cædmon contemplatively stared at the online bio. 'How fascinating. Dr Lyon is an expert in the ancient languages of the Near East. Is there an email address?'

Edie scanned the page. 'Yep. M Lyon at c-u-a dot e-d-u.'

'May I?' He gestured to the netbook; Edie obliged the request, sliding the computer to his side of the table.

The direct approach usually the one that bore fruit, he typed a pithy message.

Dr Lyon,

I am an associate of Dr Jason Lovett. During the course of our recent excavation in Rhode Island, we uncovered an unusual artefact with an incised script which we believe to be of Near Eastern derivation. Would you be interested in examining a digital photo of the artefact and rendering a translation?

Thank you, sir, for your kind consideration. I look forward to your response.

Cædmon Aisquith

'Yes, I know, I bent the truth somewhat.'

'How about an out-and-out lie?' Edie indignantly huffed. 'You barely knew Jason Lovett. And we did not discover the *artefact* in Rhode Island. Which, by the way, makes it sound like you found nothing more interesting than an old potsherd.'

'If I reveal the truth, I doubt very much that I will be able to secure Dr Lyon's cooperation.'

'What exactly do you expect this professor emeritus to do, translate the Emerald Tablet? If so, then . . . then you deceived me.'

'I did no such thing!' he exclaimed in his defence, the accusation baseless.

'All right, we found the Emerald Tablet. The treasure

hunt is over.' Reaching across the table, she grabbed hold of his wrist. 'But we *cannot* under any circumstances tell anyone that we found it. Death follows in that thing's wake.'

'Do you not trust me to be careful?'

Releasing his wrist, she laughed caustically. 'I know what this is all about. Since you've secured the Emerald Tablet, you can rest easy, assured that Rico Suave won't be selling the relic to some terrorist group. Which means that you can now turn your attention to vindicating your academic credibility. God, Cædmon! You really are a piece of work. Two men have been murdered and all you can think about is your next book. *Testis sum agnitio.* Am I right?' She pointedly glanced at the silver ring on his right hand.

Recognizing a trap, Cædmon considered how best to reply. For the last six days, his focus had been on the hunt. Now that he had the Emerald Tablet, he was unsure how to proceed, suddenly aware that the relic might actually contain a secret of historic magnitude.

'We'll cross that bridge when we come to it,' he said at last, a noncommittal cliché the best he could manage.

Edie's gaze narrowed. 'Given that it's early spring, I imagine the Rubicon is very cold and very deep.'

Cædmon hit the SEND button. 'No doubt it is.'

About to hand Edie the netbook, he stopped in mid-motion, noticing that the corpulent diner at the next table had turned an unhealthy shade of madder red. Suddenly, without warning, their neighbour banged a beefy fist on the table, cutlery and water glass crashing to the floor. In the next instant, he began to spasmodically flail, white froth bubbling between his lips. Gasping for air, the rotund gastronome clutched the area over his heart . . . right before he slumped forward, his face landing in the half-eaten Belgian S'more.

The waffle originally intended for Edie.

81

'Quick! Someone! Call 911!'

With that hoarse yell, a frantic melee erupted inside Chow Hounds eatery. Waiters dashed willy-nilly. Several patrons rushed to the table offering assistance to the rotund diner. Several more, small children in tow, headed for the door. One impolite lout aimed his mobile camera at the frenzied scene.

Edie turned to Cædmon, a stricken expression on her face. 'Is he . . .?'

'Poisoned, I believe.' Given the fat man's lifeless gaze, Cædmon didn't hold out much hope for resuscitation.

'But . . . that . . . that was my waffle,' she croaked. A split-second later, realization dawning, she shivered violently. 'He's here, isn't he?'

Cædmon assumed that she referred to Rubin Woolf's murderer.

'In Washington? Most definitely. On the premises? Not entirely certain.' Cædmon quickly surveyed the colourful eatery, searching for a six-foot-tall, trim, stylishly dressed man. *No one fitted the bill.* If the bastard was on the premises, he'd taken cover. Which meant they had two options: escape via the front entrance or exit through the kitchen located in the rear of the building.

He glanced at the Belgian S'more smeared all over the dead patron's face. He suspected the waffle had been poisoned in the kitchen before the waiter set the plate on the table. If so, the murderous bastard might still be lurking there. Waiting for them to sneak out the back exit.

Cædmon grabbed the netbook and handed it to Edie. Mind made up, he put a hand on her back and bustled her towards the front door. A gamble, to be sure. For all he knew, the bastard was standing outside on the pavement. He slung an arm around Edie's shoulder. Meagre protection, at best. Particularly if their enemy carried a weapon.

Outside, he scrutinized the environs. A rambunctious quartet milled nearby, having just exited a departing cab. In the distance, he heard the wail of a siren. The ambulance was on its way. *A wasted effort.* But not his concern. He had to get Edie to safety.

Edie tugged at his arm, urging him to veer to the left. 'The car's parked down the street.'

'Too risky,' he informed her, worried that the murderous bastard may have spotted the cherry-red Mini. Parked on a lightly trafficked side street, it was the perfect place to waylay them.

Hoping to confound their assailant, Cædmon grabbed Edie's hand and ran across the street, heading for an establishment fronted with blue opaque glass. Emblazoned on the plate-glass door was the silhouette of a woman holding a ridiculously long cigarette holder to her lips. Below that, in a fancy script, was the name of the watering hole – C'est Bleu.

Yanking the door open, he ushered Edie across the threshold and into a dimly lit lounge.

Cædmon waited for his pupils to dilate so he could better see in the murky, smoke-filled depths. It took a few seconds for his middle-aged eyes to make the adjustment. To their immediate right was a sleek bar that glowed with an other-worldly blue light. To their left, a bank of mirrors reflected that ghostly blue light. Despite the woefully inadequate lighting, he could see that the habitués of C'est Bleu were a smartly dressed lot, approximately sixty of them scattered about the lounge.

The biggest surprise was that the back wall did double-duty as a movie screen, an old black-and-white subtitled film currently being projected on to the wall. The movie looked familiar. Perhaps *Ascenseur pour l'énchafaud.* He wasn't sure.

'I think this place is about to give birth to the cool,' Edie hissed in a lowered voice.

The observation was spot on, the quintessentially 'cool' jazz strains of Miles Davis pulsing through the sound system. Moreover, the place reeked with a blasé pretentiousness that was off-putting to everyone save the clientele.

They headed towards the other end of the glowing blue bar, as far away from the front door as possible.

Edie grabbed his hand. 'Now what?'

Not exactly sure, love.

Hit with an uneasy premonition, Cædmon glanced back at the front entrance . . . in time to see a lone man enter the lounge. *Six feet in height. Trim physique.* Several females seated in the near vicinity slyly turned their heads in the newcomer's direction.

'It's Rico Suave,' Edie murmured . . . just before she loudly hacked, her lungs violently reacting to all of the cigarette smoke.

The man at the door instantly turned in their direction.

Even in the dim blue light, Cædmon and Edie cast an easily identifiable silhouette – a six-foot-three male and a woman with corkscrew curls.

'Blast,' Cædmon muttered under his breath.

Brainstorming on the run, he ushered Edie in the direction of a dimly lit hall. Within moments, they found themselves in a vestibule of some sort, the walls covered in a metallic paper that cast a lunar hue on the narrow hall. Cædmon opened the first door he came upon – the ladies' lavatory – and pushed Edie across the threshold. *Out of sight.*

'Stay put!'

'But I—'

'Under no circumstances are you to leave the loo!' he interjected, shortchanging her objection.

Order issued, he strode back to the lounge. The beautiful bastard was nowhere in sight.

Unnerved rather than relieved, he purposefully marched in front of the makeshift movie screen, briefly sharing the screen with Jeanne Moreau. For those few moments, the projector cast a harsh light on to a tall red-headed bugger with a satchel clutched to his chest. The gauche move incited a good bit of notice, the conversational drone punctuated with audible curses. *Perfect.* He wanted to make it easy for the bastard to find him. To lure him away from the vestibule on the other side of the lounge. To let the bastard see that *he* was the one carrying the bulky case that contained the coveted prize.

No sooner was Cædmon out of the projector's glare than he came upon a swinging door ornamented with silver studs. A small sign affixed to the middle of the door read 'Private'. No time to squabble over semantics, he shoved his shoulder against the door and stepped inside. As he did, a beam of garish yellow light momentarily invaded the lounge, provoking yet another round of muttered curses.

Finding himself in a small storeroom illuminated with a bare bulb, he searched for something, *anything*, that could be used as a weapon. He suspected that he only had a few seconds to arm himself.

'Damn,' he muttered, the room was stocked with oversized items, not a one of which weighed less than four stone. *Industrial vacuums, floor buffers and stacked cocktail tables.* Not a single liquor bottle or fire extinguisher to be had.

Quickly opting for Plan B, he wedged himself into a narrow alcove on the far side of the room. In desperate need of a weapon, he opened the leather satchel strapped around his chest and removed the metal case that contained the Emerald Tablet. Grasping the sturdy case with both hands, he stood at the ready. *Waiting* . . .

The swinging door turned on its hinge. The loud creak sent a bone-jangling shiver down his spine. Cædmon slowed his breathing, listening as his nemesis cautiously prowled around the storeroom. No doubt wondering where the hell he was hiding.

Cædmon suddenly caught a whiff of sandalwood. His cue.

Lurching from the alcove, metal case hoisted in the air, he swung it towards the bastard's head, making contact with the other man's jaw. A sickening, yet satisfying, *crunch* coincided with a wounded grunt of pain. A dazed look in his eyes, the younger man swayed unsteadily before collapsing on the floor in an ungainly heap. Blood gushed from his nostrils, staining his fashionable suede jacket. A battered Apollo.

Still clutching the case, Cædmon stood over the unconscious bastard, conflicted. All it would take was a firm grasp of the head and one vigorous twist. *Problem solved.* Jason Lovett and Rubin Woolf could rest in peace. So, too, the overweight glutton at the eatery. Strong-armed justice at its most violent.

Realizing that he'd just contemplated killing the defenceless man sprawled at his feet, Cædmon's breath caught in his throat. The fact that his nemesis was unconscious left a foul taste in his mouth. Although God knows the beautiful bastard deserved a fate worse than a blackened eye and a bashed jaw.

'Shag it!' he muttered, shoving the metal case back in the satchel. He needed to collect Edie and get out of C'est Bleu before the bloodied beast revived, a wounded animal always more ferocious.

Grateful for the reprieve, he hurriedly strode across the lounge, ignoring the disdainful glances and indignant whispers that followed in his wake.

Reaching the vestibule, he came to an abrupt halt, his heart slamming against his ribcage.

The door to the ladies' loo was ajar.

With no thought to propriety, he charged through the doorway . . . and promptly started to cough, gagging on the cloying perfume that permeated the diminutive space. A *femme fatale* had recently doused herself.

Christ! Where was Edie? At a glance, he could see that the lavatory was empty.

Spinning on his heel, he charged across the hall to the gents'.

It, too, was vacant.

Standing in the middle of the vestibule, he turned full circle. Which is when he saw a phosphorescent red glow out of the corner of his eye. A sign at the far end of the hallway marking an emergency exit. He ran down the hall and forcefully shoved both hands against the panic bar.

On the other side of the exit was a deserted alley that reeked of urine, stale perspiration and a dead animal carcass. No time to take stock, he ran towards the nearest street, that being Edie's most likely avenue of escape.

Assuming, of course, that she had even exited the building. The bastard could have had an accomplice who—

Don't think it!

An opportunity to escape had presented itself and she had seized it. Edie Miller was, if anything, resourceful.

Emerging from the alley, breathless, he came to a full stop, caught in the bright beam of an automobile's headlight. The car careened to a screeching halt, the back end wildly fishtailing. The next instant, the passenger door flew open.

Edie leaned across the gear stick. 'Get in!'

82

'All is lost!'

'Do not give up hope,' Mercurius beseeched, trying to calm his distraught *amoretto*. 'We have come far together. Be strong, Saviour. Much is at stake.'

'But the *archimalakas* has the relic!'

'I know . . . let me think.'

'You must always remember, little one, that you were named for the Bringer of the Light.'

'Do not fear the Light, Merkür. For it will lead you to your life's purpose.'

Though he did not know it at the time, being only five years of age, Osman and Moshe had entrusted him with a momentous responsibility – to bring the great work that they had begun to fruition. To fulfil their vision and liberate the anguished masses from this hideously flawed creation. This godless earth where we are daily force-fed the hypocrisy that misery is a blessing in disguise and suffering an ordeal that must be endured in order to enter the kingdom of God. Not even Moses dared to pass that canard off as 'truth'.

The Light *did* work in mysterious ways, man being unable to fathom cause and effect until after the fact. More than forty years ago, in Amman, Jordan, Mercurius had uncovered a single word embedded in the text of the Copper Scroll. *Akhenaton.* That single, startling word implied a connection, however tenuous, between the Hebrews of the Old Testament and ancient Egypt. Frightened by an anonymous act of vandalism, he'd never published his findings. Instead, he cowered in silence.

But when the Greek crone had unceremoniously thrust a loose-leaf manuscript at him seven years ago, Mercurius had been given an unbelievable gift. One bequeathed to him in 1943. The *true* history of the Hebrew tribes and their connection to the Pharaoh Akhenaton.

Within days of that miraculous encounter at his childhood home, he'd been given yet another gift . . . the beautiful young man, Saviour Panos. Firmly grounded in the material world, his *amoretto* was the dark to his light. Together, they made a perfect whole. Old and young. Cerebral and visceral. *Erastes* and *eromenos.*

Cause and effect.

The two of them would give a great gift to a world at war with itself. A gift that had the power to engender a spiritual awakening of mankind's collective soul. A gift that would bind up all the wounds. A way to usher the victimized inhabitants of this planet to the Lost Heaven. The only true utopia. Paradise regained.

He was the Bringer of Light. It was his sacred duty to see that it happened.

But he *had* to acquire the Emerald Tablet. Without it, the *Luminarium* was just empty words. In the same way that the Emerald Tablet was worthless without the encryption key contained in the pages of the *Luminarium.*

Cause and effect.

Now was not the time to cower in silence. For evil *is* birthed in silence. How many stood silent while Osman and Moshe were led to the waiting train? A scene repeated thousands of times across the whole of Europe.

Now was the time for action.

He'd vowed that no man would *ever* profit from the Emerald Tablet. Clearly, the Brit intended to do just that. To sell it to the highest bidder. *Why else would Cædmon Aisquith have gone to such lengths to find the sacred relic?* And now that he'd unearthed the sacred relic, what lengths would he . . .

Yes! Of course! The path was so clear . . . so brilliantly illuminated.

Excited, Mercurius clutched the phone tightly. He would atone for his sins after the Emerald Tablet had been retrieved.

'*Amoretto*, you must listen *very* carefully. There *is* a way to retrieve the sacred relic.'

A deadly way, to be certain. But with so much at stake, he refused to stand silent.

83

Exhausted, Edie plopped gracelessly into one of the upholstered Louis VI chairs scattered about the hotel lobby, the events of the last hour having unravelled at breakneck speed.

Which was about how fast she drove down 14th Street, flooring it through two red lights to get to the Willard Hotel. The marble-columned, overly-plush lobby had 'safety' written all over it. *How could any harm come to you in this magnificent old-world edifice?* The stalwart doorman would keep the bogeyman at bay.

She glanced over her shoulder; Cædmon was still at the concierge desk on the other side of the lobby. No sooner had they pushed through the revolving door than he'd trotted off, keen to check the metal case into the hotel vault.

Self-conscious of the fact that she was underdressed for the upscale lobby – decked out in a wrinkled pea coat and stained jeans – Edie smoothed a hand over her tangled curls. *She probably looked like one of those big-haired women in a Gustav Klimt painting.* Cædmon was equally dishevelled, but speaking the Queen's English meant that he got away with a lot; Americans were enamoured with well-spoken Brits.

At the moment, she was far from enamoured.

Hearing the melodic strains of a Chopin sonata, she peered behind the columned promenade adjacent to the lobby. A tuxedoed pianist was finessing the ivory. An image flashed across her mind's eye – *Rubin Woolf, decked out in his smoking jacket, seated at a white baby grand playing* . . .

'Would you care for something to drink?'

Startled, Edie jerked her head. A pleasant-faced cocktail waiter, holding an empty tray, stood beside her.

'Sorry, I, um, didn't see you,' she sputtered. 'A drink? Yes. Perfect. Although I'm drawing a big blank.' She self-consciously laughed. Not only did she look like a bag lady, she was starting to sound like one.

'May I suggest a Silver Bullet? It's a Martini with—'

'No Martinis!'

The waiter contemplatively tapped a finger against his chin. 'You strike me as the Kir royale type.'

'Sounds wonderful. Make it two, please. Someone will be joining me.'

A few moments later, Cædmon approached. 'I say, posh accommodations,' he wryly remarked, seating himself in the Louis VI chair opposite her. He ran a hand over his jaw. 'Although that shave at C'est Bleu was so close, I damned near nicked myself.'

'It could have been worse . . . you could have had a dagger thrown at your back,' she snapped, annoyed by his facetious remark.

Cædmon lowered his hand. Head cocked to the side, he frowned. 'Considering that we escaped unscathed, you're uncharacteristically taciturn.'

Taciturn? Try terrified.

The waiter returned, setting two champagne flutes on the table. Flipping his empty tray, he unobtrusively took his leave. Cædmon raised a questioning brow.

'Kir royale.' She shrugged. 'I needed a pick-me-up.'

'The French monks who created crème de cassis thought it a curative for wretchedness.'

Edie raised her flute in mock salute. 'Bring on the crème de cassis. I've had all the wretchedness I can handle for one day. And speaking of which, we absolutely *cannot* go public with the Emerald Tablet,' she blurted, deciding to lay all her cards on the table. 'If the secret of creation *is* contained within the ancient pictograph that's inlaid on the tablet, the ramifications are mind-boggling.'

'No need to worry. I wasn't planning on running off half-cocked.' One side of his mouth twitched. 'At least not until we know what we're dealing with.'

'Is that why you asked Dr Lyon to translate the tablet? So you'll know what you're dealing with? Or are you planning to perform a little alchemical mojo, see if you can replicate the Big Bang theory of creation?'

An annoyed expression flashed across his face. 'I am convinced that the Emerald Tablet was the reason behind the Templars' demise.'

'Okay, fine,' she muttered, readily conceding the point. 'Isn't it enough to know that the Emerald Tablet is real, that it does actually exist? Earlier today, we made a horrible mistake. We should *never* have dug it up. But it's not too late. We can return it to—'

'I *cannot* and I *will* not,' Cædmon interjected, jaw tightly set, blue eyes glittering.

'Our having custody of the Emerald Tablet is wrong on so many levels, I don't even know where to begin. No, wait! How about starting with the dead man at Chow Hounds? Who, by the way, was an innocent bystander.'

'Yes, Jesus wept. Unfortunately, blood and treasure go hand-in-hand. Better the corpulent bystander than one of us.'

Edie gripped the stem of her champagne flute, on the verge of slinging the contents in his face.

'Christ! Did I just say that?' Wearing a stunned expression, Cædmon shook his head. Dr Jekyll regaining his sanity. 'Forgive me. But the fact of the matter still remains . . . the Emerald Tablet is a discovery of the first magnitude. Now that our grave concerns about the relic falling into the hands of a terrorist have been doused, there's no reason why—'

'Listen to you! What are you going to do? Haul it back to Oxford so you can wave it in the face of all those dons at Queen's College who dissed your dissertation? Because I'm beginning to think that's what this deadly scavenger hunt was all about – redeeming your academic reputation. You'd love nothing more than to rub the Oxford crowd's face in it. "See, I was right all along!"'

'Nothing so crass, I can assure you. And you know full well why I went to such lengths to find the relic, the horrific fate of Atlantis never far from my mind.'

'But you do seek vindication,' she pressed.

Long moments passed, the drawn-out silence instilling a weighty sense of consequence to the unanswered accusation.

'For nearly fourteen years I've had to live with the disgrace of being shown the door,' he said after a lengthy pause. 'Don't you understand, Edie, the Emerald Tablet is *the link* between ancient Egypt and the Knights Templar. I've waited my entire adult life for such a discovery. So, to answer your question, *yes*, I seek vindication.'

The admission gave Edie no satisfaction. 'How can you put your personal vanity and ambition above the concerns of mankind?'

Cædmon threw his hands up. 'Ah! So now I'm Atlas, forced to bear the weight of the world on my shoulders. I've put too much blood, sweat, toil and tears into this venture to back away from it.'

'Don't go all Winston Churchill on me.'

'I seek only the truth.'

'Oh, yeah, truth . . . the coin of your realm,' she deadpanned. 'And, of course, let's not forget about knowledge. That's your – what do they call it? – oh, yeah, your Bushidō. The code that you live by.'

'You cannot sway me. My mind is made up.'

'But you haven't even considered the dire—' Edie stopped in mid-sentence. *Wasted breath*. She'd have better luck convincing a stranger to wire her money.

Cædmon reached for the netbook.

A few minutes later, he smiled, his good humour returned. 'I've already received a reply from Dr Lyon. How curious. No typed message, but he did send an attachment.'

'Great,' she muttered as he pecked at the keyboard. 'Maybe after dinner we can all do a little skinny-dipping in the hidden stream of knowledge.'

His smile instantly vanished, replaced by a thunderstruck expression.

'What's the matter?' Not giving him a chance to answer, Edie grabbed the netbook and swivelled it in her direction. A half-second later, she slapped a hand over her mouth, afraid she was going to upchuck the Kir royale. 'Oh, my God!'

'Trust me . . . there's no evidence of God in *that*.'

That being a photograph of Dr Lyon, naked, submerged in a tub of pink bath water. Everything else was coloured red, hair, cheeks and shoulders all streaked with crimson blood. *Mouth gaping. Eyes bulging.* His withered face frozen in a death mask of sheer terror. Above the tub, a blood-red octogram star had been scrawled on the white ceramic tiles. A horrific piece of graffiti.

Edie wrapped her arms around her waist and closed her eyes. *It did no good.* She could still see a frail, white-haired man peering up from his watery grave.

'Such a bloody, pointless murder . . . killing for the sake of killing.' Cædmon reached for his untouched champagne flute and took a long swig. Mauve-coloured liquid sloshed in the glass, his hand visibly shaking. 'We are dealing with a man without conscience. That rare breed who takes a sadistic delight in bloodletting.'

'What do we do now?' she asked, barely able to get the words out.

Expression grim, Cædmon said, 'We go to ground.'

84

'Dark-eyed night.'

And a damned dreary one at that. The clear skies which prevailed earlier had given way to a pluvial close of day.

Removing his hand from the steering wheel, Cædmon flipped on the Mini's windscreen wipers, the rain coming down in blinding sheets. He cast his driving companion a sideways glance. 'Since you're treating me like a leper, I presume you're still peeved.'

'Try outraged.' Edie shot him a mutinous glare. 'How in God's name did Rico Suave find Dr Lyon?'

Having braved Edie's ire more than a few times, Cædmon was determined to remain calm. To be the staid voice of British reason in the eye of an American storm.

'I suspect the bastard used an electronic listening device to eavesdrop on our conversation at Chow Hounds. If so, he would have overheard the discussion regarding Dr Lyon. Catholic University is only two miles from the eatery. A ten-minute drive at most. No doubt the professor resided in the near vicinity.'

What he didn't mention – *why invite additional scorn?* – was his suspicion that no sooner did the beautiful bastard revive from the head-bashing than he went on a murderous rampage. A predator, their adversary had a marked predilection for defenceless victims.

Like Edie Miller.

Which was the reason why they were en route to Baltimore-Washington International Airport. According to the concierge at the Willard, there was a flight for London boarding at four o'clock the next morning. Six hours hence. He'd already contacted his old group leader at MI 5 and made arrangements for Edie to be picked up at Gatwick and taken to a safe house. Yet another reason for her ire; she didn't like being shuttled across the Atlantic and orphaned out to strangers.

Cædmon flipped the indicator and veered on to the northbound ramp of the Rock Creek Parkway. This late at night, there were few motorists on the winding, tree-lined thoroughfare.

'If you were just tilting at windmills, I could accept that,' Edie said out of the proverbial blue. 'But you actually found the Emerald Tablet and because you couldn't keep the discovery to yourself, an *innocent* old man was murdered. His death is on your hands.'

'Oh, for pity's sake! That's total nonsense.'

'From where I'm sitting, the flame is high and your fiddle is seriously out of tune.'

Patience tried, he tightened his grip on the steering wheel. 'Rather than trade barbs, we need to take stock.'

'Just listen to you. You're like a junkie in denial.' Accusation levelled, Edie ponderously sighed. 'It's my own damned fault. I loved the fact that you were a brainiac. An iconoclast. A Renaissance man.'

It didn't escape his notice that Edie used the past tense for that most cherished of verbs. 'And "hell hath no fury like a woman scorned".'

'Can the literary quotes.'

'Quotations.'

The instant he said it, he felt like a bastard, the conversation having devolved into a juvenile tit-for-tat. 'I know that you're angry, Edie. However, you *will* get on that plane tomorrow morning and you *will* – Christ!' he abruptly hissed, furiously pumping the brake pedal with his right foot. *No resistance! None whatsoever.*

His spine stiffened, levering away from the car seat. He shot Edie a quick sideways glance. 'Are you securely belted into your seat?'

'Why, what's the matter?'

Still stomping on the malfunctioning pedal, he shifted into a lower gear. 'The brakes just went out on the Mini.'

'But we're going downhill!' There was no mistaking the terror in her voice. 'If we crash into a tree, we'll never survive.'

'As I'm well aware,' he grated through clenched teeth. With the wet road conditions, if he yanked on the handbrake they'd jack-knife for certain. He sucked in a loud, choppy breath.

He glanced at the speedometer. *Bugger!* Twenty-five hundred pounds of steel picking up speed with each passing second.

Edie frantically pointed to the right side of the windscreen. 'There's a grassy field at the bottom of the hill. That might be a good place to stop this sucker.'

'Right.' He flipped on the full beams, able to see that the grassy expanse was bordered in dense shrubbery. He could use the terrain to advantage. 'Is the Mini equipped with airbags?'

'Passenger and driver side.'

Thank God. They might actually survive the ordeal. Assuming he could plough into a thick hedgerow rather than a sturdy oak.

As they raced towards the bottom of the hill, the trees that lined the parkway passed in a dizzying blur. The downshifting had slowed the Mini a bit, but not enough that he could safely engage the handbrake.

They hit the bottom of the hill doing 42 m.p.h. A snail's pace by Formula One standards, a potentially deadly speed without brakes. Spotting a clearing between the trees, he forcefully yanked on the steering wheel. The Mini jumped the concrete kerb, momentarily airborne. A split-second later, the car shook on its frame, hitting the grassy expanse with a bone-jarring impact. Cædmon immediately jerked on the steering wheel, first in one direction, then the other, trying to create enough friction to slow the Mini.

'Damn!'

He'd yanked too hard, the car whirling into a dizzying spin.

'We're going to crash!' Edie shrieked – right before she leaned over and pulled on the handbrake.

All four tyres instantly locked, the Mini skidding sideways. On a crash course with a cluster of saplings.

'Brace for impact!' he hollered as the vehicle smashed into the spindly grove of young trees, both airbags exploding on contact.

The collision happened too quickly to process. *Shattered glass. Sheared wood. Crunched metal. An ear-splitting scream.* Engine stalled, the Mini came to a shuddering halt.

'Edie, are you all right?'

'I . . . I think so,' she feebly replied, her voice muffled by the airbag.

His eyes filled with grateful tears. 'If I can remove the ignition key, I might be able to punch a hole in the—'

Without warning, the driver's-side door flew open. An instant later, his airbag deflated with a loud *whoosh*. Movements slowed by pain, he turned to the Good Samaritan who'd come to their assistance.

Christ!

Battered face illuminated by a piercing beam of light, his nemesis leaned into the car.

'Surprise,' the once-beautiful bastard intoned in a slurred voice, dragging the word out to three syllables. While the right side of his face was still comely, the left side was disfigured by a bruised jaw and an ugly gash on his upper cheek. A malevolent, two-faced Janus.

Cædmon made a quick grab for the ignition keys.

Only to stop in mid-motion when he felt the barrel of a revolver shoved against his left temple. Uncomprehending at first, it suddenly dawned on him that the bastard was responsible for the brake failure.

'*Very* slowly, remove the car keys and hand them to me.'

Forced to acquiesce, a loaded gun an effective means of ensuring compliance, Cædmon did as ordered.

'What's going on?' Edie asked, her inflated airbag obstructing the view.

Still holding the revolver to his head, the other man punctured a hole in Edie's airbag with the sharp blade that he had clutched in his left hand. That done, he stepped back from the open door.

Beside him, Cædmon heard a terrified gasp.

Whatever you do, Edie, don't give the bastard a reason to pull the trigger.

'Englishman, out!' The other man roughly gestured, using his gun like a traffic baton.

Biting back a groan, Cædmon slowly hoisted himself out of the wrecked vehicle, every muscle in his body protesting at the movement. Breathing heavily, he stood beside the demolished front-end, his knees wobbling unsteadily, hit with a nauseating bolt of pain. The pouring rain felt like tiny shards of glass pelting him in the face.

He surreptitiously glanced about. Parked behind the mangled Mini was an Audi A6. The engine still running, its halogen headlamps illuminated the crash scene, the ethereal glow revealing wisps of smoke and saw-toothed saplings.

Revolver held at the ready, the bastard walked over to Edie's side of the Mini and yanked open the door. 'Give me the leather bag at your feet.'

Edie wordlessly complied, handing over the satchel. The contents were rifled through. Moments later, he shoved the bag at her chest. Muttering a curse, the bastard stormed to the back of the Mini and opened the boot. He removed two soft-sided pieces of luggage which he unzipped and unceremoniously dumped on to the ground, the contents strewn all over the wet grass.

'Where is it?'

Taking a deep breath, Cædmon hoped to God the answer didn't sound their death knell. 'The relic is in the vault of the Willard Hotel.' Then, applying a whitewash, he said, 'I'm the only one who can access the code to retrieve it. And I will only do so provided no harm comes to Miss Miller.'

‘The woman can retrieve the relic.’

‘Not true.’

The other man’s eyes narrowed. ‘You lie.’ Reaching into his jacket pocket, he removed a mobile phone which he tossed on to Edie’s lap. ‘The woman will retrieve the relic from the safe. She will then call the number programmed on the phone. She will not call the police. She will do only as she is instructed.’ Although he referred to Edie in the third person, the two-faced bastard bent slightly at the waist so he could peer at her malevolently.

‘If she disobeys, I will kill the Englishman.’

85

Cædmon examined the windowless room.

The décor consisted of two wooden chairs, one of which he was seated in, a metal desk, a heavy steel door and a bare light bulb in a ceiling socket. The sturdy concrete walls were painted an uninspiring shade of dun, the concrete floor a dark green, the paint peeling from both surfaces in ragged strips. Overhead, an exposed pipe dripped rusty water in a continuous and annoying *plonk-plonk*.

There was one other pipe in the room – a solid metal pipe securely attached to the concrete wall with heavy-duty straps. He knew it was securely attached because he was handcuffed to the blasted thing and had had no luck yanking it free from the wall.

At least I don't see any electrodes, Cædmon thought with a measure of relief. *How bad can it get?*

Earlier, gun barrel pressed to the back of his head, he'd been 'ushered' into the basement of a nineteenth-century bank building currently undergoing renovation. Scaffolding, sawhorses and plastic sheeting were strewn about the gutted upstairs interior. A negligent workman had been kind enough to leave a string of electric lights turned on, so they wouldn't break their bloody necks as they trespassed. Since he'd been forced to drive the Audi, Cædmon knew the bank was located in the vicinity of Catholic

University. The bastard had probably reconnoitred the site earlier in the evening en route to his murderous rendezvous with the unfortunate Dr Lyon.

Thank God the bastard had taken him hostage instead of Edie.

Even in her distraught state, Edie had to know that if she handed over the Emerald Tablet to their nemesis, she would be rewarded with a bullet to the brain. Cædmon prayed that her sense of survival was strong. That she used the cell phone to call a taxi. And that she took the taxi directly to BWI airport. He didn't care which plane she boarded so long as she left the DC area.

On the other side of the room, the steel door suddenly swung open with a jarring reverberation. A jaunty hitch in his step, the once-handsome man strolled through the metal door frame, the bare bulb casting an unflattering light on his hideously swollen jaw.

He calmly placed a hammer with curved claw and a pair of slip-joint pliers on top of the metal table. 'The upstairs is being completely refurbished to make way for a discotheque. I'm not entirely certain, but I believe it will be called *La Banque*.'

'How unoriginal,' Cædmon muttered, taking silent note of the hardware. It implied ominously that he would be 'put to the question' – the quaint medieval euphemism for torture.

As though he were a mind reader, his captor forcefully shoved the metal table in his direction, butting the short end against his waist. Cædmon grunted, the wind knocked out of him.

'How careless. My apologies.' Placing a hand over his heart, the bastard smiled insincerely. A grotesque parody given his battered left side. 'I have yet to introduce myself. I am Saviour Panos.'

Saviour. Cædmon snorted caustically. The bastard's mother certainly played a cruel joke on the world the day she bestowed that name upon her son.

Panos seated himself sideways on, presenting Cædmon with a view of his still beautiful right side. 'Did you know that you have me to thank for the successful retrieval of the Emerald Tablet?'

'Indeed?'

'There was a police officer in Meridian Hill Park. Probably still is.' Panos punctuated the addendum with another insincere smile. 'Unless someone has found him.' Reaching behind him, he removed a heavy revolver from his waistband and set it next to the hammer and pliers.

Belatedly realizing that the weapon Panos had been brandishing was the dead policeman's service revolver, Cædmon's belly painfully tightened.

'Good God.'

'That depends on which god one prays to . . . the god of Light or the god of Darkness.'

Cædmon wondered if his captor obliquely referred to the octogram star, comprised of two perfect squares. Light and Darkness. The union of opposites.

'I take it that you are an occultist.'

Raising his hand, Panos lightly caressed Cædmon's cheek. 'Can you take it? Do you want to take it?'

Cædmon instantly recoiled, banging his head on the concrete wall behind him. The conversation had suddenly veered in an unexpected direction.

'I'm curious about your woman . . . does she give you

pleasure?' The picture of nonchalance, Panos draped his upper arm over the back of the chair.

Cædmon refused to answer.

'I will take your silence as a "yes". She's very beautiful. Usually women don't arouse me, but if I had the right woman—'

'Don't even think about it, you bastard!' Cædmon exclaimed, the other man's verbal blade cutting deep.

'You are in no position to stop me. From doing *anything*.'

To prove the point, Panos rammed his elbow into Cædmon's chin, slamming the left side of his face into the metal pipe attached to the wall.

Jaw clenched, he swallowed a deep-throated bellow as a burst of excruciating pain instantly radiated across his cheekbone. Like a bear caught in a trap, he futilely pulled against the handcuff that restrained his right wrist. When that got him nowhere, he went for his captor's throat with his uncuffed left hand.

The other man chuckled, six inches out of reach. 'Just desserts, my English friend.'

Also chuckling, Cædmon spat out a mouthful of blood and spittle. His aim true, the disgusting gob hit Panos directly in the face.

The smirk instantly vanished. 'For your sake, I hope the curly-haired bitch loves you. If not . . .' He let the threat dangle.

'*I loved the fact that you were a brainiac. An iconoclast. A Renaissance man.*' Prior to the brake failure, Edie had used the word 'love' in the past tense. Not exactly the sentiments of an enamoured woman.

Despite the throbbing pain, he summoned a cocky grin. 'She's mad about me.'

Snarling, his face twisted with rage, Panos grabbed the hammer.

Cædmon braced himself.

Bring on the lions.

86

'Oh, my God!'

Edie stood at the hotel window. Cell phone clasped in her right hand, she began to shake. Afraid she might collapse, she grabbed hold of the window frame. A photograph of Cædmon was displayed on the small LCD screen, unconscious, blood-splattered. *Beaten to a pulp.* A little welcome-to-your-room present from Rico Suave.

Horrified, she stared at the photo, the need to scream so strong, she didn't know if she could control it. Instead, she threw the cell phone across the room, the device landing harmlessly on the plush wall-to-wall. Then, like a deflated balloon, she slowly slid down the wall on to the carpet. Knees drawn to her chest, she wrapped her arms around her legs and rocked to and fro. Paralyzed with fear. Sobbing, praying . . . *begging.*

Please keep him alive.

Trapped in a bell jar, a prisoner, she could only peer through the glass.

When she was eleven years old, she'd walked into the trailer and discovered her dead mother on the floor, an empty needle in her arm. Grief-stricken, she'd laid down beside her mother on that stained, threadbare avocado-green carpet until a neighbour found her the next morning.

She was now on the verge of that same stupefied kind of shock.

Determined *not* to slip over the edge, Edie lifted her head from her knees. The driving rain cast distorted shadows across her huddled body, the night animated with shadows. Dark, murderous shadows.

Earlier in the day, she'd pleaded with Cædmon to turn and walk away from the Emerald Tablet. Just like Benjamin Franklin had done more than two hundred years ago. It couldn't have been easy for the inquisitive genius, but Franklin knew the staggering fallout that would ensue if the Emerald Tablet fell into the wrong hands. Men would lie, steal and kill to learn the secret of creation. As Rico Suave had so pitilessly demonstrated. But Cædmon had been hell-bent. And now they had to contend with a fiend from hell.

To escape the monster, she'd sought refuge in a small hotel in DC's Chinatown district. Mentally and physically exhausted, she'd picked up a take-out order of kimchi and bulgogi from the late-night Korean restaurant on the corner. She hadn't eaten since early afternoon and needed to recharge.

She glanced at the unopened food cartons that she'd put on the desk, suddenly nauseated by the smell of cabbage and beef.

Worried that the outcome of Cædmon's abduction was a *fait accompli*, she felt a deepening sense of dread. They were dealing with a preternatural killer who, from the onset, had been one step ahead of them.

How the hell did Rico Suave find them? Rhode Island, London, Philly, DC – somehow he'd always managed to put in an unwelcome appearance.

Okay, he probably trailed them from DC *to Arcadia in the*

Audi, she thought, the fog slightly clearing. When the arrows started to fly, she and Cædmon had been forced to abandon the netbook computer. A casualty of war. It could be that Rico retrieved the netbook and discovered the online booking that had been made for London.

But how in God's name did the fiend track them to the Christ Church burial ground? And then, a day later, track them to the Willard? Because, obviously, that's what he'd done. And then he went the extra mile, locating the Mini in the valet parking lot and sabotaging her brakes. For all she knew, he'd been shadowing them the entire day.

Hit with a niggling suspicion, Edie crawled across the carpeted floor and snatched her leather satchel off the bed. Unzipping it, she rummaged around and removed a hard-bound notebook. She flipped it open. That's when she felt it – a small, nearly invisible strip. She reached over and turned on the nightstand lamp. Holding the notebook near the bulb, she saw what appeared to be a clear Band-aid stuck on the inside cover.

A magnetic tracking strip!

As she sat there mired in fear, the bastard, transmitting device in hand, was simply waiting for her to retrieve the Emerald Tablet from the Willard hotel. The device would indicate *exactly* when she stepped foot in the hotel lobby. He could then follow her, forcibly take custody of the relic . . . and pull the trigger.

Fear now trumped by rage, Edie shoved herself upright, strode across the room and snatched the container of kimchi off the desk. Opening it, she smashed the magnetic strip into the fiery cabbage concoction, her nostrils twitching from the sudden burst of cayenne pepper. She then headed over to the window; a benefit of being on the third floor, the window actually opened.

For nearly five minutes, she stood at the ready, container in hand. A white pick-up truck stopped for a red light directly beneath the window. The rap music blaring from the truck's sound system meant –

Taking aim, Edie tossed the food carton.

– the driver didn't hear the *thump!* in the truck bed when the kimchi plopped all over the ribbed cargo space.

Mission accomplished, she walked over and grabbed the discarded cell phone off the floor. She set it on the nightstand. Rage a clarifying antidote for fear, she began to devise a plan of action.

Not having a weapon was most definitely a handicap.

No! That wasn't true. Granted, her weapon didn't come with round-nosed bullets, but it *was* deadly.

Edie smiled mirthlessly.

The devil may have demanded a dance, but she would pick the tune.

87

The hammer came down on Cædmon's left hand with such violent force, he screamed in agony. The pain unbearable, he retched all over the table. One did not have to be a trained physician to know that more than a few carpal bones had been broken.

Trapped between the conscious and unconscious worlds, he sagged against his chair, his chin dropping on to his vomit-splattered chest. An instant later, he slipped into the latter world.

How many minutes passed, he had no idea, blissfully unaware of the passage of time.

Consciousness returned piecemeal, bogged down with an excruciating pain centred in his mutilated left hand.

Focus on something other than the pain, he silently ordered.

An impossible command, the very act of pulling air into his lungs an agonizing labour.

Not entirely certain of his whereabouts, Cædmon glanced around the windowless room. As if on cue, the steel door on the far side of the room swung on a rusty hinge.

A stylishly attired man with a battered face entered the room. 'My stoic Englishman has finally opened his beautiful blue eyes. I trust that you're enjoying yourself.' Smiling, he fixed his gaze on Cædmon's bloodied and mangled hand.

As though a bucket of ice water had just been tossed on his head, he instantly revived.

'A jolly good time was had by all,' he snarled, glaring at the sadistic bastard. Hatred the only weapon in his arsenal.

'And to think the night is still young.'

Cædmon inwardly groaned. Mystics, the chronically obsessed, serial killers, they all shared a common trait – insomnia, able to function on little more than a cat nap.

Saviour Panos seated himself at the table. 'We have much in common, you and I.'

'We breathe the same air . . . that's all that we have in common.'

'A cunning man, even now, face bashed, hand broken, you are trying to figure out a way to disarm—' He broke off in mid-stream and glanced at the mobile clipped to his waist, the device emitting a muffled *whhrrr*. 'Ah! Your lady love has finally returned my earlier call. I took the liberty of photographing you while you slept. A little memento to ensure her cooperation.'

Smirking, Panos took the call. 'Perfect timing! My sleeping beauty has just aroused.'

Cædmon felt the sting of tears, Edie was no match for a monster like Saviour Panos. *Why in God's name didn't you go to the airport?* Although he hadn't done the tossing, he knew that Edie had been thrown to the wolves. His fault.

Forgive me, love.

A few seconds into the call, Panos's mocking expression morphed into one of thunderous rage.

Jabbing his finger against the mobile, he disconnected the call. 'That bitch!'

Hearing the rage in the other man's voice, Cædmon suffered a bum-clenching burst of panic.

Damn it, love. What in God's name have you done?

88

The dark night of the soul.

What was that from? She couldn't remember, literary quotations were Cædmon's specialty. Didn't matter. Probably popped into her head because the exchange with Saviour Panos would soon take place, with Edie waiting in a pitch-dark chamber. A woe-is-me kind of place to be sure.

She'd devised a simple plan for the exchange – use the Emerald Tablet like a Trojan horse to entice the enemy into dropping his guard. Why overpower when you can outwit? Better to slay the dragon without breaking a sweat or raising a battleaxe. Kill or be killed. *What else could she do?* You can't negotiate with a monster. Besides, the alternative was unthinkable. *Cædmon, his head awkwardly slumped, face swollen, hand mangled.* She'd make penance once her beloved was safe.

Then there was the bigger picture – if Rico Suave got a hold of the Emerald Tablet, she feared he would sell it to the highest bidder. A ruthless despot. A maniacal madman. And if Rico actually had the encryption key to unlock the Genesis code, the despot or madman could *create* a catastrophic burst of energy.

'Abandon all hope ye who enter here,' she muttered. In Atlantis, they didn't even live to tell the tale.

Benjamin Franklin had been right – leave creation to

the Almighty, mortal man was ill-equipped to handle such heady power.

Closing her eyes, she breathed deeply and visualized, *yet again*, how the exchange would unfold. To prevent a deadly mishap, her mind had to be free. Clear. Totally focused. Be deceptive. Be decisive. Be all you can be. *I am woman, hear me roar.*

Edie snorted derisively. Who the hell was she kidding? She was petrified, her heart pounding in her throat, the sound echoing in her ears. Non sequiturs *and* anatomically impossible. *But, oh, so true.* One misstep and her well-laid plan would go the way of the mouse. The enemy had beauty, brains and, lest she forget, bullets. But – and she had to keep reminding herself of this – she had the element of surprise. And a secret weapon. A cannon to his revolver.

Her cheapy Timex emitted a tinny *beep-beep.* Edie pushed the metal nubbin to turn off the alarm. The show was scheduled to start in ten minutes. '*We'll make the exchange at three. Do not be late. And if you lay another hand on Cædmon, I* WILL *tie a cinder block to the Emerald Tablet and toss it in the Potomac.*'

Unable to see in the inky darkness, she gingerly moved her right hand. Butting up against the camping lantern, she switched it on. The fluorescent bulb cast a surreal white light on the Templars' subterranean sanctuary. *Yawgoog's Cave.* The eight stern-faced knights carved on to the chamber walls had creeped her out, the reason why the lantern had been turned off.

Scrambling to her feet, Edie took one last look at the

Emerald Tablet that she'd earlier placed in the niche behind the stone altar.

The jewel finally returned to its proper setting.

She took another deep breath. 'Time to gird my loins.'

Whatever that meant.

89

Conniving bitch!

She'd carefully planned every detail. The yellow flags leading the way through the forest. The rope ladder extending from the stone slab to the cave entrance. The strategically placed lanterns to illuminate the subterranean cavern. Such a cunning spider.

Saviour would take great joy in plunging a stiletto in the black widow's belly. And he would make the Englishman watch as he did it.

Focusing on that calming image, he tried *not* to think about the fact that he was standing at the entrance to a most forbidding place.

'You might find this interesting; caves are symbolic of birth and burial,' Aisquith conversationally mentioned. 'No doubt, that's why so many of mythology's sacrificial saviours are born in caves. Only the good die young, eh?'

Saviour glared at the battered Brit. '*As to thialo!*'

'*Fila mou to kolo*,' his captive calmly replied.

The bastard spoke Greek!

'Kiss your own ass,' he muttered under his breath. 'And don't forget who has the gun.' To make sure he remembered, Saviour waved the revolver in front of the other man's face. Although not so close that Aisquith might foolishly make a grab for it. Because of the rope ladder, he'd had no choice but to cuff the Englishman's hands in front of him rather than behind.

They'd gone no more than twenty feet when Saviour pulled up short. His heart slamming against his chest.

'*Christos!*' he exclaimed, recoiling.

It was a daimon come to life!

Aisquith chortled. 'Steady, old boy. You might inadvertently fire your weapon. With all this stone and rock, the discharged bullet could easily ricochet and hit the wrong target.'

'Do not mock me!'

'Wouldn't dream of it.' Sneering, the Brit gestured to the stone grotesque. 'Allow me to introduce you to Asmodeus. The demon of lust and King of the Nine Hells.'

Saviour tightened his grip on the gun handle. 'Take your pick, Englishman.'

'How amusing. Come. We mustn't tarry. I believe the lady said three o'clock. A most portentous hour of the day.'

Uncertain what that meant, Saviour jutted his chin at the dimly lit passageway.

As they made their way through the narrow chasm, he silently conceded that 'the lady' wasn't like any other woman he'd ever met. She intended to launch an attack. *Why else would she have gone to so much trouble?* Dictating the time and place for the exchange. Choosing a dark place of 'birth and burial'.

And soon he *would* be reborn. He'd lived twenty-five years with nothing to show for it. No accomplishments. Not one single thing that he could point to and say 'I did this' or 'I made that'. Fucking. That's all he'd ever done . . . until he met his beloved mentor.

Mercurius had assured him that everything would be all right. That he had nothing to fear. That he had a plan to create the world anew. A better world. *No*, a perfect world. A world in which there was no disease to steal our cherished friends. And where a mother loves her only son.

Birth and burial.

Her funeral, not his.

90

The two men entered the Templar sanctuary. One carried a sturdy revolver in his right hand. The other had both wrists cuffed together.

Edie stifled a horrified gasp.

'Hello, love.'

Drained of animating colour, Cædmon's face appeared spectre pale. The right side of his face, that is. The left side was a bruised and swollen mess. As though he'd gone five rounds in the Octagon with an Ultimate Fighter. That, or survived the bar fight from hell.

Her gaze moved from his battered face to his manacled wrists. A soiled, makeshift bandage had been wrapped around his left hand. She winced, well aware that dirt, germs and open wounds did not mix.

'I can see from your aghast expression that the photograph didn't do me justice,' Cædmon sardonically remarked. 'You have my companion to thank for that.' He jutted his chin at the armed man standing beside him. 'Allow me to introduce Saviour Panos.'

Having taken a position in front of the stone altar, Edie folded her arms across her chest. If her plan was to succeed, she *had* to stick to the script. 'You're fifteen minutes late, *Saviour*.' The fact that Panos's left visage was, like Cædmon's, a grotesque parody of the right aroused no sympathy in her.

'We ran into traffic.' Wearing a smug smile, Panos placed his free hand on Cædmon's shoulder. 'And would you deprive me of an additional fifteen minutes with my new English friend?'

His jaw set tight, his mouth little more than a taut slash, Cædmon stared straight ahead.

Hang in there, Cædmon. The train is about to leave the station.

'Gee, you certainly know how to make a girl feel unwanted. And speaking of girls, there she be . . . the Emerald Tablet.' Edie gestured towards the niche. 'Yours for the taking.' She'd set the lantern on the stone altar, aiming it directly at the coveted relic, the inlaid gold script of the Eight Precepts gleaming in the fluorescent beam.

What man could refuse so gorgeous an object?

An awestruck expression on his face, Panos strode across the chamber. *But in the wrong direction!* Bypassing the niche completely.

'What the—' Edie caught herself in mid-curse. Flabbergasted, she watched as the dark-haired man came to a halt in front of a carved pilaster that was set between two octagonal walls.

Raising his hand, Panos caressed a bas-relief carving of an eight-pointed star that was set in the middle of the pilaster. 'It's beautiful.'

The octogram. The same symbol that Panos had scrawled at each of the murder scenes.

Admittedly baffled, Edie wondered what she was missing. Saviour Panos had killed three men to get the Emerald Tablet and yet, since entering the sanctuary, he'd given the relic little more than a passing glance.

'Ah, yes, the octogram. In Islamic art it's known as the

khatim sulayman,' Cædmon remarked. 'You clearly have an affinity for the symbol.'

An affinity? Was Cædmon being for real? Try deadly obsession.

'According to legend, King Solomon used the symbol to capture an evil *jinn*. A *jinn*, of course, being a demon similar to Asmodeus,' Cædmon continued in a surreally calm tone of voice. One that belied the deeply etched lines of pain that furrowed his brow.

Why was Cædmon placating the bastard? And ruining her carefully conceived plan.

Prior to their arrival, she'd spent two hours on her hands and knees painstakingly examining every square inch of the sanctuary. In addition to the concealed trap that she'd fallen into when she and Cædmon had first discovered the chamber, she found one other trap. This one cunningly placed dead centre in front of the niche. Emphasis on the word *dead*.

And to lure the bad guy, she'd placed her colourful bait – the Emerald Tablet – in the carved-out recess. All she had to do was get Panos to walk over to the niche *before* he pulled the trigger and killed them. Because she was fairly certain that was *his* plan.

'You ought to check out the octogram that's on the back of the Emerald Tablet,' Edie said enticingly, hoping to nudge the monster in the right direction. 'It's a real beaut. Takes up the whole backside of the relic. In fact, it's my understanding that the octogram is *the* key to unlock the secret of creation. That's why the Emerald Tablet is such a holy relic.'

The sales pitch took, Panos *finally* deigning to glance at the green crystalline tablet displayed in the niche.

‘He will be so pleased,’ Panos cryptically murmured as he stepped towards the altar.

Holding her breath, Edie counted the steps until the bastard unexpectedly plunged to his death.

Out of the corner of her eye, she caught a quick-moving blur. Turning her head, she saw Cædmon, a feral gleam in his eyes, rush towards the altar.

Right towards the concealed death trap!

91

'Cædmon, don't!'

To Edie's horror, he ignored the shouted plea.

An instant later, like uncoiled springs, Cædmon's cuffed wrists thrust upward into the air . . . before looping over the top of Panos's head. With a grunt, he yanked the other man against his chest, strangling him with the metal chain that linked the two cuffs.

Panos thrashed wildly against Cædmon, the two men no more than three feet from the trap. Having a height advantage, Cædmon managed to hold firm. *Grimacing. Grunting.* His face a mask of pained determination. With his left hand, Panos impotently clawed at Cædmon's face. In his right hand, the Greek still held fast to the revolver. Given their close proximity, he obviously realized that he risked shooting himself if he fired it.

Edie, hands fearfully clasped to her mouth, stood frozen in place. With no weapon at the ready, she was afraid to intervene. Afraid she might break Cædmon's deadly focus. Given the amount of pain that he *had* to be suffering, what she was witnessing was nothing less than heroic. Superhuman, in fact.

Face beginning to turn blue, Panos suddenly used his revolver in an unexpected manner – he forcibly rammed the butt of the weapon against Cædmon's battered left hand.

'Fucking bloody bastard!'

Cædmon raised his manacled wrists, releasing the hold on his blue-faced captive. Gasping, he recoiled from the other man.

Oh, God!

With a sickening sense of certainty, Edie knew how the violent tableau would end. As soon as Rico Suave caught his breath – which could be any second – he would kill Cædmon!

As though reading her mind, Panos bared his teeth and growled. A savage animal. 'I'm going to blow a hole in your conniving heart, *boutso gliftie*!' he hissed, his malice recharged.

Hearing his intention so bluntly put propelled Edie into action. Like a snapped rubber band, she lunged forward, her survival instincts kicking in. *Literally.*

Falling back on the six weeks of kick-boxing that she'd taken at the YMCA, she quickly advanced on her target. She'd done the course three years ago, so there was only one move she actually remembered. Probably because it was the only one she'd mastered with wham-bam proficiency – the side kick. Able to hear her instructor's voice in her head – *Slide! Chamber! Kick!* – Edie assumed an offensive posture. Funnelling her fear into one dynamic, quick motion, she smashed her hiking boot into Saviour Panos's crotch.

The wailing howl that ensued was perversely gratifying.

As expected, the wounded gunman doubled-over – a defensive move programmed into the male DNA – shielding his groin from another attack. Bleating, he muttered what sounded like a string of foul epithets in a foreign language.

Cædmon quickly jabbed his right knee upward, catching Panos in the chin. The hard-hitting knee strike sent Panos reeling backward. The younger man gracelessly windmilled his arms, attempting to regain his balance. Still holding the revolver, he crashed into the stone altar.

Edie instinctively ducked, afraid the loaded gun would accidentally discharge.

Grunting, Panos bounced off the edge of the rough-hewn altar, staggered several feet and –

– plunged through the concealed death trap in front of the niche!

Vanishing without so much as a whimper. Or a foul-mouthed curse.

Cædmon, slack-jawed, stared at the gaping hole. 'My God.'

Edie exuberantly thrust her right fist into the air. Recalling her favourite episode of *Lassie*, she happily exclaimed, 'Timmy's in the well!' *Yeah, boy!*

Euphoric, she rushed over to Cædmon, who calmly peered into the hole. 'A deadly fall from grace,' he said dispassionately. No love lost.

Her cheeks moistened with tears, it took every measure of self-control *not* to fling herself at her battered warrior. Instead, she stopped a handbreadth in front of Cædmon. Ever so gently, she brushed her fingers against his bruised cheek.

'Worse for wear,' he said matter-of-factly, pre-empting her enquiry. 'Let's leave it at that.' Then, one side of his mouth quirking upward, 'Your bravado gave me quite the scare. I don't know whether to kiss you or throttle you.'

'I'll settle for the former. The latter will have to wait until I'm suited up in my fishnet stockings and black leather corset.' She laughed shakily, her emotions all over the map. 'Aren't you the one who said that "bluff can move mountains"? Although . . .' She glanced at the hole in the floor. 'As crazy as it sounds, I wish it hadn't come to this.'

'I'm afraid that nothing short of death would have stopped him. Survival of the fittest at its most horrific.'

Sidestepping the death trap, she walked over to the niche behind the altar. 'All that trouble and he never did take the bait.' She removed the relic and carefully retraced her steps, purposefully *not* peeking into the hole. 'I don't know about you, but I am ready to blow this joint.'

No sooner were the words out of her mouth than the skin on the back of her neck prickled. In that instant, she intuitively knew . . . a dark shadow loomed behind them. She warily turned her head towards the entrance to the sanctuary, half expecting to see Saviour Panos – Rasputin-like – having survived the deadly plummet.

'Good God,' Cædmon uttered.

Her thoughts exactly, stunned to see an armed white-haired man standing in the entryway.

'I . . . I don't . . . don't understand,' she sputtered. 'We thought you were dead.'

92

'Still among the living, as you can plainly see.'

Cædmon gaped at the resurrected gunman, shocked. 'I am as confused as Miss Miller. How can you be both death and . . .'

'Alive? A bit of smoke and mirrors, as they say. Or porcelain and bathwater, in this case. Please forgive the subterfuge. A necessary ploy to force your hand. We have not been properly introduced. My birth name is Merkür de Léon. Americanized many years ago to Lyon. Spelled with a "y",' he added, obviously amused by the 'ploy'.

Still flabbergasted, Cædmon stared at the elderly man who all along had been pulling the puppet strings. *The kindly Dr Lyon.* Professor Emeritus at Catholic University. Although not so kindly that he didn't carry a firearm. A Smith & Wesson 9mm revolver. Eight rounds in the clip, one in the chamber. Which meant that Dr Lyon, Professor Emeritus, had nine shots available to him. Of course, he only needed two to kill them. An easy enough prospect given that he and Edie were utterly defenceless. Nowhere to hide. And nowhere to run.

'Where is Saviour?' Dr Lyon scanned the room, his eyes suspiciously narrowing.

Cædmon quickly glanced at Edie. A warning. *Whatever you do, love, don't reveal that his homunculus tumbled into the pits of hell.*

'Your neophyte suffered an unexpected bout of claustrophobia which prompted his early departure.'

'Yeah, he had a real bad case of spelunkphobia.' Edie snickered.

'Since there's only the one exit, Saviour ordered us to retrieve the relic while he awaits our egress *above* ground. I'm surprised you didn't cross paths.' Cædmon strove for a calm façade, ignoring the searing bolts of pain that continuously pulsed from his battered left hand. Refusing to show any weakness. *Smoke and mirrors.*

With a nod of the head, Dr Lyon accepted the deceit as payment in full.

'All in all, well done, sir!' Cædmon congratulated him with hale good humour. 'We respectfully concede the field and award you the prize. Edie, if you would be so kind as to set the Emerald Tablet on the stone altar where Dr Lyon may properly examine it.'

'Um, right . . . be happy to.' Always a dependable teammate, Edie did as instructed.

Like guests summoned to dinner, the three of them gathered at the altar: Dr Lyon at the head of the table, Cædmon at the foot, and Edie, the hapless diner in the middle. And, of course, the silent, uninvited guest Saviour Panos who'd been cast into the pit just prior to the dinner gong.

Dr Lyon's eyes glimmered with unshed tears as he stared at his 'dinner plate'. Utterly bedazzled. As Cædmon had been when he first set eyes on the sacred relic.

'I'm admittedly curious as to how you learned of the Emerald Tablet,' Cædmon conversationally remarked.

Long moments passed before Dr Lyon finally tore his

gaze away from the relic. 'I was approached by Jason Lovett regarding the Paleo-Hebrew inscription that he unearthed in Arcadia.'

'Paleo-Hebrew is an ancient version of the Semitic language,' Cædmon said in a quick aside to Edie.

Like a lover caressing his beloved, Dr Lyon smoothed his hand over the intricate gold-inlaid design, Edie having set the relic on the altar backside up. 'The Templar inscription proved to be a Latin transliteration. Properly translated, it reads "Thoth's stone".'

'Aka the Emerald Tablet,' Edie said. 'Which is how you knew that the Templars had taken the relic to their secret New World colony.'

'No sooner did I read Dr Lovett's extraordinary email than I knew it was the fourth and final sign.'

Taken aback, Cædmon's head jerked. 'Do you honestly believe that the hand of providence—'

'I *am* the chosen one!' Dr Lyon snapped. 'It is my destiny to have found the Emerald Tablet.'

Although tempted to point out that *he and Edie* unearthed the sacred relic, Cædmon held his tongue.

'Oh, puh-leeze! This guy's clearly delusional,' Edie scoffed, subtlety not her strong suit. 'I don't know why we're even wasting our breath talking to you.'

'Perhaps because I am the one holding the gun.'

At hearing the ironic riposte, Edie openly glared.

'Do you by any chance know *how* the Genesis code works?' Cædmon politely enquired, hoping to smooth the rough waters. A calm sea might buy them more time.

'The Emerald Tablet is an ingeniously crafted cryptogram that unlocks the sequences of the Divine Harmonic,'

Dr Lyon replied, back to speaking in a measured professorial tone.

The Divine Harmonic.

Cædmon raised a quizzical brow, unfamiliar with the term.

Using the index finger of his left hand as a pointer, Dr Lyon indicated the circular wreath of intertwined characters. 'The pictograph is fashioned from the letters of the Paleo-Hebrew alphabet. Each letter, when spoken aloud, has a specific tone that generates a unique pulse and vibration. Not only can sound and vibration alter physical matter, but it can *create* physical matter if correctly sequenced.'

Edie turned to Cædmon. 'Tell me it ain't so.'

'I cannot,' Cædmon honestly replied, grappling with this latest revelation. 'Dr Lyon's claim is scientifically possible. Indeed, there is a branch of science known as Cymatics that studies modal phenomenon, specifically examining the interaction of sound, vibration and frequency. The results of these experiments tend to prove Dr Lyon's assertion that sound and vibration can affect physical matter.' He hesitated, well aware that the Cymatic research had also proved something else. Something utterly astounding.

Dr Lyon wordlessly lifted his chin in Cædmon's direction, silently commanding him to continue.

'Right.' He took a deep breath, worried that, rather than dousing the flame with a wet flannel, he was about to splash gasoline on to the fire. 'The Cymatic researchers also discovered that when the letters of the ancient Hebrew language are spoken aloud, the ensuing tonal vibration *alters* physical matter. This result could not be replicated with any modern-day language.' He shrugged, forced to capitulate under the onerous weight of the scientific evidence. 'One can only speculate that there is a universal harmonic contained within the ancient Hebrew language that has the inherent ability to reconfigure physical reality.'

Edie snapped her fingers. 'Yeah, don't you remember? In *The Book of Moses*, Benjamin Franklin mentioned the Egyptian-styled ritual that he attended and the "ungodly chant" that was sung.'

'Garbled polyglot without the encryption key.' Dr Lyon shrugged dismissively. 'The *order* of each vibratory sound is the key.'

'Holy crap!' Edie turned to him, wide-eyed. 'That can only mean one thing – he's got the encryption key.'

The older man opened his mouth. Then just as quickly closed it. Neither confirming nor denying.

'Come now. You are among friends. Or at least unarmed dinner companions,' Cædmon coaxed with forced humour.

'Yes, I have the encryption key,' Dr Lyon finally confessed. 'Some years back, I inherited a rare document that chronicles the entire history of the Emerald Tablet dating back to Atlantis and the High Priest Thoth. Entitled the *Luminarium*, it was composed by a Muslim *Ma'min* and a Jewish Kabbalist in the mid-twentieth century. Prior to their deportation to Auschwitz.'

'My God,' Edie murmured, like Cædmon, horrified. The mere mention of the place conjured a ghastly image.

'I've never heard of the *Luminarium*.'

'Only one copy of the manuscript exists. Within its pages, the secret of the Divine Harmonic is revealed.' Dr Lyon paused, garnering their full attention. 'As well as a detailed plan to end the violent depravity that permeates this world.'

Edie immediately swung her gaze towards the head of the table. 'Why am I suddenly getting a *very* bad feeling?'

'The wise authors of the *Luminarium* knew that evil cannot be contained,' Dr Lyon continued, an excited glimmer in his eyes. 'It must be destroyed. Only then can our earthly souls ascend to the Lost Heaven, our true home. In the Lost Heaven, violence does not exist. There is only the Light. In all its purity and goodness.' Taking a deep breath, Dr Lyon placed his palm upon the Emerald Tablet, his pose reminiscent of a witness swearing upon a Bible before taking the stand. 'I intend to follow in Thoth's hallowed footsteps. Just as the Atlantean High Priest destroyed war-mongering Atlantis twelve thousand years ago, I intend to use the Divine Harmonic to destroy this flawed creation.'

Hearing that, Edie gasped.

'God save me from over-reaching zealots,' Cædmon muttered, the reality of Dr Lyon's scheme hitting him straight on. Like a fist of fives to the underbelly.

'All of which explains why Benjamin Franklin, John Adams and Thomas Jefferson went to such lengths to hide the Emerald Tablet,' Edie exclaimed, her cheeks flushed with heated colour. 'So that people like *you* would not get it into their head to play God.'

'One cannot permit evil to exist if one has it in one's power to eradicate that evil,' Dr Lyon calmly replied.

'Making *you* the ultimate Decider. Oh, *that's* rich!'

Dr Lyon picked up the Emerald Tablet with his left hand and clasped it to his chest. 'Unlike you, I have the courage of my convictions. And I will heal humankind by ending the violence and brutality. Once and for all. This is my *gift* to the planet, to reunite *every* living soul with the Light. Only then can you and I, and indeed every inhabitant of this battle-scarred planet, be made whole.'

'I'd like to point out that good people do inhabit the planet.' Although damned difficult, Cædmon kept his tone neutral.

'And they shall inherit the Lost Heaven. I can think of no better reward. By initiating the harmonic sequence, I will liberate the suffering masses from this cesspool of evil.'

Edie snorted derisively. 'Thank you, but I'd rather jump into the deep-end of the cesspool than—'

'Surely the world is not so far gone that we need contemplate so drastic a solution?' Cædmon said over the top of her. Well aware that Dr Lyon's gun was loaded, he didn't think it wise to antagonize the man.

'Sadly, there's no such thing as a utopian safe haven. No New Atlantis. No New Jerusalem. The dark fire burns too bright. Several miles from this very spot there's a mass grave with the butchered remains of three hundred innocents . . . I rest my case.'

The professor's startling declaration of intent cast a lunar shadow across the altar. In the pit of his tightening stomach, Cædmon feared that they were dealing with a madman.

'So the solution is to kill *everyone*? That gives a whole new meaning to the word overkill.' Edie shook her head in disgust.

'When you are free of this dark world, you will thank me.'

'For committing an act of radical nihilism? I think not,'

Cædmon retorted, refusing to go an inch, let alone ride the full mile.

The older man smiled. 'I prefer to think of it as *sacred* nihilism. Indeed, I could have done like everyone else and anaesthetized the pain of existence with narcotics or alcohol or—' He stopped in mid-stream. Frowning, he stepped around the stone altar and peered down . . . directly into the gaping hole below.

Cædmon was able to see on Dr Lyon's face the *exact* moment that the recognition dawned.

A split-second after that, as though the older man had been bitten by a snake and succumbed to paralysis the instant the poisonous venom entered his bloodstream, Merkür de Léon stood motionless. Totally and completely disorientated.

Then, just as Cædmon feared, he imploded.

Spinning on his heel, his hand violently shaking, he aimed the Smith & Wesson, first at Cædmon, then at Edie. Glaring.

Whether by accident or design, Dr Lyon fired a shot, the bullet ricocheting off the wall near the entrance.

Bloody hell!

Afraid the next shot would hit its mark, Cædmon grabbed the lantern on the stone altar and flung it to the floor.

Plunging the sanctuary into primeval darkness.

93

I can't see anything!

Terrified, Edie shrieked.

The high-pitched sound reverberated off the stone walls. Endlessly echoing. Deafening even to her own ears. *Oh, God!* She was totally disorientated. Pitch-black darkness, fear and uncertainty all compressed into a painful cranial throb that felt like it would detonate at any moment.

A split-second later, a second bullet discharged, whistling past her head, lodging in the pilaster behind her. She heard several pieces of stone, blasted free, pelt the ground.

'Hit the floor!' Cædmon ordered, his disembodied voice echoing off the sanctuary walls.

Gripped with terror, she reflexively dropped to the ground. On the other side of the sanctuary, she could hear Dr Lyon's erratic breathing. *Or was that her erratic breathing?* Edie held her breath, afraid Dr Death would home in on her serrated exhalations.

Shifting into high gear, she crawled away from where Dr Lyon had been standing.

At least, she *hoped* she was moving *away* from the monster. She couldn't see a damned thing. Trying to make as little noise as possible, she winced every time the tip of her hiking boot scuffed the uneven stone surface.

'Three blind mice . . . see how they run,' Dr Lyon taunted. Not sounding the least bit afraid. His courage no doubt bolstered by the fact that he had a loaded pistol clasped in his hands.

That or the crazy old coot could see in the dark.

Like she wasn't scared enough, *that* thought sent a shiver of pure panic up her spine. Edie wondered how long they could play the avoidance game. Although the sanctuary was fairly large, with a diameter of some twenty-five feet, at some point they were bound to bump into each other.

If she could just find Cædmon, maybe they could escape together before their would-be killer figured out they'd gone AWOL.

No sooner did that plan cross her mind than she brushed up against something warm. *A body!* She instinctively jerked, started to scurry away. A strong hand grabbed her ankle.

'It's me, love.'

Cædmon! Thank God!

Relief instantly morphed into panic as another gunshot ringing out.

'You will both pay for the heinous crime that you committed,' Dr Lyon announced.

Edie's stomach painfully knotted. She frantically reached out, grabbing hold of the first thing that her hand came into contact with – Cædmon's kneecap. Although which one, she had no idea. 'We have to turn the lantern back on!'

He leaned close to her, his nose bumping against her cheek. 'I'm afraid that the lantern's a lost cause,' he whispered in her ear.

'I have a second one in my duffel bag. It's on the other side of the cave. All I have to do is crawl—'

'No!' he hissed, his warm breathing hitting her full in the face. 'Any idea how many death traps are in the cave?'

'There's two of them . . . the one behind the altar and the one that I fell into before.'

'Right. I want you to stay put while I go after the bastard.'

'Are you crazy? Not only are you handcuffed, but you have a broken hand.'

'Trust me, love . . . he *will* kill you.'

'Like you're gonna get off with only a slap on the wrist. Not only do I have two good hands, but I've got a mean side kick in case you missed the earlier show. So I want you to stay . . .' Edie swept her arm to-and-fro across the stone floor.

Where before there had been a hard knee and a warm body, there was nothing but thin air.

Cædmon was gone!

94

'O dark dark dark. They all go into the dark.'

The transplanted bugger T. S. Eliot had no blasted idea just how abysmally dark it could get.

Hampered by the handcuffs, Cædmon had to crawl, crab-like, on his knees and elbows, wrists held off the ground. He bit back the pain that ferociously pulsed from his mutilated hand. Surrounded by Stygian blackness, he navigated by sound. A difficult feat in a cave where each and every thud reverberated off the octagonal stone walls in a distorted echo.

Knowing there was a second death trap, he painstakingly moved forward a few inches at a time. Every now and again he stopped, listened, made a course adjustment. *A blind, battered fool.* But what choice did he have? If he and Edie called retreat and left the cave, the bastard would put a bullet in each of their backs.

While Dr Lyon had a gun, he also had at least seventy winters on his head. Putting the older man at a distinct disadvantage. Or so Cædmon hoped, his plan to catch the bastard unawares.

Hearing a muffled wheeze – one that definitely did not emanate from Edie – he headed in that direction. Hope renewed.

The chain that yoked the two cuffs together softly jangled.

Almost instantaneously, a shot rang out. The bullet hit

the floor a few feet from Cædmon, spraying his face with stone chips.

Bloody hell!

The bastard was standing there – wherever *there* was – with his ears pricked. Listening. Firing each and every time he heard so much as a peep. By his count, Dr Lyon had five bullets left in the clip. Ample ammunition to kill them.

Cædmon froze. Stilled his breathing. Focused on the palpable silence until he heard – *Yes!* – an almost imperceptible breath.

The old man was close. *Very close.*

Knowing it was now or never, Cædmon surged forward, butting his head against Dr Lyon's shins – knocking his legs out from under him. The older man hit the ground with a thud. One that induced a pain-wracked bellow.

The attack cost Cædmon, an agonizing burst of pain exploding in his left hand. He bit back a scream, unable to follow up on the initial attack.

Seconds later, catching his breath, he awkwardly crawled several feet, swiping the ground with his manacled hands, searching for the fallen gunman. He came up empty-handed.

Where in God's name was . . .

A lantern was suddenly switched on, the cave flooded with fluorescent light.

Cædmon blinked, willing his pupils to make the adjustment speedily. Squinting, he glanced up . . . just in time to see Dr Lyon, standing over him. Still clinging to the Emerald Tablet, he aimed his small black pistol at Cædmon. The kill shot – when it came – would slam directly into the centre of his forehead.

Cædmon gulped a deep breath. No doubt his last. Standing near the altar, Edie screamed.

'I'm sorry,' the older man murmured, eyes filled with tears.

'I'm not!' a deep voice intoned.

What happened next occurred with such stunning rapidity that Cædmon struggled to process the lightning-fast chain of action and reaction – *Dr Lyon glanced up. Gasped. Redirected his 9mm pistol at the new threat. Cædmon peered behind him. His turn to gasp* – the Narragansett Indian, Tonto Sinclair, a Winchester bolt-action rifle held to his shoulder, stood in the entryway to the sanctuary.

Just then, a bullet rang out. Fired from Dr Lyon's pistol. A split-second later, another shot, this one from Tonto Sinclair's rifle. Cædmon watched in stunned amazement as a high-speed bullet hit the Emerald Tablet. *Actually ricocheting off the damn thing!* As though it were sheathed in Kevlar, the relic proved impenetrable.

The impact of the high-velocity shot forcefully thrust Dr Lyon backward. Like a wobbly child's top, the older man spun to the left. He then staggered several steps, still – *amazingly* – keeping his hold on the sacred relic.

Suddenly realizing that the older man was veering towards the second death trap, Cædmon unthinkingly shouted, 'Stop!'

Too late.

Like his beautiful paramour, Dr Lyon instantly vanished, plummeting to . . .

. . . *the abyss.*

95

A moment of stunned silence ensued.

Only to be shattered when the Indian rifleman deftly yanked the bolt handle on his weapon, ejecting the spent shell casing. Grim-faced, he closed the bolt, chambering the next round.

'Something tells me that we're not out of the cave just yet,' Edie murmured. In her right hand, she held a lantern, its white beam skittishly jerking about. Evidence of her jittery unease.

Tonto Sinclair strolled over to the gaping hole and peered down. 'What do you wanna bet there's no big white rabbit down there?'

'You have my gratitude, Mr Sinclair,' Cædmon said, well aware that the Indian had saved his life.

Resting the rifle in the crook of his arm, Sinclair stared at him with hooded eyes. 'Last I heard, white men still speak with forked tongue. And I didn't take out the bastard to save your ass.'

'Indeed? Which begs the question . . . why did you pull the trigger?'

'You're a smart motherfucker. Figure it out.'

'Mr Sinclair did it to prevent Yawgoog's Stone from being removed from the cave,' Edie said, walking towards them. She fixed her gaze on the rifleman, her earlier fear replaced with a calm certainty. 'Isn't that right?'

'Smart lady. It's been more than four centuries, but Yawgoog's Stone has finally been returned. The curse on my people will be lifted.' The harsh tone had noticeably softened.

'You mentioned Yawgoog's Stone when we first met, but . . . Did you know then that Yawgoog's Stone and the fabled Emerald Tablet were one and the same?' *That Yawgoog's Stone was the link between the Knights Templar and the Egyptian pharaoh Akhenaton.*

'Jason Lovett was using me to find Yawgoog's gold. The scrawny shit was on a treasure hunt. He didn't believe that Yawgoog entrusted my people with the sacred stone. Or if Lovett did believe, he didn't care.'

Cædmon stood silent. Guilty of the same crime as the ill-fated archaeologist. From the beginning, he had suspected that the legendary Yawgoog was a Knight Templar. Or, at the very least, a descendant of the fugitive knights. But he'd given little thought to the relationship that may have existed between the Templars and the Narragansett. Simply put, it had no bearing on his investigation. *His treasure hunt.*

A treasure hunt that had just came to a startling finale, the Emerald Tablet flushed down the proverbial drain.

His initial relief having congealed into hollow regret, Cædmon walked over and examined the gaping hole. *Deep?* Most assuredly. But certainly not bottomless. With the proper equipment, he could . . .

'Let it go, Cædmon.' Standing beside him, Edie took hold of his right hand. Under the pitiless glare of the fluorescent light, her skin appeared translucent. Her deep-set brown eyes heart-wrenchingly serious.

Although she uttered but four simple words, Cædmon had the distinct impression that he'd just been presented with an ultimatum . . . Edie or the relic.

He cast one more glance at the pit. Then took a deep breath.

'Right.'

Epilogue

Two weeks later

Washington, DC

'A rave success, love.'

'Why, thank you, kind sir.'

Smiling, Edie placed a hand on Cædmon's crooked elbow. Turning her head, she waved a final farewell to the gallery owner who'd hosted her photo exhibition. Entitled *The Glory: Women of Axum*, the collection of documentary-style photographs had been favourably reviewed in the *Washington Post*'s Art & Style section. At the opening, Cædmon heard the adjectives 'luminous', 'thought-provoking' and 'stunning' freely bandied about. He couldn't have been more proud.

'A celebration is in order. Fancy a drink?'

'How about a round of ouzo at Zorba's?'

Cædmon glanced at the Greek taverna on the other side of Connecticut Avenue. 'I think not. Perhaps the wine bar up the street?'

'Sounds like a plan.'

As they strolled along the pavement – heavily trafficked at the five o'clock hour – a passing pedestrian accidentally jostled Cædmon on his left side. He winced, pain management still an issue.

Last week, he'd undergone the first round of

reconstructive surgery on his mangled hand. Despite the near-constant pain, his orthopaedic surgeon remained confident that, with the proper rehabilitative therapy, he could expect an eighty per cent recovery.

Mercifully, his right hand had not been injured.

Cædmon glanced at the bandaged appendage, trying to put a 'happy spin' – as Edie liked to say – on a bleak situation.

Although there was ample reason to rejoice, he thought, taking note of the soft chiaroscuro blush that suffused the congested cityscape with a heavenly glow. In the grassy median that separated the lanes of traffic, yellow jonquils jauntily swayed. For some inexplicable reason, it made him feel like a new man.

Inspired, he turned his head to the curly-haired maid who walked beside him. 'For the longest time, I had no anchor in my life.'

'What about knowledge?' Edie glanced at the silver ring on his unbandaged hand.

'A course heading. A direction to sail the ship. But without an anchor, a man cannot put into harbour.'

'Am I hearing this correctly?' She could barely contain her laughter. 'Did you just compare me to a barnacle-encrusted anchor?'

'I did. How bloody unromantic is that?' He shook his head, not exactly certain how to make amends. Then, hit with a brilliant idea, he came to a complete standstill and pulled Edie into his arms, kissing her full on the lips.

It was long moments before he finally pulled away. And then only because the public display had elicited three catcalls and two appreciative whistles.

‘Umm, fly me to the moon.’ Brown eyes gleaming, Edie batted her lashes. ‘Care to tag along? The in-flight movie is not to be missed.’

‘I am completely enamoured.’ Slinging his right arm around her shoulders, they continued down the street.

‘You’re enamoured because spring is in the air. When a young man’s fancy turns to skirt-chasing.’ Edie flirtatiously raised the hem of her colourful skirt several inches.

‘Curiously enough, Thoth was the Egyptian guardian of the vernal equinox.’

‘Speaking of which, I know that you’re disappointed about losing the “missing link” between the Knights Templar and—’

‘Bugger the Templars.’

Now it was Cædmon’s turn to glance at the silver ring. *Testis sum agnitio.* Although fascinated as ever with the elusive and enigmatic Templars, he’d vowed that he would never again let his passion overcome his reason, Edie having rightfully accused him of being ‘obsessed’.

‘I don’t know about you, but I’m still grappling with the fact that Dr Lyon *seemed* like a kindly grandfather. The sort who wouldn’t harm an annoying fly.’

‘“One can smile, and smile, and be a villain.”’ The instant he said it, he apologetically grimaced. Of late, Edie had taken to calling him ‘Quetzalquotel’. ‘Pardon the literary lapse.’

‘In America, we like our villains scaled and horned. It’s easier to pass judgement when something is clearly black or clearly white.’

‘Grey does have a way of mucking things up. That said, Rubin Woolf had mentioned that the Jewish Kabbalists of Spain were the guardians of the Emerald Tablet prior to the Knights Templar.'

Edie cocked her head to one side, gaze narrowing. 'Do I *really* want to hear this?'

Quite honestly, he didn't know.

'It's entirely possible that there are other relics or esoteric secrets to be uncovered in Spain,' he continued, deciding to plough his furrow. Come what may. 'Given that the Templars were granted land tracts in Catalonia, Valencia and Aragon during the Middle Ages and that there were established Jewish communities in those same regions, the Iberian Peninsula might prove a fascinating place to conduct research for my next book.' He hesitated, suddenly worried that he'd botched things so badly with the Emerald Tablet that Edie no longer wished to assist him.

He nervously cleared his throat. 'Er, that said, would you be interested in—'

'Gee, Big Red. I thought you'd never ask.'

Acknowledgements

My thanks to Ria Palov for creating the book illustrations.

C. M. Palov

He just wanted a decent book to read ...

Not too much to ask, is it? It was in 1935 when Allen Lane, Managing Director of Bodley Head Publishers, stood on a platform at Exeter railway station looking for something good to read on his journey back to London. His choice was limited to popular magazines and poor-quality paperbacks – the same choice faced every day by the vast majority of readers, few of whom could afford hardbacks. Lane's disappointment and subsequent anger at the range of books generally available led him to found a company – and change the world.

'We believed in the existence in this country of a vast reading public for intelligent books at a low price, and staked everything on it'
Sir Allen Lane, 1902–1970, founder of Penguin Books

The quality paperback had arrived – and not just in bookshops. Lane was adamant that his Penguins should appear in chain stores and tobacconists, and should cost no more than a packet of cigarettes.

Reading habits (and cigarette prices) have changed since 1935, but Penguin still believes in publishing the best books for everybody to enjoy. We still believe that good design costs no more than bad design, and we still believe that quality books published passionately and responsibly make the world a better place.

So wherever you see the little bird – whether it's on a piece of prize-winning literary fiction or a celebrity autobiography, political tour de force or historical masterpiece, a serial-killer thriller, reference book, world classic or a piece of pure escapism – you can bet that it represents the very best that the genre has to offer.

Whatever you like to read – trust Penguin.

read more
www.penguin.co.uk